The Diplomat of Florence

A Novel of Machiavelli and the Borgias

Anthony R Wildman

The Diplomat of Florence

Plutus Publishing Australia

To Robert, as always.

Also by Anthony R Wildman:

What News on the Rialto?:
The Lost Years of William Shakespeare

As a prince is forced to know how to act like a beast, he must learn from the fox and the lion; because the lion is defenceless against traps and a fox is defenceless against wolves. Therefore, one must be a fox in order to recognise traps, and a lion to frighten off wolves.

Niccolò Machiavelli, *The Prince*

Principal Characters

In Florence

The Machiavelli Family

Niccolò Machiavelli, Second Secretary to the Florentine Republic
Bernardo Machiavelli, Niccolò's father
Primavera Machiavelli, Niccolò's elder sister
Totto Machiavelli, Niccolò's younger brother
Marietta Corsini, Niccolò's wife

At the Chancellery

Marcello Adriani, Chancellor of the Florentine Republic
Antonio della Valle, Secretary to Marcello Adriani
Biagio Buonaccorsi
Agostino Vespucci
Filippo Casavecchia

Florentine Politicians

Piero Soderini
Francesco Soderini
Giovanni Ridolfi
Antonio Delvigna
Giovanni Guadagni
Luca degli Albizzi
Francesco della Casa
Pierfrancesco Tosinghi
Alamanno Salviati
Jacopo Salviati
Francesco Taddei
Bernardo Rucellai
Niccolò Zati

Florentine Ambassadors

Ricciardo Becci , Ambassador to the Holy See
Lorenzo Lenzi, Ambassador to the King of France

The Borgias and Their Lieutenants

Pope Alexander VI
Cesare Borgia, Duke of Valentinois and Duke of the Romagna
Alessandro Spanocchi, Borgia's treasurer
Michelotto Corella, Cesare's most trusted lieutenant
Ramiro da Lorqua, Governor-General of the Romagna
Agapito Geraldini, Cesare's principal secretary

In Rome

Giuliano della Rovere, Cardinal, later Pope Julius II
Asciano Sforza, Cardinal

Borgia's Captains

Vitellozzo Vitelli, Lord of Città del Castello
Paolo Orsini, Condottiero from the Roman Orsini family
Giulio Orsini, Paolo's cousin
Gianpaolo Baglioni, Lord of Perugia
Oliverotto Euffreducci, Lord of Fermo

Rulers of the Romagna and other North Italian States

Caterina Sforza, Countess of Forlì
Antonio Baldraccani, Secretary to Caterina Sforza
Guidobaldo da Montefeltro, Duke of Urbino
Jacopo d'Appiano, Lord of Piombino
Giovanni Bentivoglio, Lord of Bologna
Pandolfo Petrucci, Lord of Siena

At the French Court

Louis XII, King of France
Georges d'Amboise, Cardinal of Rouen, Louis' chief counsellor
Jean de Beaumont, French general
Gian Jacopo Trivulzio, Italian condottiero from Milan

Others

Leonardo da Vinci, Artist, philosopher and engineer
Salai, Leonardo's apprentice

Notes for the Reader

'The past is a foreign country; they do things differently there.' So L.P Hartley wrote in *The Go-Between*; for many readers, this book may be doubly foreign, in that it is set five hundred or so years in the past and most of the action takes place in a country with which they may not be familiar. I thought it might be useful, therefore, to include a few notes on terms that appear in the text that will help modern, English-speaking readers navigate Italy at the turn of the sixteenth century.

Gonfaloniere	Literally 'Flag Bearer', it is the title given to the senior magistrate of the Florentine Republic; his authority was quite limited - think more Chairman of the Board than CEO.
Signoria	The nine officials who were elected (usually by lot) as the most senior governing committee of the republic. They were known as the *Priors*.
Signor	Today, the simple equivalent of our 'Mr', but in Renaissance Italy it was more formal, more like 'My Lord'.
Podestà	The senior legal official of a city or town; typically, the Podestà would hail from another city or country, since this would help ensure their independence in a society where client relationships made that a difficult thing to achieve.
Messer	A shortening of the Italian word 'Messere', commonly used as a title of respect for judges and other senior officials.
Ser	Another shortening, this time of the word 'Sere', and used typically as we would use the word 'Sir' (though its use doesn't specifically imply knighthood, just seniority)
Condottiero	A mercenary, or soldier of fortune (plural *condottieri*). The term comes from the word 'condotta', which in Italian means 'contract'
Loggia	An open sided gallery, usually used for public purposes in Italian cities and towns.

Ottimati	The name that was given to the aristocratic faction that had traditionally provided Florence with its magistrates before Savonarola's reforms.
Popoleschi	The 'popular' faction, supporters of Savonarola and therefore by extension of the common people, though in reality most were still of aristocratic origin.
Frateschi	The name that was given to the bands of young boys and girls who Savonarola recruited as acolytes in his cause.

Central Italy in 1500

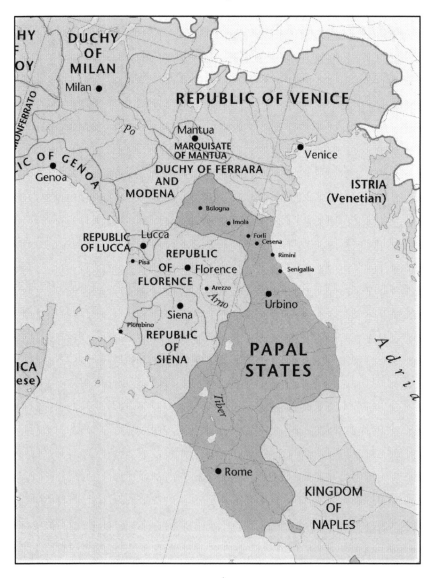

Part One—Shadows and Clouds

Chapter 1—The Preacher

'Throw out everything that is noxious to the health of the soul. Let everyone live for God and not for the world. Live in simplicity and in charity.'

The preacher was barely visible to all except those members of the congregation who were closest to the pulpit of the Cathedral of Santa Maria del Fiore. But the frame of this small, gaunt man concealed powerful lungs and a passionate spirit, which combined to hurl his words to the very back of the cathedral, where Niccolò Machiavelli was standing, near the entrance portico.

'Here it comes,' he murmured. 'The Great Denunciation.'

'You merchants and bankers, you think you can buy everything with money. You weigh your wives and daughters down with gold, and you pay the artisans to paint you as saints. But do you really think the Virgin Mary went about dressed in fine silks and draped with golden earrings? Do you? You should destroy these idolatrous images, abandon your palaces, and go back to the simple ways of Christ!'

A sigh rippled through the crowd.

'We will all die, my brethren, the rich and poor, the old and the young, the infirm and the strong, all will turn to ashes. But those who have abandoned Christ will leave behind a special stench, and no absolution offered by the corrupt priests of the Church of Rome will erase that stench from the nostrils of the faithful. Those priests, who pretend to live by holy orders, who absolve the worst sins of the rich in return for a handful of coins, but demand a week's wages from the poor for the same indulgences, they will be condemned to hellfire for all eternity. And the worst sink of iniquity is Rome itself! Yes! Rome is a cess-pool of wickedness and lechery, and all the vices known to man are practised there.'

Now there were shouts here and there, as the people grew more agitated. This was an old song that they had heard repeated many times in the preacher's sermons.

'The time is coming, my brothers, when all will be swept away, when these evil men who rule our church and our state are turned out by the sword of the righteous. I know this because God came to me and showed me a vision.' He paused, the fervent, prominent eyes sweeping across the crowd, gauging their mood. 'I saw a sword over Italy, quivering. Then, all of a sudden, the sword turned its point downwards, and amid a tempest, it set about scourging all the evil-doers in the land.'

The crowd was hushed, now: they had heard the preacher talk about his visions before, and they knew that there was something extraordinary coming.

'What did this mean? I, Fra Girolamo Savonarola, I will tell you: Florentines, that sword is that of the king of France! It is he who will cleanse Italy of the stink of corruption!'

As the crowd erupted into excited chatter, a tall, elegant young man gave out a snort of derision, loud enough to attract disapproving stares from those around him. Not that Agostino Vespucci gave a fig for that. 'King Charles is in Italy for more temporal reasons, I'll wager. Come on Nico, let's get out of here: he'll be raving for another hour at least.'

Niccolò fought the urge to giggle at the shocked looks on the faces of the people around them as he turned to follow his friend down the crowded nave towards the cathedral's main doors. Only an aristocrat like Agostino could get away with showing such disdain for Savonarola and all his works.

Emerging from the chilly shadow cast by the immense cathedral into bright sunshine, they hurried across to their favourite tavern, a low-roofed place with a jolly striped canopy that extended out into the piazza and sheltered a rough table and benches which they proceeded to colonise, shouting for wine and food as they sat down.

'On the way, lads,' fat Carlo the innkeeper said; he bawled instructions at one of his serving girls and then looked curiously at the four students. 'Been listening to the friar have you? And what song was he singing today?'

'The same as all his other sermons,' Agostino sniffed, picking at a thread on the sleeve of his padded and slashed doublet. 'Fire and damnation unless we all go about wearing ashes and sack-cloth. We should give up all material things, he says, and establish the City of God on the Arno.'

4

Carlo's face split into a red-cheeked grin. 'Florence as a new Jerusalem? He's barking up the wrong tree there, I'd reckon. Can't see all them Medici and Albizzi and the rest giving up their finery, can you?'

'You're right Carlo,' Niccolò laughed. 'No matter what Savonarola says, Florentines will keep on amassing money and spending it on paintings and sculptures to stuff into their grand palazzi, Carnival will always be a drunken riot, and the bum-boys in Sant' Ambrogio will continue to offer their arses to anyone who will give them a few scudi for the pleasure. There are so many delicious vices to choose from if you are a Florentine!'

'Still, Brother Savonarola has a point, I reckon, when he says the devil uses the rich to oppress the poor. Rich folks say that poor people only have themselves to blame for their misery, but when these great men force shopkeepers to sell their shops and farmers their land for a trifle, when they pay a pittance to labourers and artisans for their work, is it any wonder that people turn to thievery and prostitution?'

Having made this pronouncement, Carlo turned and waddled back into the inner recesses of the tavern, leaving the two friends to exchange bemused looks.

'Carlo doesn't exactly look like he's on the bones of his arse, does he?' Agostino laughed. 'I know for a fact he does very well out of this place, and what is more he owns a couple of warehouses down by the river which bring in a good income.'

Niccolò was unsurprised by his friend's knowledge of the finances of their friendly tavern-keeper: Agostino's sources of information were mysterious but comprehensive, and he always seemed to know the most surprising things about people.

'That might be true, Agostino, but Carlo is not so different from the rest of that crowd in the cathedral. There were plenty of poor artisans and beggars, for sure, but surely you noticed that there were also lots of well-off gentlemen and ladies swooning over every word, even as Savonarola denounces them. It's as if they go there wanting to be condemned.'

Agostino's reply was cut short by the chaos that enveloped them as the arrival of food and drinks coincided with the appearance of two more friends, students like themselves, shouting greetings and hurling orders at the poor harassed serving-girls. In appearance the newcomers were a mismatched pair: Filippo Casavecchia, the taller and leaner of the two, was perfectly and fashionably turned out in tight-fitting blue doublet and scarlet hose, covered with a short turquoise tabard that made no concession to the cold. His companion, Biagio Buonaccorsi, was almost the opposite, his chubby figure carelessly dressed in rumpled clothes that clearly had not had the attention of a laundress for some time, and his shoulder-length hair was in need of a comb.

'New hat, Casa?' Niccolò asked once everyone had settled down. 'Come into some money?'

Casavecchia removed the hat in question, an elaborate blue silk affair decorated with a long feather, and regarded it critically.

'It is elegant, isn't it? The latest fashion in Venice, or so the vendor in the market by the Ponte Vecchio told me. It was a gift from my uncle.'

'Never mind his damned hat,' Biagio said excitedly, 'you won't believe the news we heard there: the French have occupied Pisa and declared that they will restore it to its ancient liberty!'

That got everyone's attention, much to Biagio's satisfaction. King Charles VIII of France had entered Italy a month before with a huge army, intent on enforcing his claim to the throne of Naples. One after another, the states of northern Italy had thrown themselves at his feet; the Florentines had temporised, making vague promises of support, but that had not prevented the king from invading Florentine territory. The fortresses at Sarzana, Pietresanta and Livorno had all been taken, which was bad enough, but to lose Pisa was a body-blow, for the city was Florence's western gateway to the sea, and the jewel in the Florentine crown.

'And have a look at this.' Rummaging in the big purse that hung from his belt, Biagio extracted a leaflet which he slapped down on the table so that everyone could see. 'These are appearing all over the city, posted on walls and left in churches. I found this one blowing about the courtyard of the Studio.' The Studio was the official name of Florence's university, where they all studied together.

The leaflet was a cheaply printed effort, and most of its message was yet another exhortation to Florentines to think less of Mammon and more of God, but it was the headline at the top that was particularly arresting:

Oh, Most Christian King of France, free the people of Florence from the yoke of Tyranny!

'Savonarola was just singing the same tune just now in the cathedral,' Agostino said, frowning. 'But his message was that the French king was coming to cleanse us of our moral corruption, not to overthrow the government.'

'Is that what this means?' Casavecchia asked.

'Don't be naïve, Casa, what else could it mean? Whoever printed this—and we can be sure it was printed with Savonarola's approval—is calling for the downfall of Piero de' Medici and his friends.'

'But Piero is hardly a tyrant. After all, he is subject to the will of the Signoria, like everyone else.'

'Which is stuffed full of Medici supporters, as are all the other government committees.' Niccolò was brusque. 'Agostino is right; this is a call for King Charles to overthrow the government.'

'And replace it with what?' Biagio wanted to know.

'If the good friar is to be believed, the kingdom of God, though I expect the king of France might have a few other ideas. Let's see what Adriani has to say this afternoon; he always has original thoughts on matters political.' Marcello Adriani was their lecturer for the afternoon at the Studio, Florence's university.

'He won't be having any thoughts today,' Biagio said, again happy to be the first with the news, 'other than where the nearest latrine might be; apparently he has come down with a case of the flux. No lectures this afternoon.'

After a few not very sincere expressions of sympathy for their lecturer's illness, the friends indulged in another hour's drinking, talking, and harassing the serving-girls. By the time their impromptu party broke up, Niccolò was a little tipsy as he made his way through the crowded streets of Florence. It was late in the afternoon when he walked onto the Ponte Vecchio, and the butchers were starting to close up their stalls. Frowning, he came to a halt, guiltily remembering that the housekeeper had asked him to buy something for their supper that evening.

'Ho, there, young Niccolò, looking for something? You'd better be quick, or I'll be closed before you've finished your wool-gathering!'

'I'm not gathering wool, Marco, I am thinking.' Niccolò was indignant. 'It's different.'

'Looks the same to me. Come on, my wife will scream the house down if I am late for dinner.'

'All right, all right. Angelina wanted some beef. Three pounds or so, she said.'

The burly young butcher rummaged among the bleeding carcasses on his counter and set about chopping and cutting with the dexterity of long practice. In a few minutes, the required amount of meat had been carved, weighed and wrapped. 'There you are. And take some chicken livers as well, fresh today, on me.'

'Hah! You will do anything to keep Angelina sweet on you, Marco. Now, how much are you going to rob me for the rest?'

Agreeing on a price after a few minutes' good-natured haggling, Niccolò paid over the required coins and was on his way across the bridge and into his home district of Santo Spirito. Casa Machiavelli was much like its neighbours—four stories tall with a small warehouse on the ground floor where they stored the wine and oil produced on the family farm in the hills, the brown stone façade above punctured by windows whose green-painted shutters had been thrown wide open to admit as much light and air as possible from the narrow street.

Having delivered his parcels to the housekeeper, Niccolò went in search of his father and found him in his library, where he almost always spent the afternoon. Bernardo Machiavelli was proud of his collection of books, his most prized possessions, and spent many hours each day interrogating them. He was busy translating the writings of the ancient Roman historian Titus Livius from Latin to Italian, a project that had been commissioned by one of Bernardo's wealthier acquaintances, for which he was being paid a gratifyingly fat fee.

'Hello father,' Niccolò said, dropping his satchel on a chair. 'Angelina says there is bread and cheese, and some of her pickled onions, whenever you are ready.'

Bernardo looked up from his book, mildly irritated at the interruption. 'Yes, all right. You're home early.'

'Marcello Adriani is ill, so we were all allowed the afternoon off. Have you seen this?'

Bernardo picked up his spectacles and peered at the leaflet. 'Well, well. The yoke of tyranny, indeed. I suppose they mean Piero and his friends.'

'Who else would they mean? Is there anyone else who could be described as a "tyrant" in Florence?'

'Piero is just a boy, though he thinks he is a prince and entitled to princely trappings.' Bernardo was dismissive. 'Lorenzo would never have been criticised so, not even through the side of the mouth like this.'

'True enough, father,' Niccolò said. 'Though they didn't call him "Lorenzo the Magnificent" without cause: all that money spent on building palazzi and country houses, and all the paintings and sculpture to adorn them. He lived like a prince, so it is hardly surprising that his son thinks he is royal.'

'Who are the Medici anyway? Jumped up wool traders. There are plenty of other wealthy and ancient families in Florence who could claim the right to lead us.'

Niccolò smiled, always amused when his father's snobbish streak came out. It was true, though, that the old Florentine families had always resented the Medici dominance of the government, even as they acquiesced in it, fawning on Lorenzo while they muttered insults behind his back. When Lorenzo had died, two years back, they had wasted no time investing his twenty-year-old son Piero with all of his father's authority, even as they expressed doubts about his ability. Since then, the chorus of complaints had grown ever louder and more insistent.

'Anyway, I doubt King Charles is much interested in changing the government of Florence,' Bernardo went on. 'He just wants us to stand aside while he marches through Tuscany on the way south to Rome and Naples.'

'Oh? You don't think he has been sent by God, like Savonarola says, to scourge us of our wickedness and licentiousness, and cleanse the corruption of the church?'

9

That provoked a predictable outburst. 'Savonarola! That charlatan. But I suppose in these gullible times foolish men will believe in the ravings of a friar from…where *is* he from? Ferrara?' Bernardo sniffed his contempt. 'No doubt we shall soon see the government of the Medici replaced by the government of priests, and decisions made by the consultation of entrails.'

We are nearly at that point now, Niccolò thought as he left his father to his books and went to get something to eat. Savonarola's outburst anointing King Charles as the scourge of Florentine vice was hardly new: he had been prophesying some such thing every week for months. But as the French army got closer, more and more people had crowded into the cathedral, and his credibility had soared. The great lords of the Signoria were increasingly afraid of him, and there was even a Savonarolan party beginning to emerge, dedicated, so they said, to his aims and ideals.

As for Piero de' Medici, Niccolò hadn't ever really given him much thought. Lorenzo had come to power in the year that Niccolò was born, the third generation of the Medici dynasty to hold power in the republic. His death had been a shock, but Piero's accession had just seemed inevitable at the time, and if the aristocrats had doubts about his ability they didn't say so in public, at least not at first. For Niccolò and his university friends, it seemed to be no bad thing that the government of an old man was about to be replaced by that of a man who was more or less their own age. His father was right about one thing, though. Where old Lorenzo had charmed his critics, Piero seemed to go out of his way to antagonise them, and that would lead to nothing good.

As Angelina fussed about getting the evening's supper onto the table, Niccolò pulled his dog-eared copy of Dante's *Divine Comedy* from his pocket and propped it open to read while he devoured bread and some hard pecorino cheese. There was little point in thinking any more about politics, he decided, since the Machiavelli family was hardly likely to be able to have any influence over them, so he might as well lose himself for a while in the great master's poetry. Before long, he was climbing Mount Purgatory with Dante and Virgil, oblivious to the growing cacophony around him as the various members of the household arrived for supper.

*

Under the portico surrounding the courtyard of the Studio, the dice clicked and clattered as they rolled across the flagstones, rolled to a halt, and announced their verdict—four, two, six.

'*Zara*, dammit!' muttered Filippo Casavecchia, the loser for this throw, having guessed wrongly the total of the dice thrown by his opponent. 'And by just one! You have the devil's luck, Niccolò.'

'Whene'er a game of dice is broken up, the one who loses sorrowing stays behind, and learns, as sadly he repeats the throws…'

'Yes, all right, Agostino, you know your Dante. But I'm not far behind. Another few throws and I'll get even.'

'Very well, Casa,' Niccolò agreed. 'But just three more. After that, like Dante I am abandoning you to purgatory.'

Casavecchia took up the dice again and was about to throw when a commotion coming from the gate connecting the courtyard to the street caught their attention.

'Go and find out what's happening will you, Biagio?'

Niccolò thought for a moment that Biagio might protest at this peremptory request, delivered with a cool expectation of obedience. But after a moment's hesitation and the smallest of grimaces, Biagio shrugged and ambled over to the gate.

'It's a march of some kind. I think something is going on. Come and see for yourselves.'

When the friends got to the gate, they were confronted by a crowd of citizens tramping determinedly down the narrow street, shouting the same slogans over and over, 'The People and Liberty! Down with the Medici!' It was only then that Niccolò realised that the bells were ringing from the direction of the Piazza della Signoria. That was usually a signal for the citizenry to go to the piazza for an emergency assembly. Without giving it a second thought, they gathered up their dice and joined the jostling, cheering throng.

'No idea what is happening, my young friend,' the jolly-looking man marching next to him said in answer to Niccolò's query. 'But someone said

11

that the Signoria has locked that brat Piero out of their palazzo. It's the end of the Medici, I reckon.'

That *was* sensational news if it was true. Criticism of Piero had become deafening over the last few weeks, particularly since he had decided, without any authority from the Signoria, to dash off to the camp of King Charles and make all sorts of promises if he would refrain from attacking Florence. People had been particularly incensed when Piero had agreed that the French could keep all of the fortresses and towns they had taken, including Pisa.

Emerging from the narrow street into the broad expanse of the piazza, they found themselves at the back of a huge crowd gathered around the tall, fortress-like Palazzo della Signoria, the headquarters of the Florentine government standing on the south-east corner of the square. Held aloft on tall poles carried by their proud flag-bearers, the banners and pennons of the city's districts flapped and snapped in the breeze above the mutter of the crowd. From every side came shouts: 'The People and Liberty! Long Live Florence! Down with the Medici!'

A memory came to the surface of his mind: fifteen years ago, when he had been just a boy approaching his ninth birthday, his father had come home in a state of white-faced shock, taking pains to double lock the doors and close all the shutters. Bad men had attacked Lorenzo de' Medici and his brother Giuliano, he said, and the city is in an uproar. Niccolò had never seen his father look so frightened as he told his mother in a low voice that the conspirators had killed Giuliano, and no-one knew whether Lorenzo had survived.

When he was older, his father had told him the rest of the story, how the population seemed to lose its collective mind, running wildly around the city torching the conspirators' houses and stringing them up from the battlements of the government palazzo. Lorenzo had, of course, survived the attack though he had been badly wounded, and he had wreaked terrible vengeance on the surviving conspirators and their families. With a shudder, he wondered whether history was about to repeat itself.

Three long trumpet blasts rang out, and slowly the noise subsided into a gentle murmur. A man appeared on the small balcony projecting from the centre of the palazzo and began to read a proclamation. From their position at the back of the crowd, Niccolò and his friends could hear nothing clearly, but the gist was conveyed quickly enough in hurried summaries that passed from mouth to mouth.

'He says that Piero de' Medici and his brother Giovanni are banished from the city,' the jolly man in front of them said. 'He is an outlaw, and any man who kills Piero will earn a reward of two thousand ducats.'

'That's a lot of money.' Biagio whistled. 'If I were Piero, I would be on a horse out of Florence right now.'

Piero was apparently of the same view. That evening, when the friends gathered at Carlo's tavern to chew over the day's events, the story was being told that Piero and Giovanni had gathered their households and ridden out of the city towards Bologna. Stunningly, it seemed that the rule of the Medici really was over.

Chapter 2 – The Republic of God

Florence, November 1494

Ten days after Piero's ignominious flight, Charles VIII of France entered Florence in triumph, welcomed by a supine Signoria and an apprehensive populace who watched his vast army march through the Frediano gate in shuffling silence. Standing in the crowd with Agostino as the king arrived in the Piazza della Signoria, Niccolò was astonished at the sight of this apparently irresistible conqueror, a small, ugly man with a hunched back, bowlegs and a limping gait.

'*That's* the mighty King of France?' Agostino was equally amazed. 'He looks like a troll dragged up from the underworld!'

'Yet that dwarf has humiliated all northern Italy,' Niccolò said pensively, 'and stripped us of our defences. He might have got rid of Piero de' Medici for us, but what, I wonder, will he do next?'

'Well, I hope he moves on soon. We've got a dozen of his bloody soldiers quartered on us. They are eating like locusts and drinking us dry, and there isn't a maid in the house who hasn't had her arse pinched, or worse!'

Niccolò laughed in sympathy. His home, too, had been forced to house some of the French troops, much to the distress of his father and the rest of his family. 'He might be saying he comes as a friend, but he is behaving like a conqueror.'

'Which is what he is.' Agostino was sour. 'Though we, the vanquished, seem to have neglected to put up any kind of resistance. I fear Florence has simply swapped one master for another.'

That assessment seemed chillingly accurate over the days that followed, as Florence came to feel like an occupied city. French soldiers were everywhere, the Florentines' weapons were confiscated, and detachments of French soldiers were eyed with wary resentment by those few Florentines who had not locked themselves in their houses either in fear or as a mute form of protest.

In the Machiavelli household, hosting a couple of French soldiers placed a strain on everyone. His father retreated to his study and his books, refusing to have anything to do with them, and his sister Primavera likewise stayed her

14

room, leaving Niccolò and his brother Totto to manage the household staff and ensure that there was as little friction as possible with the soldiers.

Not that they seemed particularly dangerous to Niccolò. They were both country lads, one big and muscle-bound, the other willowy and pasty-faced. After a few days, Niccolò and Totto got used to their presence and chatted to them in a mixture of Latin and the few words of French that Niccolò had acquired from somewhere in his eclectic reading. For conquering heroes, they seemed surprisingly nervous, and they kept asking how many armed men Florence could raise if put to it; a question that betrayed the cause of their anxiety.

Niccolò couldn't resist a teasing answer. 'As to that *messieurs*, I am told that at the sound of the city bells more than a hundred thousand armed men could be summoned from the countryside.' Whether that was true or not, he had no idea, but it seemed to impress the two Frenchmen while doing nothing to ease their nerves, as he had intended.

He was not alone in wanting to do something to unsettle these unwelcome invaders. Going to and from the Studio, he was startled to hear taunts shouted down from the windows of houses, directed at passing detachments of French soldiery. One day he had to duck to avoid stones that came hurtling from a doorway in the direction of a passing soldier. Then he noticed piles of wood appearing on street corners, which residents had nonchalantly placed, with every appearance of innocent intent, in a perfect position to barricade the streets in a hurry.

No one knew how long the French would stay or what price would be required for them to leave, but rumours went around that Charles had told the Signoria that he would sack the city unless they paid him two hundred thousand ducats and accepted the return of Piero de' Medici, an appalling prospect.

Then, suddenly, the occupation was over. The two soldiers billeted on the Machiavellis joined their comrades and marched out of the city, drums beating and trumpets blaring.

'So what happened?' Niccolò asked Agostino when he and Biagio met him in the Piazza della Signoria to watch a new statue being erected in front of the palazzo. 'You always seem to know what goes on in the Signoria.'

Agostino had an uncle who was currently serving his three-month term on the Signoria, and who often treated his nephew to an account of the goings-on behind the bluff brown stones of the government palazzo. Agostino, in his turn, clearly enjoyed the status it gave him when he was able to pass on the latest to his friends.

'It seems that we owe our liberation to Piero Capponi. You know, the former ambassador. King Charles told the Signoria that if they didn't agree to his demands, the city would be sacked at the sound of his trumpets. "In that case," Piero said, "if you sound your trumpets, we shall toll our bells!" And then he tore the draft treaty in half and walked out. That was enough to get Charles back to the negotiating table.'

Niccolò laughed, remembering his half-joking jibe at the two French soldiers. Perhaps the King of France had been told the same story.

'We still have to pay him a hundred and twenty thousand ducats,' Agostino went on, 'but he has at least agreed to return our fortresses to us.'

'What about Pisa?' Filippo Casavecchia joined them, pushing his way through the crowd in time to hear the last few words. 'Is he going to make them give up their rebellion?'

The citizens of Pisa had remained defiant. Having once been given their independence from Florence, they weren't about to give it up easily. 'All Charles promised was that he would deal with the Pisans when he has finished his Naples campaign,' said Agostino.

Not much of a promise, Niccolò thought. He was about to say so when a cheer went up from the people who had been waiting for Donatello's fine bronze statue of Judith decapitating the giant Holofernes to be levered into place in its new home in front of the palazzo. It had been seized and removed from the Palazzo Medici as part repayment of the debts owed to the state by the now-exiled Piero, and an enthusiastic Agostino assured them that it was an exquisite work by the great master. Niccolò, no aesthete, was happy to take his word for it.

'So what happens next?' Biagio asked of no one in particular as the crowd began to break up.

16

'I don't know,' Niccolò replied, blowing on his hands to keep them warm. 'But think of it—for the first time in our lifetimes, we are free to make a real republic, a place where every citizen can speak his mind and where every virtuous man can become a prince! We have recovered our freedom and we must preserve it at any peril!'

'As the Pisans are doing?' Casavecchia mischievously punctured Niccolò's excited rhetoric.

He was rewarded with a frown. 'Of course they defend their liberty. If we value ours, we should negotiate and make them our allies, not fight them.'

The words had come unbidden and unexamined, and were more than a little heretical, for Pisa was regarded by all Florentines as theirs almost by right, cheerfully ignoring the fact that it had its own long history before it ever became part of Florence's Tuscan empire. The sentiments surprised him as much as they did his companions, but he said nothing to soften them, letting his words hang in the chilly air. For him, they had the ring of truth, no matter how unpalatable they might be to his fellow-citizens.

'Well, there goes any chance of you being elected to the Signoria!' Biagio's loud laugh caused heads to turn among the slowly dispersing crowd.

'No chance of that, anyway.' Niccolò smiled back. It was true—serving in the government was an unpaid occupation, something that only those of independent means could undertake; means that the Machiavelli family did not have. 'Come on, let's get out of this cold. I heard that there is a new tavern behind Santa Croce that serves ravioli in broth so good that they are queuing down the street for it. And I've just enough in my purse to buy us a round.'

*

'How, in the name of God, can an assembly of three and a half thousand members ever work?'

The question came from an indignant Marcello Virgilio Adriani, a prematurely balding scholar and lecturer of considerable renown and impeccably aristocratic antecedents who was formally one of their lecturers, but who had become more of a friend and mentor to the four students. They had gathered as they did every week, under the porticoes of the university, ostensibly to study classical literature and poetry together. Inevitably, the talk turned quickly to political developments, as the Republic of Florence was reshaped and reborn before their eyes.

Things had moved swiftly after the French departed. The old and long-disused mechanisms of Republican government swung creakily into action, and various assemblies had been called to debate the future constitution, mostly stacked with supporters of a newly-energised Girolamo Savonarola, whose ideas they championed with vigour.

After much vigorous debate, it was decided that the new republic should continue to be governed by the institutions that had always existed, even under the Medici: a small Signoria that served for a few months at a time, chaired by a gonfaloniere drawn from their number. But Savonarola had also proposed that the ultimate legislative supremacy should be vested in a huge new body, to be called the Great Council.

'I know what my Uncle Guidantonio thinks about it,' Agostino said. '"The people lack the discretion to choose wise men over the ignorant, so this new assembly will just be a great crowd of ignorant oafs. A disaster, in short". That's what he told the Signoria last week.'

The others nodded and muttered a chorus of assent, though Niccolò couldn't tell if they really agreed with Guidantonio Vespucci's assessment or were simply impressed because he was, after all, a senior aristocrat and a member of the Signoria.

He had a slightly different opinion. 'There is something noble, surely, about trying to establish a broad franchise to reflect the will of the people. Otherwise, we will end up with another government of oligarchs, which, you have to admit, has not been such a successful model of late.'

'Really, Niccolò?' Biagio was startled. 'I wouldn't have picked you as a Savonarolan!'

'Neither I am, Biagio. Can you see me giving up whores and dice in favour of a life of austerity and celibacy? No, I think the good friar's ideas about a Republic of God are unrealistic, to say the least. And Florence is the last place where any man of sense would try to establish such a thing.'

'Savonarola is hardly a man of sense.' Filippo Casavecchia snorted. 'A man of nonsense, more like.'

18

'Still, Niccolò makes a good point,' Adriani said, cutting short the group's laughter. 'Surely a well-ordered republic should have a means to reflect the will of the people as a whole, even if that will might be, let us say, ill-informed from time to time? So how can the natural excesses of the mob be restrained, Niccolò?'

'Well, the Romans had a solution to this very dilemma.'

He waited patiently while his friends engaged in the ritual rolling of the eyes and groans with which they always responded to his citations from Roman history; they thought he was obsessed with Roman constitutional theory. Nor were they entirely wrong. Helping his father with his translation of Livy had given him a profound respect for the inherent genius of the ancient Roman Republic, and he thought there were lessons that his own time could learn from their forebears.

'They too invested the sovereignty of the state in the people,' he pressed on. 'But they had the wisdom to subject their decisions to the deliberations of the aristocracy, people who were bred to government and who could take the long view of things.'

'SPQR,' Adriani murmured. '*Senatus Populus Que Romanus*. The Senate and the People of Rome, together. Yes, quite so, Niccolò. Yet I fear that our republic will find it difficult to arrive at such a balance. The people would not trust a senate made up of the *ottimati*, half of whom would rather have the Medici back than allow the people a say in government.'

'And they probably wouldn't be wrong in that,' Agostino said sardonically. 'You watch as the aristocrats fight back. They are just using Savonarola, you know, fawning on his every word because he sways the sentiments of the people, but they will turn on him sooner rather than later, mark my words.'

Over the weeks and months that followed, though, it seemed that Agostino was wrong. Far from turning on the friar, the aristocratic party, the *ottimati*, seemed powerless to stop him. The new council was elected and a Signoria and gonfaloniere chosen from its members, various other committees were formed to advise on foreign and domestic policies, and life seemed to settle down into a new, more tranquil pattern.

For Niccolò, this new tranquillity had a perverse effect. He became restless and bored with his everyday round. His formal studies came to an end, and

19

though he saw his former friends from time to time, his life increasingly revolved around domestic concerns.

The Machiavelli were an old family, but they had never acquired any great wealth. Niccolò's patrimony consisted of the townhouse in the Oltrarno, a small farm in the hills outside Florence, and one or two other properties dotted around the city. It was enough to feed the family and ensure they would never want for the necessities of life, and when the time came for him to inherit, he would be able to live the life of a gentleman, albeit a modest one.

The trouble was, that seemed like a very dull prospect indeed. Tending the farm and managing a modest rent-roll were hardly taxing occupations and spending all his remaining time in the library seemed pointless, particularly at a time when it seemed as though history itself was unfolding all around him. Yet he could not for the life of him think what else he could do. The city's newly febrile political atmosphere had set off in him an incoherent desire to participate, to act, to influence events, but without money, and lots of it, getting into a position of influence seemed impossible.

So he had little choice but to watch, impotent, as the public life of Florence took its course. It was a course that became increasingly tense when it became apparent that Savonarola had been in deadly earnest when he talked of establishing Florence as a City of God. The city's youth, always restless and susceptible to the wiles of rabble-rousers, unexpectedly became his foot-soldiers. Gangs calling themselves the friar's *frateschi* roamed the streets, chanting hymns which they interrupted only to hurl abuse to anyone who had deviated from the strictly conservative dress codes that the new Great Council had passed into law as one of its first acts.

'It's all just too much to bear,' a petulant Filippo Casavecchia groused one afternoon at Carlo's tavern. 'One of the brats actually threw a ripe fig at me, just because the colour of my doublet was too bright, or something.'

It *was* pretty garish, Niccolò thought, bright yellow striped with green. 'Oh I don't know, Casa, they might just have good taste.'

While Niccolò was enjoying Casavecchia's spluttering outrage at that remark, Agostino thumped the table with his tankard, and then, since that didn't get the response he was after, he jumped on the table and stood looking down at them, hands on hips and a stern look on his face.

'Signori, I propose that we establish a new confraternity to give some relief to our fellow Florentines from the mischief of these over-zealous children!'

'Oh, I like that, Agostino!' Biagio laughed. 'And what shall we call it?'

'How about "The Company of Pleasure"? Hey Carlo, get us some paper and a pen: Nico, you're our wordsmith, you can write the rules!'

By now the whole tavern was listening, enjoying the performance. Pen and paper procured, Niccolò stared out into the piazza for a moment, and then began writing, reading aloud as he did so, with frequent interruptions from his friends.

'Item: No man older than thirty years old can be a member of the company. No old lechers here!'

'But the women can be of any age, surely?' Biagio contributed. 'And the Head of the Company can be either a man or a woman.'

'Speaking of which, we need a method of electing the company head. How about this: Of the men, the first Head will be he who has the longest nose; of the women, she who has the smallest feet.' Niccolò's suggestion was met with howls of laughter: it was well known that the size of the nose and feet corresponded inversely to the size of the private parts of each sex.

'Company members must always speak badly of each other, and reveal each others' faults without hesitation.' That came from someone in the crowd that had gathered around them, setting off a storm of other suggestions. Niccolò hurried to write them all down, and then, finally added a last flourish before calling a halt to proceedings:

> It is resolved that no-one is ever to show by external
> signs the thoughts in his mind; rather, the contrary will
> be done, and he who knows best how to pretend or tell
> lies merits the most commendation.

As a kind of intellectual protest against the strictures of the *frateschi*, the articles for the Company of Pleasure had a certain juvenile amusement value, though Niccolò and his friends were careful not to make sure everyone knew it was a joke, and he stuffed the articles themselves into the bottom of one of the coffers in the Machiavelli house that contained boring legal documents, to make sure they couldn't accidentally see the light of day. He wasn't at all sure that Savonarola's acolytes had much of a sense of humour.

The friar himself delivered sermon after sermon, claiming to have had more visions sent directly from God, and denouncing the new pope, Alexander VI, who remained strangely tolerant, doing nothing to stop the priest's harangues. Then the friar's genius for political theatre inspired another outrage—the so-called 'bonfire of the vanities'—when, on Palm Sunday of 1496, many of the city's artistic treasures were piled up and burned, along with the clothes and possessions of those who the *frateschi* considered immoral.

'He's finally gone too far,' was Agostino's verdict in the aftermath of the bonfire.

'Do you think so? It seems to me that half the city is appalled, but the other half is in ecstasy!'

'That may be so, Niccolò, but it adds one more log to a different bonfire—the one that the aristocrats are building under Pope Alexander.'

'So your uncle says." Niccolò was playful; Agostino's frequent citation of his uncle as the authority on everything that the *ottimati* were thinking had become something of a joke among the little group of friends.

Agostino had the grace to laugh. 'Yes, of course. But I hear the same from many others, I promise you.'

This time, at least, Agostino was right, though it took another year and a half before the pope finally excommunicated Savonarola and forbade him to preach for a hundred and twenty days. Even that didn't silence him, for he simply went to work with his pen, writing treatise after treatise which his supporters printed and circulated throughout the city.

But something had changed. The people of Florence began to entertain doubts about the charismatic friar they had adopted as their own, and the drab, dour society that he and his followers had imposed on them. Increasingly, parades of the *frateschi* were interrupted by Florentine toughs who pelted them with stones and wrested the crosses from their hands, threatening the boys with beatings or worse. An abortive attempt by Piero de' Medici to attack the city set the nerves further on edge. Then there was an outbreak of the plague, necessitating tough sanitary measures that drove people off the streets into a sullen quarantine until it passed.

In August, a plot came to light—five highly respected citizens were accused of planning the return of the Medici to Florence. The evidence against them seemed to be flimsy and extracted under torture. Nevertheless, the Signoria, still dominated by Savonarola's partisans, condemned them to death, and worse, refused their right of appeal to the Great Council under a law originally proposed by Savonarola himself. The Dominican remained silent throughout the whole episode, and the execution of the supposed conspirators provoked furious denunciations from every quarter.

Through all this, Niccolò remained an ambivalent observer. He supported the new republic, had high hopes for it, but this latest outrage was, for him, unbearable. 'How can they do it, father?' he all but shouted when he heard the news. 'Surely there is nothing more foolish than to make a law and not observe it.'

'What, you think that has never happened before?' His father was mild.

'Only in tyrannies. If a law is regarded as generally useful, it should be observed equally by all, no matter who proposed it or who opposed it.' Niccolò was insistent. 'By allowing his partisans to ignore his laws, Savonarola shows that he is no better than his enemies, and a tyrant in all but name.'

Bernardo raised his shoulders in a shrug. 'Calm yourself, son. There is nothing you can do about it. Now, do something useful and help me with these ledgers. I can't make head or tail of them.'

Which just about sums up my life, Niccolò thought sourly. While significant events unfolded in Florence and the wider world, he, Niccolò Machiavelli, was stuck trying to make sense of his father's impossibly confused bookkeeping and wondering what he was going to do with his life.

Then, in the new year of 1498, everything changed.

Chapter 3—A New Republic

It was Ricciardo Becci who set in train the events that changed Niccolò's life forever. A friend of his father's, Becci had been living in Rome for the last three years, where he was Florentine ambassador to the court of Pope Alexander VI.

On his way back to the Holy City after a short visit to Florence for consultations with the Signoria, he had called at the family farm at the little hamlet of Sant' Andrea in Percussina, intending to share a cup of wine with his old friend Bernardo before continuing on his way south. But the weather had turned foul, and torrential rain made the road impassable, so the diplomat had been glad to accept the offer of dinner and a bed for the night. Niccolò's father retired soon after supper, pleading tiredness, leaving his son alone with their guest. Their talk soon turned to the febrile state of the city's politics.

'I tell you, Niccolò, this state of affairs cannot last much longer. The Signoria knows we cannot continue to allow this mad priest to incite the common people against the pope for much longer, but they are too afraid of him and what the mob might do to them if they oppose him, to do anything about it. And that fool Popoleschi isn't worth a pig's ear as gonfaloniere. Just dithers and wrings his hands.'

Niccolò struggled to keep a straight face. The stocky, bluff man sitting across from him in front of the fire in his father's study didn't look much like a diplomat and he didn't talk like one. He wondered if Becci was this blunt when dealing with the smooth cardinals and bishops in Rome. Perhaps he had just had too much of the rough red wine, made from the Machiavelli family's grapes, with which he had been plied over dinner.

'I am told that the Signoria have at least decided that the cathedral is too prominent a place for his sermons and that they have ordered him to confine his preaching to San Marco.'

That caused one of Becci's bushy eyebrows to rise. 'Your sources of information are impressive, young man. That was only decided yesterday. It might help; San Marco is on the edge of the city, and the monastery church is much smaller than the cathedral. If Savonarola had any sense at all, he'd take the hint and tone things down. But I don't think he will. He has truly come to believe that he has been sent by God to reform us all.'

'And the pope? What will his next move be?'

The ambassador frowned slightly, as if assessing what he could safely share. 'Piero de' Medici,' he said, eventually. 'Some of Alexander's advisers have been in talks with Piero's envoys and they are urging the pope to provide the necessary arms and soldiers to enable him to return to Florence and get rid of Savonarola.'

'But surely they cannot be serious?' Niccolò was surprised by his vehemence and it occurred to him, too late, that his outburst might seem impertinent to the older man. But he couldn't stop now. 'The pope would spend a great deal of money on a very chancy venture. It's not as if Piero has proven himself much of a leader, and surely Florence would find herself plunged into bloody civil war!'

'I suspect the pope knows that.' Becci was dry. 'Whatever Alexander's faults, he is not a fool. But he is running out of alternatives. If the government of Florence cannot shut Savonarola up, his only other option is to place the city under interdict.'

That, Niccolò knew, would be a calamity, perhaps even worse than civil war. An interdict would mean that the church would no longer look favourably on the city's citizens, and its priests would no longer conduct mass, take confession, bury the dead. In short, the people of Florence would be deprived of all spiritual comfort.

Pondering the implications of that reduced him to silence. Then a streak of irreverence emerged that occasionally startled his friends when he let his self-control slip. 'But it might not be such a bad thing,' he said, with the beginnings of a mischievous smile. 'After all, the people might discover that they don't need priests to intervene with God after all. And then where would Savonarola be?'

Becci stared at him, then roared with laughter. 'I see you have a rare sense of humour, young man,' he said when he eventually caught his breath. 'Though it's just as well we are out here in the country where no one can hear you, otherwise you might find yourself strung up by some of Savonarola's damned *frateschi*!'

25

He had meant it as a joke, but even as he joined the ambassador in laughter, another thought came into Niccolò's mind. 'You know, Ser Ricciardo, I was talking to one of the Franciscans last week, outside Santa Croce, and he was bemoaning the loss of income from donations and bequests that his order has suffered since Savonarola came to power. It's all going to the Dominicans, instead. Apparently, the faithful think that they have a better chance of getting to heaven if they donate to Savonarola's order rather than theirs.'

'You do surprise me, Niccolò. Is there anyone in Florence you don't talk to?'

'Well, I *listen* to everyone. But the point is, it is not in the interests of every priest in the city to see Savonarola and his Dominicans so powerful. The Franciscans at least might be pleased to see him brought down a peg...' Now he had Becci's interest. 'So if the good brothers of St Francis at Santa Croce could be brought to challenge Savonarola's claims to be a prophet, he might at the least be distracted from his attacks on the pope. That is a thought worth pursuing.'

The diplomat's dark eyes considered that. 'Niccolò, you have an original way of thinking. Sooner or later, the wheel will turn, and we will have a government that will be better equipped to use your talents. When that time comes, nominate yourself for public office. I will support you, that I promise.'

Niccolò was taken aback, for though he had considered government service, he had been discouraged by the chaos of the republic's current politics. And then there was the fact that the most prestigious positions were unpaid, which meant that they were usually won by men who had far greater means at their disposal than Niccolò Machiavelli and could afford to devote the greater part of their life to politics. Even to win one of the lesser positions, which were considered less honourable but which were paid a stipend, would require the active support of a network of patrons and friends. He could think of several people who would gladly offer their help if he chose to run, but Becci's offer would carry significant weight.

He simply nodded and stammered his thanks, and they passed on to other subjects. But the idea of public office kept buzzing around in the back of his head, long after he had retired for the night. By the time he eventually fell asleep, he knew that this was where his life was going to go.

The next morning, as Becci was about to climb into the saddle and resume his journey, he paused and turned to his hosts. 'Niccolò, it occurs to me that it

26

might be very useful if I could have a reliable report on the priest's next sermon.'

'Consider it done, Ser Ricciardo.'

With which, the Florentine ambassador to the Holy See had mounted his horse, which was skittish and keen to get on its way, and shouted a last farewell as he headed south along the muddy road, his horse's hooves kicking up mud as he went.

'What was that about?' His father was obviously mystified.

'Nothing, just a little job that he wanted me to do for him.'

Niccolò returned his father's enquiring look with a level stare that defied him to ask more; after a few seconds, Bernardo shrugged and turned to go back inside.

*

> Still expounding Exodus and coming to that passage, where it says that Moses slew an Egyptian, he said that the Egyptian represented evildoers and Moses the preacher who slew them by exposing their vices. Then he added, and this is what he was driving at, that he wanted to give the Egyptian another stab wound, a big one. He said that God had told him that there was someone in Florence who sought to make himself a tyrant, and that he was engaged in dealings and schemes in order to succeed, and that the desire to drive out the friar, to excommunicate the friar, and to persecute the friar meant nothing else than to seek to create a tyrant...

As he sat in his father's library penning these words later that afternoon, Niccolò remembered the excited speculation that had run, whispering, around San Marco's church. To whom might Savonarola be referring? Who was it that was using the pope's excommunication of this holy man to set up a tyranny that would tear down everything he and they had built since the end of the Medici regime?

Names were whispered, some of them so ludicrous that Niccolò, leaning carelessly against the wall and trying to keep an expression of gullible enthusiasm on his face while his brain feverishly recorded every word, had almost had a fit of giggles. The cheap rhetorical trick that Savonarola was employing was contemptible, stirring up the crowd with a non-existent threat, cloaked in a 'vision' he said he had had from God.

It had always seemed strange to Niccolò that God, who had a pope and all those bishops to choose from for his confidences, should instead have picked this Dominican mendicant friar as his mouthpiece. Of course, no one had ever actually heard the voice of God whispering in Savonarola's ear, except the preacher himself, since the Almighty apparently preferred to communicate late at night when Savonarola was alone in his cell. But as he looked around the crowd that filled the church and spilled out into the piazza beyond, he felt he was alone in his scepticism.

Then Savonarola's sermon had taken a new tack. Perhaps realising that the Signoria was so afraid of him that he no longer needed to defer to them and that planting the idea in the minds of the people that the republic was under threat from some internal conspiracy would be sufficient to keep them confused, he had instead turned the full force of his denunciations against the pope.

> *He seeks to set them at odds with the Supreme Pontiff and says of the pope what could be said of the wickedest person you might imagine. Thus, in my judgement, he acts in accordance with the times and turns his coat accordingly...'*

And that, Niccolò thought as he absently scribbled a few more closing lines to his report, was the key, for it was evident that Savonarola had no intention of being turned aside from his course of confrontation with the pope and the church. If Ambassador Becci had been hoping that he would have some good news to report to the pontiff, he was going to be sadly disappointed. The Florentine Signoria was cowed, and Savonarola seemed to be the unchallenged master of Florence.

Yet, barely a month later, everything changed.

It was the Franciscan monks of Santa Croce who had lit the fire which turned into a conflagration. No one seemed to know who'd really started it, but one of the Savonarola's fellow priests on the other side of the city at San Marco had taken exception to a sermon by one of the Franciscans that attacked Fra Girolamo in violent terms. The upshot was an extraordinary challenge—that the two priests should walk through fire to see which of them was telling the truth.

Hearing of this madness from an uncharacteristically excited Agostino Vespucci, Niccolò was startled, and he wondered whether ambassador Becci had taken up his idea, even though he had meant it as a joke, and somehow contrived to incite the Franciscans to this act of defiance.

'What is it that the Apostle Matthew says?' Agostino exclaimed, 'that "a depraved and adulterous people look for miraculous signs"? Though surely there should be some less homicidal way to put this to the test!'

'Perhaps they will both die, and the people will see that these tricksters are mere conjurers, mountebanks whose promises of paradise on earth are just so much hollow nonsense.'

Agostino looked shocked by that remark, not so much because of the words as because his friend had dropped his mask of circumspection and revealed his real sentiments. He took a furtive look around the piazza to see if they had been overheard. 'Be careful, Nico, or you'll find yourself hauled up in front of the justices.'

Agostino was right to remind him that speaking so freely could be dangerous. But neither of them could have foreseen how swiftly the end would come.

The so-called trial by fire, when the appointed day came, turned into a farce. Ludicrously, the two friars spent hours quibbling with each other about the terms of the trial, infuriating the big crowd that gathered to witness this extraordinary event. The supporters of each side began to accuse the other's protagonist of wanting to get out of it.

Then a torrential downpour appeared, sweeping across the city and drenching the platform upon which the oil-soaked wood and kindling were piled. When the whole thing was finally called off, and the disgruntled crowd dispersed, still shouting imprecations at each other, Niccolò knew that

Savonarola's authority was fatally weakened. For the first time, the ordinary people on whose support his career had been built hurled abuse at the friar as he was hustled away from the piazza surrounded by guards.

A few days later, the news came that king Charles VIII was dead, back home in France after his failed campaign to conquer Naples.

'The great prophet didn't predict *that*,' was Agostino's acerbic comment. 'So much for the French king's sword sweeping away all vice. You watch, the nobility will take their chance now.'

Agostino was simply repeating the views of his uncle Guidantonio, one of the leaders of the aristocratic party, but Niccolò had no doubt that his prediction would come true. It didn't take long; in early April a mob attacked the houses of several prominent Savonarolans, giving the authorities the excuse they needed to proclaim the friar an outlaw. Savonarola and two of his fellow Dominicans were arrested and thrown into prison, and after a few days it was proclaimed throughout the city that the friar had confessed to all sorts of crimes, including conspiring to take over the government.

That last seemed particularly implausible to Niccolò, and he said so to his father.

'Why would he conspire in secret to achieve the aims he expounded so loudly in public? He and his partisans were well on the way to controlling the government anyway.'

'After a few drops of the *strappado* most men will confess to anything,' was Bernardo's dour assessment. Niccolò shuddered at the thought of it: this method of torture, in which the victim's arms are tied behind his back and strapped to a machine that jerks the body into the air, usually wrenching his arms from his sockets, was excruciatingly painful and few men could endure more than a few 'drops'.

Another two uneasy weeks went by, and then it was announced that Savonarola and his two accomplices had been found guilty of treason, and condemned to death. On the appointed day, Niccolò stayed home, obeying his father's nervous demand that all of the family stay off the streets while the city's temper was so disturbed. It was from an excited Biagio that he heard the details.

30

'They were hung in chains on a platform that was constructed overnight in the Piazza della Signoria, and then the bodies were burnt. And the noise! Apparently gunpowder was mixed with the fuel, so all anyone could hear was the crack of explosions.'

'And the crowd? How did they react?'

'Silent, mostly. It was as if they were witnessing a martyrdom. Very eerie.'

'Savonarola as a saint? He would have been appalled at the very idea that his bones might become an object of veneration among the faithful.'

'No chance of that. The city fathers have commanded that his remains be tossed into the Arno.'

And so the turbulent rule of Girolamo Savonarola was over. His partisans were unceremoniously ejected from office, causing new elections to be held for the vacancies thus created. Among the new appointments was Marcello Virgilio Adriani, chosen as chancellor and first secretary of the republic, a post primarily responsible for foreign affairs. He was also the titular head of the chancellery office, which dealt with all of the republic's correspondence and kept the records of the deliberations of the Signoria and the other committees that collectively formed the government. It was Adriani who asked Niccolò to put his name forward for the position of second secretary.

'You would be perfect,' Adriani said when they met at the new chancellor's house. 'After all these years of factionalism, we need people in the chancellery who are non-political. I know you had your criticisms of Savonarola, but I don't know anyone who would say that you were a member of any of the parties either for or against him. Besides, Becci speaks well of you. He says you write a fine report and are a shrewd observer of the behaviour of men. There will be others who will covet the post—it has a salary of one hundred and ninety florins, after all—but I think you will find you have enough supporters to secure it.'

Niccolò needed little persuasion. The second secretary's formal responsibilities were for relations with the republic's subject states and territories, but in the overloaded and overworked chancellery office, the boundaries between the various posts were, he knew, fairly porous, and the second secretary was often called on to undertake all kinds of diplomatic missions. Adriani, an intelligent and charming but rather lazy individual,

31

would likely confine himself to the more ceremonial aspects of his job, and delegate everything else to his subordinate. That would suit Niccolò perfectly well, for he could see that it was an opportunity to be at the centre of things.

But first, he had to secure the position. He was not wealthy and could not bribe his way into office as others could, and so he tackled the task in the only way he knew—by hard work. Having put his name in formal nomination, he crisscrossed the city, talking to everyone he knew who might influence the final election, offering soothing condolences to those who had been supporters of Savonarola, expounding his views more forcefully to those who had been his opponents and, to the surprisingly large number of people who, like himself, had been nervously neutral through the recent turmoil, he emphasised his literary skills, so important in a position that handled all the city's correspondence.

The ballot, when it came, was decisive, and he beat three other candidates by a handy margin of votes. He was now Second Secretary of the Florentine Republic.

Chapter 4—A Cardinal becomes a Duke

Florence, June 1498

'That must be your desk,' Biagio said, pointing at a table at the far end of the room, a long and narrow chamber that opened off the Hall of the Lilies, the magnificent room where the Signoria met, and state receptions were held.

Niccolò's satisfaction at his own election had been sweetened when he learned that all three of his friends from the Studio had also won places in the chancellery. Arriving at the entrance of the Palazzo della Signoria that morning, he had been unsurprised to see the ever-eager Biagio waiting for him, a good hour before anyone else was likely to turn up, let alone Casa or Agostino, who were habitually late risers. Bounding up the three flights of stairs like exuberant schoolboys, unable to contain their excitement, they had arrived breathless at the portal to their new kingdom.

The morning sun spilled through three tall windows into a room that looked like an abandoned battlefield. Books, papers, ink pots and pens littered every surface. A forlorn-looking hatstand stood in one corner, its only burden a single cap; in another, a pile of ledgers teetered on the top of a coffer, threatening to tumble to the floor at any moment. Dodging between the desks and chairs that filled almost every available inch of space, Niccolò slid into the big cross-legged chair that sat behind the big table and contemplated the mess of papers and files strewn across its polished wooden top, abandoned when its previous tenant, Alessandro Braccesi, had been dismissed. Poor Alessandro, left stranded on the wrong side of the river by the fall of Savonarola.

'Don't feel too sorry for him.' Biagio was reading his mind. 'He picked the wrong horse to back, that's all.'

'Easy to do in Florentine politics. We could find ourselves in the same position easily enough.'

'Come on, Nico, don't be such a pessimist! Not today, anyway. After all, Alessandro's misfortune turned out to be your good luck, didn't it?'

Which was true enough, though he felt that Biagio was undervaluing his efforts to give Fortune's wheel a nudge in the right direction. But then the Buonaccorsi were sufficiently wealthy and well-connected that it had needed

33

little exertion on Biagio's part to secure his place in the chancellery. The same was true of both Agostino and Casa, whose names and connections had pretty well guaranteed them a position. Niccolò was, when he came to think about it, probably the poorest man in the entire chancellery.

It was not in his nature to brood on such things, which was just as well, for the political upheavals of the last few months had paralysed the workings of the chancellery office. There was a great deal of work to do, for which he would need all of the energy he could muster. Correspondence had piled up unanswered; the records of various meetings of the Signoria left in a deplorable state, no more than rough drafts that were yet to be fair-copied and filed; and the roll of citizens eligible to participate in elections and the lists of those who met the requirements to be elected for office were not up to date. As if all that wasn't enough to contend with, there was a new government in place, a new gonfaloniere and Signoria, and a new Committee of the Ten of War, the body responsible for formulating policy for the management of all matters military.

Of course, he and Biagio and Agostino and the others were just clerks, public servants whose job was to record and give effect to the decisions of their masters, who were the actual decision-makers in Florence. For the most part, their work was prosaic: minuting meetings, copying and filing executive orders, and composing letters to foreign princes and potentates. They might be at the heart of government, but what their superiors actually wanted was a fair hand with the pen and a high work-rate. Any views they might happen to have on the great affairs of the day they could keep to themselves.

Niccolò had arrived at the chancellery with a head full of cloudy but elevated ideas about how government should work and, with visions of himself offering humble but compelling policy advice to the grandees of the Signoria, only to find that the only opinions they sought from him concerned such vital issues as the appropriate titles with which to address a letter to the Duke of Ferrara, or the correct procedures for voting in the Great Council.

For the first week or two, it all felt like a great come down from the excited high hopes of that first day, and he struggled to fight off depression. It was some unexpectedly practical advice from his father that had eventually lifted his mood.

'My son,' Bernardo said with a gentle smile, after listening to a half-hour rant from Niccolò on the subject of his impotence, 'I have believed all my life

34

in the power of the pen. Those who write history determine the way future generations will see and understand what has happened. In the same way, those who write the letters and record the minutes soon find themselves being consulted about what is to be written, not just its form. Know what they want to say before they know it themselves and, before long, you will find that the lords of the Signoria will be asking your opinion on everything.'

So unexpectedly pragmatic was this advice, coming as it did from his woolly-headed father, that Niccolò just stared at the older man for a few moments, before grasping him in a hug and kissing him on both cheeks. 'Papa, you have lightened my load no end. I shall follow your counsel to the letter and become the best, most well-informed and most thoughtful secretary in the history of the republic!'

Aristotle and Livy and Caesar and the rest could offer him little guidance in this, so he reluctantly pushed them to the back of his mind and instead thought about the problems that faced him in practical terms. His first priority must be to bring the workings of the chancellery office up to a reasonable state of efficiency. He knew what had to be done, but felt hampered by his lack of authority, for though he had the grand title of second secretary, in reality, he was no more than first among equals with his other colleagues in the chancellery office. True, he was responsible for making sure the work got done and for allocating the various tasks to the other secretaries, but beyond that, his powers were limited.

His solution was a combination of hard work and patience. He worked exhaustingly long hours, making sure that every letter he wrote, every minute he formulated, every memorandum he composed, was as perfect as could be, as a model to the others. He went out of his way to offer help and assistance to any of the others who seemed to need it and listened patiently to their complaints about the impossible or confused directives issued by their political masters. Invariably, the other secretaries came away from these meetings with suggestions as to how they might best deal with their problems and, before long, he found that his authority in the chancellery office was unquestioned. Agostino and Biagio, meanwhile, were soon recognised as his lieutenants, as was Filippo Casavecchia, whose unfailing good humour soon endeared him to the rest of the chancellery clerks.

As summer gave way to autumn, he and his colleagues had cleared away the backlog of correspondence and instituted new procedures so the complicated routines of the office were managed efficiently. Not everything was perfect, of course; nothing much, except perhaps time, would solve the various schisms that rent the Great Council, creating endless confusion, and the sheer volume of paper that flowed through the chancellery was still overwhelming. But all in all, considering the chaotic state of the office he had inherited, Niccolò was pleased with their progress.

Understanding the politics of the newly-reconstituted republic was another matter altogether.

The end of Savonarola had not meant the end of factions. The *popoleschi*, the party of the people, now repudiated Savonarola, refusing even to speak his name; they were nevertheless determined to maintain the broad-based democratic system that he had championed, in particular the fifteen hundred elected representatives of the Great Council, seeing it as the one body that ensured that the people had a real and powerful voice in the government. That didn't suit the *ottimati* at all, who still wanted to return as much power as possible to aristocratic hands. Some of them, it was rumoured, were even prepared to invite the Medici to return. The two parties were deeply suspicious of each other, and every piece of legislation soon became a proxy for their ongoing war.

Then there were all the complicated networks of patronage, linking the great families of Florence with their retainers and supporters and dependants in a web of promises and favours that often crossed factional lines. Discerning the true interests of the council's members and getting any decision from its executive committee, the Signoria, involved a great deal of careful negotiation and a lot of tiptoeing to avoid stepping on the wrong shoes.

The short tenure of the members of the Signoria was another complication that might have rendered the government of Florence completely impotent were it not for the fact that those elected to the Signoria were usually full-time politicians. They were wealthy enough that they could devote a significant amount of time to the affairs of the republic, attending the Great Council, serving on various committees, meeting others of their class informally at their palazzi or social events. By the time they were elected to the Signoria, most were at least aware of the critical issues of the day.

Even so, they relied on the permanent public servants of the chancellery to help them through procedure and to ensure that there was some kind of continuity of policy. Niccolò and his colleagues were the only people in the Palazzo della Signoria who knew intimately how the rickety, clumsy structure of the Florentine government actually worked, how decisions had been taken, and what political traps had been sprung or avoided. And this, Niccolò realised, was the key to acquiring some influence, limited though it may be, over the republic's policy.

The grinding work of setting the chancellery to rights had been a crash course in government, and Niccolò set out to use this newly acquired knowledge to his advantage. He was always available with a ready ear whenever any of the priors, as the members of the Signoria were called, came looking for some record or state paper. After a while he found himself the recipient of their private commentary on the goings-on in the Hall of the Lilies next door, to which he listened politely, occasionally offering up pithy comments that his interlocutors received with amusement if he had judged his man well or a dignified silence if he had not.

Thus encouraged, he began to offer advice that went beyond the mechanics of protocol and procedure, always delivered with the diffidence and humility due to their rank as the masters of Florence. Some of the priors were disdainful since they regarded him as not much more than a superior sort of servant, and gave him an astonished stare, as though a donkey had suddenly delivered an oration in Latin. But others, usually those who were secure enough not to feel threatened by him, listened politely, if noncommittally, now and then demonstrating their approval with a smile or a nod. Little by little, they got used to him and, before long, even the least perceptive of them began to show that they appreciated his interventions. Then, within a few months of his taking office, the Signoria showed their growing confidence in him by appointing him as secretary to the Committee of the Ten, the council responsible for the management of military affairs.

The day after this latest appointment was announced, Niccolò was at his desk, privately enjoying a moment of satisfaction at this state of affairs, when Filippo Casavecchia brought the entire office to a standstill by letting out a squawk loud enough to cause everyone in the office to look up.

'What is it, Casa?' Agostino called across the room. 'Your tailor's bill come in?'

37

The laughter that remark caused was good-natured, for the fussy Casavecchia spent an inordinate proportion of his salary on clothes, much to the amusement of the far wealthier Agostino, a man who, though always immaculately dressed, was indifferent to all matters of fashion.

Sending a glare and a dismissive wave of the hand in his colleague's direction, Casavecchia made his way across to Niccolò's desk and handed him the sheet of paper he had been holding. 'What do you make of this? Here, halfway down.'

It was a despatch from Ricciardo Becci in Rome. Machiavelli's eyes skimmed down the page to the item his colleague had pointed out.

'Ah. I see why you were so surprised,' he said to the room at large. 'It seems that one of Pope Alexander's sons has renounced holy orders, given up his cardinal's hat, and is to become a soldier! And the French king has made him a duke, duke of...' He consulted the paper again. 'That's it, duke of Valentinois.'

'Well, that certainly doesn't happen every day,' Biagio said. 'Most churchmen would walk over hot coals to get a cardinal's red hat and shoes. It must be unprecedented for one of them to want to give them up.'

'Which son?' Casavecchia asked. 'There are so many of them.'

Every pope seemed to come to the Throne of St Peter accompanied by a cloud of relatives—nephews, nieces, cousins and occasionally, even unacknowledged illegitimate sons who might be presented to the world in another guise. Alexander, the former Cardinal Rodrigo Borgia, was no different, except that he made no effort to hide the paternity of his children and was ever eager to promote them to positions of power and authority whenever the opportunity presented.

'Cesare,' Niccolò answered. 'Bishop of Pamplona and archbishop of Valencia. He's the eldest of the brood now, I think, since Juan died last year.'

'Wasn't there a rumour that this Cesare was responsible for his brother's murder?'

The mysterious death of Juan Borgia, Captain-General of the Papal Armies, had caused a sensation at the time. Headstrong, arrogant and incompetent, the list of people who might have wanted to kill him was a long one. So when

38

Juan's body had been fished out of the Tiber bearing the signs of a brutal death by stabbing but, strangely, still wearing his jewels and rings and with coins still in his wallet, rumours began to fly, all of which had been duly reported by the Florentine ambassador in the despatches Niccolò had read in his first days in the chancellery.

His natural scepticism, however, made him cautious. 'So it is said. But I am not so sure. Fratricide is a dreadful crime.' He glanced around the room, suddenly conscious that everyone had stopped work and was listening to his every word. 'And even the most ruthless churchman might blanch at committing it.'

'Well, guilty of fratricide or no, this particular ruthless churchman seems to have translated himself into a duke.' Agostino was thoughtful. 'What prize, I wonder, was the King of France awarded in return?'

That was a good question. Niccolò picked up the despatch again, skimming down to the next paragraph.

'Ser Ricciardo says that the pope has annulled Louis' marriage.' King Louis XII had succeeded his brother Charles in April and had immediately applied to the pope for a divorce from his supposedly sterile wife. 'You remember, he set up a commission of prelates in France to examine the issue back in July. They must have completed their work and given Pope Alexander the excuse he needed to release the king from the bonds of matrimony to a barren wife. A dukedom for the pope's son seems to have been the price for such an expeditious outcome.'

He handed the despatch back to Casavecchia, who was responsible for copying it into the letter-book and including the most important points in the daily bulletin summarising the day's despatches that went across the hall to the gonfaloniere and the other members of the Signoria every afternoon. The momentary excitement over, peace and quiet were restored as the room went back to work on the never-ending piles of paperwork. Before long, the only sound was that of quills scratching across paper and the occasional muttered exclamation when a word seemed particularly hard to make out, or an error was made in transcription. Niccolò himself, returning to the task of composing a particularly vexing letter to the commander of the garrison at Volterra, gave no more thought that day to the question of Cesare Borgia.

A few weeks later, the Florentine ambassador to Rome himself turned up, having been summoned to report in person to the new Signoria. Afterwards, he dropped into the chancellery office and, clapping Niccolò on the shoulder with a force that made the younger man wince, taking the opportunity in his big, booming voice to congratulate him in person on his appointment.

'I told you this was the place for you, Niccolò! It looks like you've taken to it like a frog to a lily-pond. And the Signoria is pleased with you, I can tell you that. Come on, walk with me and we'll have a chat about what's what.'

Niccolò was disconcerted by Becci's loud praise, and his cheeks were flushed as they walked out of the chancellery office under the collective gaze of the other secretaries. Outside, the piazza was sweltering under the late summer's sun, and they sought shelter under the vaulted arches of the great Loggia that ran along the southern side of the piazza, where vendors of fruit and vegetables had set themselves up, as they were permitted to do when the portico wasn't being used for any governmental purpose.

Pacing up and down along its length, Niccolò listened in respectful silence as the older man declaimed on the strengths and weaknesses—mostly weaknesses, in the ambassador's view—of the new Signoria and gonfaloniere, with whom he had been closeted for most of the day.

'The old Medici system had its problems, and God knows I don't want them back again, but at least you knew who you were dealing with and there was some kind of consistency to the policy of the state. To change the government every few months makes that impossible. I've just spent two hours explaining to this lot of priors exactly what I told their predecessors three months ago! And then, once they have the facts, they are either too intimidated by them to make any decisions at all or they blunder about in ignorance, thinking they can do what their predecessors could not. It's enough to try a saint.'

All of which Niccolò entirely sympathised with for he wrestled with the same problems every day. But complaining about it would do no good, and he sought to direct the ambassador's thoughts into more constructive channels. 'We were startled to read in your despatch a few weeks ago, Ser Ricciardo, of the decision by the pope's son to repudiate holy orders and become a soldier.'

'And a French duke to boot! He is being sent off to France in a few weeks, carrying the king's annulment with him. There is even talk that he is being promised a princess as a bride! They are flying high, the Borgias.'

40

'What kind of man is this Cesare? No one seems to know much about him here.'

'Made to be a soldier, I would say. Very athletic. Cardinal Sforza told me that the day after the consistory approved his renunciation, Borgia turned up in his hunting park with a dozen henchmen, and proceeded to kill eight bulls, one after another, with his men cheering him on! Since then, hardly a day has gone by when there hasn't been some story or another of his physical exploits. It's as if he wants to prove to the world that he should never have been made a priest in the first place.'

Niccolò thought about that as they made a turn at one end of the loggia. 'But he's a soldier without an army, at least for now.'

'That's true, though King Louis is taken with him and is said to be keen to offer him a command in his army.'

'An army that is intended for where? Milan?'

'You're sharp today, Niccolò. Yes, that does seem likely. Louis has barely got his feet settled on the royal footstool, but I imagine he has not forgotten that he has a better claim to the Duchy of Milan through his mother than *Il Moro* has.' Ludovico Sforza, the Duke of Milan, owed his nickname—The Moor—to his dark complexion. 'I imagine the duke is spending a lot of time looking over his shoulder and wondering when a French army will appear from over the Alps, this time uninvited.'

Becci was sardonic. Four years before, it had been the Duke of Milan who had, for reasons of his own, invited Louis' vainglorious predecessor to march through Lombardy in his campaign to conquer Naples. By thus opening Italy's northern door Ludovico had caused mayhem: the fall of the Medici and everything that followed in Florence, while Pope Alexander had had the fright of his life when French cannons had been trained on the walls of Rome. All this had flowed from Ludovico's incompetent scheming, so if Charles' successor chose to attack Milan, none of the other states of northern Italy would shed a tear.

'But what does the pope gain by drawing closer to France?'

The ambassador gave him a sideways look. 'Indulge me Niccolò, while I give you a little lecture in the realities of Italian politics. You know of course

41

that apart from all the little states, Ferrara and Lucca and so on, the peninsula is dominated by five powers: Venice, Milan and us in the north, the kingdom of Naples in the south, with the pope and his territory wedged between. Keeping a balance between these five has always been our policy, as it is that of the pope. Why do you think that is?'

Niccolò thought for a moment. 'Because we are the weakest of the five?'

'Bravo, young man. Yes. Milan and Venice can both command powerful armies and, in the case of Venice, a powerful navy. Naples occupies all of the southern half of Italy as well as Sicily, and is both rich and well-armed. What is more, the royal house hails from Aragon, and so King Ferdinand has the backing of the kings of Spain. The pope has great wealth and prestige, and controls a great swathe of land from Ravenna all the way down to Gaeta, near Naples. We, on the other hand, control barely half of Tuscany, have no standing army, and rely on our wealth and our wits to survive.'

'So our aim in foreign policy is to play each of the other powers off against each other, trying to make sure that none of them is strong enough to crush the others. Yes, I see.'

'Good. But not everything is entirely as it seems. For one thing, the papal territories are actually barely under the pope's control. Travel through the region around Rome, and you pass castle after castle from which you will make out the flags of the Orsini and the Colonna and the other great Roman families, who are always ready to rebel against papal authority. So the pope is not as powerful as he seems, and has to devote most of his energy to making sure that he is able to keep what little control he has over his own back yard.'

'Then there is the Romagna,' Niccolò said thoughtfully. This region, between the Apennine mountains on the eastern border of Tuscany and the Adriatic Sea, was even more lawless, dominated by petty princes who hired their little armies out to anyone who would pay them. 'I suppose this pope says he will rein in the Romagna lords?'

'Yes, just as every one of his predecessors has,' Becci nodded. 'But he has no hope of succeeding there if he also faces the prospect of another French invasion. Alexander is terrified of the prospect.'

'And so he draws ever closer to France,' Niccolò said, 'no doubt hoping to avoid having to again face a French army outside Rome.'

Becci laughed. 'Oh, he's just following the fashion. It can't have escaped your notice that all the states in the north of Italy have been falling over themselves to ally with the French, ourselves included. Charles really upset the apple-cart when he invaded four years ago.'

A glance at the clock on the tower of the Palazzo della Signoria told Niccolò that it was high time for him to return to his desk. 'I must get back to work, Ser Ricciardo. Thank you for your time. As always, I learn something new from every conversation with you. Even though most of these matters are properly in the domain of Ser Marcello, it is always helpful for a humble servant of the state such as me to get the value of your insights.'

Becci looked at him. 'By God, Machiavelli, you do lay it on. No wonder the Signoria thinks you have the makings of a diplomat.'

Niccolò felt himself blushing once more. He hadn't meant to be quite so obsequious; it was just a habit he had acquired in dealing with all the various members of the government, the Signoria, the members of the War Committee and the other committees, the legislators of the Great Council, most of whom were so puffed up with their own importance that they barely noticed his flattery.

Seeing his embarrassment, the ambassador gave him a friendly laugh and an encouraging squeeze of the shoulder. 'You keep doing what you are doing, my boy. Everyone likes you and everyone talks to you, and that is a priceless quality in a diplomat. Now, I must go too.'

And so they had parted, Niccolò back to the pile of correspondence that awaited him on his desk, Ambassador Becci to his lodgings to collect his servant before starting out on the long road south to Rome.

Settling back behind his desk, and ignoring the curious looks from his subordinates, Niccolò indulged himself in a momentary daydream, in which he, Niccolò Machiavelli, was appointed as an ambassador representing the interests of the Florentine Republic in some all-important negotiation with a foreign potentate. It would happen one day, he was sure. But for now, there were the records of the last meeting of the War Committee to be reviewed and corrected, a task that seemed just a little more tedious than usual.

Chapter 5—Trouble in Castrocaro

You're a lucky bastard!

Niccolò laughed out loud when he saw the words that Biagio Buonaccorsi had scribbled across one corner of formal instructions issued by the Signoria for his first important independent mission.

Biagio said it again later that afternoon as they sat under the shade of a tree, one of a small grove that stood between the unfinished palazzo being built by Luca Pitti and the cluster of houses surrounding the church and piazza of Santa Felicità in Santo Spirito. Despite the distant hammering coming from the palazzo, it was a peaceful spot on that late July afternoon. They had taken a rare break from their labours in the chancellery and slipped across to the other side of the river, where they cajoled the Machiavelli housekeeper into providing them with a flask of wine, some meat and cheese, and half a dozen oranges.

Peeling the last of the oranges, Niccolò laughed at his friend's outburst, which had been occasioned by the instructions he had received that morning directing him to leave the following day on a mission to the court of the famous, formidable and, it was reported, beautiful Contessa Caterina Sforza, Lady of Forlì and Imola. 'It's business, Biagio, nothing else. Do you think I am going there to seduce her?'

Biagio made a choking sound, indignant laughter competing with his attempt to swallow an orange segment. 'Of course not!' A pip was ejected and fired across the grass. 'I just meant you are lucky to have a chance to get out of the office for a while, that's all.'

'If you say so.' Niccolò was equable, choosing not to point out that Biagio had talked of almost nothing else except the legendary Contessa as they'd walked over there. 'Anyway, I will only be gone a few days, a week at the most. I'll be back before you know it.'

'Leaving us to swelter away under the supervision of that shit-eating bastard della Valle.'

'Antonio! What has he done to get under your skin?'

'Nothing yet. But you know what he's like—as soon as you are out of sight, he'll be in the office, poking around, making those oh-so-superior comments he likes to make, with his bloody patrician nose in the air.'

It was all Niccolò could do not to burst out laughing. Antonio della Valle was exactly as Biagio had described him—a jumped-up pompous young man who seemed to think his position as secretary to Niccolò's superior, Chancellor Adriani, gave him the right to lord it over the other secretaries and notaries of the chancellery. By longstanding tradition, it was his responsibility to check on the progress of the office whenever the second secretary was absent. So far, that had only happened once, three months before, when Niccolò had been sent on his first independent mission to the military camp outside Pisa where a mercenary captain, Jacopo di Piombino, had been threatening to withdraw his services unless he received more money. That absence had only been for a few days, but it was all the time that della Valle had needed to make his unwelcome presence felt in the office. Niccolò had had to spend half a day smoothing down various feathers when he'd got back.

'Come on, Biagio, you can't take him too seriously. He's reached the pinnacle of his career already, and he knows it. You should follow Agostino's example and just ignore him.'

'It's all right for Agostino, he comes from a real patrician family and della Valle can't afford to offend him.'

That was true; Niccolò had greatly enjoyed the moment when Agostino, subjected to some officious enquiry, had fixed Antonio della Valle with such a look of affronted astonishment that the Secretary to the Chancellor had blanched, stammered, then bolted from the office in haste, leaving behind a room full of laughter.

'Come on, we'd better get back,' Niccolò said, hauling himself to his feet. Biagio followed suit and they set off down the street towards the Ponte Vecchio. He slipped an arm across his friend's shoulders. 'You know, it's the work we do that matters. All Antonio does is fetch and carry for Adriani and help him write those tediously long odes to the majesty of the republic that he has to deliver to the Great Council. No one will remember him after he's gone.'

This seemed to cheer Biagio up. 'You're right. It's just that he gets under my skin.'

'Don't let him. And listen, while I'm away, I'm relying on you to keep me informed of what is going on here—not just in the chancellery, but what they are saying in the Signoria and elsewhere. Write as often as you need to, and no-one else needs to see your letters; they can just be between you and me.'

'Don't worry, Niccolò, you can rely on me.'

Machiavelli squeezed his arm and smiled his private smile. That was the way to handle Biagio, make him feel like he was your confidant, the person you most trusted in the world. Not that doing so required any dissembling on his part, for he knew that Biagio was bone-loyal. But he didn't have the self-confidence of Agostino Vespucci and needed constant reassurance that his status was inviolable. And Niccolò did need to have someone keeping an eye on office politics while he was gone, for it was not just Antonio della Valle who was happy to find fault when his back was turned. This wasn't a task he could give to anyone else—Agostino was bored by such grubby matters and Filippo Casavecchia, for all his charm, was too flighty to be relied on.

The next morning, he was on his way, riding east along the south bank of the Arno in the brilliant morning sunlight, feeling as excited as a schoolboy to be freed from the confines of the office where he had spent most of his waking hours for the last year. That day, he was no mere clerk, but the independent agent and proud representative of a great republic. He startled both himself and his horse by laughing out loud at the prospect. Then his more sardonic self admonished him that, at this rate, he would be more puffed up with self-importance than even Antonio della Valle by the time he got to Forlì. He reminded himself that, notwithstanding the long and precise set of written instructions he had been given, his task was quite straightforward.

The Florentine government had determined that the time was right, the King of France having promised his support, to commence a campaign to recover Pisa, which had been in Florentine hands for almost a hundred years until Charles VIII had taken it into his head to restore their independence. The *condottiero* Ottaviano Riario had been engaged to provide a mercenary troop to help in this endeavour over a year ago but had quit the contract after only a few months, claiming he had been underpaid. Now the Signoria had been approached by his mother, the Contessa Caterina Sforza, asking for Ottaviano to be re-engaged on the same terms as before.

The Florentines, always alert to the possibility of a bargain, had decided to accept the *condottiero*'s services, but at a much lower salary. It was this that Niccolò was to negotiate; as he saw it, this was a repeat of his mission to deal with Jacopo di Piombino, though he acknowledged that the Lady of Forlì was, by reputation at least, an altogether more formidable opponent.

Marcello Adriani had emphasised as much when he had given him his instructions the day before. 'You will need to keep your wits about you, Niccolò. Caterina Sforza hasn't held on to Forlì and Imola all these years by being soft. Not that she is above using her femininity when it suits her, but she has a shrewd brain at work underneath. I don't know what game she is playing with this sudden renewal of interest in committing her son's soldiers to us, but the fact is that we need them, so you must to make sure that we don't lose her goodwill.'

'While offering to pay her less money for her services than before,' Niccolò said.

With someone more conscious of his dignity than Marcello Adriani, such a remark might have been considered impertinent, but the chancellor shared Niccolò's wry sense of the absurd, and he'd just smiled. 'You know our masters. If there is a bargain to be had, they want it, even if good sense says that they should pass it by. Speaking of which, in the interests of getting the maximum value from your journey, there's something else I want you to look into on your way to Forlì. Castrocaro.'

'The feud?'

'Yes. The Signoria is worried that any new outbreak of strife there will weaken the border. You saw the report—it seems that the old quarrel is starting up again.'

Niccolò had indeed seen the report. Castrocaro was a small place, but its fortress was an important link in the chain of defences between Tuscany and the Romagna, the papal territory that curled around their eastern border. An old vendetta between the Naldi and the Corbizo families had settled into a sullen truce over the last few years, but apparently, there had been some new disturbances that suggested the feud might break into the open again.

'The War Committee also want an inventory done of the military supplies there,' he'd said, one hand thoughtfully rubbing his chin. 'That can be my excuse to visit, and then I can interview the local families and see what's going on.'

'Good man,' Adriani had replied. 'I'm told that one Guerrino del Bello is the fellow at the centre of it all. Make sure you talk to him.'

He arrived in Castrocaro on the afternoon of the second day of his journey, having stopped overnight at a particularly cheap and vile roadside hostel in the tiny hamlet of San Benedetto. Though he was not expected at the fortress, the commandant responded quickly and respectfully when Niccolò showed him his authorisation from the Signoria. The inventory of supplies of cannonballs and saltpetre stored in the fortress was soon completed and he decided to raise the question of the feud.

'Ah. I was wondering why the Signoria should have sent such an illustrious servant to deal with a routine matter of munitions.' The commander, who seemed to be a simple and guileless soldier, looked at him with a worried expression.

'Alas, my simple ruse is easily penetrated,' he said with a smile. 'Don't worry, the Signoria just wants to know what is going on and whether there is anything to worry about.'

'That's a laugh. This whole thing started with the Signoria in the first place. Not this one, the last lot. They sent me a message to say that they had a suspicion that Dionigio Naldi, the exiled head of the family, had plans to enter Castrocaro to do some mischief to the Corbizo family, with the help of a fellow named Golferelli. I sent my sergeants to arrest this Golferelli, but unfortunately, he got away and fled the town. The next thing I know, the Naldi are claiming that my actions were taken at the behest of the Corbizzi and that they were cancelling the truce! It took me weeks to smooth everything down and get everyone back on talking terms.'

'And this fellow Guerrino del Bello? In Florence, they told me I should talk to him. How is he involved?'

The commander looked a little rueful, one hand rubbing the back of his neck. 'That *was* a mistake on my part. I was told that del Bello was conspiring with some members of the Corbizzi family to foment trouble. I went to his house, where he was having dinner with four of his friends, demanded that they break up, and told his friends to leave the town. Guerrino slammed the door in my face. Frankly, the intelligence I had was a little dubious, so I decided to take no further action. But I think he is still pretty angry with me.'

'I see. Well, I'd better go and see him at least, then I'm sure we can wrap this matter up.'

Leaving the commander to complete the paperwork for the inventory, Niccolò walked down the hill into the town to find del Bello's house. As it happened, young Guerrino was not at home, but his father, a straight-backed and white-haired old man, was happy to welcome him inside and to talk about his son's misdemeanour. Niccolò soon warmed to the del Bello patriarch, who was quick to acknowledge that his son had been disobedient and had acted hastily in denying the demands of the commander. But he insisted that they were loyal to Florence. 'It's a matter of simple hospitality, signor. It is not right to ask us to send out into the night friends and relatives who we have received as our guests. The commander should have known better.'

With which Niccolò found himself agreeing. Assuring the old man that all would be well, he decided to walk up to the piazza to see what else he could find out. The place boasted only a single tavern, and the owner and his few patrons knew by then exactly who he was, the word having flown down from the Castello within a heartbeat of his arrival.

Not surprisingly, he was greeted with the wariness of villagers everywhere in the presence of officialdom. The offer of a round of drinks loosened their tongues a little, and a few crude jokes he had picked up from his farmhands at Sant' Andrea did the rest. After half an hour's chat about the weather, the local crops, the state of the roads and the peccadillos of the local mayor (addicted to chasing young maids half his age, apparently), they began to talk about the subject that Niccolò was really interested in—the old feud between the Naldi and Corbizi families.

'Let me tell you, Messer Machiavelli, no one here wants that fight to break out again.' The tavern-keeper joined in the conversation, thumping his counter in emphasis. 'It took long enough to end it, and there was a lot of property damaged before it was done. Even a knifing or two. No, the fires of that feud need to be kept well tamped-down.'

The others in the tavern nodded and murmured their agreement.

'What about this business with Guerrino del Bello? I notice he isn't in town…'

'You met old Bello del Bello, did you not, signor?' asked the local priest, who had been listening quietly to the conversation. 'What was your impression of him?'

'He seemed an upstanding sort of fellow, I would say.'

'Well, he and his son are like two peas in a pod. We all heard the story, and your Florentine commander went to some trouble to apologise for the disturbance he caused in the town. Guerrino was in the right of it, but he made no trouble. No, signor, the Bellos are peace-makers, not peace-breakers.'

Niccolò nodded. Clearly, the inhabitants were united in their desire to ensure that the town returned to its usual tranquillity, and there seemed little more to be said on the subject.

'Mind you,' someone else said, 'if there is going to be trouble hereabouts, it will come from outside Castrocaro.'

The speaker of these words—a grizzled-looking farmer in his middle years—earned a few sharp looks from his fellow citizens.

'What do you mean?' Niccolò asked.

'What he means,' said the tavern-keeper, 'is that we can keep the peace in our town and in our own way, but when the soldiers of the Lady of Forlì come calling, there is little we can do.'

'Oh? There has been some trouble?'

'You could say that. Yesterday, a dozen crossbowmen wearing the Naldi colours raided and robbed a farmhouse just a mile from here. Three men were wounded. It's a bad business.'

'Naldi livery, you say?'

'When Dionigio Naldi and his cousins were exiled, they went off and formed a company of *condottieri*. Their current employer is Lady Caterina.'

A mile away, and therefore well within Florentine territory. What was Caterina Sforza doing, allowing her soldiers to attack a Florentine village at the very time she was trying to get employment for her son's mercenaries with the republic? It made little sense.

'Listen here, Messer Machiavelli,' the tavern keeper said, intense. 'You seem like a sensible sort of man, so I'll tell you straight what we all think. We owe our allegiance to Florence, but we are afraid that your government is too preoccupied with its own matters to look after little Castrocaro and won't be there when we need it.'

'But the Romagna is peaceful enough at present,' Niccolò said, amiably. 'Surely you don't expect an attack from there?'

'I don't know, signor. But we hear all sorts of rumours. And let me tell you, we don't trust the Lady Caterina at all. These raids have been happening too often.'

Niccolò nodded and solemnly promised to convey their concerns—there seemed little point in repeating promises of Florentine protection which they obviously didn't believe—and then proceeded to lighten the atmosphere with another round of drinks.

Later that night, he put everything he had learned into a despatch, trying to convey something of the anxiety of the townspeople. Everything suggested that Castrocaro was secure enough for the time being, and the disturbances he had been asked to investigate appeared to be nothing. But something was boiling in the pan, that was clear.

Chapter 6—The Tigress of Forlì

Forlì, July 1499

Eager to get on with his commission, Niccolò left Castrocaro at daybreak to complete the short journey to Forlì. Dropping down out of the hills to the edge of the Po valley, he approached the formidable walls of a city that was one of the critical strongpoints along the ancient Via Aemelia, the arrow-straight Roman road that skirted the Apennines and connected Milan with the Adriatic coast at Rimini.

Word of his coming had been sent by regular courier some days before, and he was admitted without difficulty at the western gate. From there, he was directed to the sprawling Ravellino Fortress on the edge of the city. Within its extensive outer fortifications were the usual collection of stables, smithies, armourers and barracks to be expected in a building whose primary function was military. Beyond these stood an elegant palazzo, the residence of the Contessa Caterina, surrounded by its gardens, and beyond that, again the forbidding four-towered form of the Citadel, the last bastion of defence in an impressive complex.

His arrival might have been expected, but Her Excellency was clearly not holding her breath waiting for him to appear. With the barest of courtesies, he was curtly informed that the contessa was presently engaged with other business and had no time to see him then. He was to come back later. Keeping his temper with difficulty, Niccolò made a pretence of apologising for having caused any inconvenience by his early arrival and took his leave. Having seen to the quartering of his horse, he decided to walk back into the city and have a look around. In his dusty travelling clothes he was an anonymous figure—just another of the many itinerants who thronged the town. It grew steadily warmer as he wandered through clean and well-ordered streets thronged with well-dressed, prosperous-looking citizens.

In front of the Duomo, a market had been set up, selling all manner of goods. One of the stalls displayed portraits of the contessa, some of them just crude prints, others quite finely painted likenesses. Curious about the woman he was about to meet, he picked one up. If the portraitist had got it right, she was undoubtedly beautiful. A long and graceful neck supported a fine-boned oval face framed in long tresses of red hair artfully curled into ringlets. The artist had painted her in half-profile, from which position a pair of shrewd eyes seemed to look mockingly at the viewer. Remembering that Biagio had asked him to send back one of these portraits, he began haggling a price with the vendor.

'Do you sell many of these pictures?' he asked once they had agreed a price and the vendor was wrapping the picture in a grubby piece of cloth.

'You would be amazed, signor. It seems that every household in Forlì wants a picture of our contessa to hang on their walls or in their place of business. Though it's not so often that a Florentine gentleman like yourself wants one.'

'It's for a friend,' Niccolò said, offering a deprecatory smile. 'He is fascinated by Contessa Caterina, though quite why I don't know.'

The vendor nodded at that. 'Not so hard to understand. How many female rulers do you know of, in Italy or anywhere? Let alone any who have kept their state for as long as she has. She is a remarkable woman, signor, wouldn't you say?'

True enough, Niccolò thought as he walked away from the market, the newly-wrapped likeness tucked under his arm. As he walked, he reviewed what he knew of her history. Born the illegitimate daughter of Galleazzo Sforza, the late Duke of Milan, brought up at the Milanese court and betrothed to Girolamo Riario, Lord of Imola, at age ten. Growing to womanhood, she survived half a dozen pregnancies, and numerous conspiracies in Rome, where her husband served his uncle—or, some said, his father—Pope Sixtus IV.

Riario had been assassinated a decade ago and she had acquired the lordships of both Imola and Forlì, ruling in place of her young son, Ottaviano. In rapid succession, she had married one of her stable grooms (also murdered in yet another conspiracy), then Giovanni di Pierfrancesco, a Florentine aristocrat, who had led her into her present alliance with Florence. Then, ten months ago, her beloved Giovanni had died after an illness and the contessa had been left once again to rule her domains all alone.

Her fierce *condottiero* father had insisted she be trained in the use of arms as well as the other more usual, more gentle arts. These skills she had found more than one occasion to use and with a courage that had stunned her opponents. In Rome, twenty years old and pregnant, she had commanded her husband's troops when they'd occupied the papal fortress of Castel Sant'

Angelo in an attempt to control the election of a new pope after the death of Sixtus IV.

Most famously, when her first husband had died in the chaos of an assassination plot, she had locked herself up in the Ravaldino, abandoning her children as hostages to her husband's murderers. That they had seriously underestimated her became apparent when she defied them from the walls of the fortress. The conspirators threatened to kill her children to which she responded by yanking up her skirts and pointing to her genitals, shouting down that she had the means to make more of them! The conspiracy collapsed and the contessa had engaged in a fierce orgy of revenge, imprisoning and killing the assassins and their families.

This was the woman he was about to confront. Back in the lodgings they had allotted him in the fortress, he slipped the painting into his saddlebag and changed from his travelling clothes into garments more appropriate to a formal audience. Half an hour later, he was waiting in an anteroom to be admitted to her presence, nervously reviewing his instructions.

The big wooden doors finally swung open and he was ushered through a deserted audience hall into a smaller side chamber that held only two people— the Contessa herself and a spare, grey-haired and middle-aged man who stood beside her chair, his hands folded in front of him and his black eyes impassive.

Niccolò approached and made an appropriate genuflection, sufficient to communicate respect without indicating servility. Kissing the proffered hand, he straightened and looked the contessa full in the face for the first time. His first irreverent thought was that Biagio would have been disappointed had he been here. The girl whose likeness the painter had captured was still there in the mature woman who sat regarding him with a cool and imperious stare, but her face was lined with the marks of strain—crow's feet radiated from the edges of her eyes and two severe frown lines between them. The famous red hair, where it peeked from beneath her elaborate headdress, was coarse and dull, and the application of paint to her face didn't entirely disguise an ageing complexion.

'Messer Machiavelli, you are most welcome to our court.'

The voice was harsh; more commanding than beguiling. 'Your Excellency, I thank you for your welcome and the courtesies shown by your servants. I regret that my early arrival was inconvenient to you and I am grateful that you have so speedily made this time available to receive me.'

If she knew that her servants, far from showing him any courtesy, had dismissed him with great disdain when he had arrived that morning, she gave no sign of it. Instead, she indicated the older man standing beside her chair. 'You will not have made the acquaintance, I don't suppose, of Messer Giovanni da Casale. He represents my uncle here in Forlì.'

As he made a small nod of recognition, Niccolò thought rapidly about why da Casale might be here. He was a senior adviser to the Ludovico Sforza, who had seized control of the Dukedom of Milan following the death of his brother, Caterina's father. Perhaps his presence was meant to convey that the contessa was not without options—if Florence did not meet her terms, she would snuggle up even closer to Milan and its tricky duke, which could cause concern in Florence if King Louis was indeed preparing to attack Milan as Ricciardo Becci had suggested. She might even turn against her old friends, the Florentines.

Make sure you don't lose her goodwill, Adriani had said. Not surprising—the last thing the Signoria would want is to have a weakness on their eastern border if there was a possibility they would have a French army rampaging around to their north. This was going to be more difficult than he'd thought. 'Excellency, the hour is late, so if you will allow, I will come to the point.' A nod authorised him to continue, using the formal language of diplomacy. 'My lords of the Signoria of Florence desire me to convey to you their earnest desire that the time will come when they may show how highly they value those who have loyally served our republic and have shared our fortunes, as Your Excellency has ever done.'

Neither face showed any change of expression at this pleasantry and Niccolò hurried on. 'However, I must inform Your Excellency that your request to renew the contract for the services of your son Ottaviano and his army gives rise to certain difficulties. As you know, Signor Ottaviano broke off the contract by which he had been engaged before its designated time had expired. This necessitated the hire of new troops to replace him, at considerable expense to the Florentine treasury, which is already stretched to its limits.'

The only response from the contessa was a minute arching of an eyebrow. It was da Casale who spoke, his tone carefully neutral. 'So you do not propose to renew the contract?'

'I simply wish to convey the difficulties with which the Signoria finds itself contending. The original contract having been broken and the Florentine treasury being exposed to heavy additional charges. As a result, my lords of the Signoria wish to make it clear that they believe they are under no *obligation* to renew the engagement of Signor Ottaviano.'

'But?' Da Casale said, lips turned down in impatience.

'My Lady,' Niccolò said, addressing himself to the contessa rather than her adviser, 'out of the love that the republic bears you and in consideration of the services you have rendered her in the past, the Signoria has authorised me to offer a renewal of the contract, but on a peace footing and at compensation for this year not to exceed ten thousand ducats.'

Through a tempestuous life, Caterina Sforza had learned to school her emotions when she needed to. That much was evident as she leaned forward a little in her chair and fixed Niccolò with a stare that conveyed her displeasure even as she employed honeyed words in her response. 'I have always, Messer Machiavelli, been satisfied with the words that the Signoria have used to me. Their actions, on the other hand, have not always been so pleasing. This seems to be one of those occasions. You talk of the costs to your treasury; this I understand. But you should also understand that Florence has never paid the rate of compensation that would be commensurate with the value of my services. You get us cheap, Messer Machiavelli.

'Nevertheless, I will not dispute on this point, nor will I dispute whether or not Florence is bound to renew the agreement. All I can say is that I have faith that you will eventually see sense and will not now show yourselves ungrateful to one who has for many, many years done more for you than any of your other allies. Your Signoria has clearly taken considerable time to discuss and consider this proposition before putting it to me, and I would not want to insult them by replying in haste, so I must take some time to consider my answer.'

With which she stood and offered her hand in dismissal. Niccolò bowed and pressed his lips against the cold emerald set in her ring. 'Of course, Your Excellency, such a decision must be given proper consideration. I beg that you will think quickly upon our proposal, however, so that I may return and

56

communicate it to the Signoria as soon as may be.' He hesitated for a moment, remembering another item from his instructions. 'If I may ask one more question of Your Excellency? The Signoria has written to you on a previous occasion requesting that you supply us with cannonballs and a quantity of saltpetre. They have asked me to request, most respectfully, an answer to their query.'

'You may tell the Signoria that I have neither. And I am greatly in need of both.'

For the first time in the interview, Niccolò saw a flash of anger in the otherwise impassive eyes. She seemed on the verge of saying something else, then thought better of it, settling instead on a silent stare at the Florentine envoy. Niccolò held her gaze for a moment, glanced at the dour and still silent Da Casale, then nodded and retreated to the door.

Later, in the early evening, he was in his room overlooking the palace gardens, scratching away at his report to the Signoria when he was interrupted by a knock at the door. Opening it, he was confronted by a stout and grey-bearded gentleman of middle age, who announced himself as Antonio Baldraccani, Her Excellency's secretary. *Now the real negotiation will begin*, Niccolò thought as he ushered his guest into the room and offered him the only chair, while he remained standing.

After a few opening pleasantries, Baldraccani came straight to business. 'You should know, Messer Machiavelli, that the Lady Caterina has received a request from her uncle, the illustrious and mighty Duke of Milan, asking her to send him fifty men-at-arms and fifty mounted crossbowmen.'

Why did duke Ludovico suddenly need soldiers? He remembered his conversation with ambassador Becci. Perhaps Il Moro thought he was about to be invaded and was desperately shoring up his defences.

'He has further agreed to engage her services on the same terms as those your republic offered last year, which you have now reduced,' the secretary went on. 'You see the difficulty this makes for the contessa? She would not be able to excuse herself to the duke if she accepted the conditions offered by you, which are discreditable, as opposed to his, which are highly honourable. And of course, there is the obligation by blood to the duke. And so she finds herself at a loss and cannot decide promptly on a reply.'

'There is little I can say to you, Signor Baldraccani, other than to repeat that we are constrained by the limits of our treasury and can offer no more than the ten thousand ducats I have already mentioned.'

'Even though your republic has increased the pay of the other *condottieri* in its service?'

That is sly, Niccolò thought. This secretary was well informed about the pay of the Florentine army.

'As I explained to Her Excellency,' he said with growing impatience. 'Florence is bound to these other mercenaries, who have continued to perform to their contracts. We are under no such obligation to her son, who abandoned his responsibilities. It is only out of respect for the contessa's long loyalty to us that we are offering a renewal on terms we believe are appropriate for the case.'

Baldraccani looked glum, then threw his hands up in defeat. 'All I can say is that my lady is desirous of renewing her son's engagement with Florence, but that she must consider these other offers, which will take time. I beg of you, Messer Machiavelli, write to your Signoria and assure them of her goodwill.'

As he placed his hand on the door-latch, the secretary turned back. 'You asked the contessa whether we could spare artillery balls and saltpetre, and my lady made it clear we could not. However, she asked me to say that, should you require gunpowder or soldiers, other than those belonging to My Lord Ottaviano, she would be prepared to part with some of them, if a price can be agreed.'

'The Signoria will be most grateful, I am sure.' He did his best to sound appreciative of this small olive branch. Another question occurred to him. 'Tell me, Signor Baldraccani, how long has Messer da Casale been at court?'

The contessa's secretary visibly debated with himself how to answer. Perhaps there might be some jealousy between this secretary, who had presumably served Caterina Sforza for a long time, and the blow-in from the court of Milan.

'As to that, Messer Machiavelli, he has been in Forlì for two months, at the behest of her uncle.' Another hesitation. 'The contessa values his advice greatly and makes no decision without him.' With which, Baldraccani nodded his farewell, and left.

After the secretary had gone, Niccolò pondered for a while. Perhaps he was getting somewhere, after all. The limited offer of war supplies suggested that the contessa was prepared to give some ground; a signal that she might be prepared to accept something less than her original demand for the use of her son's troops. How genuine was she in her protestations of loyalty?

And how to explain the presence of da Casale? Something in the tone of the secretary's words had hinted that perhaps the presence of the Milanese was unwelcome. Had he been sent to try and detach the contessa from her alliance with Florence? After all, her bond there was the fruit of her marriage to a man now dead for ten months, and she had blood ties with Milan.

Making up his mind, he pulled out a new sheet of paper from the supply he kept in his satchel, dipped his pen in ink, and began to write. Half an hour later, having provided his masters with a detailed account of his meetings so far, he began writing his conclusions.

> *Mere words and arguments will not go far in satisfying Her Excellency unless supported by acts. If Your Lordships were to make some acknowledgement to the contessa for her past services or increase the compensation under the new engagement, you would be sure to preserve her friendship.*

The pen stopped for a moment. Should he recommend an amount of compensation that might satisfy the contessa or was that exceeding his remit? Of course, the Signoria had expected that just presenting their demands would do the trick and they had given him limited authority to negotiate. Yet he was the man on the spot and if this matter was to be concluded satisfactorily, he was sure that they would have to offer something. Naturally, the skinflints in Florence would not want to hear that they had to pay anything more, which seemed to Niccolò to be stupid and short-sighted. Caterina Sforza was a valuable long-term ally, and pushing her into the arms of her volatile and unpredictable uncle did not seem to be sensible policy. That thought decided him and he started writing again.

59

I believe the way to content Her Excellency would be to increase the pay for this year to twelve thousand ducats. This at least is my opinion, in which I admit I may be mistaken; it is difficult to judge whether she is more favourably inclined to her uncle the duke or to our republic. On the one hand, for the present Giovanni da Casale seems to rule everything and may easily sway the undecided mind of the contessa. But on the other, I also think she foresees the possibility that the Duke of Milan will be attacked by France and does not know what security there would be for her should she attach herself to him under those circumstances.

Sanding the despatch and sealing it, Niccolò hoped that his arguments would have some sway over the thinking of the Signoria. The regular courier to Florence was waiting in the courtyard of the fortress and, as he watched the young man swing into his saddle and trot out of the gate, he felt satisfied he had done all he could for now. He would just have to wait until he received a reply.

Waking the following morning, he decided that there was little point in seeking another appointment with the lady Caterina until he had something useful to communicate. Indeed Baldraccani had indicated as much when applied to. So he was left to his own devices meantime. There was plenty of private correspondence to go through. A long letter from Biagio reminded him to send him a likeness of the contessa (he would get a nice surprise when the courier arrived) and complained extensively about Antonio della Valle (Niccolò laughed out loud when he read that Biagio wished poor Antonio 'bloody shit in his arsehole'). A shorter, more sardonic note from Agostino made fun of the office antics and gave him an admirably concise summary of various conversations he'd had with members of the Signoria that touched on his mission here. Then there were official reports that had been forwarded for his consideration on various routine matters, less amusing to read but important nevertheless.

With his usual efficiency, he had soon dealt with it all, writing half a dozen letters to various people and packing them off with the daily courier. Bored, he decided to walk back into the town. In the piazza, he had just stopped to chat again to the vendor who had sold him the picture of the contessa when there was a great tumult as a troop of soldiers marched into the middle of the square. Niccolò had no experience in counting troops, but it looked to him as if there were about five hundred ordinary men-at-arms, followed by another fifty crossbowmen. Well-equipped and uniformed, they tramped through the piazza, trumpets blaring and drums banging, the Sforza flag snapping in the breeze atop its tall pole held by a strutting flagbearer. In their lead was a tall, muscular young man wearing a magnificently plumed helmet.

'Who's that?' Niccolò asked the picture seller as the column tramped past them in perfect order.

'That's Dionigio Naldi, one of the contessa's captains. He's off to Milan, so rumour says, with his troop.'

Naldi. The exiled head of one of the factions that seemed to be causing such trouble in Castrocaro. 'I am no military man, but they do seem to be well-drilled.'

'Aye. The Lady Caterina oversees them herself.' The picture seller was obviously proud of the martial skills of the Contessa of Forlì. 'A right tartar, they say she is. The soldiers are more frightened of her than any of their captains, and the captains shit themselves when they see her coming.'

Niccolò laughed and wandered off, thoughtful. Over the course of the day, he made a point of talking to as many people as he could—ordinary people, tradesmen, vendors and the like, and people of the middle sort, merchants and traders, farmers in from the country. His Florentine accent was not particularly remarkable in a town where so many of his countrymen were employed at the court and he had a way of putting people at ease that encouraged them to open up and talk.

What he heard was that, strong though Caterina's grip on the city might appear, she was not in fact at all popular. Paying the soldiers required money and that meant imposing ever-higher taxes; not a great way to inspire affection. It seemed that the incident he had heard about at Castrocaro was not isolated— many of the country people suspected her soldiers of fomenting lawlessness in the countryside. Not for the first time, Niccolò wondered whether she had her soldiers entirely under control; they were mercenaries, after all.

Not that Caterina Sforza seemed to care very much about any of that. From behind the walls of her fortress, she could afford to ignore the disaffection without. Still, Niccolò wondered what would happen if some foreign power came along and offered to relieve the people of Forlì of her presence. She might well find that having control of the fortress would be no substitute for the support of her people.

The next day, young Ardingo, the tireless courier who rode back and forth between Forlì and Florence, delivered the Signoria's reply to his report. As soon as he had read the contents, he hurried off to find Baldraccani to ask for an audience with the contessa. An hour later, he was again in the same little room off the audience hall, approaching the Lady of Forlì, the despatch clutched in his hand. Da Casale was not there this time and the contessa was accompanied only by the faithful Baldraccani.

'Excellency, I have received a reply to my despatch of the seventeenth.'

'So Baldraccani has already informed me. Let us hope that they have come to an intelligent decision.'

'I think you will find they have, my lady.' Niccolò smiled, unable to resist a theatrical flourish as unrolled the despatch and affected to read the contents, though he had already committed the key points to memory. 'Their lordships of the Florentine Signoria send you their greetings and, having considered at some length the despatch which I sent to them and, in particular, the views that I expounded therein, have consented to increase the payment for the services of Lord Ottaviano to twelve thousand ducats.'

He had not expected that the contessa would leap from her chair and cover him with kisses on hearing this news, for the price offered was well short of her expectations. But neither did he expect that she would just sit there, stony-faced and silent, making no reaction at all.

'This offer does not meet with your approval, Lady Caterina?' He was unable to keep the surprise out of his voice. 'May I reassure Your Excellency again of Florence's continuing goodwill and determination to ensure the honour and safety of Your Excellency.'

At last she stirred and the flinty eyes softened. 'I am sorry, Messer Machiavelli, if I appear less enthusiastic than you expected. Of course, I am gratified that your Signoria has seen fit to increase their offer and naturally my loyalty to Florence is undimmed. But I must consider the respect that I owe to my uncle before coming to a decision.'

Milan again! Surely the woman could not be seriously considering throwing herself into the arms of Ludovico Sforza. Blood relative or no, he was a slippery devil and short-sighted to boot. He was about to open his mouth in protest when he was forestalled by a gesture and a mild cough from Baldraccani. 'Messer Machiavelli, we are allies of Florence and shall remain so. If it is possible to do so with honour, we will of course accept your government's offer.'

Niccolò felt a small glimmer of hope. Notwithstanding the carefully-hedged words, perhaps he had achieved his objective after all, and without too much difficulty. But his optimism was immediately punctured by Baldracanni's next words. 'However, I ask you to consider this, Messer Secretary. We must justify this step before the world, and in a way that does honour and credit to my lady's government of these lands.' There was a glint of mischief in the secretary's eyes as he fixed Niccolò with a firm stare. 'Our alliance with Florence has hitherto been an informal one, subject to the continued goodwill between our states. To strengthen our bond, we would ask your government to bind itself to defend, protect and maintain the integrity of my lady Caterina's various dominions, in a formal treaty.'

Niccolò struggled to prevent the irritation he felt showing on his face. However strategically important Forlì and Imola might be, the Lady Caterina's domains constituted little more than a statelet, a client who owed fealty to the Republic of Florence. She was not an equal and had no right to demand formal treaties and the like. The idea was preposterous and he had no doubt what the Signoria would say. 'My lady, I regret that I am in no position to answer you on this point. My instructions do not go so far as to permit me to enter into negotiations for a treaty and I fear that I must refer the question to the Signoria.'

Who would, no doubt, send a much more senior member of the patriciate to undertake any such negotiation, assuming that they would entertain such an outlandish idea in the first place. He consoled himself with the thought that he had at least achieved the more limited objective of negotiating a reduced price for her son's services.

'Of course,' the contessa said, rising. Unexpectedly, she offered him a warm smile, the first he had received from her since they had first met. 'I had expected that you would need to consult your superiors. But may I ask you, Messer Machiavelli, to urge them to consider our request most carefully? You have been persuasive so far and I do not doubt that your views on all these matters are held in high esteem in Florence. I have other appointments, but you may wish to consult further with Antonio; he knows my mind on this matter.'

After the contessa had left, he turned to Baldraccani, barely able to contain his anger. 'Well, Antonio? What is going on? Surely you know that the Signoria will not countenance such an arrangement. And I can't believe she is going to switch her allegiances from Florence to Milan!'

The contessa's secretary spread his hands in a deprecatory gesture. 'Come and walk with me, Niccolò. It is close in here, don't you think?'

Outside in the pine-scented cool of the gardens, they walked in silence for a bit, and then Baldraccani indicated a stone bench on which to sit. 'Lady Caterina's concern is not with money, though she does believe that her son is entitled to be paid what he is worth. She will remain loyal to Florence. She well recognises how fickle her uncle is and how precarious his throne if King Louis chooses to prosecute with arms his claim to the duchy. He is unlikely to be able to guarantee her safety and the security of her state.'

The light of understanding began to creep into a corner of Niccolò's mind. Caterina Sforza was in fear of her security. That was why she was making this surprising demand. But from whom was she in danger? Not France, surely— King Louis wanted Milan, not Forlì or Imola.

'I see you perceive my drift,' Baldraccani said. 'And no doubt you are wondering what has caused her such unease. Have you been keeping an eye on Rome, Niccolò?'

Machiavelli thought for a moment. 'There have been reports that Alexander wants to launch another crusade. But doesn't every pope do that?'

'Yes. But what if the target of the crusade is closer to home than far-off Jerusalem? The Romagna perhaps?'

The glimmer became a flood of light. Though they behaved as though they were independent, in theory, all the rulers of the petty states of the Romagna, including Caterina Sforza, were technically vassals of the papacy, which claimed suzerainty over the whole area. Alexander well knew, from his long experience as Chancellor of the Holy See, what a thorn in the side of the papacy the lawless Romagna could be.

Niccolò remembered something else. 'His son, Cesare. The one who swapped a cardinal's hat for a ducal coronet. Doesn't he have military aspirations?'

'Valentino, they're calling him. Our information is that he has been stirring the pope up to launch a campaign in the Romagna to bring all of the cities here to heel. He sees himself, I think, as its future ruler. And so my lady fears that she will be squashed in any such campaign, and is desirous, therefore, of a more formal pact with her old friends in Florence.'

It was an intelligent strategy, he had to concede. Valentino's dukedom was the price the pope had extracted for annulling Louis's marriage. No doubt the French king's gratitude would extend further, perhaps even to the provision of troops to fight a campaign in the Romagna. And since king Charles' invasion four years before, Florence was, notionally at least, an ally of France, so if Caterina Sforza could tie herself formally to the republic, she might win immunity against the Papal Army, should they materialise. And yet...

'All this seems a little far-fetched, Antonio. You and your mistress are, I think, panicking too soon. These are merely rumours, and even if Cesare Borgia were by some miracle to be made commander of an army substantial enough to conquer the Romagna, the military history of his family would hardly inspire confidence!'

'So you will do nothing to prosecute our request?'

'I will report it and I will recommend that the Signoria give it the most earnest consideration. But they will say no.'

Baldraccani's disappointment was obvious. 'Florence may come to regret its short-sightedness,' he said bitterly. 'For if the Romagna falls to the Borgia, who is to say that they will stop there?'

'And the matter of Ottaviano's troops? And the gunpowder and other supplies?'

'What answer can you expect?' Baldraccani shrugged. 'We face an uncertain future and must husband our resources.'

So he was to depart Forlì empty-handed, without even the promise of munitions that the Signoria had asked for. Resentment at the presumption and

65

arrogance of this petty ruler welled up inside him and it took all of his self-control to remain civil as he bade farewell to the contessa's secretary.

As he began the long ride home the next day, pondering everything that he had learned, Baldraccani's words rang in his head. Niccolò truly believed what he had said—that it was premature to worry about the possibility of an invasion by an untried general leading troops that as yet did not exist—but something else told him that, in the long and tangled history of northern Italy, stranger things had happened.

Chapter 7—Death of a Condottiero

Florence, August 1499

He returned to Florence on the first day of August, reporting immediately to Marcello Adriani, who listened impassively as Niccolò poured out his frustration with the fickle Lady of Forlì. At the end, the chancellor was perfectly phlegmatic about the whole episode.

'Don't be too upset, Niccolò,' he said placidly, his hands crossed on his stomach as he leaned back in the fine gilded chair in his office on the priors' side of the palazzo. 'The Signoria thought it worth the attempt, but they would have been astonished if you had succeeded. No one will think the worse of you. In fact, they were much impressed by the quality of your reports from both Castrocaro and Forlì.

'As for the demand for a formal alliance, it is of course out of the question, though as you promised to put it to the Signoria, we shall do so. They may be prepared to send someone to negotiate, but I doubt it. We have too many other concerns at the moment to be troubled very much by the Contessa Caterina Sforza.'

Which was as Niccolò had expected. Still, he felt a pang of bitterness. He had brooded on the whole episode all the way back from Forlì, and the more he thought about it, the more he was convinced that the republic was pursuing a foolish policy with respect to minor allies like the Lady of Forlì. Florence was, it seemed to him, an unreliable partner for such small states, more interested in saving a few thousand florins than in cultivating a secure, long-lasting friendship. He could not help but think that the Signoria would eventually come to regret its parsimony.

And then there was the question of Cesare Borgia and the pope's ambitions for the Romagna. Were Secretary Baldraccani and his mistress jumping at shadows or did they face a real threat? It was hard to be sure, but there was no doubt that the atmosphere he had detected in Castrocaro and in Forlì itself was uneasy, to say the least. Where it came from, he did not know, but some instinct told him that there were real dangers here, hidden just below the surface like rocks in a slow-flowing stream.

'…and by now the siege should have commenced.'

Niccolò brought his attention back to Adriani. What was he talking about? Ah, yes, the siege of Pisa, the planning for which had been underway for some time. 'With Vitelli still in command?'

'Yes, though Rucellai and the others are still suspicious of the good commander's intentions,' Adriani said. 'I think they would believe him unfaithful even if he handed them Pisa on a platter without the loss of a single life or florin!'

Paolo Vitelli was probably the most famous mercenary captain in Italy and he had been engaged by the Florentines to conduct the campaign that would, it was hoped, finally force Pisa into submission. Niccolò, in his capacity as Secretary to the War Committee, had read with some bemusement the correspondence that had gone back and forth between the arrogant *condottiero* and the Signoria. Vitelli's strategy was to occupy the towns and villages surrounding Pisa to strangle her. This, he maintained, would be cheaper in men and money than a direct siege. Niccolò thought he was probably right.

But this was not a popular idea with some members of the Signoria, who were deeply distrustful of the great captain's motivations. He was in league with Venice and Milan, they whispered, who would like nothing more than to ruin them with a long campaign. Though Vitelli rather scornfully maintained he might know a thing or two more about soldiering than any soft-handed Florentine merchant, he had, in the end, agreed to undertake a direct siege of the recalcitrant Pisan Republic.

'I am not so sure that Pisa is worth it either.'

The sentiment, expressed so baldly—more directly than Machiavelli had intended—startled his superior. 'What can you mean, Niccolò? Pisa has been ours for damned near a hundred years! Agreeing to this new republic of theirs was the price we had to pay to appease Charles VIII, God rot his soul. Getting Pisa back is an article of faith for the Signoria and they will pay any price to do so!'

'*Any* price? Do you really think so, Marcello?' Suddenly Niccolò was impatient and he jumped to his feet in agitation, his arms chopping up and down as he made his points. 'It's the Pisans who are prepared to pay any price, not us. We hire mercenary armies and then quibble endlessly about their pay, while the Pisans are arming every male capable of fighting. They will fight to the end because they are defending their own homes and their own soil against

68

us. If we are to prevail, we will have to reduce the city to rubble and enslave all its citizens. Are we, civilised men, going to do that? Does our genteel Signoria have the stomach for such measures?

'And think, Marcello, what the world would say of us if we did succeed in such a way! We would be despised, and rightly so. For a republic like ours, rooted in the consent of the people, to make war, a punitive war to the end, on a sister-republic is shameful. It would be better for us and the Pisans if we were to leave them in peace and negotiate a durable pact between us for our mutual defence and benefit instead. But we haven't even tried diplomacy, to see if there might be some common ground.'

He came to a halt, exasperated. Adriani had not moved during his diatribe, had just sat with an expression of mild interest in his clear blue eyes and the tolerant smile that Machiavelli knew from the Florentine Studio as he used to listen as his undergraduate charges stretched their rhetorical wings for the first time. 'You hadn't better let too many members of the Signoria hear you talk like that, my young friend, or you could find yourself out of a job!' The chancellor's warning was delivered with a laugh, robbing it of its sting. 'Though there is some truth in what you say, I'll admit. But the die is cast and we shall all have to wait and see how it falls.'

*

A week later, the halls of the Palazzo della Signoria were ringing with two astounding pieces of news. The first was delivered by a breathless courier from the war-camp at Pisa and seemed to vindicate those who had advocated a direct attack. Paolo Vitelli and his soldiers had assaulted a part of the walls that had seemed weakest and had battered a breach with his cannons, through which his troops had poured, forcing the defenders back into the city itself.

Word of this surprising victory soon spread beyond the walls of the government palazzo and, in hours, there were throngs of joyous citizens out in the piazza and invading the courtyards of the palazzo itself, shouting their excitement and waving banners. It seemed obvious that a complete victory was only days away.

The other item was even more momentous but arrived in quieter fashion in the daily despatches from the Florentine envoy in Milan. A French army had been gathering for some months in Lyon, presumably intended for the long-heralded assault on Milan to enforce King Louis' claim to the duchy. It had finally crossed the border and was marching through Lombardy. Ludovico Sforza was in a panic and sending desperate appeals for help to the Italian states.

There was no chance he would get it, Niccolò was certain. The duke's foolishness in allowing Louis' predecessor into his domains, thereby causing great distress to every Italian city and principality all the way down to Rome, was unlikely to be forgotten. He could almost hear the cries of outrage that would come from the Signoria when he presented them with the ducal plea that afternoon.

Reading through the details of the despatch again, one particular item caught his eye—the pope's son, Duke Valentino, was accompanying the French army, leading a company of cavalry. So Cesare Borgia had got an actual military command at last, albeit a small one. Niccolò remembered reading in another of the many reports that crossed his desk that Borgia had married only two months ago, not to an Aragonese princess, in the end, but to Charlotte d'Albret, a French girl who whose father was the powerful Duke of Guienne and whose brother was the King of Navarre. Apparently, he had boasted that their union had been consummated eight times on their wedding night; an impressive effort. Niccolò wondered that the young man had found the will and the energy to leave the marriage bed at all to join in this invasion.

But it was the news from Pisa that filled every moment of his waking day over the next few weeks, as the Signoria and the War Committee held meeting after meeting to debate the republic's next steps once the war was finally won. To call some of the sessions 'debates' was perhaps a stretch, taken up as they were with endless speeches about the splendour of Florentine arms, the bravery of her (paid) soldiers, and the terms that would be offered to the vanquished Pisans.

Yet something nagged at the back of Machiavelli's mind. As the weeks went by, there was silence from the besieging army, which seemed ominous. Saying as much to the newly-elected Gonfaloniere Guasconi achieved nothing except to earn him a rebuke as a foolish pessimist.

Then at the end of August came the perplexing news that, instead of rushing in and finishing off the conquest of Pisa, Vitelli's army was immobilised in their siege lines, apparently struck by an outbreak of camp-fever. The Pisans had taken the opportunity to repair their walls, and, far from being finally defeated, were more defiant than ever.

The people of Florence, having been led to believe that a triumph was imminent, responded with fury and Niccolò found himself virtually imprisoned, along with the rest of the government, in the Palazzo della Signoria. In a panic, the Signoria ordered Vitelli to halt the campaign (a singularly pointless decision, Niccolò thought, since it seemed to have come to a halt of its own accord) and appointed commissioners to go to Pisa and investigate.

Then, a few days later, another despatch from Milan contained the equally astounding news that Ludovico Sforza, faced with a French army at his gates, had fled the city, ending Sforza rule over Lombardy. For the second time in five years, Italy was being trampled by an invader, with unpredictable consequences.

Beyond another bout of hand-wringing, a despondent Signoria had little time to think about the events to their north, given the crisis nearer at hand. Vitelli had many enemies, particularly among those who had so strenuously advocated the very strategy that had led to the current disaster. Trying to deflect any possible blame from themselves, they accused the *condottiero* of being a traitor. Why else, they demanded, had Vitelli's men not charged into Pisa as soon as they had made their breach?

The captain had his defenders. The army was short of ammunition and cannons, they said. It had been decided to wait until these defects were remedied so that the outcome of the final assault would be more certain.

Then the sickness had struck, something no one could have predicted. All these things might well have been true, though Niccolò for one, knowing the plentiful state of munitions and cannon that were at the disposal of the Florentine armies, was more than a little sceptical, but they cut little ice with a magistracy determined to find a scapegoat for the failure.

One afternoon, Niccolò was talking to Gonfaloniere Guasconi in the lofty and gilded Hall of Lilies, when they were interrupted by a group of priors. Their spokesman seemed to be Bernardo Rucellai, a wily Savonarolan who had nevertheless managed to survive the change of regime with his influence intact.

'Something has to be done about Vitelli, Guasconi!' Rucellai was abrupt, ignoring Machiavelli entirely and focusing all his fury on the gonfaloniere. 'He has betrayed us all and should be hanged in the piazza as a traitor!'

Guasconi, a naturally dignified and courteous man, visibly recoiled at this assault. 'My dear Bernardo,' was his mild response, once he had recovered himself, 'I think we all agree that *something* must be done. But what proof do you have of his guilt?'

'Proof? What more proof do you need than the failure of the army before Pisa? We are agreed,' he gestured to the group of men standing behind him, who nodded and murmured their assent, 'that he is guilty and must be punished. And if you will not do so, I intend to move a motion in the Signoria this afternoon to have him arrested.'

In the face of such vehemence, Guasconi's courage, never a quality in great abundance, gave way completely and he muttered his agreement.

The Signoria meeting that afternoon was chaotic, and Niccolò struggled to keep coherent minutes, so strenuous were the arguments. But eventually it was agreed that Vitelli should be summoned to a meeting to discuss the reorganisation of the army, and there arrested.

Back in his office making a fair copy of the minutes and drafting the necessary summons to the mercenary captain, Niccolò was filled with foreboding. After all, it was the Signoria itself that had originally decided to halt the campaign, rather than wait for Vitelli's explanations and recommendations for prosecuting the war, so they were as responsible for the fiasco as their general. Was Vitelli a traitor? It was hard to know. He wondered too about the motives of Rucellai and his confederates—the man had been a close friend of Lorenzo de' Medici, and he remained an ardent *ottimato*. Was it possible that Rucellai was himself the traitor, serving the exiled Piero de' Medici's interests by disrupting the Florentine campaign against Pisa and bringing the government into disrepute with the people?

*

Two days later, the former captain of the Florentine armies was imprisoned in the dungeon below the Palazzo della Signoria. Niccolò, absent on family business on the other side of the river, knew nothing of subsequent events until, summoned by a brief note from Biagio, he hurried back to the centre of the city. There, just outside the entrance to the Palazzo della Signoria, he was confronted with a sight that made his stomach churn—the decapitated head of Paolo Vitelli, stuck on a pole with a flaming torch next to it so that the citizens of Florence would be able to see it in the gathering darkness.

Pushing his way through a small crowd that seemed more subdued than elated, he looked up. Vitelli's sightless eyes were wide open, looking down his long nose; Niccolò felt as if the dead man was accusing him in some obscure way. He shuddered and went into the building.

Upstairs everything was hushed, the members of the Signoria evidently having retired to their private apartments. In the chancellery, only Biagio and Agostino were still at work, though in a distracted and desultory fashion. He paused at the door and poured himself a glass of wine, something he rarely indulged when in the office. It was a signal for the others to jump up from their desks and come over to join him.

'What happened?' he asked, emptying the glass in one go, pouring another and gesturing for his friends to help themselves. 'I thought the commission was to examine him, not condemn him outright.'

'No one seems to know exactly what went on, Niccolò,' Agostino said. 'They questioned him in the usual way, then they subjected him to harder methods of interrogation, accusing him of all sorts of treacheries. He admitted nothing, it seems, saying that he had always intended to resume the siege once he had recovered from illness.'

'And the next thing anyone knew,' Biagio took up the story, 'there was a headsman and a block down in the courtyard and he was executed. The greatest mercenary commander in Italy, condemned and killed without trial despite having done nothing that showed any lack of good faith. What will the world think of our republic now?'

'There's worse news,' Agostino said. 'The prosecutors were sent to arrest Paolo's brother Vitellozzo, but he seems to have slipped out of the city, swearing to avenge his brother's death with Florentine blood. And he'll have our army with which to do it since Paolo's soldiers will follow no one else. What a disaster.'

With which sentiment Niccolò could only agree.

When eventually he read the formal minutes of the commission that had executed this bloody deed, Niccolò saw that there had been no real evidence against the mercenary, just gossip and hearsay, unfounded accusations supported by nothing but the calumnies muttered in the piazzas, loggias and streets of Florence by its agitated citizens, stirred up by leaders whose motivations were questionable.

'What mercenary commander will accept a contract with Florence now,' Niccolò demanded of Marcello Adriani when they met some days later, 'knowing that any failure on their part might result in such an ignominious end?'

'Someone had to be blamed, Niccolò, since the mob was baying for blood.'

'And he who builds on the mob builds on sand.' Niccolò was scornful. 'Vitelli might well have been a traitor but it seems to me that if the rule of law means anything, his guilt should have been established in court, where his accusers could produce proof if they had any. And even if he was guilty, surely some penalty short of death might have been imposed? In the ancient Roman republic, they merely fined those of their captains who failed, or confiscated their property…'

'I hear your father speaking,' Adriani said with a smile. 'He can always find a precedent somewhere in Livy. But look, Niccolò, we are not in ancient Rome. We are in modern Florence, and our armies are commanded by mercenary captains whose wealth, their fortresses, their lands, their cash, are all out of our reach. Capital punishment is the only sanction we have.'

A dubious conclusion, Niccolò thought, but since Adriani's complacency was impenetrable, he dropped the discussion and changed the subject to other less controversial matters. Yet as he made his way home through the quiet streets that evening, his mind came back to the problem. Adriani was right— mercenary captains could not be fined or have their goods confiscated. But what followed from that might be a different answer. If Florence armed her own citizens, just as Pisa had, she would no longer rely on the fickle *condottiere* and the commanders of her armies would have a stake in the success or failure of her campaigns.

That thought found a lodging somewhere in his mind and there it would settle until circumstances interrupted its slumber. One thing he was sure of— that day's events would cast a long shadow into the future.

74

Part Two—A Fox Among Wolves

Chapter 8—The Lion Springs

Florence, February 1500

'Duke Valentino entered Rome like a new Caesar. Having waited in the cold and rain for three hours at the gate of Santa Maria del Popolo, along with all the other ambassadors and members of the Curia, we were treated to the sight of the duke, flanked by cardinals and escorted by a hundred pages all dressed in finest black, riding into the city at the head of his army. There was considerable trouble when the duke's army—Gascons and Swiss—met the papal soldiers sent to meet them, though Don Cesare quickly settled it. The march resumed with Vitellozzo Vitelli at the head of the soldiers...'

At the mention of the name of Paolo Vitelli's brother, the members of the Signoria shifted uncomfortably in their seats, exchanging uneasy glances with each other.

'At the Vatican,' Chancellor Adriani continued, peering short-sightedly at the despatch from ambassador Becci in Rome, 'Duke Valentino was greeted by the holy father, who seemed unable to decide whether to laugh or cry with joy at the triumph of his son and so did both alternately. Cannon fire was heard from the Castel Sant'Angelo, the reverberations from the salutes bringing down several windows and shutters in the Vatican Palace, so loud were they...'

Niccolò stopped listening; he had read the ambassador's report that morning and was well aware of its contents. A gust of the cold February wind caused the window shutters to give a loud rattle and he tugged his coat closer around him to keep out the draft that eddied through the room. Though he took care to keep his face in its usual expression of alert interest, his mind wandered elsewhere, thinking about the chain of events that had led to this day.

It had begun just a few weeks after Vitelli's death, with an extraordinary announcement from the pope, who had issued a bull relieving his vicars in Rimini, Imola, Forlì, Camerino and Faenza of their authority, and excommunicating them to boot. All of these city-states were in the Romagna, and the vicars deposed were the *de facto* rulers of their respective territories, all of them tough and ruthless *condottiere* commanding substantial military forces.

As if that weren't enough, Pope Alexander had then issued another bull deposing Guidobaldo da Montefeltro, the powerful Duke of Urbino, whose territory stood between the Romagna and the sea. No clearer signal could have been sent of the pope's intentions—to pacify at last the turbulent and unruly region that had always owed nominal fealty to the church, but which was, to all intents and purposes, lawless.

In Florence, all this news was greeted with surprise, but also with some indifference. Papal declarations were all well and good, it was thought, but where was the pontiff going to get the military force necessary to enforce his will?

The answer to that question came a month later, when Cesare Borgia, who had last been heard of marching with King Louis in triumph into Milan, appeared at the head of an army of nearly eight thousand French soldiers and marched on the city of Imola, where the citizens took fright and surrendered with almost no resistance. Niccolò had noted with wry amusement that the commander of the fortress at Imola was none other than Dionigio Naldi, who had promptly deserted his mistress and gone over to join forces with Borgia.

Then, just six days later, Forlì itself had opened the city gates, and Caterina Sforza had once more found herself besieged in the Ravaldino. By the time the new year had dawned, and with it a new century, Cesare's guns had battered a hole in the walls of that formidable fortress. In the ensuing chaos, the contessa had been captured.

'It would have been safer for her had she not been hated by her people,' was the acid judgement that he passed in his report to the Signoria summarising all these events. He could not regret the fall of the arrogant Contessa Sforza and her tiny statelet, and perhaps some good would come from having a pacified Romagna on their eastern border. Yet he also thought of Secretary Baldraccani's parting words and wondered whether this new lion's appetite would be sated with these conquests or whether its ravening jaws would turn towards Florence herself.

For now, though, the reappearance of that perennial plotter Ludovico Sforza had drawn the beast's fangs. Somehow, he had managed to raise a substantial force of mercenaries and was marching on Milan, causing King Louis to demand the return of his soldiers. The young Borgia had no choice but to make the best of things by leaving a few troops to garrison his new possessions and return to Rome for his triumph, hauling the unfortunate Caterina with him. It was reported that she had been used by Duke Valentino for his pleasure, before being unceremoniously imprisoned in the dungeons of the Castel Sant'Angelo.

Chancellor Adriani had finished speaking, and the current gonfaloniere, Antonio Delvigna, invited discussion. Niccolò took up his pen to do his duty and record the deliberations of the Signoria.

'It seems to me that there is little to be concerned about,' said Giovanni Guadagni, one of the new priors, a rather ponderous man given to making pompous announcements about subjects upon which he had lavished little thought. 'What, after all, are Forlì and Imola? Just border towns of little importance in themselves. And we are well rid of the Sforza woman; a female ruler is an abomination against nature, anyway.'

There were nods around the table from the less experienced members of the Signoria. Others, more thoughtful, recognised that Guadagni was talking nonsense, though none of them said so, save one.

At the opposite end of the table from Niccolò, Piero Soderini, lately ambassador to France, shook his head. 'I disagree.' Though he spoke in an even tone of voice, there was something authoritative about this lean-faced man that commanded the instant attention of his colleagues. 'It seems to me that there is some larger design at work here. When the pope supplanted his vicars in the Romagna, he named his son as a replacement for all of them. If he intended nothing more than to bring his errant subjects to order, why would he make Duke Valentino their ruler? Why would he not replace each of them separately with favoured appointees? No, I think he is planning to make Cesare Borgia into a power in north Italy. In which case, Imola and Forlì are just the first steps.'

That provoked a hum of comment, some of the priors nodding in agreement, others shaking their heads, unable to believe that Pope Alexander could be so ambitious. Forgetting for a moment his role as a neutral recorder of the Signoria's deliberations, Niccolò found himself nodding thoughtfully in agreement with Soderini.

'What do you think, Machiavelli?'

Adriani's question caught him by surprise, though the encouraging smile on his superior's face reassured him that it had not been asked in order to embarrass him. They had been discussing this very subject earlier in the day, and the chancellor knew precisely what his thoughts were. To be asked to express them in open council was, however, an unusual mark of confidence.

'Signori, in my opinion, Ser Piero is correct,' he said. 'This Cesare is a bold and ambitious man, according to all reports, and while Pope Alexander may wish for nothing more than to see the Romagna pacified, I think that Duke Valentino wants for himself nothing less than a kingdom.'

'So Imola and Forlì are just the start? Is that what you are saying?' The gonfaloniere was querulous, as if annoyed that he had to take the words of a mere secretary seriously.

'Yes, my lord gonfaloniere, that is exactly what I am saying.' Having been thus committed by Adriani, Niccolò wasn't about to back away. 'Signor Soderini has already told us that Cesare has the affection of King Louis, who can provide him with armies he needs, and the church can provide him with the necessary funds to pay and supply them. But he also knows very well that the favour of princes is fickle, and that the pope, though his health is said to be good, is as mortal as any man. Therefore, I think he will resume his campaign as soon as circumstances allow while he can still rely on these two supports.'

'Messer Machiavelli is right,' Soderini said, giving him a warm smile. 'Though it is probably the young bull which is in this case leading the old bull by the nose.' The reference to bulls, the Borgia family emblem, caused a ripple of laughter around the table. 'But if he is also right that this is just the beginning of a longer strategy by the pope to bring the Romagna to heel, we face a new and potentially perilous situation on our eastern borders.'

'How so, Ser Piero?' The query came from another of the newly sworn priors near the foot of the table. 'These petty tyrants have been troublesome enough over many years. Surely it would be to our benefit if they were brought under control?'

'Think about it, man.' Soderini was impatient. 'The Romagna provides a buffer between our territory and that of the Duchy of Ferrara and, beyond that, the Venetian Republic. While it was ungovernable it posed no threat to our eastern trade routes, but a strong state governed by a determined warlord would be a different matter. We should resist, I think, with every means at our disposal.'

'Yet what can we do?' Giovanni Guadagni now sounded less pompous and just a little frightened. 'We have no army and must depend on mercenaries to defend our territory.'

The other members of the Signoria broke into fevered chatter, fearful and outraged all at once.

'France.' With a single word, Soderini regained their attention. 'Louis may favour young Cesare Borgia, but he is also pledged in alliance to us. For now, he is preoccupied with Ludovico Sforza, but it is my guess that the Milanese will soon enough be weary of their tiresome duke and throw him out once again. When Louis has restored his state in Lombardy, it will occur to him that an unrestrained Borgia bull rampaging through northern Italy will not be in his best interests.'

That was shrewd, Niccolò thought as he plied his pen to record the discussion. Piero Soderini had been on an embassy to France the previous year, during which he had successfully extracted from King Louis a promise to provide troops to help with the siege of Pisa, and no doubt he knew the minds of both the king and his principal adviser, George D'Amboise, the Cardinal-Archbishop of Rouen.

'So we just wait until Louis has dealt with Ludovico and see what happens?' The gonfaloniere sounded confused.

'Yes, for now,' Soderini said. 'But we should send a new embassy to Milan to press him to send the soldiers to Pisa that he promised and, at the same time, try to remind him of the value of the Florentine alliance.'

'Well then, let it be so decided,' the gonfaloniere said. 'Now, let us move on to our other business…'

When the meeting finally concluded some hours later, Piero Soderini intercepted Niccolò as he was gathering up his papers and preparing to return to his office on the other side of the Palazzo. 'Niccolò, thank you for your support on the matter of Borgia. It was helpful.'

'Of course, Ser Piero. To be honest, I was surprised and flattered that the Signoria should wish to hear my opinion at all. I am, after all, a mere secretary.'

'Oh, rather more than that, I think. Chancellor Adriani speaks highly of you and we were impressed by your despatches from Castrocaro and Forlì, for their

81

accuracy and also for your observations, which seemed to get to the heart of things.'

Niccolò inclined his head in modest acceptance of the compliment. He did not know Piero Soderini well, except by reputation, but he seemed to be an approachable, sensible sort of fellow, the kind of man to whom people listened when he spoke. Emboldened, he decided to share the concern that had been worrying him ever since the appalling events of the previous year. 'It troubles me, Ser Piero, that the republic, for all her wealth, seems to be so dependent for her security on forces that cannot be easily controlled—foreign mercenaries and foreign kings. This Borgia threat may be too great to be defeated in the old way, by the disbursement of great quantities of gold.'

'It troubles me, too, Niccolò.' Soderini nodded. 'But what is the alternative? We cannot afford a standing army. No, for now, I think we must make do with mercenaries and alliances to preserve our independence. For which we will need diplomats like you!' Soderini issued a rare laugh, clapped Machiavelli on the shoulder, and made his farewells.

Watching him go, Niccolò was thoughtful. He had studied the history of the ancient Roman Republic before it was corrupted by the tyranny of the emperors, and those studies had taught him that it was incorruptible citizens like Piero Soderini, dedicated to the service of the state but not ambitious for themselves, who were the soul of any republican state. He hoped that Florence could call upon enough such good men to provide a government wise enough to steer them through the troubles that he knew lay ahead.

That evening, when he arrived at the family house in Santo Spirito, still preoccupied with the events of the day, it took his mind a few moments to realise that it seemed peculiarly hushed. Normally, as he climbed the stairs to the first floor where the central living apartments were located, he would have been greeted by the yapping of his widowed sister's annoying pet dogs, mingled with the welcoming sound of family chatter as they gathered over the evening meal (an event at which he was invariably a late arrival).

But the dogs were nowhere in evidence and the main hall was deserted. It was only as he dropped his satchel on the big table in the middle of the room that he heard the sound of voices in quiet conversation coming from an adjoining small parlour. He recognised them as belonging to his sister

Primavera and his younger brother Totto, who both jumped to their feet as he put his head around the door.

'Oh, Niccolò!' He felt the wet from his sister's tears on his cheek as she threw her arms around him. Though she was older than him by a few years, Primavera was as delicate and unworldly as he was the opposite and she had always treated him as though he were the elder and she the younger.

'What is it? What has happened?' Even as he held her, his eyes met Totto's across her shoulder and he knew the answer.

'Father has been taken ill,' Totto said, his voice grave. 'We found him in the library, collapsed at his desk. When he woke, he couldn't move his arms or legs and his speech was unclear, slurred, as though he were drunk.'

'Where is he?'

'Upstairs in his bed. Doctor Bartolomeo has been with him all afternoon. He has only just left.'

'God. Why didn't you send for me?'

'We would have,' Primavera said, dabbing her eyes with a handkerchief, 'but you are always so busy, and there was nothing you could have done anyway that the doctor wasn't already doing.'

He felt a stab of anger and was about to vent it with some words that would have been unkind before he caught himself. They were right, of course. He had been guilty often enough of ignoring the family's affairs, so absorbed was he in his work, and had been known to respond with impatience when they intruded. He could understand their reluctance to send for him, even in this crisis.

They took him upstairs to the big bedroom, where his father lay propped up on pillows in his massive old bed. He was shocked by the old man's appearance. When Niccolò had left this morning, his father had been his usual self, talking enthusiastically about the Roman texts he was translating from Latin to Italian, a task he found infinitely more engaging than managing the family's farm and other business interests. Yet here he was, a few scant hours later, hardly more than a corpse, his face entirely drained of colour. One corner of his mouth drooped and a tiny bead of spittle had caught in the corner of his

83

lips. He did not move and it was only the black eyes, following his eldest son as he crossed the room, that gave any sign that he was still alive.

Niccolò sat down on the bed and took his father's hand. They had never been particularly close, but he had always felt an affection for this rather dreamy and impractical man to whom he owed his love of books and learning. He remembered sitting on his father's lap as a boy, wrapped in wiry arms that held a book in front of them, from which he read to his avid son. He could still smell the paper and see his father's hand passing across the words as he sounded them. And it had been in Bernardo's treasured library, built up over decades of collecting, that he had discovered Livy and Caesar and Suetonius, the poetry of Petrarch and Dante, the plays of Aeschylus.

As an adult, Niccolò had spent many happy hours disputing back and forth the meaning of this text or that, a cheerful and uncomplicated relationship that had lasted into his time at the Studio. Someone had once said that they seemed more like brothers than father and son. The only source of disagreement between them was Bernardo's lack of interest in the management of the family assets. Only a few days ago, he had lost his temper when it had become apparent that Bernardo had forgotten—forgotten!—to collect payment for a shipment of wine from Sant'Andrea into the city. But at that moment those differences seemed inconsequential as he looked at the familiar face, for once unable to find the right words.

'The doctors say that he cannot speak but he can hear us,' Totto said from behind him.

Bernardo's face contorted and a small noise emerged from the twisted mouth, little more than a grunt. Niccolò squeezed his father's hand. 'Don't try to talk, Father, if it distresses you. I'm sure this will pass and you will be talking again soon. In the meantime, rest. We will make sure you get the best of care.'

The eyes blinked and a tear formed at one corner and rolled down his cheek. Primavera leaned across from the other side of the bed and wiped it away. 'I'll sit with Father for a while,' she said. 'You and Totto should talk.'

Niccolò nodded and rose. The two brothers withdrew into the big hall and settled themselves on chairs before the fire. 'What does Doctor Bartolomeo say? Will he get better?'

Totto looked wretched. 'He doesn't know. It is apoplexy, he says, a disease that is mysterious. The only treatment is rest. Sometimes the patient recovers, sometimes not. There is no way to tell which way it will progress.'

'Well, we will just have to do the best we can to keep him comfortable and warm, and pray.'

Not that praying would do much good. He was no atheist and he was devout in his attendance at the family church of Santa Felicità, but his sceptical streak, never far from the surface, made him doubt that God spent much time listening to every prayer sent heavenwards by his children. Niccolò preferred to rely on his own earthly efforts as much as possible, even if in this case those efforts consisted of not much more than ensuring that his father's comfort was seen to and that the doctor called regularly.

Over the month that followed, there seemed to be some improvement— speech came back, halting and stammering, and though he remained bedridden, the patient reported some feeling returning to his limbs. April's spring sunshine, accompanied though it was by ferocious showers and winds that rattled the shutters, seemed to brighten Bernardo up even more and they began to harbour hopes that he would recover completely.

Niccolò had little choice but to suppress his natural anxiety about his father since his work continued to demand all his time and energy as the turbulence continued in northern Italy.

As Piero Soderini had predicted, Ludovico Sforza's triumphant return to Milan turned to ignominious defeat in April, when he was defeated and imprisoned after his people had turned against him once more. The Florentine ambassadors at the court of King Louis, having offered their most enthusiastic congratulations, took the opportunity to remind the king that he had promised aid to Florence in her campaign against Pisa. This was met with some impatience, but eventually, the French agreed to send six and a half thousand troops... provided Florence paid the exorbitant price of twenty-four thousand ducats a month for their services! The Signoria nearly had a collective attack of apoplexy themselves when they heard the terms, but had little option but to endorse them and hope that the soldiers would enable them to defeat Pisa before the treasury was bankrupted.

Between meetings of the Signoria, sessions of the War Committee and the river of routine correspondence that ran through the chancellery offices no matter what the state of the republic's foreign affairs, Niccolò had little time to spend at his father's bedside, though he was never far from his thoughts. Like his siblings, he observed the small signs of improvement, the slow and painfully halting return of speech and the improved pallor and began to harbour some hope. Even the doctor, usually as pessimistic as all his tribe, began to express guarded optimism for a full recovery.

And then, as stunningly unexpected as a bolt of lightning from a clear blue sky, his father died.

Niccolò was at the Palazzo della Signoria when a messenger had slipped into the Hall of Lilies, where a committee of the Great Council was meeting, and passed him a scrawled note from his brother. He had felt himself turn pale and afterwards remembered only that he had stammered his excuses and left, the committee members staring open-mouthed at this strange behaviour from their normally unflappable secretary.

Outside, he had stood staring up into the hot blue sky, trying to master his emotions. And then, tears starting from his eyes, he walked home. By the time he reached the house, he was back in control of himself, and able to offer some comfort to his sister and brother. They told him that Bernardo had passed away while he was sleeping, something no one had expected, and when he went up to see the body, it looked as though he was asleep still.

Over the following weeks, Niccolò found himself burdened with the aftermath of his father's death. There was the funeral to arrange, then the endless legal details of the will, fortunately straightforward but time-consuming nevertheless. He was now the head of the Machiavelli family and that meant he had to take responsibility for managing the family's properties and the farm, seeing to the welfare of his sisters and brother and attempting to deal with the surprising number of creditors that Bernardo had left behind. Happily, the latter were accommodating, perhaps in deference to his growing prominence in the government.

Totto, as directionless at twenty-five as he had been at the same age, was recruited to take care of as much of the family business as he could, something he took on with enthusiasm, though Niccolò suspected he had about as much business acumen as their late father. Even so, any help was welcome, given that his work remained unrelenting.

He was still deeply mired in all these concerns when Piero Soderini pulled him aside after a particularly tedious meeting of the War Committee that had mostly been spent going in circles debating yet another demand from King Louis for more money—twelve thousand ducats this time, as a contribution to the cost of his garrison at Milan.

'When the Signoria meets this afternoon,' Soderini said, with no preamble, 'I intend to propose that we send new commissioners to the army at Pisa. I will also propose your name as one of those commissioners.'

Niccolò was astonished and humbled. Piero Soderini was an increasingly influential voice in the government, and he did not doubt that if he was proposing Niccolò's name, it would be accepted without demur. 'I am honoured, Ser Piero, that you should consider me suited to such a task. I promise I shall not disappoint.'

'Well, you might want to know the terms on which you are being despatched before you make any rash promises!' Soderini was wry. 'As usual, the Signoria will ask you and your fellow commissioners to do the impossible—appease the French soldiery without spending any money.'

'Ah.' Niccolò's hand went to his chin.

King Louis had, at last, despatched the promised troops to besiege Pisa. But there were rumours that there was disaffection in the camp that had been set up outside the city, the soldiery complaining that they had not been paid. They seemed to believe that Florence was responsible for this deficiency, even though they were paid directly from the French, not the Florentine treasury. The reports that had come from the camp painted a picture that was as murky as the muddy Arno, so Niccolò could see sense in despatching commissioners to get to the bottom of things.

'I don't know who the other commissioners will be,' Soderini broke into his thoughts, 'Luca degli Albizzi will lead, most probably. And perhaps Francesco della Casa as his second. Both are good men, but neither is as astute as you, Niccolò, so we'll be relying on you.'

If Soderini thought these were the men who should undertake such a mission, it was almost certain that they would indeed be chosen. And so it proved—by the end of the day, he had his instructions, and the next day the three of them, accompanied by two servants, set off on the road to Pisa.

Chapter 9—The Revolt of the Swiss

Pisa, July 1500

The sights and sounds of the army camp before Pisa were much as he remembered from his first visit in April of the year before, though that had been a different army under a different commander. Plodding along the muddy road beside the Arno, they were a mile or so away when the three Florentine commissioners and their small retinue of servants saw columns of smoke from dozens of cooking fires. It was late afternoon, and no doubt the besieging soldiers would soon be settling down for their evening meal. Niccolò felt his stomach give a rumble in anticipation. They had not eaten since mid-morning and that had been a meagre repast of cheese and bread, hastily consumed by the roadside.

As they drew closer, he heard the familiar clamour of the camp. A low hum of human voices was the constant background, pierced from time to time with shouted orders and curses, over which more distinct sounds could be made out, carried across the flat plain by a gentle breeze. There was the chime of iron on iron from the armourers' shops, the whinny of horses and the jangle of their harnesses, the rumble and creak of wagons. But Niccolò also noted that there was nothing that might indicate any fighting was going on, no boom of cannons or roars of defiance at a stubborn enemy. They might have been approaching a peaceful country town rather than a martial encampment.

'Halt! Who might you be, then?'

The peremptory query came from one of a pair of slovenly-looking sentries who stood guard at one of the gates in the rough stockade that marked the edge of the camp. He spoke Italian, though it was heavily inflected with a foreign accent that Niccolò couldn't identify.

'I am Luca degli Albizzi, Commissioner of the Republic of Florence,' their chief announced with all the dignity and hauteur that came naturally to a senior member of the Florentine aristocracy, 'come to inspect the camp with my two colleagues here, Signor della Casa and Messer Machiavelli.'

His words were met with barely-concealed contempt and a sneer. 'Florentines, eh? Just what we need, a few more bloody shopkeepers to give orders and sit around drinking wine while we do all the fighting,' the guard said, spitting out of the side of his mouth. He reached out a dirty and calloused hand. 'Papers?'

'We will show our commission to no one other than General de Beaumont.' Albizzi's face was taut with anger. 'It will go hard with you, I promise, if you do not admit us immediately and conduct us to his quarters.'

The two sentries conferred in a low undertone that was inaudible to the three mounted men. Niccolò could feel the fury emanating from della Casa, and a glance in his direction confirmed that the naturally florid face was turning an unhealthy shade of red. An explosion, Niccolò thought, could not be far away, which would not be helpful.

Fortunately, the commotion at the gate had caught the attention of an officer, who arrived just in time to forestall the impending detonation, exercising an authority that, Niccolò noted, was only grudgingly accepted by the two sentries, with mutterings and dark looks.

'I am sorry, signori, you were expected later today.' The officer was genuinely apologetic. 'If you will come with me, I will conduct you to your quarters.'

As they followed the captain through the makeshift gate, Niccolò looked around with interest, trying to gauge the mood. The camp seemed orderly enough, but he sensed an odd atmosphere. When he had visited Jacopo di Piombino's siege camp a year ago, there had been bustle and energy, a sense of purpose. This camp had none of that. It seemed almost torpid. The knots of soldiers, mostly Gascons and tough-looking Swiss mercenaries, looked surprisingly dishevelled. Some of the glances they received as they passed verged on murderous and were occasionally accompanied by low-voiced curses. Certainly, none appeared to have any interest in the enemy, perched behind the long grey walls that he could see across the open ground behind the camp.

They came to a substantial-looking structure, half-tent and half-wooden house, which the officer indicated were to be their quarters. Inside, the space was sparsely furnished, though perfectly adequate for what they anticipated would be a short stay.

While his colleagues bustled about directing the servants as they unpacked, Niccolò took the officer aside. 'What's going on, captain?' he asked in a low voice. 'I am no soldier, but all does not seem to me to be well in the camp.'

The captain nodded, seeming relieved that one of the commissioners had raised the subject. 'Signor de Beaumont charged me to tell you and your colleagues of the true state of affairs as soon as I had an opportunity to talk to you in private.'

Jean de Beaumont was the well-respected French commander of the army, appointed at the specific request of Piero Soderini, who had met him in Paris. Niccolò looked around the room. The unpacking was almost done and he caught the eye of Francesco della Casa, whose face had by now returned to its normal colour. With a nod of his head, he hinted that they should send the servants off to their quarters.

As soon as they were alone, he turned back to the captain.

'General de Beaumont wished me to advise you that there are serious problems in the camp.' The officer was blunt. 'The main one being that the men haven't been paid, for which they are blaming Florence. They say that yours is a nation of shopkeepers who would short-change their own mothers if they thought there was a profit in it. Signor de Beaumont is most concerned for the situation and fears that the soldiers will mutiny if they are not paid soon.'

'But how can that be?' Albizzi was puzzled. 'The army is being paid by France, not Florence.'

'True, signor, but Florence has been tardy in sending their share of the costs of the siege to Paris and that is being used as an excuse by the king's officials to hold back the army's pay.'

The three commissioners looked at each other. What the officer had said was true, for the Florentine government was having great difficulty meeting its obligations to the French king, but it was disconcerting to hear that this was common knowledge in the camp.

'Where is General de Beaumont?'

'In his quarters. He asked me to conduct you there with an invitation to join him for dinner as soon as you are settled.'

So, without further ado, they walked the short distance to the army commander's quarters. De Beaumont received them with flourishes of courtesy and conducted them immediately to the table which had been set ready for dinner. Over the next hour, the conversation was carried on in a confusing mixture of Italian, French or, when neither of the other languages could provide the required expression, Latin.

The French commander, though perfectly courteous and urbane, at first seemed reluctant to address the purpose of their mission, contenting himself with fussing over the food and wine, and general inanities such as the weather (unseasonally poor for campaigning) and the state of the army's provisions (adequate, evidently, though they lacked sufficient supplies of wine). Eventually, Albizzi coaxed him around to the state of the army's morale.

'It is not good, I am afraid, as I am sure my officers must have told you,' he said, a mournful look on his face. 'The Florentine mercenaries seem content enough, but the Swiss and the Gascons are noisy in their complaints about everything.'

'Everything?' della Casa asked, exchanging a sceptical look with his colleagues.

'Well, mostly about money. They haven't been paid for some months.' The general seemed surprisingly complacent about this fact.

'Why have they not been paid, General?' It was Niccolò's turn to take up the interrogation. 'This is the responsibility of the French treasury and therefore of yourself, is it not?'

De Beaumont looked unhappy. 'Signori, the fact is that my king has withheld payment because your government has been delinquent in making their contribution to the costs of the campaign. And so I do not have, here in the camp, the necessary gold to pay them.'

'And your captain told us that this is known among the soldiers, who blame Florence for their lack of pay.' Niccolò was acid.

'Alas, that is so. I do not know how that information got out, but it is all over the camp. I had assumed that, knowing this, your Signoria would be sending with you at least some of the arrears.'

91

'General,' Albizzi said, looking uncomfortable, 'you must know that the fee which King Louis demanded for these Swiss and Gascon mercenaries who are causing us so much trouble was, to say the least, exorbitant. When we agreed to pay it, we were hopeful that the campaign could be brought to a swift conclusion, thus enabling us to meet His Majesty's terms without difficulty. But the siege has dragged on and so we find that our treasury is depleted.'

'Florence can and will pay, do not fear,' della Casa interrupted, impatience etched on his face, 'but it will take some time. Until the situation has been rectified, we look to you to keep order in the camp and ensure that the soldiers stay loyal and bent to their tasks.'

De Beaumont did not seem at all surprised to hear this news. But neither did he seem much inclined to take any firm action to restore discipline. Niccolò was becoming increasingly disenchanted with the French commander, who did not at all fit his idea of a strong war-leader.

'I will do what I can,' was all the general offered. 'But matters have gone too far to be easily settled with a few words and promises.' He looked sadly around the table before a new idea seemed to come to him. 'It might help if we could improve their rations. Perhaps if we could procure an additional supply of wine? Their food is adequate, but they do moan about the lack of wine.'

De Beaumont seemed not to notice the astonished looks that this remark induced on the faces of his three guests and was equally unperturbed when they abruptly brought the evening to an end at the first opportunity and returned to their quarters.

'Did I hear him right, Luca?' Niccolò burst out as soon as they were through the door. 'Did he seriously suggest that his problems would be solved if we could provide the soldiers with more to drink? Or did I misunderstand him completely?'

Albizzi shrugged and shook his head in frustration. 'No, you heard correctly, though I grant the conversation was hard to follow.'

It was Niccolò's turn to shake his head. 'I am no soldier, but I have read my Livy and Caesar, and Frontinus. Those generals would have punished insolence from their subordinates most severely, not sought to mollify them with wine! Is he stupid or incompetent?'

'Calm down, Niccolò,' della Casa said. 'He's an experienced soldier and, what is more, he is the commander we asked for. Surely we should trust his judgement?'

'Francesco is right, Niccolò,' Albizzi decided. 'Look, send off to Cascina for a few barrels of wine and let's see if he is right, eh?'

Niccolò looked from one to the other. He was not at all sure they could take Beaumont at his word, but he was the junior member of the delegation so, in the end, he nodded and extracted writing materials from his satchel so he could write the despatch to ask for the barrels of wine that were going to have such a miraculous effect.

Miraculous or no, the wine had not yet arrived a few days later when the Gascons up and left the camp in a body, abandoning their comrades and making off with weapons and provisions. Then the Swiss, usually the most disciplined of troops in any mercenary army, started to disobey orders. The camp rang with whistles and catcalls, and the exasperated shouts of the officers whose orders were being ignored. Throughout, the three commissioners could do little other than remain in their quarters, furiously writing despatches back to Florence.

Niccolò and Albizzi were in the middle of composing one such message when the door-flap of their tent was thrust open and a dozen Swiss mercenaries, armed to the teeth, stamped their way in. Albizzi was a refined gentleman of middle years with considerable natural authority; even so, Niccolò thought, it must have taken considerable courage for him to stand and face these menacing professional soldiers who, from the expressions on their faces, were not there to exchange pleasantries.

'Gentlemen,' he said, 'we are, as you see, at our work. If you have some business with us, please state what it is.'

One of the mercenaries, a stocky man with flashing black eyes and a long scar that ran down the left side of his face, stepped forward from among his fellows and stood before the commissioner, hands firmly planted on hips and bearded chin thrust out in belligerence. 'You are the representative of this shopkeeper-republic for whom we are fighting and dying?'

There wasn't a lot of evidence that anyone was either fighting or dying, Niccolò wanted to say, though he had the sense to stay silent.

93

'Yes, we are the Florentine Commissioners. I am Luca degli Albizzi. My colleague here is Niccolò Machiavelli. But you know this, else you would not be here. So I ask again, what is your business?'

Albizzi's tone remained admirably level. Niccolò wasn't so sure he could have stayed as calm in the face of these men.

'Tell him, Sergeant Alberic,' one of the soldiers shouted, in a guttural accent. 'Tell him we want our money.'

The leader, Alberic, waved a hand to silence his follower. 'Commissioner, the issue is this—we haven't been paid. We belong to the company of Antonius Buner and we were employed by your piss-republic three months ago. There are a hundred and fifty of us, and not one of us has yet seen a *scuda* by way of payment. We want to know what you are going to do about it.'

Albizzi glanced across at Niccolò, who replied with the smallest of shrugs, trying to look much calmer than he felt. 'Sergeant, I fear I know nothing of these matters. Your pay comes from the royal treasury in Paris, not from Florence.'

He got no further as a growl of disapproval emerged from a dozen angry throats behind the sergeant. Hands flew to waists and daggers were drawn from scabbards with a rasping sound that terrified Niccolò. Where, he wondered, were the French officers who were supposed to be commanding this rabble?

'Gentlemen, there is no need for violence.' Albizzi's voice was still calm. 'What I said is the truth—it is France, not Florence, that owes you your pay. But if you wish, I will write letters to the Florentine Signoria, urging them to meet your grievances. Deputise two of your number to carry the letters and they can add their voices to mine.'

There was silence before the mercenaries' leader spoke again. 'Very well, Messer Commissioner, write your letters. Send them to your damned Signoria. But I tell you this, if we do not get a satisfactory reply within forty-eight hours, we will return and we shall take our pay in your blood!'

With that, he turned on his heel and pushed through his companions out of the tent. The others followed, with black looks at the two Florentines.

When they were once more alone, Albizzi collapsed into his chair. Niccolò hastened to pour them both a glass of wine, his hand trembling as he did so.

'Dear God, Machiavelli, I thought we were both going to die. Where in the name of all that is holy are these men's officers?'

As if on cue, two French officers burst through the tent opening. Despite his shock at the whole episode, it was all Niccolò could do not to burst into unseemly laughter at the hand-wringing and stream of concerned platitudes that emerged from the mouths of the newcomers.

'Signori,' he said, interrupting their flow with a gesture of impatience. 'Your protestations are all very well, but it seems to me that you ought to have better control over these men. Is this how King Louis manages his armies? Surely not!'

As he was saying these words, the bulky form of de Beaumont himself came into the tent, closely followed by della Casa, who had been out visiting some of the Florentine mercenary commanders. Dismissing his officers with a few words, the French general proceeded to add his apologies for what had just occurred. 'But I fear that there is worse to come. This complaint is mirrored all over the camp and I expect that a general mutiny is not far off. And in all honesty, I do not know what to do about it.'

After de Beaumont had gone, della Casa poured himself a glass of wine and turned to his colleagues, a black scowl on his face. 'I don't know why Soderini thought he was the right man for this expedition. He doesn't seem to have any idea how to bring his troops under control. And from everything I've been hearing from our Florentine captains, the whole camp is in chaos.'

'It does seem as if he expected an incident like this,' Niccolò observed. 'And he seems more despondent than angry about it. I would have expected more determination in so senior an officer.'

'I am not even sure that he wants to win this campaign,' della Casa said. 'Our captains have been telling me the strangest stories. For example, the French seem to have been allowing cannon balls and powder and provisions to reach Pisa by the river, even though they say they are in control of the Arno's mouth. I am not at all sure we can trust the French. After all, the longer the campaign goes on, the more it will drain our treasury.'

'They do seem to have excuses for everything. Apparently, it's all our fault for not providing enough munitions, though we have met their every request, and more.' Albizzi's disgust was palpable. 'Well, let's send that letter off and see what tomorrow brings.'

But what the following day brought was an escalation rather than a resolution of the crisis. At three in the afternoon, the sergeant, Alberico, appeared once more at the entrance of their tent, but this time there were a hundred or more angry soldiers behind him.

'Signor degli Albizzi, I am afraid that my comrades no longer trust in the goodwill of your republic, and we demand that you pay, right now, all that is owed to us.'

Once again, Luca degli Albizzi drew himself up to his full height and summoned all his considerable dignity. 'Might I ask, sergeant, what has occasioned this change of heart? We sent off our letters with two of your men this very morning as we promised. We can hardly have an answer back from Florence yet!'

The sergeant had the good grace to look a little uncomfortable, but then adopted the same aggressive stance as the day before. 'As to that, signor, whether the answer comes today or tomorrow or in a week is of no consequence, for we do not trust that your damned Signoria will deal honestly with us, thieving hucksters that they are.'

The argument went on for some time, Luca degli Albizzi standing his ground patiently and calmly, the sergeant growing ever more agitated, and the soldiers behind him growling and shouting their disapproval of the whole process. Machiavelli and della Casa could do little but stand in silent admiration of their chief's composure, afraid to interject lest they make matters worse.

Then, without warning, the soldiers seemed to lose all self-control. Half a dozen of them surged forward, almost knocking over the sergeant in the process, and grasped the startled Albizzi under the armpits. In moments, they had hustled him out of the tent, leaving Machiavelli and della Casa standing in stunned silence behind them, listening to the noise of the soldiers' progress through the camp until it receded into the distance.

'We must tell the Signoria,' Niccolò said, his numbed mind falling back on habit. He moved towards the table where papers and writing materials had been scattered by the altercation, sat and scribbled a short note, signed and sanded it. *Finding a courier might be a challenge,* he thought absently.

Della Casa seemed just as dazed as Niccolò. He wandered around the tent, picking up overturned furniture and carefully placing it back in position as if that would restore sense and sanity to the world.

The appearance of de Beaumont, trailed as usual by his hand-wringing lieutenants, was no surprise. *Why are you never on hand when you can be of some use?* Niccolò thought sourly. He cut off the inevitable flow of apologies with a gesture. 'Signor de Beaumont, this must be sent instantly to Florence. I would be obliged if you would arrange a reliable courier, if such a person can be found in this chaos.'

'Of course, Messer Machiavelli, of course.' De Beaumont was pleasingly obsequious. He handed the note to one of the flutterers, who dashed out of the tent, holding Niccolò's short letter at arm's length, as though it were poisoned.

'Where have they taken our colleague?' Della Casa was peremptory, the respect he had initially felt for the Frenchman now wholly dissolved. 'And what are you proposing to do to recover him?'

'I have sent men to follow them and report back, but beyond that, I fear there is little that I can do. The camp is a powder-keg, and we must avoid setting a match to it.'

That earned him a look of withering contempt from della Casa. But however frustrating it might seem, in fact the general was probably right. They would have to wait and see what the rebels would do next. As far as de Beaumont's scouts could tell, Luca degli Albizzi had been taken perhaps half a mile towards the walls of Pisa and had been deposited in the middle of a camp of about five hundred mercenaries. They would allow no one to come any closer.

For the whole of that night and most of the following day, there was no news at all. The two remaining Florentine commissioners felt completely powerless. They importuned de Beaumont to do something, anything, to recover their captured colleague, but to no avail. The Frenchman seemed to be paralysed.

It was late in the afternoon that, finally, their missing colleague reappeared, accompanied by two of de Beaumont's French soldiers. Though physically he seemed none the worse, his pallor was white and there were dark marks of exhaustion under his eyes. Dismissing the soldiers, Niccolò and della Casa helped him into a chair and poured him wine.

'Thank you, my friends, thank you. It is sweet indeed to be among friendly faces again. I hope never again to suffer the pain and affliction that I have felt over the last day and a half.'

'What happened, Luca?' Della Casa brushed aside his colleague's sufferings, which seemed a little insensitive to Niccolò, though Albizzi was not offended.

'They threatened me with my life if I did not immediately guarantee that Florence would pay the arrears owed, not just to their company, but also to an entire army of some five hundred men. What was more, if I did not settle with them, they said they would seize all our cannon and march on Florence themselves! Whether they are capable of such a thing I do not know, but they seemed quite determined.'

Albizzi took another deep draught of the wine before continuing. 'I told them that I would personally stand surety for the sum they required, though it was manifestly impossible for me to do anything while I was being held captive. This seemed to carry some weight, and eventually, they allowed me to write to the Signoria and to send letters to those of my friends who might be able to raise a sufficient sum to satisfy them. Once that was done, they were satisfied and released me.'

'And now where are they, these rebels?'

'It was hard to make it out in that barbaric patois of theirs, but I think they plan to move tonight towards San Giovanni alla Vena, and then go by the Lucca road to Pietrasanta. They say they will await the pleasure of the king there. The Gascons have, it seems, already marched and will be waiting for them on Lucchese territory.'

'So virtually the whole the army has deserted, except for our own troops.' Niccolò said.

Their gloom at this realisation was not lifted by the arrival of de Beaumont, who dispensed once more ritual regrets at the treatment of the Florentine commissioner, which they heard out with a politeness that barely concealed their ire. The general then proceeded to confirm the dire state of the army. 'I still have a core of loyal soldiers, some of the Gascons and, of course, there are your troops, but without additional reinforcements, we will be vulnerable to any sallies from Pisa. And we need to secure Cascina and Pontedera.'

98

These two towns were the keys to the eastern approaches to Pisa and they also guarded the western approach to Florence. The desertions had left both without garrisons.

'Jacopo da Piombino?' Niccolò's suggestion was tentative, conscious as he was that de Beaumont, whatever his failings, was a far more experienced military commander than either he or his colleagues. 'Perhaps we could ask the Signoria to direct him to concentrate his army upon Cascina?'

'Is he reliable?' De Beaumont's question was hardly unreasonable in the circumstances.

'I think so,' Niccolò said. When he had visited the Lord of Piombino at his camp the year before, he had been impressed by the discipline with which he managed his army. 'I haven't seen or spoken to him for over a year, but since we renegotiated his *condotta* last March he has proven faithful and effective.'

Albizzi nodded his agreement. 'Niccolò is right, General. I will send to the Signoria today to ask that Piombino be redeployed to Cascina forthwith. If that meets with your approval?'

His army half-melted around him, the beleaguered de Beaumont had little option but to agree, with a distracted wave of his hand. No doubt the greater part of his mind was busy composing an explanation to King Louis for this disaster.

The reply to their despatches came back a few days later, the Signoria having evidently spent a full day debating the disaster. Their lordships agreed to the proposed redeployment of Jacopo di Piombino and further requested that they seek de Beaumont's agreement to move all their remaining cannons and munitions to Cascina to procure their safety and ensure the defensibility of that strategic town. The siege of Pisa was, to all intents and purposes, over.

The three commissioners were also permitted to return to Florence. Quitting what remained of the camp, a sea of rubbish and discarded equipment among the sagging tents and forlorn banners, they rode in silence, contemplating the unhappy task ahead of them of reporting on the debacle.

Chapter 10—A Mission to France

Italy and France, July 1500

A sense of frustrated powerlessness accompanied the three envoys like an unwanted street urchin all the way home. They talked desultorily about how they would justify themselves to the Signoria when they got to Florence, but their heart wasn't in it, and they arrived in the city shrouded in an invisible pall of gloom. But they were to be surprised.

'Don't worry, Nico,' Biagio said when they met in the customs courtyard of the government palazzo. 'The priors are outraged over everything that happened in Pisa, angrier at the French than you and the others.'

When the Signoria met later that afternoon, Biagio was proved right. He and his fellow commissioners were greeted with applause and a series of speeches expressing the fury of the Florentine Republic at their treatment. Then Gonfaloniere Delvigna called the meeting to order, beginning a debate that was to last for the rest of the day.

Resuming his role as official recorder of the Signoria's deliberations, Niccolò listened with growing dismay as the discussion began to verge on the hysterical. As the scale of the disaster sank in, bombast gave way to despair and the priors started to jump at every shadow, real and imagined.

'What will happen if the pope resumes his campaign in the Romagna?' one of them asked, panic in his voice. 'What then? We don't have enough soldiers to fight against Borgia and the Pisans both!'

That seemed an improbability to Niccolò since all Cesare Borgia's conquests had been made using French troops, which were no longer available to him. He wanted to say so but, lacking a specific invitation to speak from the gonfaloniere, he had to remain a mute witness as the storm of impotent hand-wringing eventually wore itself out.

A far more pressing concern was the damage to their reputation at the French court. 'De Beaumont will no doubt even now be on his way to King Louis, full of justification for his failure,' Piero Soderini said, 'and no doubt he will blame us for the whole debacle.'

'Will he be believed? After all, it was the French and Swiss troops who deserted their posts, not ours.'

'I don't know, Antonio. But who is to gainsay him? We have few friends at the court.'

'And so long as the French hold Lombardy we need their alliance if we are to counter the influence of Venice and guard against any designs the pope might still have on the rest of the Romagna.' This from Jacopo Salviati, one of the more experienced and respected priors.

'Exactly so.' Gonfaloniere Delvigna looked around the table. 'Then it seems to me, signori, that we must send ambassadors to King Louis to ensure that he fully understands exactly what happened at Pisa.'

That proposal met with universal approval, as did the next statement from Piero Soderini.

'And who better to convey what happened than our envoys, Francesco della Casa and young Niccolò Machiavelli here. I think we can excuse poor Luca, who has suffered enough on behalf of his country! But Francesco and Niccolò were on the spot, after all, and can convince the king of our blamelessness.'

Niccolò did his best, not entirely successfully, to hide his surprise at this proposal. Yet in some ways it felt appropriate. After all, he had just passed his thirty-first birthday, he had been in office for almost exactly three years, and he had now acquired some experience of diplomacy. So it was with a mix of pride and apprehension that he stammered his consent to undertake this commission.

*

> *You will proceed with all possible despatch, even to riding post if your strength permits it, to Lyon, or wherever you learn that his most Christian Majesty is to be found.*

With these words, which were followed by several pages of detailed and specific instructions, Niccolò and Francesco della Casa were to be despatched to France as special emissaries to King Louis XII. The essence of their mission was to protest the failure of the French army before Pisa and to say whatever they needed to say to persuade the king that the failure was none of Florence's doing.

'No doubt de Beaumont will have despatched agents to Lyon already,' Chancellor Adriani told them when he handed them the commission. 'And no doubt they will be telling him that it was all our fault, that we failed to provide sufficient munitions and other supplies and so on. You were both in the camp and you know what happened, so you are perfect ambassadors to convince Louis that we were not at fault.'

Niccolò skimmed through the commission with his customary speed. 'So we are to blame de Beaumont as energetically as possible,' he said. 'It also says that we should not hesitate to charge him with cowardice and corruption. Is that wise? De Beaumont was the general we requested, after all, and he is well thought of by the king.'

'I tend to agree with you. But feelings in the Signoria were much inflamed against him, and you know what they are like once they have got an idea into their heads. Look, you must use your judgement to decide exactly how to proceed. Lenzi will be able to give you more exact guidance.'

Lorenzo Lenzi was one of the two permanent ambassadors to the French court, to whom they were to report on their arrival in Lyon. The other, Francesco Gualterotti, was due to return to Florence soon and was unlikely to be in Lyon when they arrived.

'And what of the French king's promise of more troops to renew the campaign?' della Casa asked. 'Are we expected to convey the Signoria's views on that as well?'

To the astonishment of the Signoria, King Louis, on hearing of the debacle at Pisa, had written in the warmest terms, deploring the failure and offering a new army to renew the campaign. But the Florentines were becoming warier of the value of outside help for this enterprise and of the king's motives in offering it. As it was, the remnants of de Beaumont's army still sat on Tuscan soil, ravaging the countryside all around them. If the French reinforced that army with still more troops, was it not possible that they would never leave and would turn their arms against Florence itself? The debate had raged for half a day, until eventually they had decided, respectfully, to decline the offer, a decision that had not as yet been communicated to King Louis.

'You have no such instructions,' Adriani said, with stiff formality. 'No doubt the Signoria will write in due course or communicate their intentions to Lenzi. Leave it alone, Francesco. It will just complicate your job to have to deal with that question as well.'

'Which means,' Niccolò said to della Casa after the chancellor had gone, 'that our lords of the Signoria are in a funk. They don't want to offend Louis, but they don't know how to tell him they don't want his help.'

Della Casa laughed. 'I swear, you grow more cynical by the day, Niccolò. Mind you, you're probably right this time. Tell me, how is Primavera?'

Niccolò's sister had fallen ill with a summer fever. At first, it had seemed nothing, a passing illness that she would shake off, but after a few weeks she was still bedridden, and showed no sign of improvement, despite all the efforts of the family doctor. 'We fear for her life, Francesco. To tell the truth, this commission comes at a bad time for me—my father's affairs are still not settled, there is an endless pile of paperwork that has to be dealt with, and now this.'

Della Casa gave his arm a sympathetic squeeze. 'I'm sorry to hear that, Niccolò. But at least you have Totto to help out.'

Though Niccolò nodded his agreement, he knew that Totto was too young and inexperienced to shoulder much of the burden that should rightly fall on his shoulders as the head of the Machiavelli family. Yet what choice did he have? Turning down this commission was unthinkable, and besides, Adriani had assured him that he would be back in a few weeks. He just had to hope that Primavera would recover in that time and that Totto would rise to the challenge.

*

The two emissaries left Florence through the city's eastern gate the following day, accompanied by two pack mules and a servant apiece. After a day and night on the road, they arrived in Bologna, one of the principal cities of the Romagna. There, they enjoyed the hospitality of Giovanni Bentivoglio, the wily *condottiero* who had ruled the papal city for almost forty years. He was also the only one of the vicars in the Romagna who had not been deposed by Pope Alexander.

'The old bastard doesn't dare,' he said when they joined him for dinner in his vast Venetian-style palazzo. 'My hold on Bologna is secure enough, and the people support me. He would have a fight on his hands if he ever tried to get rid of me.'

'And you are not worried about his son?' Niccolò asked. He decided he rather liked this tall, grey-haired old man. 'His new possessions in the Romagna are not so far from your territory, after all.'

'Well, he is a little close for comfort, I grant you that. But I can hold him off, I expect. No doubt Florence would offer support if it came to war.'

It was more a question than a statement, but they could in all good conscience not do more than offer vague noises of encouragement, and though their host's demeanour did not change, they both sensed that he was a little disappointed with them as they left early the next morning to begin the long journey across northern Italy, a journey that, at that season, was less than comfortable.

The July heat beat down on the dusty roads and by the middle of each day the heads of both horses and men were drooping as they plodded along. Though they all wore big kerchiefs to keep the dust from their mouths and noses, the clouds of pesky insects that accompanied them got into their ears and eyes and stung the horses, making them restive and difficult to manage.

Their safe-conduct procured them decent accommodation in the towns and cities of Italy, but as they moved further away, climbing up through the Alps towards the French border, they were obliged to put themselves up at increasingly dilapidated inns and hostels that were all they could afford on their minuscule salaries (della Casa, the senior envoy, was paid eight lire a day, while Niccolò received a mere four), usually sharing a room with their servants.

Rats were their constant companions in these places, and one morning Niccolò awoke to find his boots half gnawed through and full of rat droppings, and his court clothes similarly ruined. Della Casa could barely restrain his mirth, which probably contributed to Niccolò's uncharacteristic burst of rage at his hapless servant, who should have known better than to leave his possessions on the floor where the rats could get at them.

Adding to their misery, the quality of the food deteriorated as they got further and further away from the familiarities of home. Della Casa was proud of his iron constitution and bragged that he could eat and drink anything without his stomach being upset. But the food provided at the French inns proved to be his undoing, with its unaccustomed spices and sketchy cooking, and he spent several uncomfortable days on the road after over-indulging one night. Niccolò was unaffected, being more abstemious by habit, though his servant also succumbed. Niccolò regarded this as some form of divine justice for his carelessness with his master's clothes.

Along the way, he got to know his fellow envoy a little better. Francesco was several years older and, though he carried an old Florentine name, he was not much wealthier than Niccolò, a point that caused the disparity in their pay to rankle. Though they had known each other for some years, they had not worked together before the mission to Pisa, an experience that had made them firm friends. Thick-set and florid, della Casa shared Niccolò's sanguine outlook on life, seeing things as they were, rather than as he would like them to be. And he enjoyed a good joke, laughing uproariously when amused by one of Niccolò's sly tales.

Their journey, though tedious and uncomfortable, passed without incident until, having finally descended on the other side of the Alps, they arrived at the little town of Aiguebelle, just a few days' ride from Lyon. The inn where they ended up that night was particularly villainous, their room hot and stuffy and the bedding lice-ridden. Even so, Niccolò had learned the knack of sleeping in even the most uncomfortable conditions and had fallen into unconsciousness as soon as his head hit the pillow. From this blissful state, he was rudely summoned just before dawn by a violent shaking being administered by Francesco della Casa, whose anxious face he could barely make out in the dim light. 'They've gone, Niccolò!'

'Who has gone? Where?' Niccolò shook his head to dispel the last vestiges of sleep. What on earth was Francesco on about?

'The bloody servants. They've run off and taken everything with them!'

He pushed himself upright and looked around the room. When they had gone to sleep last night, there had been four of them, as usual. He and della Casa had taken the two narrow cots, and the servants had laid themselves down on the rough bedding that they carried with them. Now, sure enough, they had gone, along with the big saddlebags that had contained their clothes and other possessions. All that was left was Niccolò's satchel, which contained their instructions and safe-conduct, his well-thumbed copy of Dante's *Divine Comedy*, and what was left of his money. Everything else was gone. 'Are you sure they haven't just started saddling the horses early?'

'The innkeeper says he saw them riding off on them, along with the pack-horses, an hour before dawn.'

'Then why didn't the poltroon come and tell us?'

'He's French.' Della Casa's shrug was eloquent, conveying his disgust with every member of that race. 'The more relevant question is, what now? Do you have any money?'

Niccolò opened his satchel and rummaged in the bottom, bringing out a small purse. 'There's not much. Probably enough to buy a couple of nags and pay for the rest of the journey to Lyon if we are frugal, but that is about all. We will need clothes if we are to appear appropriately at court, and we'll need to hire some new servants, though God knows how we will do that. Let's hope that there is a draft for our salaries waiting for us in Lyon. And perhaps Lenzi can help out. Damn it, why would they have done this?'

Niccolò wondered guiltily whether his loss of temper a few days before might have been the cause of their misfortune, but then dismissed the thought—servants who made mistakes were accustomed to putting up with much more severe mistreatment than a mere tongue-lashing.

'It might be because they haven't been paid,' della Casa said, looking a little sheepish,

'What do you mean? We had enough money to pay them, didn't we?'

'Not really. You know how tight our funds have been; everything has cost more than we expected and we have to keep some money to pay for bribes and presents and what-not at the French court when we get there. So I held their pay back, told them they would be paid in full when we got to Lyon.'

Niccolò stared open-mouthed at his colleague. 'Francesco! What were you thinking? And now the rascals have decided to make off with everything we own in place of their back-wages! What a bloody disaster.'

Two tell-tale red spots appeared on della Casa's cheeks, which Niccolò knew presaged a full-scale explosion. A shouting-match would do neither of them any good, so he decided that retreat might be wiser. 'Ah well, I don't suppose that there was anything else you could do. It's the Signoria's fault. If they were paying me at parity with you, we wouldn't have had to cut corners. Come on, let's go and see if we can find some horses and get on our way.'

Having begrudgingly paid the innkeeper who had so signally failed to look after their interests, they bought a couple of poor broken-winded nags from the local stables, the best that they could afford with what was left of their funds, and went on their way to Lyon, which they reached three days later.

Ambassador Lenzi was, when they arrived at the door of his modest lodging in the middle of the town, sympathetic to their plight, though he seemed to think that such mishaps were far from unusual, the typical hazards of a diplomat on the road. The good news was that he was in a position to help re-equip them, albeit modestly, from funds that he had received from Florence for such purposes.

The bad news, delivered once they had settled over supper in the tavern occupying the ground floor of the ambassador's lodging, confirmed a suspicion that had crept into Niccolò's mind as they rode through the city.

'The court has left,' Lenzi said, efficiently devouring a braised chicken leg. 'They moved on to Nevers two days ago. It's three days' ride away, so you'll catch them if you can find some horses and men tomorrow.'

That explained why the town had seemed surprisingly quiet for a place where the King of France was supposed to be in residence. Then Niccolò realised what else Lenzi had said. 'We? Aren't you going to Nevers as well?'

'Not me, I'm going back to Florence. My embassy is finished and the Signoria have recalled me. Not a minute too soon, frankly.'

Machiavelli and della Casa looked at each other. No one in Florence had mentioned that Lenzi had been recalled. With the other permanent ambassador, Gualterotti, also on his way back to Italy, they would be left to deal with the French king and his advisers alone. That was not something either of them had envisaged.

'I can see this is news to you both,' Lenzi said. The smile on his face suggested he was enjoying their discomfiture, prompting the nasty suspicion to enter Niccolò's head that he and della Casa were deliberately being left as scapegoats should their mission go awry. After all, they were both fairly junior and much more dispensable than aristocrats like Lenzi and Gualterotti.

'I'm sure we will survive,' della Casa said, showing more confidence than Niccolò felt. 'But if you can offer us any advice before we go...'

'Of course, of course.' Lenzi was now positively jovial. 'Look, I will give you some written instructions tomorrow, but the most important thing is this— your best friend and worst enemy at the court of the King of France is Georges d'Amboise, Cardinal-Archbishop of Rouen, and the architect of the king's policy in Italy. Get him on your side and anything is possible. Lose his friendship, and you might as well just turn around and go back to Florence. Go and see him first and follow his advice in everything.'

'He is well-disposed towards us?' della Casa asked.

'Yes, though within limits. King Louis seeks to manipulate affairs in Italy by playing each city off against the others. This is an old game and d'Amboise is a master at it. But for now, he is favourably disposed towards us as a counter to the pope's ambitions in the Romagna.'

Cesare Borgia again, Niccolò thought. That young man's ambitions seemed to be worrying everybody.

'The Signoria instructed us to explain all that happened before Pisa,' he said, turning the discussion to a different question that had been vexing him. 'But they particularly wanted us to place the blame on de Beaumont. Does this seem advisable to you?'

Lenzi looked as if he had been scalded. 'My dear boy, do not do any such thing! De Beaumont and d'Amboise are old friends and political allies. Accusing de Beaumont would lose you his support in an instant. No, I suggest you put all the blame on the Italians, the Lucchese and the Sienese, whose agents I have no doubt were at the bottom of it all, stirring up sedition among the troops.'

That theory had, Niccolò remembered, been advanced in the debates in the Signoria, but without any evidence. For himself, he had seen little sign that

108

there were any such agents at work in the camp, though that did not make the idea impossible.

'And what about the king's offer of a renewal of the siege?' della Casa turned to the other question that they had discussed endlessly on their long journey. 'Has the Signoria given you any instructions on that front?'

'None whatever,' Lenzi said cheerfully. He leaned forward, drawing them into a conspiratorial huddle. 'I would try and avoid talking about it if I were you. But if the subject does come up, this is what I would suggest you do. First, play on the king's conscience. Tell him that the Pisans are ravaging our countryside, which would not have happened had we not relied on the French, and in so doing disbanded our forces so that we could pay for his. Secondly, suggest that a small force, say two hundred lances, would be welcomed on Pisan territory, should he be so disposed as to send them. But do not say that Florence is prepared to pay for any new army, nor for any arrears of pay due to the disbanded troops from the previous siege. You have no instructions on that front, clear?'

In the end, they had two days to ponder Lenzi's words, and the many more instructions besides that he included in a lengthy memorandum he sent them the next day. They were two long and frustrating days, for, try as they might, they could not find horses to take them on to Nevers. The whole of Lyons and the countryside around it having been stripped of virtually all supplies by the royal household. Even servants were hard to come by, especially since, after their recent experience, they were disposed to be particularly careful in their choice of personnel. And then there were supplies for the journey to be purchased and new clothes appropriate to one of the most impressive courts in Christendom to be found, all of which took up every waking minute. By the time they were finally ready to leave, their meagre funds were all but exhausted.

Lenzi was helpful, assisting with their various purchases and arranging for some additional money to be provided against their future salaries, the drafts for which had (of course!) not yet caught up with them. Money was going to be a constant worry and Niccolò decided that enduring penury in silence would serve neither him nor the republic well. So he wrote off to the Signoria and the War Committee, begging most humbly for them to increase his salary. For good measure, he had also sent messages to Biagio and Totto, asking them to do what they could on his behalf.

109

At last, though, there was nothing else for them to do, and they were ready to depart.

'Don't forget, boys,' the ebullient ambassador said as he saw them off, 'when you meet the cardinal, don't try and argue about any point on which he has formed a definite judgement, whether you like it or not. For in the end, where Georges d'Amboise wants to go, there you too will end up going.'

Chapter 11—An Interview with a King

Nevers, France, August 1500

That advice was still ringing in their ears when, dusty and tired, they arrived at the little town of Nevers, perched on its sandy bend of the Loire. Here they found all the bustle that had been so absent in Lyon. The streets were crowded with people, self-important retainers in royal livery mingling with the ordinary townsfolk, all hurrying about trying to keep up with the demands of hundreds of noble Frenchmen and their retinues. Somewhere, a pair of trumpets blasted out a fanfare announcing the arrival into the town (or perhaps the departure) of some duke or count. Ahead of them, a cart piled high with provisions of every kind had broken a wheel, blocking their way to the grand-ducal palace, wherein the king and his court were presently residing.

Eventually, having picked their way around the cart and the knot of angry people surrounding it, they found themselves at the gates to the courtyard of the grand chateau. The guards seemed unwilling at first to let them go any further, and they had to wait until higher authority was summoned in the form of a gorgeously-dressed captain who inspected their safe-conduct, by now tattered and grubby and almost illegible. After giving them a long look up and down, he finally waved them through.

'Your men can take the horses around the back,' he told them as he scribbled a note on a portable writing table being held by one of his men. 'You'll find the cardinal on the second floor. Give the footmen this and they'll take you to him.'

Anticipating that they would not have an opportunity to change their clothes until they were settled into their accommodation, they had done their best to make themselves presentable by wearing court gowns over their riding clothes before leaving Lyons that morning. Even so, they were somewhat dusty, a condition they could do little to rectify as they were conducted up the stairs and into the apartments of Cardinal d'Amboise by a supercilious footman who bade them wait in an anteroom while he informed his master of their presence. After only a few minutes, they were directed through the door with a casual flick of the fingers that conveyed the footman's disdain perfectly.

The man who rose from his desk and crossed the carpeted floor to greet them in perfect Italian was portly, to say the least. Below the magnificent robes, there was a substantial body that was clearly used to good living, but which nevertheless moved with surprising grace. The cardinal's face, below its elegant red hat, was sharp-boned and narrow, not at all the jolly visage usually associated with fat men. His eyes, black, bright and cunning, conveyed nothing except mild curiosity.

With a little nervous clearing of his throat, della Casa launched into the opening remarks they had rehearsed on the road, explaining why they were there and commending themselves to his care, as a friend of Florence.

'Messieurs, I am glad that your Signoria has sent you to us,' the cardinal responded, his voice a deep and cordial baritone. 'The king was deeply troubled by the news of the insurrection before Pisa when he heard of it and wrote to your government to say so, as you know. Although this is now an old affair, over and done with, I am sure His Majesty will want to hear your account of it.'

'Thank you, Your Eminence. We will be most gratified to obtain an audience whenever a suitable opportunity should occur.'

As della Casa was speaking, the door to the anteroom opened, and the same haughty servant came in and handed the cardinal a note. On scanning its contents, the cardinal's face turned crafty, the eyebrows lifting ever so slightly, the broad smile narrowing. 'What better time than at present? When I was told you were here, I sent straightaway to the king and he has commanded you to an immediate audience.'

This they had not anticipated and Niccolò felt a flutter of anxiety deep down in his stomach. How absurd it all was—he, Niccolò di Bernardo Machiavelli, a mere secretary from a minor Florentine family, was about to be presented to one of the most powerful kings in Europe. The urge to giggle fought with his nerves as they moved through the various anterooms towards the royal apartments, each filled with courtiers who bowed and scraped as the cardinal came by, their eyes curious about the two newcomers to court.

As they walked, d'Amboise kept up a one-sided conversation, consisting mostly of pithy observations, delivered with no care as to whether they could be heard, about the various people who made obsequious obeisance to the cardinal as they passed. Machiavelli and della Casa responded with nothing

112

more adventurous than nods and murmurs. Then, just as they were about to enter the king's receiving chamber, the cardinal asked the question they did not want to answer. 'What, Signor della Casa, does your government intend to do about my king's proposal to recommence the siege of Pisa?'

Della Casa opened his mouth to begin the reply they had carefully rehearsed, when the door swung open and a footman announced them, thus saving him the necessity of any response at all.

The room into which they were ushered was broad and light, with a range of tall windows that admitted the sunshine from the courtyard outside. Tapestries hung on the walls and the floor was covered with fresh rushes. The furniture was sparse, just one or two benches and tables, a few chairs, all elegantly made. At the far end of the room, sitting casually in a tall chair of state, was his Most Catholic Majesty, Louis XII. He was in conversation with a military man, who Niccolò thought was Florimond Robertet, one of the king's most senior commanders, and another man, a grizzled-looking Italian who he didn't immediately recognise.

'Gianjacopo Trivulzio,' della Casa muttered in a low voice as the doorman announced their arrival, 'the Governor of Milan. We will need to be careful what we say in front of him.'

They moved forward, bowing, and as Cardinal d'Amboise made a few remarks introducing them and explaining their presence, Niccolò had his first chance to look properly at the king, who had been elevated to his throne so unexpectedly just two years before. At thirty-eight, he was in his physical prime, the broad shoulders under the sumptuous green velvet of his doublet suggesting the body of an athlete. Beneath a simple black hat decorated with an enormous ruby, black hair hung fashionably long down to his shoulders and framed a jowly face dominated by the long Valois nose that ended above a pinched mouth and prominent chin. Hooded blue eyes regarded them with an air of impatient self-confidence as he waited for his chief minister to finish the introductions.

'You are welcome to our court, messieurs.' The king's voice was surprisingly soft. 'We were pleased when the cardinal informed us of your arrival, for we are most interested to learn more of the events outside Pisa in these past months and to understand what the intentions of your republic might

113

be for the future. We care much for the welfare of our friends in Florence and are determined to sustain them in their efforts to bring the Pisans to their duty.'

Della Casa's response was, as they had rehearsed on the road, soothing and conciliatory, emphasising the great discredit that the failure had brought both to the king and their beloved republic but making it sound as if it had all been an act of nature, like a flood or a fire, rather than a failure of men.

'As we were ourselves present in the camp,' he went on, turning to the substance of their commission, 'their lordships of the Signoria have sent us to explain to Your Majesty the circumstances and details, and to convey our indignation at the treatment of our commissioner, Signor degli Albizzi, who was carried off and held prisoner by the Swiss. Further, their lordships also required us to explain that the cause of the raising of the siege was in no way due to any act of commission or neglect on the part of our republic...'

While della Casa proceeded with his formal speech, Niccolò watched the expressions on the faces of the king and his ministers. Louis remained inscrutable, his fingers absently twisting one of his rings, but otherwise completely still. D'Amboise maintained a friendly and encouraging smile. On the other hand, the two soldiers scowled at the implication that French arms had been inadequate to the task of subduing Pisa. When della Casa had finished speaking, the king exchanged glances with them before he spoke. 'But come now, monsieur, surely this failure cannot all be laid at the feet of our armies?' His voice was still affable, as though making a friendly enquiry about a matter of little import. 'It has been reported to us, in some detail, that considerable blame must attach to your republic and its governors.'

'My Lord King, it grieves us to hear that you have received such reports,' della Casa said soothingly. 'But to our certain knowledge, Florence has met all the demands that were placed upon us by your generals during the campaign. Perhaps you could enlighten us as to the specific points at which it is said that we have failed Your Majesty?'

With a gesture, the king directed them to Cardinal d'Amboise. 'We are told that the Florentines failed to provide adequate supplies of munitions and provisions. That this contributed to the general state of decay in the army. And there was the matter of your soldiers' failure to secure an important bridge, allowing the Pisans to sally out, to the detriment of all.' D'Amboise was at first stern, but his expression softened a little as he went on. 'But gentlemen, let us

114

not say any more on the subject, else we will find ourselves in endless recriminations. All this is in the past, and we need rather to consider the future.'

They should have taken the hint and allowed the conversation to move on. But della Casa was not prepared to let it lie. 'My Lord Cardinal, I do not know who has been advising you on this matter,' he said, looking not at the cardinal, but at the Italian *condottiero*, Trivulzio, 'but I must protest that we met every request for provisions and munitions that General de Beaumont sent us, and frequently exceeded his demands. What you may not have been told, seigneurs, is that there was much waste in the camp, which we can easily detail—'

A gesture from the king brought della Casa to a stammering halt. 'Enough. As My Lord Cardinal has said, it will profit us nothing to spend our time in recriminations over who was at fault. For the present, we readily acknowledge the perfidy of our Gascon troops and the infamy of our Swiss mercenaries in carrying off your commissioner. Sadly, they are in the habit of acting this way and have practised similar extortions wherever they are employed. We will also concede that perhaps our General de Beaumont should have more thoroughly enforced obedience from the soldiery under his command. This question our commissioners will examine in due course.'

'If Your Majesty will permit,' Niccolò was cautious, conscious of his status as the junior envoy, 'it is true that there was a great lack of discipline in the camp and indeed this was the real cause of all the disorder. But throughout, we found General de Beaumont to be jealous of Your Majesty's honour, and friendly to our country. Had others shown equal goodwill, we should no doubt have been victorious.'

The cardinal's approving nod told him that he had hit the right mark. No doubt de Beaumont had jealous rivals whispering in the king's ear. Perhaps one of them was general Robertet, who was still scowling at them. By defending him, Niccolò had, he hoped, bought them some credit with the all-powerful cardinal.

The king seemed mollified. 'Indeed, and no doubt our commissioners will get to the truth of things, though there is no doubt that this enterprise has ended in a manner prejudicial to yourselves and with little credit to me.' The unreadable blue eyes rested on Machiavelli, who did his best to project a calm he did not feel as the king's tone of voice became tinged with impatience. 'But that, as My Lord Cardinal says, is water under the bridge. More importantly, we must come to some decision as to what had best be done next. We have made our views known to your Signoria and have offered men and arms to resume the campaign. Since you were most recently in Florence and must know the mind of your government, I ask you to let us have their answer.'

It was the question that d'Amboise had asked them, just before they came into the audience chamber, the question to which they were under the strictest instructions not to respond.

It was della Casa's right and responsibility to convey their inability to tell the king what he wanted to hear, but before his colleague could say a word, Niccolò found himself speaking. 'My Lord King, we have no orders from the Signoria on this point. Our instructions were confined to the events that occurred in the camp, at which we were personally present.' The king's angry frown at these words should have been a warning, but something prompted Niccolò to keep talking, thinking on his feet. 'Your Majesty, the people of Florence have been involved for many years in an onerous and financially ruinous war. Seeing the unhappy and unexpected outcome of this last enterprise, they have lost the confidence, courage and strength necessary to embark on another such uncertain campaign.

'But if Your Majesty were to conquer Pisa by the force of your arms, then restore her into our hands, we could then be sure that there would be a reward for the expenses that we should have to incur anew. If that were the case, we confidently believe that the Signoria would happily and amply compensate Your Majesty for your outlays.'

When he finished speaking, Niccolò looked from face to face, feeling pleased with himself and his elegant formulation of a proposal that would meet the demands both of King Louis and Florence—let the king take Pisa, turn it over to the Florentines, then they would pay him.

He was completely taken aback when Georges d'Amboise' face clouded over and his fists clenched in anger. 'What are you saying, Monsieur Machiavelli? That we should make war for the benefit of Florence at our own expense?'

Niccolò opened his mouth to reply but finding no words that might mollify the angry churchman, closed it again, feeling foolish.

'My Lord Cardinal, no!' Della Casa came to his rescue. 'What Niccolò meant, but perhaps did not make clear, was that France should be fully reimbursed for all expenses incurred after placing Pisa in our hands.'

'Even so, you suggest that we should find the funds from our treasury in the first instance and only when our arms are successful will those funds be repaid. It seems to me that this proposal would leave France with all the risk and Florence with all the profit!'

'Your Eminence,' Niccolò returned to the fray, having recovered himself and feeling that he should do what he could to rescue them from his blunder, 'this was but a suggestion on my part and does not represent settled Florentine policy on this question, upon which, as monsieur della Casa has said, we have no instructions.'

This seemed sufficient to mollify the cardinal. The soldiers, Niccolò noticed, were now grinning at their discomfiture.

'Messieurs,' the king said, leaning a little forward in his chair and raising an admonitory finger. 'there is a treaty between our two states. You know that I will always do my duty in accordance with its provisions, and I expect your Signoria to do the same. If, on the other hand, they should fail to do so, I think I could be excused if I abandoned my obligations.'

Louis paused to allow that statement to hang in the air. Thoroughly chastened, both emissaries held their tongues. When the king spoke again, it was in a low voice, almost as if he were musing out loud. 'Of course, once we have resumed the campaign, Pisa and Montepulciano and all the other places, should we win them, would be in my control. If I then choose to return them, it would be merely from my desire to keep to my engagements.'

Meaning, Niccolò thought, *that even if the Florentines pay the French to win back their territory for them, there is no guarantee that he will keep his side of the bargain.* The point was clear. They were being given a lesson in the realities of power, for no matter how many ducats the Florentines could outlay, it was the French king who possessed the armies.

'Your Majesty,' della Casa said, clearly anxious to bring matters to a conclusion, 'we will most likely receive from the Signoria a definite reply on these questions very soon and will convey their answer as soon as it is obtained.'

The king sat back again in his chair, and waved a languid hand, satisfied that he had got his point across. 'It is important that they do so, as quickly as may be so that we can decide whether or not to disband those of our infantry who remain on Florentine soil at the disposal of your republic. And I fully expect Florence to meet the charges involved in their maintenance until they are discharged and the cost of returning them to their home soil, in accordance with the terms of the treaty between us.'

With which he stood, indicating that the audience was at an end. Making their obeisance, the two ambassadors backed towards the door, leaving a distinctly chilly atmosphere behind them.

Chapter 12—Intrigue in Montargis

Montargis, France, August 1500

'I'm sorry, Francesco. I don't know why I said it. It just seemed such an elegant solution.'

They were in their temporary quarters for the night, a poky attic room in a small inn that their servants had managed to procure while they had been having their audience with the French king. Though it was hardly comfortable, it did not matter, since the court was moving on to Montargis in the morning and they would be accompanying it.

'Never mind, Niccolò, it's not your fault. The Signoria must have known that the French would want to know whether they were going to accept their offer or not and should have given us instructions on the subject, particularly since they knew we would be alone here, without support from the regular ambassadors. You did the best you could.'

Niccolò didn't feel as if he deserved this restrained response from his colleague, but was grateful for it, nevertheless. They had just finished writing a long despatch to Florence, putting the best light they could on the day's meetings. But nothing could disguise the fact that, far from winning the king's support, they had come perilously close to losing it entirely. If they were to recover, they would depend even more on the goodwill of Georges d'Amboise.

The following morning, the two envoys were up early, joining the vast cavalcade that jostled its way out of town, heading for the court's next destination—the little town of Montargis. It wasn't until later that afternoon that, having found new lodgings and settled themselves in, they were able to track down the cardinal and try to resurrect their reputation with him and the king. It did not start well.

'Messieurs, you should understand that every day there are accusations and complaints that are being levelled against your government,' the cardinal said, counting off on his fingers. 'You have been most reluctant to take any measures of your own to recommence the siege; you have been unwilling to admit any French garrisons onto your territory, despite the clear military necessity; you have refused to pay for the return home of the Swiss soldiery, even though such payment was explicit in the treaty between us; and it is Florence that should take full responsibility for the debacle before Pisa.'

'Eminence, we can only state again what we said yesterday,' della Casa said, barely waiting for the cardinal to finish his recitation. 'Florence has done everything asked of her under the terms of the treaty. The purpose of our mission here is to enable you to satisfy yourself of this and we are willing to submit to the strictest investigation on this point. As for the Swiss, surely Your Eminence can understand our reluctance to pay for them, given that they have not performed the service for which they were contracted?'

The cardinal waved an impatient hand. A sly look came onto the severe face. 'Messieurs, I know you are honourable men, representing your government as ably as you can, but it is difficult to gauge the sincerity of your expressions of support, given the degree to which Florentines are disunited among themselves.'

'My Lord Cardinal, let me assure you that on all important matters, Florentines are entirely united.' Della Casa's flustered indignation was not feigned.

Niccolò was more interested in trying to understand what point the cardinal was trying to make. 'Where, eminence, did you hear such a thing? From the Lucchese?'

There had been envoys from the Lucca present at the French court until recently. The Lucchese had many reasons to want to undermine the Florentine relationship with the French and there were those in the Signoria who believed that Lucca had been behind the revolt of the Swiss, though of this there was no proof.

'No, Monsieur Machiavelli, not the Lucchese. This has been told to us by Frenchmen who are in Florence, reporting their conversations with prominent Florentines.'

Conversations with those of the *ottimati* who secretly wanted the Medici to return, in other words. 'Your Eminence would do well to reflect on the character of those who are making such reports to your countrymen.' Niccolò could not entirely restrain his annoyance. 'There is, of course, always lively division and discussion among our people and at the Signoria; this is to be expected in a Republic. But those men who are charged with the government

120

are, as Francesco said, entirely united on all matters of importance. The views of those who are outside the government might well be of interest, but Your Eminence should weigh their real value and motives carefully.'

Cardinal d'Amboise stared at him. Niccolò held his gaze, feeling much as a mouse might when confronted by a hungry snake.

'You think that I do not?' The cardinal's brows rose. 'But let us return to the central issue—Pisa. We are astonished that, after importuning us for so long for assistance to reduce the place and return it to your sovereignty, you should be so unwilling to resume the siege, unless it be at the expense of France.'

Niccolò's mistake from the day before was back to haunt them. He was surprised when della Casa decided to make another attempt to persuade the cardinal of the idea's merits. 'Your Eminence, let me say again that Florence will do its duty. But you should not be surprised that we mistrust the future, given the failures of the past. We lack men, money and resources to undertake a fresh enterprise on this scale. But for your king, whose resources are so much greater than ours, it would be an inconsiderable war to undertake.'

'If France were to assume the siege as its own,' Niccolò added, eagerly following his colleague's lead, 'no doubt it would be more certain of success. And that success, once achieved, would bring even greater glory to the name of King Louis, being undertaken wholly in his name and by his arms alone.'

'Let there be no doubt either, monseigneur,' della Casa continued, 'that the Signoria will recompense France for all of the expenses undertaken in the project immediately upon the return of Pisa.'

The cardinal, who had remained stern and unsmiling through this verbal onslaught, seemed about to respond in anger, but then his expression softened. 'Your zeal in supporting the interests of your country is to be commended, messieurs. You cannot be faulted on that front. But the truth is you cannot guarantee that the Signoria will agree to this proposal of yours, can you? And you have already said that you are not empowered to negotiate on their behalf, so I can see no point in further discussing this matter, at least until your masters have agreed to pay for the Swiss or you have received some further instructions.'

Della Casa's response was stillborn as d'Amboise raised a hand to silence him. 'I am not insensible to your plight, my friends. You were despatched here to tell us what you know of the unfortunate events at Pisa, which you have done, ably. But you appear to have no useful instructions with respect to these other matters which are of such importance to France. And you expected, no doubt, to have the support of your regular ambassadors.

'In short, I perceive that you are labouring under great difficulties to represent your masters of the Signoria, who have sent you here in a fog of uncertainty. You are to be commended for your tenacity in holding to your positions, but I am afraid, messieurs, that you are more than a little out of your depth here.'

With some difficulty, Niccolò controlled his urge to offer a heated reply; an involuntary movement of his colleague's arm told him that della Casa was doing the same.

'I do not mean this unkindly,' the cardinal went on, the same steady and appraising look in his eyes, 'but I am a realist. I would advise you to write to your Signoria, convey our dissatisfaction with them and reiterate the demands we have made. When you have a reply, we can talk further. Until then, I see no possible value in further discussions. Good day to you both.'

*

'I truly do not know why we are here, Nico,' Della Casa said morosely, back in their lodgings. 'We have, after all, discharged our responsibilities and done all we could. The Signoria ought to recall us and send properly accredited ambassadors who can deal with these questions with authority.'

After that Della Casa sank steadily into melancholy, rarely rising from his bed before noon and drinking heavily in the little tavern near their lodgings that was favoured by the other Italians at the court, and which had become their informal headquarters.

Niccolò was sympathetic and felt just as frustrated as his colleague, but he decided that he was not going to be dragged down into the pit of despair. He would make the most of this extraordinary opportunity to serve his country. So he kept himself busy from early morning until late at night, doing his best to suck up as much information as he could about this strange travelling circus that was the court of the King of France, condensing what he had learned into detailed despatches that could be sent to Florence whenever they could scrape together the money to pay for a courier.

King Louis' court was, he had been told, much smaller than that of his predecessor, the late King Charles VIII. Yet it was a marvel of organisation, managed by thirty-four officials whose unenviable task it was to move ahead of the court and find lodgings for everyone, from the highest nobles down to the meanest servants. Even the little band of women of pleasure who accompanied the court were always found a discreet house somewhere.

So efficient was this system that, within a few days of the court arriving at Montargis, everyone was settled and routines established, and the little town absorbed the imposition of several hundred people with little disruption. To be sure, the streets were crowded with officials and soldiers hurrying about, and the townspeople had the same harried air he had observed at Nevers. Still, he found it surprising, given the scale of the imposition, that there were no fights in the streets, there was no more rubbish accumulating in the gutters than usual, and the general air was that of a busy market-day.

What was impossible to miss were the Italians. Fully a third of the court comprised his countrymen, all of them dissatisfied in one way or another. There were many Milanese, of course, busily ingratiating themselves with their new masters. The other cities of north Italy—Siena, Lucca, Ferrara—all had their representatives, minnows darting among the sharks. Then there were the many Neapolitans, exiles from the court of King Frederick, who were full of plots to entice King Louis to follow in his predecessor's footsteps and invade Naples. The Venetians also kept an ambassador with the court, whose agents were everywhere, stirring up the other Italians and generally making mischief. Even the pope had a permanent ambassador, the resplendent Monseigneur d'Arles, who had rented a substantial house at his own expense for the duration of the court's stay at Montargis.

Niccolò, leaving his unhappy colleague to wallow in his misery, spent his days talking with as many members of the Italian contingent as he could. He decided that he might as well act as if he had the standing of a full ambassador, rather than a mere junior envoy, calculating that his countrymen would admire his bravado, even if they knew that the truth was something different. And it appealed to his well-developed sense of the absurd.

Each city and state naturally congregated in their preferred venue, sometimes a tavern, sometimes the house of one of their number. Moving from one to the other, he soon became a welcome presence at drinking parties, card games and talking sessions. In the company of those who were educated, he deployed his skills as a scholar, dazzling them with the epithets of ancient philosophers, apt verses from Dante and Aeschylus, and long, erudite discussions on Greek and Roman history. With the soldiers and minor courtiers, he told the jokes and seamy stories that had always amused his friends back in Florence. Before long, every Italian at the court of King Louis knew Niccolò Machiavelli, the somewhat curious but very likeable Florentine ambassador.

He listened, too. Fortunately, his countrymen were a garrulous lot, eager to exchange gossip and tell tales about their experiences with the French, all the while puffing themselves up to make sure that he knew just how important, how very influential they were. One of the most talkative turned out to be Gianjacopo Trivulzio, the Milanese who had stood scowling at them during their first audience with the king. Though he had been treated with great respect by the king and cardinal, it seemed that the *condottiero* was touchy about perceived slights to his reputation, as Niccolò discovered when, meeting him on the steps of the church one morning after mass, he was treated to a surprising outburst against the French.

'They are riding high now,' he said, making no effort to lower his voice, which caused several heads to turn and listen with undisguised interest, 'and so they are insolent. But they are cowardly underneath. If you can resist their first onslaught, they become depressed and easily discouraged. I tell you, Machiavelli, leading an army made up of such men is no easy task. The king doesn't understand it.'

Niccolò nodded encouragingly while steering his outspoken countryman away from the crowd. He didn't particularly like this rather shifty Milanese, whose outward bluffness disguised a devious mind, but he thought he had a point. The image of the craven French general at Pisa came into his head. 'General de Beaumont—'

'De Beaumont!' Trivulzio was scathing. 'Exactly the type I mean. The failure of your Pisa campaign is entirely and wholly his fault. The Swiss and Gascons frightened him half to death. And when the French try to say that errors were committed by all parties, they are just trying to make Florence share the responsibility of the faults that were all their own!'

Clearly, Niccolò's assessment that de Beaumont had enemies at court was correct. 'Florence can, I think, bear the calumny,' he said, offering his most sardonic smile. 'But the king seems fixated on the question of paying the Swiss, which is a more difficult problem for us.'

'The French, my young friend, are more eager for money than for blood. Louis has Milan now, and he would like to get Naples if he can. But both he and d'Amboise are loath to empty their treasury in the pursuit of these aims. And why would he, when he can get what he wants by playing off the Italian states, one against the other?'

What the *condottiero* had said was sadly all too true—the French king could rely upon the inability of the various Italian states to see beyond their narrow self-interest. This was as true for Florence as it was for Venice, Siena, Ferrara and all the rest. The Florentines wanted Pisa, but they wanted someone else to do the fighting for them and they wanted to pay as little as they could for it.

'Take the Neapolitan exiles,' Trivulgio went on, oblivious to Niccolò's thoughtful silence. 'Pisa foiled one of their plots. They had convinced the king that he could take the money that you Florentines had promised and use it to mount the campaign to unseat King Frederick in Naples. The pope offered financial support to the whole enterprise too. But the Neapolitans assumed, of course, that Pisa would fall easily and cheaply. It didn't, and now your government is slow in paying up, so the king has gone cool on the idea. Needless to say, the Neapolitans are furious with him, though they are too cowardly to say so.'

Niccolò nodded. 'I heard the other day that King Frederick is sending ambassadors to Louis to discuss an accommodation.'

'Much good it will do them. The king and the cardinal will play for time; they need to renew the treaty with Emperor Maximilian first. Then we will see what happens.'

Though France and the Holy Roman Empire were nominally at peace, the French conquest of Milan had strained their relationship with the emperor, whose wife was yet another Sforza, Bianca Maria. Imperial ambassadors were expected at any moment to discuss the treaty between the two powers.

As they parted, Trivulgio expressing an affection for Florence and her representatives that Niccolò knew was entirely insincere, he was left in a thoughtful mood, sifting through the various things the soldier had said. It was the comments about the pope that he found most disturbing. Was the pontiff really offering financial support to King Louis for a new Neapolitan campaign? Alexander had already suffered once the depredations of a French army marching through his territory, so perhaps this time he was prepared to pay Louis off, hoping to avoid another such humiliation.

Rumours swirled around the town in confused eddies, and the papal ambassador's residence seemed to be at the epicentre of many of them, so it was a stroke of good luck when Niccolò struck up a conversation one night in a tavern with one of the ambassador's secretaries, Alessandro Spannochi. Well into his cups after what had apparently been a trying day, it took no time at all for Niccolò to get him talking. He was, it transpired, a younger son of the pope's chief banker, seconded to Monseigneur d'Arles from the papal household. Though he had only arrived from Rome a few days before, he seemed remarkably knowledgeable. And he was happy to share that knowledge with his new friend.

'It was being said in Rome when I left was that the emperor is going to tear up the treaty with France, which is why the imperial ambassadors are taking so long to find the French court. And the Venetians are desperate for help from the French against the Turks, though no-one is really taking them seriously, since they exaggerate everything.'

Niccolò had heard that too: the Venetians' discomfiture was the source of much amusement among the other Italians. But Niccolò was more interested in matters closer to home.

'And what do you hear about the Romagna, Alessandro? In Florence we were amazed to hear of Duke Valentino's successes there. And I heard that the Holy Father has asked the king to supply troops and money to besiege Faenza...'

'"His Majesty has done enough for the pope and his son."' Spannochi gave a creditable impersonation of the cardinal at his most imperious, before being overcome by a fit of giggles that turned into a violent bout of hiccoughs. Niccolò pounded him on the back a few times.

'Thank you Niccolò, you're a good fellow,' the young secretary said once he had recovered himself and accepted another beaker of wine. 'Anyway, it doesn't matter much: Cesare will eventually take Faenza with or without French help.'

Niccolò accepted this further evidence of Borgia ambition without comment, and not long after Spannochi declared that it was time for him to find his bed, something he proved unable to do without Niccolò's guiding arm to keep him upright and steer him to his lodgings.

'You really are a good fellow for a Florentine,' he said again as they parted at the door of the grand house that the papal envoy had secured for himself and his household. 'We should meet again. See whether there is any fun to be had in this town.'

The next day, a hard-riding young courier named Giancarlo Bolognino arrived on an exhausted horse, bringing a packet of letters. This proved to contain some good news, at least. The Signoria had decided to accept and pay for the quartering on Florentine territory of at least some of the French troops still loitering before Pisa. Though they were sure this would not be sufficient to mollify the cardinal, let alone the king, at least it gave them something to talk to him about.

The cardinal was happy enough to hear that there was some progress when they secured an appointment with him that afternoon, but he seemed distracted, and they soon took their leave, thankful that none of the other bones of contention had been raised. The cause of the cardinal's distraction soon became apparent. It seemed that the king had fallen from his horse that morning and injured himself, though no one seemed to know how badly.

Hastily adding this to their already long despatch, they prevailed on Bolognino to take it to Lyons, where they had a reliable mercantile contact who could pay the seven *scudi* they had promised him for the task, then send the bulging packet on to Florence. It was embarrassing to have to go to such lengths just to get despatches home. With barely enough money to pay for their lodgings and food, with nothing left over to pay for couriers or to entertain, or even to buy good clothes to replace their increasingly shabby and worn court dress, they daily endured the looks of pity and sometimes outright contempt from the other diplomats who buzzed around the court. And despite his several letters begging the Signoria to bring his pay to parity with that of della Casa, there seemed no sign that their lordships were listening.

Still, he saw no point in dwelling on their situation. It was irritating, certainly, but Niccolò was still energised by the excitement of being there, representing his city at the French court. So he suppressed his annoyance and determined to stay focused on his job.

A few days after their despatches had been sent on their way, the court was on the move once again, this time heading to Melun, on the river Seine just thirty miles south of Paris. It took a full day to get there and another to settle in, another marvel of organisation. Naturally, the royal household (without, for the moment, the king, who was recovering from his injury in a small village a few miles away) settled into the royal palace that dominated the town. As for the two Florentine ambassadors, they found themselves despatched to a small house in the northern part of the city, some distance from the palace. But at least this time they had been given better quality accommodation—they had a room each, as well as a small parlour, which was luxurious compared with the standards they had endured hitherto.

Resuming their thankless mission, they made a point of calling on Cardinal d'Amboise every other day. Though the cardinal continued to receive them with every appearance of cordiality, it was clear that his patience was beginning to wear thin, for they had nothing new to report to him, and there was little that they could usefully discuss.

Catching him in the courtyard of the chateau one day, as he was preparing to leave to join a hunting expedition in the nearby forest of Fontainebleau, they tried some crude flattery.

'Your Eminence,' Niccolò started, 'It seems to us that the king attaches more importance to the payment of the Swiss than anything else. You know that this is a difficult issue for Florence, with which our poor brains have been unable to wrestle successfully. It seems to us that if Your Eminence, being so much more an experienced man of affairs than ourselves, were to favour us with your advice, it might be possible to adjust this matter in a way that is reasonable to all.'

But Georges d'Amboise was having none of it. 'My advice, Machiavelli, is simple. Nothing can resolve your difficulties in a way that would be satisfactory to France, except that you pay for the Swiss as we have requested so many times.'

Niccolò tried another tack. 'Your Eminence, I beg you to remember that Florence has always been a faithful friend of France and we have suffered in your service, for which we merit commendation, not discouragement.

128

Consider, My Lord, the effect on the other peoples of Italy, whose loyalty you wish to cultivate, when they see His Majesty's devoted friends treated so badly.'

That earned him a sharp look and Niccolò thought that perhaps his point had registered, but any advantage was lost by della Casa, who, presumably afraid that Niccolò had again pushed the cardinal too far, launched into a rambling speech reiterating that Florence was still a faithful friend of France and that the Signoria would always be willing to render service to His Majesty.

This abject surrender seemed to bring the cardinal's patience to an end. Raising his voice so that the half dozen other courtiers gathered around could hear, he planted his fists on his hips and glared at them. 'These are mere words. Enough. I have no confidence in your arguments and I am extremely dissatisfied with your Signoria. Let that be an end of it.'

With which, he mounted his horse and, giving it a savage kick, went off at a fast trot across the courtyard, leaving the two Florentines standing in embarrassment as the remaining courtiers broke into amused chatter about the scene they had just witnessed.

Their gloom was relieved a little with the arrival the next day of a packet of personal letters. Niccolò had three, one of which was from Totto, communicating the excellent news that the Signoria had, after a tenacious campaign by him, finally agreed to give him parity in his pay with della Casa. Celebrating over a bottle of better quality wine than they had been used to, Niccolò tried to cheer his colleague up by reading extracts from his other letters, which were from Biagio and Agostino.

'Biagio, as usual, is fretting that I haven't written to him often enough, as if I had nothing else to do. But he does say that our despatches are being well-received, which is something. He wants me, would you believe, to spend a *scudo* and buy him some gloves and two small cloth purses. I don't know why he would think I have the spare money for such fripperies.' He turned the page over and saw some more writing in a different hand. 'And here's a note from Andrea Romolo. You remember him? Little fellow, with a laugh like a horse. He says they are having lots of fine parties and even Antonio della Valle is starting to become a little human. About time.'

The note from Romolo also contained some gossip which he didn't read out about a plump and pretty young whore he had been fond of. She was pining away, waiting for him to come home (unlikely, he thought).

Unexpectedly, he was overcome with a wave of homesickness. What in God's name was he doing in the middle of France, with no friends except the increasingly morose Francesco della Casa, and no money with which to buy even the simple pleasure of a good, clean girl like the one supposedly waiting for him at the house next to the Ponte della Grazie?

*

August turned into September, and suddenly Niccolò found himself even more alone. Francesco came down with a fever, and though it didn't seem that serious to Niccolò, his colleague decided that nothing would do but for him to go north to Paris to seek treatment there before it got any worse.

'Don't worry, Nico,' he said as he left, 'I will be back in a week or so, a fortnight at most.'

Niccolò smiled and gave his hand to the man who had shared so much of the journey, and who was a friend as well as a colleague. But somehow he knew that della Casa would not be back, at least not before their recall came, for he had become more and more depressed over the last few weeks, leaving the bulk of their correspondence to him, spending ever more time in the taverns. In some ways, it would be a relief not to have to spend time and energy cheering him up. Even so, losing his only reliable friend was a heavy blow.

A week later, the court moved yet again, to Blois. Before leaving Melun, he sent a long and impassioned despatch to the Signoria, trying to use every argument in his armoury to persuade them to resolve the matter of the Swiss. Louis would never assume the burden of a new war on their behalf, that much was clear. No arguments about the past faithful service of the Florentines were going to be of any service, for they were simply not being listened to.

'The French are blinded by their own power,' he wrote, 'and have consideration only for those who are well-armed or who are prepared to pay.' And as far as the French were concerned, the Florentines lacked both these qualifications.

Trying to needle his masters, he even included the most hurtful thing that he had heard said of them. 'They call you "Signor Nothing",' Gianjacopo Trivulzio had told him one afternoon. 'They see no advantage in giving ground to you, for you are powerless.'

It was high time for the Signoria to despatch new ambassadors, fully accredited and with the power to negotiate on these important issues. But until that day came, he knew his duty was clear—to keep on listening to the rumours and gossip, to sift what was important and true from that which was mere dross, and to report back to Florence everything he heard.

Chapter 13—Niccolò Alone

Blois, France, September 1500

Kicking his horse, Niccolò swore softly under his breath as it gathered speed, throwing up a small cloud of dust behind. His annoyance was not with the horse, a perfectly fine beast he had hired the day before in Blois, but with himself for having slept in.

He had arrived the evening before in the little village of Saint-Ay, about eight leagues from Blois, having heard that Cardinal d'Amboise was to stop overnight there on his way to re-join the court. He didn't know what he hoped to achieve by riding out to meet the cardinal; though he did have some news to impart, it could easily have waited for a more formal appointment. Yet he felt impatient after della Casa's departure and doing something was undoubtedly better than doing nothing.

Arriving late, he had decided not to disturb d'Amboise, resolving to call on him in the morning before the cardinal got on the road. But for once his habit of rising with the sun had failed him and he had overslept. By the time he had dressed, paid the innkeeper and saddled his horse, the cardinal's retinue had long gone. Only now, with the sun creeping towards noon, could he see the dust cloud of the cavalcade ahead of him.

The cardinal did not keep great state on the road. A mere half-dozen men-at-arms provided security, and there were another three servants trailing behind them, leading pack horses. These gave him no more than a curious glance as he passed, and the soldiers, relaxing their vigilance on this well-travelled road in the middle of peaceful France, were almost as disinterested. It was only as he drew level with the cardinal that their sergeant challenged him, causing their master to turn his head in frowning curiosity. Seeing who it was disturbing his morning's contemplation, his expression changed to one of surprise as he waved the sergeant away. 'Monsieur Machiavelli! What on earth brings you here? I had thought you in Blois.'

'Your Eminence, I wished to do you honour by meeting you upon the road and offering my humble company for the last leg of your journey. Sadly, having arrived late and risen late, I missed your departure this morning and so have hastened to catch you up.'

The cardinal gave him a long, suspicious look, and then, his face clearing, he laughed. 'Honest, at least, I'll give you that. Come on, ride beside me and we'll talk.'

So far, so good, Niccolò thought, easing his horse to a gentle trot, matching the pace of the cardinal's own splendidly caparisoned mount. Yet, having gone to all this trouble to get the cardinal's undivided attention, he could not for the moment think of how to start, so for a few minutes they rode in silence.

Perhaps sensing his new companion's difficulty, the cardinal turned and looked at him. 'So, what do you want to talk about, monsieur? The same old tales of Florentine woe, no doubt?'

The words might have been mocking, but the tone was jocular and, for the first time in their dealings with the king's chief minister, he felt as though there might be a chink opening in his armour. Deciding to try and catch him on the road like this was the right decision, it seemed. But perhaps it would be better to start by imparting the small piece of positive news that he did have. 'No doubt I could entertain Your Excellency with such a recitation,' he said, trying to match the other's sardonic air, 'but I do have some positive news. As you advised, Monsieur della Casa and I asked our government to appoint new and fully accredited ambassadors to His Majesty's court. This seems to have taken some time to achieve, but I received word two days ago that they have been appointed and by now I am sure they are on their way.'

'That is good news. And the identity of these ambassadors?'

'The senior ambassador is Pierfrancesco Tosinghi. I know him well—a man of excellent background and family. His junior is to be Bernardo Ricci. All this is in official letters which I will, of course, present to His Majesty when opportunity permits.'

'Which we will have to arrange as soon as possible. No doubt His Majesty will welcome this news, as do I.'

They bumped along in silence again for a few minutes.

'Eminence, I have no wish to weary you by repeating over again all that Francesco and I have already said in defence of our republic. But until the new ambassadors arrive, I will feel it is my duty to continue to represent my country with as much honesty and vigour as I can muster.'

The cardinal said nothing, though two small frown lines appeared in his forehead.

'I know that you and the king are impatient with us and believe that we are withholding the payments that you seek out of miserliness. Perhaps this is so— I am here, not in Florence, so I cannot tell you with certainty what motivates the decisions that the Signoria makes. But I beg you to understand what I do know to be true, which is that Florence has stretched herself to her limits in support of French ambitions in Italy. We were the first, were we not, to pledge money and arms to your campaign against Milan?'

'Among the first, yes, but you took some time to come to it.'

'And we have been constant allies since. We had hoped that would engender at least some sympathy in the breast of the king. Yet instead we find ourselves subjected daily to accusations and calumnies that seek to blacken our reputation and we find that these accusations are believed by the king's counsellors.'

'You deny, then, that Florence has sent ambassadors to the Emperor? That your republic would seek to influence him against my king?'

'Eminence, I have heard that story. It came from the house of the papal ambassador. Monseigneur d'Arles is mischievous, to say the least. And the pope has ambitions of his own that might well be served by muddying the waters between Florence and France.'

It was not quite a denial, for Niccolò could not be absolutely certain about events in far-off Florence, but his words seemed to have sufficient conviction to satisfy d'Amboise. 'Well, I don't believe it either. Never have.'

'Nevertheless, such rumours abound and encourage our enemies to raise their hands against Florence. Your Eminence's influence with the king is great, and I beg of you, please do not withdraw your support for us. Rather, can you not persuade His Majesty to treat us like…' He struggled to find the right example. 'Well, like we were his children, who might err from time to time, but whom he still protects.'

'You are passionate, Machiavelli, which I respect.' That was something, at least, Niccolò thought, keeping his gaze focused on the road ahead. 'But as you are a fervent supporter of your government and its policies, so I must also support mine, and I tell you plainly again that until Florence agrees to pay for the Swiss, the king will not move on any other matter, nor will he look favourably upon your masters. In this, he is obdurate and even I cannot move him.'

'Then it would seem, Your Eminence, that you are as powerless as I, at least on these matters!'

Again, Niccolò wondered if he had gone too far; the cardinal, however, merely laughed. 'My young friend, as I am sure you will learn soon enough, no one wields absolute power, not even the King of France, who must satisfy and balance many demands in the cause of the safety of his kingdom. But enough—let us talk of something less serious. Tell me something about yourself, Machiavelli. Are you married? Do you have brothers and sisters?'

Niccolò was startled; the last thing he had expected was for this powerful man to divert the conversation into such personal channels. But, recovering himself, he stumblingly confided to the cardinal something of the story of his life, his family, the recent death of his father (the cardinal's automatic yet sincere words of condolence reminded Niccolò that the man riding next to him was, after all, an ordained priest), and his worries about his sister and his brother. Their talk moved on to more general subjects—philosophy, history, literature—and Niccolò found himself engaged in a thoroughly enjoyable discourse with the older man, who turned out to be a witty and empathetic conversationalist now that he was not dealing with affairs of state.

The morning passed in this pleasant way until eventually the walls and roofs of Blois emerged from the countryside ahead of them. Clattering across the bridge that spanned the river Loire, the little cavalcade halted in a small square just beyond the gate, where they were to part, the cardinal to go to the royal chateau on the western edge of the city, Niccolò to his modest lodgings near the cathedral.

Before they parted, the cardinal returned to business for a few moments, offering Niccolò some advice. 'I am glad that we had this chance to talk, Monsieur Machiavelli. Your position is not an easy one and your interests must perforce remain in suspense until your new ambassadors arrive. But I have come to value your candour. Do not be discouraged, continue to do your duty, and in the end all will be well.'

*

135

That evening, feeling buoyed by his afternoon ride with the cardinal, he bent his mind to composing another long despatch back to Florence, pouring all his eloquence into a series of arguments emphasising the need for the wretched question of the payments to the Swiss to be resolved and for the new ambassadors to hasten their way there.

He resumed his intelligence-gathering, visiting the other Italians in their various haunts, joining in card games with those of the French functionaries that he had befriended, and chatting with other diplomats while they stood around in the anterooms of the royal chateau, awaiting the arrival of the king and his ministers. He encountered the cardinal several times over the following days, and on each occasion, he was greeted with a smile and a handclasp. It was as if the cardinal was going out of his way to demonstrate that the remaining Florentine envoy was in his favour at least, even if his government was not. This was duly noted by the court and the other diplomats, and he started to find that he was welcomed with more enthusiasm as he made his daily rounds. Even better, he began to receive invitations to some of the more private gatherings from which he had hitherto been excluded.

One of these was to the home of the ambassador from the Holy See, Monseigneur d'Arles. The invitation did not come from that august personage himself, but rather from Alessandro Spannochi, with whom Niccolò had become fast friends. This was the first time, though, that Alessandro had invited him to the ambassador's lodgings.

Unsurprisingly, the papal ambassador had taken a house that stood almost within the shadow of the chateau where the court congregated; he could not have been closer to the king except by being housed within the chateau itself, a privilege that was reserved for the royal household.

Alessandro met him at the door, having spotted him from an upper window as he made his way down the street. 'Come on in, Niccolò, get out of the heat!' Spannochi was, as always, loudly ebullient. 'We have a card game going upstairs, mostly people you know.'

It was indeed a congenial group—several of the younger diplomats like himself, a couple of Frenchmen from the ambassador's household, and a junior secretary that he recognised from the cardinal's retinue. The card game was intense, played competitively, though not for very much money, none of the participants being wealthy enough to take great risks with their meagre pay.

Niccolò was greeted rather absently and, joining the table, was soon absorbed in the play.

Between hands there was conversation. Much of it was court gossip, tales about the mistresses of the various dignitaries of the household, scandals above stairs and below, and rumours from the world beyond the closeted confines of the court. Niccolò listened to it all and made the occasional contribution himself, rather pleased to find that, on many subjects, he was as well-informed as anybody else present.

'You are much in favour with the cardinal these days, Nico,' Alessandro said at one point when there was a break in the play to allow for the call of nature. 'It seems that not a day goes past when he does not greet you and engage in conversation.'

'Perhaps he feels sorry for me, Sandro, now I am all alone in Blois.' Niccolò laughed. 'But yes, he has been kind to me of late, though his warmth does not extend to my masters any more than does the king's.'

Alessandro, like everyone at court, knew of the Florentine difficulties. 'I fear only the arrival of new ambassadors carrying bags of silver will warm up the king.'

'I would not be so sure even that will do it.' This remark came from Nicholas Ettridge, coming back into the room, fumbling with the points of his hose after a visit to the latrine. Ettridge was an Englishman attached to the embassy of King Henry VII. 'Your countrymen are in his ear every five minutes with one scheme or another, mostly to the detriment of Florence. I heard a story the other day that will make you choke—you know that the Neapolitan exiles are pressing the king to resume the war against Pisa?'

'Yes, the cardinal mentioned it last week.'

'But I'll bet he didn't tell you that they are also telling Louis that, once he has captured Pisa, he should combine it with the other cities of Tuscany. Pietresanta, Livorno, Piombino were the names I heard, though they mean nothing to me, and create a new state under leadership that would be subservient to France. There was even talk of adding Lucca and Siena to the stable. The idea, you see, is that Louis would then have a clear path down to Naples whenever he wants it.'

137

Ettridge grinned at him, clearly waiting to see what effect his little recitation had on the Florentine envoy. Niccolò smiled calmly back, though his mind was hard at work evaluating what he had just been told. The Englishman was usually well-informed on Italian affairs; the English king had married his eldest son to the daughter of King Ferdinand of Aragon and Spain, whose cousin currently sat on the throne of Naples, so no doubt the English were keeping a close eye on the Neapolitan exiles there.

It all sounded entirely plausible until he thought about it. The towns Ettridge had mentioned were all strategically important and, notionally at least, they were Florentine possessions. He remembered his first meeting with King Louis, when the king had more or less said he could do whatever he wanted with the cities and towns of Tuscany. So he could easily see the French being attracted to such a scheme. But even if they succeeded, the pope and his territories would still be between them and Naples. Perhaps it was worth throwing a little bread into the water and waiting to see what might come to the surface.

'I doubt the king would commit to such a project unless its success was guaranteed,' he said finally, trying to sound complacent. 'And none of the places you mentioned would surrender voluntarily.'

'They can always be bought off. You Italians do seem to have a great lust for gold!'

'Sadly true.' Niccolò was wry. 'But the king and the cardinal are also reluctant to part with their money unless they are certain to get a return on it. This I know better than anyone. And besides, surely he would need the agreement of the pope if this plan were to work?'

'Which is unlikely to be forthcoming,' Alessandro said. 'Alexander's interests are closer to Rome, not Tuscany.'

'The Romagna again?' Niccolò asked. It was common knowledge among the Italians in Blois that the pope was building up a sizeable military force, but no one knew where it was to be aimed; perhaps Alessandro would let something slip.

'The Lazio, more likely. The Colonna.' Spannochi held Niccolò's gaze, blue-grey eyes seemingly innocent of any guile.

138

The Colonna family were a constant pain in the papal side, unruly *condottieri* who were allies of Naples. An attack on their castles in the Lazio might serve France's interests if the Neapolitan king was forced to divert resources to his allies' aid, weakening him in the event of a French attack. He was not sure he believed what Alessandro was saying, but he just shrugged. 'I'm sure you are right, Sandro. No doubt time will tell all.' He laughed. 'I've had enough of playing cards for one afternoon. Who wants a glass of wine?'

Later, on the way to the door after the party had finally broken up for the afternoon, he sought to satisfy his curiosity on another point. 'This Cesare, the pope's son, what is he like?'

Alessandro, his hand on the door-bolt, tilted his head as if he had never been asked such a question before and needed to consider his answer. 'I've never met anyone who is more fitted to be a soldier. He loves physical contests of every kind and wins most of them. And he's a natural leader. I've seen him with common soldiers and they adore him as much as his lieutenants. He knows how to talk to them and he takes their concerns seriously, so they know he is just in his dealings with them. He's generous with his friends and, when you are in his company, he sweeps you along with all the force of a great river.

'And he plans, my God, how he plans! Nothing is left to chance and he only gambles when he has calculated all the odds. But he is ruthless when he doesn't get his way and can be cruel in pursuit of his aims. Does that give you the picture?'

Niccolò nodded. But there was something else he wanted to know. 'He seems to have a rather homicidal nature. There was the death of his brother and now his brother-in-law.'

The death of Juan Borgia was old news, but the episode that had resulted in the death of Alfonso of Aragon, the husband of his sister Lucrezia, had shocked the French court when it had become known a few weeks before. Evidently, Alfonso had been assaulted following a dinner with the pope and injured almost to death. It was rumoured that Cesare had been responsible for the attack, though the reasons for his enmity were unknown. Then, even more shocking, a party of men, led by one Miguel de Corella, a known henchman of Cesare's, had burst into the chamber where Alfonso was recovering, saying that they had orders to arrest him because he had been implicated in a plot

139

against Cesare's life. In the ensuing struggle, Alfonso had been killed. Rumour said he was murdered, strangled by Corella.

'No one knows what happened to Juan,' Alessandro said, shrugging his shoulders. 'But Cesare says that Alfonso died resisting arrest, at his orders, because his own life was threatened. I am inclined to believe that was so, for I was walking with him in the gardens at the Vatican one day when we were narrowly missed by a crossbow bolt that Alfonso fired from his bedroom window! Why he did that, I don't know. Cesare is close to his sister. Perhaps the poor man was jealous of his brother-in-law.'

Walking home, Niccolò was thoughtful, trying to make sense of everything he had been told. Was the pope really aiming his army and his son at his over-powerful subjects in the Lazio? Somehow Niccolò doubted it. For one thing, all of Valentino's efforts so far had been directed towards the Romagna, so turning all that force on a couple of petty tyrants in the Roman backyard seemed to be something of a diversion. And notwithstanding their budding friendship, he had no reason to believe Alessandro Spannochi was telling him the truth; he was in the employ of the pope, after all.

Then there was Ettridge's tale of a plot to create a new puppet state. Though Niccolò had laughed it off, it sounded feasible, particularly if Louis finally made his mind up and committed to a Neapolitan campaign. So there was a real risk that Florence might find herself with a hostile Borgia threatening them from the east and a French-controlled principality in their former territory to the west. Still reeling from the disaster at Pisa, she would be fatally weakened and trapped between two powers who could attack her at any moment.

About the only other restraint on papal ambition in the Romagna was Florence's old rival, Venice. The Serenissima would be no more enthusiastic than the Florentines at the prospect of papal armies on their southern border. But Venice was frightened—the loss of Modone to the advancing Turkish armies in August had shaken them and they were desperate for help from wherever they could get it to defend the rest of their territory in Dalmatia.

All this he committed to a long despatch, doing his best to alert a complacent government to the dangers they faced. Though his pen hesitated over the page, he finally decided to tell them unequivocally that Cesare Borgia's real objective was the Romagna, though he had no proof to support such a conclusion other than his instincts.

He didn't have long to wait for proof that those instincts were sound. Just a few days after his report went on its way, entrusted to the most reliable courier his meagre funds could afford, the news came that Duke Valentino had left Rome at the head of an army of no less than ten thousand men, heading north-east towards the Romagna, not east towards the Lazio and the Colonna fortresses there. What had seemed to be a mere phantasm had become a frightening reality. He resolved to seek an audience with d'Amboise once again.

Arriving at the cardinal's apartments, he was told that he would have to wait since His Eminence was at present closeted with the king. In the end, he had to wait fully an hour and it was almost three in the afternoon before d'Amboise returned.

Seeing Niccolò in the anteroom, he waved for him to come into the inner chamber. 'Well, Monsieur Machiavelli, have your ambassadors made any progress or are they still taking their ease in Florence?'

Niccolò laughed. This had become something of a running joke between them. 'As to that, Your Eminence, I have no new news.'

'Hmm. We will all be dead, I expect, before these ambassadors arrive.'

'I hope not, eminence.'

The cardinal gestured to chairs placed on either side of a dormant fireplace. 'So what is on your mind, my young friend, that brings you hot-foot to my door?'

'Your Eminence will have heard, I am sure, of the departure of the pope's son, Duke Valentino, with a substantial army, aimed towards the Romagna?'

A nod from the cardinal conveyed nothing except perhaps encouragement for Niccolò to continue. 'Though I have received no new instructions from my Signoria, I am certain that I speak on their behalf when I express to you my concern at this development. This Borgia has already swallowed up Imola and Forlì. It is said he now aims to add Faenza to his state as well. Only the protection of Venice would stop him from taking Bologna, Rimini and Pesaro. Naturally, should he be successful in his aims, it would be of great concern to Florence to be faced with one such as Duke Valentino on our eastern borders, a man whose ambition seems unbridled.'

141

'I shouldn't count on Venice if I were you.' The cardinal had the look of a marketplace conjurer about to astonish his crowd by producing a rabbit from an empty hat. 'I have been told they are prepared to countenance the ambitions of the pope's son in return for help from the holy father against the Turk. In fact, they propose to appoint Valentino as captain-general of their armies and give him a palazzo in Venice to boot.'

This was bad news. Without Venetian support, Giovanni Bentivoglio in Bologna, Pandolfo Malatesta in Rimini and Giovanni Sforza in Pesaro would struggle to maintain their independence and, if they fell, Duke Valentino would be in control of the whole of the Via Aemilia and with it virtually all of the Romagna. 'And what, if I may ask, is the king's attitude to this information?'

The cardinal made a show of picking some non-existent threads from the sleeve of his gown before answering. 'His Majesty is unwilling to deny the pope anything.'

Which was different from wishing him to be victorious. Was the cardinal hinting that there was a tiny crack in the impenetrable wall of the alliance between king and pope? 'Indulge me, Your Eminence,' he said. 'The presence of France in Italy reminds me of that of the Romans in Greece.'

'How so?' Cardinal d'Amboise's question was accompanied by a half-smile. 'Let me guess, you are going to give me an apt little history lesson.'

'Bear with me, eminence. When the Romans first came into Greece, they defeated and humbled King Philip of Macedon. All the small states which were freed from Macedonian domination were drawn to the Romans, the new power in Greece. The Romans followed a simple policy—while they kept a much-weakened Macedon in check, they also maintained friendly relations with all the smaller powers. But most importantly, they never allowed any of the small states, individually or together, to gain authority in the country.'

'Let me see if I follow your analogy.' The cardinal's eyes glinted with amusement. 'We, of course, are the Romans; I am duly flattered. Milan is, I suppose, the Macedonians? And the other small cities are represented by Florence and Siena and all the rest?'

'Quite so, Your Eminence. And like the Romans, by supporting the independence of the other north Italian states, you prevent any one of them from growing powerful enough to threaten your control of Milan. But my story has a serious purpose. I fear that if France allows the pope's son to create a strong state in the Romagna, it will then be a short step for him to attack Florence. He might not be able to take the city itself, but he could severely weaken us.

'Whatever the present difficulties between us, Florence has proved her fidelity. You can trust us. But if we were to succumb, would you really want such a powerful state on your border, commanded by a man who has not yet earned your trust?'

That shot seemed to hit home. The cardinal frowned, then he nodded and leaned forward across the expanse of his desk as if about to impart a confidence. 'Niccolò, I am entirely sensible of the danger that Florence is facing and I think we both appreciate that there would be little benefit to France should your republic fall under the domination of Duke Valentino. But you know the affection with which the king regards young Borgia. I fear that I cannot sway his mind on this, particularly given the continuing refusal of the Florentine government to meet its obligations.'

So they were back at the same position once more, occupying squares at opposite ends of the board with no way of moving forward. Niccolò said nothing since there was nothing that he could say.

'But,' the cardinal resumed, his expression softening a little, 'if your Signoria will meet our principal demand for the payment of the Swiss, it is just possible I can convince His Majesty to forget all the other issues.'

It was Niccolò's turn to frown. Did he detect a subtle change of emphasis? It seemed that d'Amboise was hinting that the instant the Swiss money was paid, all would be forgiven and they would have the wholehearted support of France, though whether that support would extend to restraining papal ambitions beyond the Romagna might be another question. 'Thank you, eminence; I am sure this will be welcomed by the Signoria. I will, of course, write immediately, pressing upon them once again the urgency of resolving this matter and ensuring that Ambassador Tosinghi is instructed to conclude it satisfactorily.'

D'Amboise nodded his approval. 'If it is of assistance, I have a formal memorandum drawn up detailing our specific requirements for you to enclose with your despatch.'

This was another positive shift. The king and the cardinal had never been concrete as to what they wanted to Florentines to pay, preferring to make general demands usually mixed up with their other complaints. This had made it difficult to determine exactly how to respond. 'Such a memorandum would greatly focus their lordships' minds, of that I am sure, Your Eminence.'

'The king, I know, regrets the difficulties to which Florence has been exposed,' the cardinal said, his tone now positively encouraging, 'though he does not see how he could have taken any other course. Let your deeds show your commitment to France and all will be possible in the future.'

In other words, Niccolò thought as he made his farewells, the same message—pay up and we will make sure the pope's son is kept in check. He had not won the battle for French support yet, but for the first time, he felt as if he was making progress.

Chapter 14—Recalled at Last

Nantes, France, October 1500

The court was on the move once again, towards its next destination—the town of Nantes, four wearisome days away. The plates and silver, wall hangings and carpets, clothes chests and furniture were loaded up into wagons. Those who could afford them mounted their horses, and those who could not prepared for long days walking at the tail of the great column that marched across the old bridge and turned west, accompanied by a cloud of dust that could be seen for miles.

Niccolò, though still chronically short of money, had managed to find a French merchant who had advanced him some funds against his salary when it should eventually arrive, and so could afford a well-found and well-equipped horse. As he plodded along, surrounded by the other diplomats and minor household officials to whose company he had been consigned by the royal officers, he found himself marvelling at the fact that he was almost within striking distance of the Atlantic Ocean, having crossed the entire breadth of France in the three months that had elapsed since his departure from Florence. Three months! He had expected to be away for just a few weeks, yet here he was, still travelling and with no certainty as to when he might finally be recalled.

He worried, as the mileposts went steadily past, about what was happening at home. Poor Totto, left with the management of the house and the estate, still in disarray after the death of their father, how was he holding up? Niccolò thought with affection of the youngster's dogged campaign on his brother's behalf to get his pay increased. Totto might not be experienced in the world and he certainly showed few signs as yet of finding a vocation in life, but he had demonstrated that he could be remarkably tenacious once his mind was set to a task. Still, it was too heavy a burden to lay on such young shoulders.

What, he wondered, was going on in the chancellery office? They had expected him back long before this. He could rely on Biagio, Agostino and Casavecchia, his most trusted colleagues, to defend his interests to the best of their ability, but none of them was as adept as he at reading the cross-currents and eddies of opinion among the members of the Great Council or managing the confused egos of the members of the Signoria.

Brooding on all these questions delivered him in a melancholy frame of mind to his assigned lodgings in Nantes, where a pile of official and personal letters eventually found him a day later. Nothing in any of them did anything to improve his mood.

The most devastating piece of news was personal, though not entirely unexpected.

> *Dearest brother,*
> *There is no easy way of saying it, so I will be direct: our sister Primavera is dead. She was ill when you left, and though she seemed to recover for a while, three weeks ago she relapsed into sickness. The doctors were puzzled as to the cause and treatment, but that was of no matter anyway, for whatever they did was not enough to save her. She passed away this last week, and I am arranging for her funeral services to be held at Santa Felicità as I know you would have wished.*

The letter, its pages blotched with tears, went on to talk about practical matters as if its author could not bear to dwell on the misfortune of this news. Totto and Primavera had been close, and Niccolò experienced a wave of guilt, knowing how difficult it must have been for his brother to deal with all of this alone.

Turning to the official despatches, there was confirmation that Cesare Borgia was marching confidently towards the coast, Pesaro and Rimini his targets. But there was no further word as to the whereabouts of the promised new ambassadors. Nor was there the one piece of news he was hoping for—that the Signoria had agreed to the payment of the Swiss.

A letter from Agostino Vespucci cheered him up a little. It was full of gossip and witty wordplays which made him laugh out loud. Biagio, he said, was a Protesilaus in his interests (it took Niccolò a moment to remember that Protesilaus was the first of the Greeks to jump ashore at Troy, only to be killed). They all continued to tease poor Antonio della Valle and enjoy all-night sessions playing dice or cards. Everyone missed him, Agostino said, and wanted him to hurry home, all of which fed his growing sense of homesickness.

There was another reason he needed to get home. 'A noble citizen', his friend wrote, 'who loves you particularly, has implied that unless you are here you may lose your place altogether.' Who this well-wisher was, Agostino didn't say, though Niccolò suspected it was Piero Soderini. In any event, this was what he had feared—that there were people in Florence who would be quite happy to see his reputation destroyed and were taking advantage of this prolonged absence to undermine him.

Until now, his pride had kept him from complaining to his masters in Florence about the price he was paying for his continued devotion to their service. Even the letters he had written about his pay were couched in terms of his inability to do his job properly, rather than the considerable impost that was being imposed on his personal finances. But for the first time, he wrote a despatch that poured out his concerns and begged the Signoria to relieve him of this thankless mission.

It had been expected that the court would stay in Nantes for some time, but for reasons known only to King Louis, their stay was cut short, and as October turned to November, it was announced that that they would turn back eastwards, to the city of Tours. At least, he told himself, it was moving in the right direction, back towards his home and, hopefully, the ambassadors who were coming to relieve him.

Arriving in Tours, he found a packet of despatches waiting for him, communicating the news that Cesare Borgia had effortlessly taken both Rimini and Pesaro, two important coastal city-states ruled by ruthless but unpopular *condottieri* whose people had, it seemed, risen in revolt at the approach of Valentino's army. The duke was now laying vigorous siege to Faenza, whose people were more attached to their ruler and were putting up a stout response. But Faenza lay between Imola and Forlì and, if it fell, Borgia would be in possession of all the key cities along the Via Aemilia south of Bologna, and he would have completed, to all intents and purposes, his conquest of the Romagna.

But, dire as these events were, the Signoria was even more concerned (reading between the measured lines of the despatch, Niccolò thought that panic might be a better description) about the rumour that had reached them that Borgia had boasted that once he had taken Faenza, he would turn his attention westwards, towards Florence.

147

As it happened, the court officials had lodged him in the same little inn as Alessandro Spannochi. They hadn't seen much of each other in Nantes, so it was pleasant to have the opportunity to swap news. At first, Alessandro had little to say on the subject of Borgia's latest doings in the Romagna when they sat down for a glass of wine in the inn's little vine-covered courtyard.

'How was your last meeting with the good cardinal?' he asked. 'I hear that Florence is returning to favour once again.'

'Are there no secrets at this court?' Niccolò laughed. 'No, don't bother answering. Monseigneur d'Amboise and I seem to be getting along, though I am never entirely sure whether he is just humouring me.'

Spannochi looked at him in a quizzical fashion, his head slightly tilted to one side, and eyebrows half-raised. 'Oh, he likes you, I think. But tell me, has he said nothing to you of the latest news from Venice?'

'That the Serenissima is now preparing to abandon the Romagna, you mean? And support the pope's son in return for papal gold?'

'Yes, that, but there is something else. The Venetians have told him that a secret alliance has been made between the Bolognese, the Duke of Ferrara and the Marquis of Mantua, supposedly for mutual defence.'

Niccolò thought about that. All these city-states were potentially threatened by Cesare Borgia and lay between him and Venice, so a treaty made sense. 'No, I had not heard that particular information. Who are they supposed to be defending themselves against? Your friend Cesare?'

'Perhaps,' Alessandro replied, a twitch of amusement on his lips. 'But the ambassador told the Venetian senate that the purpose of the alliance is to combine their arms against France, with the aim of throwing them out of Italy.'

'A laudable aim, perhaps. But it seems a little ambitious. Surely they are not strong enough, even combined, to defeat the French armies?'

The smile on his friend's face broadened and Niccolò sensed he was about to get another surprise. 'Not if they are also joined by Florence. According to the ambassador, your government are the leaders in this plot.'

'But that's absurd, Sandro!' Niccolò couldn't hide his shock. 'I know the Florentine Signoria can seem inconstant and flighty, but we have been consistent in our support for King Louis. I have been telling the cardinal so day in and day out for months.'

Spannochi shrugged his broad shoulders. 'I can only tell you what I know, Nico. True or not, this is what is being fed into the ear of the cardinal and the king. If it is untrue, you must tell them so and do everything you can to counter this rumour.'

Niccolò played with his wine glass for a moment, swirling the dregs around in the bottom and looking at the lees as intently as any peasant woman trying to tell the future. The court of the King of France was a cesspit of rumour and intrigue and plot. Working out what was true and what was false demanded a shrewdness and cunning that he feared was beyond him. Why had Cardinal d'Amboise not raised this story with him? Perhaps it was some kind of test. And he sensed that Alessandro had not told him everything.

'There is something more you should know,' Spannochi said, as if reading his mind. 'Monseigneur d'Arles has also been whispering in the king's ear that the best way for France to solve the problem would be to get rid of the current government in Florence and install Piero de' Medici instead.'

The Medici bugbear again. Obviously, the entire purpose of this fictitious conspiracy was to destabilise the republican government and detach it from King Louis' affections. The fact that the papal envoy was stirring the pot meant that the whole plot originated with the Vatican... or did it? 'Alessandro, why are you telling me this?'

'Because the pope wants it to be stopped.'

Now Niccolò was completely confused. It must have been evident on his face because Spannochi laughed and threw his hands in the air in a gesture of appeasement. 'Let me explain it. The whole story started with d'Arles—it was he that came up with the idea, fed the necessary information to the Venetians through the papal ambassador there, and is making sure d'Amboise and the king believe it here. But he is acting at the instigation of Duke Valentino, not the pope; Cesare wants Florence kept off-balance and unsure of her alliances. Even better if he can detach her from France. His Holiness, however, is not so keen on that idea because he wants to keep some kind of leash on his son's ambitions.'

'And how do you know the pope's mind so well?'

'Because he sent me here to keep an eye on his ambassador, who he does not trust. Niccolò, you must also understand something about the relationship between father and son. The pope wants to see Cesare succeed in the Romagna and make it a well-governed and prosperous state instead of the chaotic and lawless territory it has always been. At the same time, he doesn't want to wreck the whole balance of power in northern Italy. But Cesare's ambitions go far beyond the Romagna and he is dragging his father along behind him. Alexander can't find the will to stop him, but he can apply the brakes now and then.'

'The young bull and the old bull,' Niccolò muttered under his breath.

'What was that?'

'Never mind. Alessandro, I am indebted to you for telling me all this. I will use it well, I promise.'

Spannochi laughed again and raised his glass. 'Let's drink. I'm glad we're friends, Nico. We serve different masters, but that's no reason we can't help each other from time to time. Here's to friendship!'

They shared another convivial glass of wine, then Niccolò left to hurry in search of the cardinal, who he found in the courtyard of the chateau where the king was lodging for the night. He was about to mount his horse to go off for his evening ride, which was something of a ritual. Though he was obviously impatient to get on his way, d'Amboise listened courteously enough to Niccolò's stammering and abbreviated presentation of the supposed plot and his anxious assurances that the rumour was entirely untrue.

Gesturing to a groom to take control of his impatient horse, the cardinal placed his hands on his hips and stared at the Florentine envoy. Niccolò could not tell whether he was angry or merely impatient at being delayed.

'Of course we knew of this supposedly secret treaty, Monsieur Machiavelli,' he eventually said. ' But now you are telling me that the papal ambassador to this court is leading us by the nose? Do I have that right?'

'Yes, eminence, that is exactly what I am saying.'

'And you insist that Florence has no part in this so-called defensive pact. You have been away from Florence for a long time, monsieur, how can you be so sure that your Signoria has not authorised such an action, and failed to advise you of the fact?'

'What you say is true, My Lord Cardinal. My government may be keeping me in ignorance, either by accident or design. But I do not believe that to be the case. I know my countrymen and I know where the interests of Florence lie. Whether there is a pact between the Bologna, Mantua and Ferrara I cannot tell, but I do know that the Florentine Signoria is much too cautious to enter into an agreement with such small states against the great power of France.'

'Your protestations do you credit, Niccolò,' the cardinal said, his face relaxing into a small smile. 'I am inclined to take your word that Florence was never involved with this malicious plan.'

He gestured to the groom to bring his horse back over and was about to mount when he stopped and turned back to Machiavelli once again. 'But one thing puzzles me, monsieur. Why would the pope wish to mislead us so? When he and my king are on such friendly terms?'

'Perhaps, eminence, you and the king should think upon the motives not of the pope, but of his son.'

'Ah. You have sung this tune before, I think.'

'But its melody rings true, My Lord Cardinal.'

'Yes, this time I think you might be right. Listen, Niccolò, you should remember that we are not easily gulled. The king's ears are long, but his belief short. He listens to everything but puts his faith only in that he can touch and prove to be true. If Florence proves herself to be constant by her deeds, she has nothing to fear. Now, I must leave you to your own devices.' He swung his bulky form up into the saddle and, with a parting wave, clattered off out of the courtyard, leaving a much relieved and thoughtful Machiavelli behind him.

A week later, a letter arrived from the new ambassador, Pierfrancesco Tosinghi, that contained the best news Niccolò had read since he had arrived in France. Not only was Tosinghi now at Moulins, less than a week's journey away, but he was pleased to inform Machiavelli that the Signoria had finally agreed to meet all the French demands. Tosinghi would present the formal letters to that effect when he arrived, but Niccolò could not resist letting the cardinal know the essentials at the first opportunity.

'That is good news indeed, Machiavelli. I was beginning to think that your government had stopped listening to you, but you have obviously been both persistent and persuasive. Come along; I was about to go and see the king, so you might as well come with me and give him the news yourself.'

This was more than Niccolò had expected, and of course he would be exceeding his instructions by presenting the fact of the Florentine agreement before the new ambassador got here; on the other hand, after all these wearisome months he was entitled to at least one small moment of triumph.

The king was alone when he and Cardinal d'Amboise arrived at his private study. At first, he seemed irritated to see his first minister accompanied by the Florentine emissary, but the cardinal used soothing words to explain Niccolò's presence and, when the good news had been relayed to him, the king's mood brightened considerably. 'Well now, monsieur, I had thought that we would never hear anything positive from your masters; they seem incapable of coming to a swift resolution on any matter. But we can, I think, forgive them for the moment and look forward to receiving your new ambassador when he arrives.'

'Thank you, Your Majesty.' Niccolò hesitated before continuing, exchanging a glance with d'Amboise, who remained utterly inscrutable. 'I do not wish to presume on Your Majesty's goodwill any further, but I feel that it is my duty to ask once again what Your Majesty's attitude will be to the aggressions of Duke Valentino in the Romagna, now that our other difficulties have been resolved.'

The king's eyes narrowed. 'Surely such matters should await the arrival of Monsieur Tosinghi, should they not?'

'Yes, yes, of course, Your Majesty. But he is still a week away, and every day the duke harasses our borders and threatens to attack us. And he now he is saying he will do so with armies provided by Your Majesty.' He had been told by Trivulzio that Borgia was making this boast. He didn't know whether it was true, but it was an alarming possibility and he was anxious to get the French to deny it. 'My Signoria would, I am sure, be glad to receive your assurance that this claim has no substance, and I am equally sure that Your Majesty would not want his honour besmirched in such a wanton way.'

The king looked at his chief minister, who shrugged. 'In matters of war, you Italians know nothing,' Niccolò was taken aback by the contempt in the cardinal's voice, but his protest was stilled by a sharp gesture as he resumed speaking. 'Duke Valentino is a talented commander, that much is true, but compared with His Majesty's generals and armies, he is an amateur. We are confident that he can be kept under control should he become over-ambitious.'

'The Italians may, as you say, know nothing of war, but you French know nothing of Italian politics, for if you did, you would never risk the balance between the powers of northern Italy being so disturbed by the ambitions of the pope's son.' Niccolò's reply was hotter than he had intended, fuelled by frustrated annoyance that the king and his chief minister could not see the obvious, despite having had it pointed out to them over and over.

To his relief, d'Amboise broke the silence with a small chuckle. 'You do have a way of making your points, Niccolò. Majesty, I rather think the young man is right. We really can't allow Cesare to use your name in this way, no matter how much he may feel he is entitled to do so. And Monsieur Machiavelli has made the case before that in the long run, it will be cheaper to contain the Borgia ambitions by preserving the independence of Florence, who has, after all, always proved to be our friend. I find I am persuaded that he is right.'

Louis nodded and returned his gaze to Machiavelli. 'You have a friend in His Eminence, I think, monsieur. Very well, we will write this day to all of our lieutenants and commanders in Italy and advise them that if the Duke of Valentinois should attempt anything against Florence or, for that matter Bologna, they should instantly march against him. That should stop his capers. See to it, Georges, will you?

'And Monsieur Machiavelli, since it seems we are unlikely to have your presence again before you are relieved, we should like to say that we have noted that you have discharged your duties with honour and honesty. Florence is lucky to have such a representative.'

With that praise ringing in his ears, Niccolò retired and all but skipped his way down the corridors of the Chateau de Tours and back to his lodgings.

Confirmation of his success arrived the following day, conveyed by Florimond Robertet, who told him that he had been instructed by the king to write to the pope and to Duke Valentino to say that he was displeased to hear that there was talk in the army in the Romagna of a pending attack on Florence, something His Majesty would in no way permit.

*

A week later, Pierfrancesco Tosinghi finally arrived. Niccolò didn't think that there was anyone he had ever greeted with more happiness in his life.

'Dear God, lad,' the big florid man boomed when he arrived at Niccolò's lodgings, 'you look worn out! And you've lost weight since last time I saw you. What have they been doing to you?'

Niccolò laughed; what Tosinghi said was true, he appeared careworn and exhausted now that he looked at himself in the mirror. 'Bad food, constant travel and endless frustration, that's all. I hope you have more joy of your commission than I have had of mine.'

'Niccolò, if I am as successful as you have been, I will be very satisfied. You do know that for most of the Signoria you are something of a paragon, don't you?'

'Really?' Niccolò was surprised, relieved and felt a little flush of pride at being so described. 'Biagio Buonaccorsi mentioned that there was some pleasure from my despatches when they were read, but other than that, I have had no reports of my standing in the government. In fact, I was worried that some wanted to see the back of me.'

'Well, they're not going to. Here.' Tosinghi handed him a small, sealed packet which, on being prised open, proved to be his formal recall. 'Niccolò, those who matter in the Signoria and the ten know how difficult and frustrating it has been for you. They also understand that, without your constant representations, we might well have lost the support of France, which is something we cannot afford right now. Representing Florence will never be an easy task, but you have done as well as any man could and I think you will find on your return that your voice will be heard with new respect. Now, where in the hell does one find a drink in this damned town?'

A week later, after one last formal interview with the king and Cardinal d'Amboise, having filled every day giving Tosinghi as thorough a briefing as he could, and having said farewell to the friends he had made at the French court, particularly Alessandro Spannochi, he was finally mounted and on the road back home. It was the fifteenth of December and he had been away for nearly six months.

Part Three—Facing the Lion

Chapter 15—A Moment of Calm

January 1501, Florence

It had been, everyone told him, the coldest winter in memory, an assertion he could easily believe as he made his way across the Ponte Santa Trinita in late January. Though the Arno wasn't frozen, chunks of ice could be seen turning among the eddies below, and the wind that swept across its surface chilled him to the bone even through his thickest cloak and three more layers of clothes he wore beneath it. Jamming his hat down more firmly on his head, he hurried across the bridge and into the relatively sheltered piazza that lay between Santa Trinita church and the bulky mass of the Palazzo Spini.

Five minutes later, he arrived outside a modest house that stood opposite the basilica of Santa Maria Novella, which faced it across a wind-blasted and snow-covered piazza, now wholly deserted, even though it was the middle of the day. Admitted by a grumpy porter, he was conducted up some stairs and through a chilly and deserted main hall to a door on the far side, upon which the porter knocked with three smart raps. When the door opened and the porter stood aside to allow him past, he was greeted by a blast of hot air from a big fireplace that blazed on one side of the room.

Standing or sitting on chairs scattered around the book-lined study were five men, all senior patricians who he knew well. Piero Soderini came forward to greet him, arms outstretched in welcome. As they embraced, Niccolò exchanged smiles over Piero's shoulder with his old comrade from the camp at Pisa, Luca degli Albizzi, looking as floridly cheerful as ever.

'Niccolò! Welcome,' Soderini said, releasing him but keeping one hand under Niccolò's elbow as they turned to face the rest of the room. 'I'm glad to see you are recovered from the rigours of your journey. You looked exhausted when you got back.'

He had indeed been exhausted when, just before Christmas, he had walked his equally worn-out horse through the Prato gate and made his way through the snow-bound streets to his house in Santo Spirito. But after a few weeks of good food, some rest and the solicitous care of Totto, who had been overjoyed to have his elder brother back, he had recovered much of his natural energy and colour. 'Thank you, Ser Piero. Florence herself has been my tonic. It's

157

amazing what a little rest and a few good home-cooked meals will do when you are at ease in your own home.'

'Well, I do feel a little guilty, Niccolò. After all, I did promise you'd only be away for a few weeks, not damned near six months! Still, you've learned a lot, which is why you are here. Now, you know everyone, I think?'

Niccolò turned to exchange greetings with the others. Standing next to Albizzi was Piero's younger brother, Francesco Soderini, Bishop of Volterra. A fleshier version of his sibling, he was known to be Piero's most trusted counsellor. In an ornate chair to one side of the fire sat Antonio Delvigna, who had again been elected as gonfaloniere for the next two months, though he had not yet taken up his post. All four were experienced and senior members of the Florentine nobility, men of considerable collective influence in the affairs of the republic.

'Well then, let's to business,' Soderini said with a brisk rubbing of hands. Seats were found for everyone, although Piero remained standing next to the fire.

The main purpose of the gathering, Soderini had told Niccolò a few days before, was to hear first-hand his conclusions from the French mission. He would, of course, prepare a formal report for the Signoria, but they wanted to listen to his thoughts first, and informally. The request had surprised him, but it was a mark of the way that perceptions of him had changed since his return. Six months before, he might have been daunted at the prospect of reporting to such men, but after his months of dealing with one of the most powerful kings in Europe and his first minister, he felt confident that he could acquit himself without disgrace. He launched into a summarised version of that long and wearing journey across the breadth of France. They heard him out in a silence interrupted only by occasional questions to clarify or seek further elaboration.

'You did very well, Niccolò, to convince d'Amboise and the king to continue to support us,' Bishop Soderini said when he had finally finished. 'What was it that swayed them in the end, do you think?'

He had thought a lot about that question on the way home. What had shocked and confused him at first, he realised, was the great gulf that had lain between what men said and what they did. For all the grand orations delivered in perfect Latin by the ambassadors and diplomats trailing the French court, what had counted in the end was raw power. All the rest was mere obfuscation. Those who had the power—the French, the Venetians, the pope—had not hesitated to use it, even as they employed honeyed words to disguise their intentions and lull their victims into false security. And those who were not in a position of strength, like Florence and her fellow Italian states, had been in no position to bargain.

'I think, My Lord Bishop,' he said carefully, 'that our mistake was to assume that King Louis and Cardinal d'Amboise would be influenced by the justice of our arguments. We may have had right on our side, but they did not take us seriously because they saw us as weak. It was only when I pointed out that both France and Florence had a shared interest in containing the ambitions of the pope and his son that the cardinal, in particular, began to listen. Though I am still to this day not certain he was wholly convinced.'

'So how long do you think the king will be prepared to keep Valentino in check?' asked Delvigna.

'For as long as we are prepared to bankroll his various excursions and ambitions in Italy, I would imagine.'

'Unless we were to grow a standing army of our own,' Albizzi murmured. 'Soldiers prepared to fight for their country, not just for pay. Then Louis would have to pay attention to us.'

Niccolò agreed with his former colleague, who was unlikely to forget for a long time his rough handling by the mercenary soldiers at that unruly camp outside Pisa, but was unsurprised when Delvigna advanced the usual objection. 'No, no. The cost of a standing army would bankrupt the state. And what would stop some dictator seizing control of the government at the head of such an army? No, our only asset is money and we will just have to use it to buy Louis off.'

'What of our own pride?' Albizzi's voice was bitter. 'Must that lie battered and bleeding in the dust while we satisfy the French lust for gold?'

'Antonio is right, Luca,' Piero Soderini soothed. 'Pride is all very well, but since we don't have the means to back it up with force, we must perforce swallow it and use our money to safeguard the state instead.'

'Which is not so easily done, the Great Council being the way it is.'

159

No one needed to elaborate on that point. Everyone in the room had grappled at one time or another with the impossibly fractured assembly from whose ranks the Signoria, the ten and all the other policy-making bodies of the Florentine Republic were drawn.

Delvigna broke the silence. 'What we need is a Doge, like the Venetians. Someone who can bang heads together until they see sense.'

'The Medicians would love that!' Albizzi was scornful. 'Just imagine, one of Piero's endless plots finally comes off, he gets to Florence with an army at his back and finds a ready-made lifetime dictatorship whose occupant he can depose and can slip his greasy backside onto the throne.'

Which was a real possibility, Niccolò knew. Piero de' Medici had never given up on the idea of a return to power in Florence and he had proven himself willing again and again to be used by others in return for their support for his schemes. He still had supporters among the *ottimati*, powerful men like his son-in-law, Alamanno Salviati, though their influence waned day by day as the memory of Medician rule faded. Even so, they remained a powerful rump, capable of influencing key appointments and decisions.

'That is a risk, certainly.' Bishop Soderini was judicious. 'Nevertheless, Antonio is correct. We need an executive who has sufficient certainty of tenure and who is in office long enough to steer a consistent path. As for the Medici, we will just have to hope that their luck holds!'

That brought a laugh from the rest of the room; Piero de' Medici was universally known as 'Piero the Unlucky'.

'The Venetian Doge does not have unlimited power,' Niccolò said, cautiously making his contribution as the laughter died away. 'Though he is in office for life, his authority is limited by their senate and the other offices of state. Could not our doge be similarly bound? Or his term could be limited, to five years perhaps?'

'Perhaps the Council of Eighty could be resuscitated and turned into something like the Venetian Senate,' Luca degli Albizzi said. 'That might be attractive to the rest of the *ottimati*. And while we might not want Piero de' Medici back in power, we may need the votes of his supporters. They might agree to something of this sort if they think there is a chance their champion will return.'

The discussion went on for another half hour, with no definite conclusions reached, though when they finally broke up and headed back out into the cold and snow, Niccolò sensed that this small group of powerful men had at least reached a consensus that something had to change and that they were determined to do something to effect it. That was a start.

Outside, the wind had died down and the cold was a little less intense. Parting from the others, he began to make his way back across the Arno to his home, deep in thought.

They were good men, all of them, and well-intentioned. And they were undoubtedly influential. But he wondered whether they would ever be able to achieve any of the reforms they talked about. Men like the Soderini brothers were increasingly rare—most of their class had hidden away on their country estates, sick of being asked to stump up loans to meet the ever-growing fiscal deficit, loans on which even the interest remained unpaid because the Great Council could not bring itself to impose additional taxes. Without their participation, the affairs of the republic remained in stasis, unable to go forward or back.

Still, their little meeting might be the start of something. Time would tell. He agreed with their aims and he resolved to do everything he could to help them move forward. If he had learned one thing in France, it was that divided counsels in the Signoria meant that urgent decisions were put off again and again. That made Florence look weak and vacillating in the face of her more determined rivals. And leadership that was only in office for two months at a time made the situation worse, as each group of magistrates passed contentious problems along to the next, unresolved. If they were to preserve their republic, something would have to change.

Not that he had many opportunities to dwell upon such questions in the months that followed. The mound of correspondence on his desk when he returned was as overwhelming as usual. And then in February, the Signoria despatched him on another mission, this time to nearby Pistoia, where the peace was being threatened by a feud that had broken out between two of the local families. Much to his chagrin, his new-found influence in the Signoria didn't cut much ice with the Pantiachi and the Cancellari, who refused to reconcile despite all his persuasive efforts. Like the dispute at Castrocaro, the roots of this feud were long lost and the hatred between the two families was too intense to be extinguished by diplomacy. He left the city depressed by the whole experience.

Back at home, his domestic life settled into new patterns. The various legal issues left behind after the deaths of his father and his sister still took up an inordinate amount of time, but the end seemed to be in sight, thanks to Totto's unflagging energy, and he drew closer to his brother as the days and weeks went by.

It was also pleasant to be back among his friends, in the familiar city he loved so much. Biagio and Agostino seemed determined to distract him from his work, dragging him away from the office as often as they could to drinking parties and card evenings in various low establishments around the town. He found their lively company and endless gossip exactly the tonics he needed to balance the sober demands of his job.

'You're becoming a dull dog!' Biagio said one afternoon not long after his return from Pistoia. 'Let's get away from here and see what amusement we can find along the river.'

'What kind of amusement do you have in mind?' he asked, all innocence.

'I did say along the river, didn't I? Come on, let's get going before Antonio comes and starts making speeches.'

Niccolò laughed and pulled his cloak off the peg on the wall beside his desk. He knew exactly what his friend had in mind. Fortunately, it was one of those rare days when he had no long, tedious committee meetings to attend and the pile of letters on his desk had been reduced to manageable proportions, so he could allow himself to be dragged away.

It was still cold out and the wind scythed through their clothing as they made their way along the banks of the river, making jokes and teasing each other. For the first time in months, Niccolò felt like the young man he was, unburdened by the cares of office and family.

Before long, they found themselves, exactly as Niccolò had expected, in an old haunt, a discreet little whorehouse in the Santa Croce quarter, close to the Ponte alle Grazie, where they warmed themselves by a roaring fire in the small front parlour.

Niccolò looked around at the everyday furnishings and the rough, faded frescoes on the walls with some affection, for he and Biagio had been going there since they'd been students together, though it had been some time since he had last indulged himself. Probably more than a year.

The madam, an ageing woman whose former beauty could still be seen if one chose to look for it below the layers of paint and mascara, went by the name of Rosalia. No one knew what her surname was or whether she had ever been married, or indeed anything at all of her history.

'Well now, if it isn't Messer Niccolò himself!' Her cracked and husky voice burst into a cackle. 'We haven't seen you here for a long time. And you look the worse for it if I may say so. Not like our Biagio here—look at him, in the pink of good health!'

'Biagio has been taking his ease, lolling about at home, while I, alas, have had to drag myself halfway across Europe in the service of my country.' He grinned to rob his remark of any implied rebuke to his friend. 'But he tells me that, though it has been a long time, I am remembered?'

'That you are. By more than one of the girls, I'd say. But one in particular has gone on and on about you, to the point of tedium. Now you two gentlemen take a seat and I will see whether she is ready to receive. As for you, Ser Biagio, your usual little poppet is also breathless with anticipation.'

She bustled off, leaving them to drink their wine—surprisingly good for such an establishment—and contemplate the pleasures to come. The girl she had spoken of was a pretty little thing, demure until she got between the sheets when she revealed appetites both voracious and inventive. Niccolò had, for a time, become quite besotted with her, common whore though she was. He felt the familiar stirring of excitement at the prospect of bedding her again.

Several hours later, the two friends retired to a nearby tavern, their lust sated and filled with the drowsy sense of contentment that usually follows such exercise.

'I should drag Antonio delle Valle around there one day,' Biagio said out of the blue after they had been chatting about nothing much for a few minutes.

163

Niccolò almost spat out the mouthful of wine he had just swallowed, so astonished was he by this remark. 'Why on earth would you want to do that? I thought you couldn't bear him!'

'Oh, well, I think I've worked out why he is so peevish and nit-picking. His wife spends half her life away, you see, up in the country. The city air disagrees with her, he says. So he doesn't have her here to give him a regular workout on the seesaw.'

Niccolò laughed even harder. He remembered Madonna Agostanza, who was as shrewish and sharp-tongued a woman as any he had ever met. Personally, he would have thought that her absence would, if anything, improve her husband's mood. 'You might be right, though if his wife ever heard what he had been up to, I expect he would soon lose the capacity to do anything at all in that line.'

Biagio laughed, then gave him a curious look. 'When you are married, Niccolò, will you forgo pleasures like the one we have just had?'

He was taken aback by the question. 'I doubt it. Whoever is foolish enough to marry me will just have to put up with me as I am, like it or not. Certainly, I don't propose to allow myself to be henpecked like della Valle!'

He laughed and changed the subject. But Biagio's flippant question disconcerted him because it made him remember that, approaching his thirty-second birthday, he was at the age when Florentine men usually exchanged the carefree joys of bachelorhood for sober domesticity. His work, the crises in his family, and his travels had left him with little energy to contemplate such a thing. But he was now the head of his branch of the Machiavelli family, responsible for the welfare of his brother and orphaned nephew and, in the weeks that followed, the idea of marriage returned again and again.

The younger, more indolent Niccolò might have left the whole question to the fates, but for his adult self, the search for a wife soon became a part-time project, returned to from time to time when his work and other responsibilities permitted. Finding a suitable candidate for matrimony was a delicate process and one for which he did not feel well-equipped. Fortunately, he could rely on the extended Machiavelli family, particularly his Uncle Piero. And Totto, who had greeted the idea of his brother getting married with hilarity, eventually entered into the whole project with great enthusiasm. Gentle feelers went out in search of a wife for Niccolò and the would-be groom waited patiently for them to bear fruit.

In the meantime, the turmoil of Italian politics continued apace. The Easter celebrations were barely over when the news came that, after a ferocious struggle, Faenza had finally fallen to Valentino's soldiers. At least the city had avoided being sacked after its defeated master, Astorre Manfredi, paid the vast sum of forty thousand ducats. Then, a few days later, Borgia marched up the Via Emilia and took the fortress of Castel Bolognese, an outpost of the city-state of Bologna. Since Giovanni Bentivoglio, *condottiero* and vicar of Bologna, was still under the nominal protection of France, this was a cheeky direct challenge to King Louis.

In the Florentine Signoria, all this provoked near-panic. A flurry of letters was sent off to be delivered to the King of France by the Florentine ambassadors following the court, reminding Louis of his promise to keep Borgia under control. That the king's wishes were being ignored became even more obvious when Borgia's army crossed the Apennines and planted themselves at Firenzuola, a mere thirty miles away from Florence. Yet another stormy Signoria meeting ensued.

'We have no choice, I tell you,' Chancellor Adriani shouted for the fourth or fifth time, his usual calm shattered by the stress. 'We have no soldiers mustered and we cannot rely on the French to keep this lion on its leash. All we can do is buy him off!'

Groans and complaints echoed around the room as the members of the Signoria once again contemplated the effect on their treasury of such a move. But the outcome was inevitable.

'Enough,' the current gonfaloniere finally said, ending the argument. 'We will despatch Piero Soderini to meet with Duke Valentino and negotiate terms. They know each other and I think Borgia respects Piero sufficiently to take him seriously.'

In the end, it cost thirty-six thousand ducats a year to enter into a treaty of alliance with Duke Valentino. Even this seemed to have minimal effect and the Florentines could only look on in frustration as he arrogantly marched his army right across Tuscany and planted himself outside Piombino, an important port city that had long been an ally of Florence. It was as if Borgia was demonstrating that he could do whatever he wanted.

In June, King Louis finally made his intentions clear by sending an army south to Rome. From there, they were to commence the campaign against Naples, long-rumoured and so not unexpected. On their way, they too left a trail of destruction through Tuscany, cutting down the crops for their own use, plundering the wine, flogging and killing those of the peasantry who tried, foolishly and uselessly, to protect their property.

'There's some good news at least,' Marcello Adriani told the Signoria in his report on the state of affairs. 'Borgia has been recalled to Rome; apparently the king is insisting that he join him in the war against Naples.'

'But he hasn't taken all of his army,' Niccolò added, rummaging among the papers in front of him for the latest report to the Committee of War from their own troops in Piombino. 'There is still a substantial force encamped around Piombino, under the command of Vitellozzo Vitelli.'

Vitellozzo, the embittered brother of Paolo Vitelli, did not sit idle in his master's absence, reducing Piombino in a matter of days. It must, Niccolò thought, have given the *condottiero* a great deal of satisfaction to have so easily deprived hated Florence of such a valuable ally. Then he too marched south to join Borgia in Rome, burning and looting whatever the French had not already destroyed. The Florentines heaved a sigh of relief. At least with all these armies occupied in the south, they would be left in peace for a while.

It was in this little moment of quiet that Niccolò's marriage project finally came to fruition. The tentative enquiries, delicately communicated by various relatives, had eventually alighted on the Corsini family. They too lived in Oltrarno and were a respected, well-connected family. Luigi Corsini had two daughters, one of whom was married to Piero del Nero, who Niccolò knew well, since he was a member of the Committee of War; the other, Marietta, at eighteen was as yet unmarried. Careful negotiations ensued between Niccolò and Luigi, with the mostly unhelpful intervention from time to time of Marietta's brother, Lanciolino.

Eventually, an initial marriage contract emerged and Niccolò was allowed to meet his bride-to-be for the first time. Of course, he had not been without independent reports on her looks and character, so he knew that she was neither deformed nor mad, but even so, he could hardly disguise his delight when he finally met her. A little shorter than himself, dark-haired and with fine skin that was, at that moment, attractively flushed, and beautiful hazel eyes that gazed at him with a frank appraising curiosity that matched his own. Her body, from what he could see of it under the modest gown, was of the solid kind that he had always preferred—a girl who he could cuddle and who would be comfortable rather than passionate was his expert appraisal.

'My dear, I hope this marriage pleases you?' he said, feeling uncharacteristically awkward.

'Of course, Signor Machiavelli, my father has spoken most favourably of you.' The response was equally formal. Then she smiled coyly. 'We both know, naturally, that whether I approve of you or not is neither here nor there, but I would like you to know that, having now laid eyes on you, nothing could make me happier than to become your wife.'

He wondered if she was teasing him. He was not, he knew, the most handsome of men, so it was unlikely that his appearance had sparked some unexpected romantic passion in her. And there was a hint of humour behind her amused vocalisation of his thoughts, something he found appealing. This might be a girl he could laugh with; no bad thing. He liked her. 'Please, none of this "Signor Machiavelli". I am Niccolò, or even Nico, if you prefer, from now on.'

She dropped a mock-curtsey. 'Nico. I like that. It is a little less severe than Niccolò. And how many babies does my lord Nico wish to bestow upon the world?'

He laughed. She was not going to be subtle, this one. 'As many as the house will hold, my dear! A veritable army of little Machiavellis!'

After that, they talked of nothing very much, but by the end of their half-hour together, Niccolò found himself thinking how much he enjoyed her company. She was not a complicated girl, but she was sweet and solicitous of his welfare and she had a coy sense of the absurd that was endearing. Her practical side came out when they turned to domestic matters and he caught the flash of inner steel as she made clear her views on the correct management of a household.

They were married in early August, at Santa Felicità. The wedding feast back at the Machiavelli house, just a short walk from the church, was modest but sufficient, and honoured by the presence of several of the more senior members of the current Signoria, as well as his friends and colleagues from the chancellery. They all made the usual ribald and obscene jokes, of course, which he bore with exuberant goodwill. But at last, they all departed and he was left to take his new bride across the threshold of their nuptial chamber, where he proceeded to discover that Marietta was, indeed, exactly the type of girl he liked, an occupation that kept them both busy until the small hours of the morning.

While his domestic life settled into a new and pleasant routine, the world outside continued on its way. Florence's emissaries and ambassadors, garrison commanders and spies sent a stream of despatches telling of the French king's triumphant campaign in the south. As Niccolò was getting married, Louis was entering Naples and deposing King Frederick IV. Then the world learned, to its astonishment, that the Neapolitan king's fate had been sealed over a year before when Louis had entered into a secret pact with King Ferdinand of Spain to divide the kingdom of Naples between them. It wasn't an alliance that would last, Niccolò thought. But at least the whole campaign had kept Louis and his armies occupied far away from Tuscany.

Summer passed into an unusually wet autumn, then a winter that was not as cold as the last. With the change of seasons, the military campaigns ceased and the armies went into winter quarters. Uneasily, the people of Tuscany went about the work of repairing the ravages of that summer with the same stolid determination with which they faced any other of the perils of that regularly afflicted their lives.

A new summer was again on its way when the ghost of Paolo Vitelli, embodied in the malign form of his brother, reappeared to disturb the uneasy peace and to propel Niccolò into another long campaign to contain the ambitions of Cesare Borgia.

Chapter 16—Trouble in Arezzo

Florence, June 1502

It was before dawn when the priors of the Signoria were awakened by the news that a messenger had arrived with urgent tidings that could not await their lordships' leisure. Struggling to shake off sleep, they dragged themselves into the Hall of Lilies to hear the news that had already been imparted to Gonfaloniere Francesco Taddei. Consternation ensued, and messengers sent to summon various servants of the state, among them Niccolò Machiavelli, who arrived bleary-eyed an hour or so later. By then, the Signoria was in the full fury of debate.

The news that had caused such dismay was of a revolt that had broken out two days before in Arezzo, a city some forty miles southeast of Florence, which had been under Florentine control for over a century. Its citizens had not only rebelled, but they had proclaimed their determination to place themselves under the protection of Borgia's captain Vitellozzo Vitelli, who was camped nearby with eight thousand troops. Worse, Vitellozzo had been joined by none other than Piero de' Medici, who had been prowling around the borders of Tuscany for most of the last year, looking for an opening.

'I have no doubt the uprising was fomented by Vitelli in the first place, at the orders of his master, and that their next step is to attack us and install the Medici again,' the agitated voice of the gonfaloniere was saying as Niccolò slipped into the room and settled himself into his accustomed place at the foot of the long council table next to Biagio Buonaccorsi who, judging from his tousled appearance, had also been summoned from his bed.

'We've been caught with our breeches down and our arse in a bucket, that's for sure,' Biagio muttered under his breath, causing Niccolò to choke as he tried to suppress an unseemly giggle. He returned his attention to the debate.

'I wouldn't be so sure.' Marcello Adriani scratched at his bald pate, a frown of concentration on his face. 'Don't forget that Piero married into the Orsini family. The Borgias hate the Orsini; the last thing that the pope would want is for them to increase their influence in Italy.'

'Yet Paolo Orsini serves as a captain in Valentino's army, does he not? Isn't that right, Machiavelli?'

169

'Yes, My Lord Gonfaloniere,' Niccolò said. 'According to our last report from Rome, at least.'

Bernardo Portinari, one of the current group of priors serving on the Signoria, was dismissive. 'He's a *condottiero*; he'll work for anyone who pays him. Anyway, it doesn't seem likely that Vitellozzo would do anything without Borgia's approval, so we must assume he was behind it.'

'Perhaps,' Adriani said. 'But we must also remember that thanks to the efforts of Niccolò here, the King of France has forbidden any attacks on either Florence or Bologna.'

Niccolò took that as a license to give his views. 'My lords, it is true that King Louis has been persuaded that his interests are best served by keeping Borgia on a leash, at least for now. Yet it does seem to me that Duke Valentino is playing with us all, as he did with Bentivoglio last year, trying to test the limits of Louis' patience with him, and our willingness to respond.'

He was uncomfortably aware that the whole table was looking expectantly at him, waiting for him to cap his analysis with a strategy that would save them. But there was no such strategy available, he realised bitterly, to a republic that could not muster a loyal army to enforce its will. 'We should remind the king of his promises to us,' he finally said, the words sounding lame in his ears, 'and ask that he reaffirm to Borgia the ban on expansion into Tuscany. That he should do so in the strongest terms possible, with soldiers if necessary.'

To his surprise, there was a general murmuring and nodding around the table, which a relieved gonfaloniere clearly took for approval, ordering that an embassy be sent to King Louis, while at the same time whatever forces they could scrape together should be sent towards Arezzo to restore Florentine control of the city. By then, the sun was coming up, and the yawning priors retired thankfully to their chambers to get some sleep. This luxury was denied to Niccolò, who had to walk across to the chancellery office so that he could draft the orders to put their lordships' decisions into motion.

The ambassadors had barely departed when yet another mud-spattered and exhausted courier arrived with even more startling news. Cesare Borgia, Duke of Valentinois and lord of the Romagna, desired the Signoria of the Florentine Republic to send him representatives authorised to come to an agreement with him on a matter 'of great importance'. What that meant, no one knew. The Signoria, in another flurry of meetings, resolved to despatch Francesco

Soderini, the Bishop of Volterra and one of the republic's most experienced diplomats. With him would go Secretary Machiavelli.

The following morning, accompanied by a couple of servants and a packhorse, they made their way along the banks of the Arno on the road to Forlì, where they had been informed that Cesare Borgia would be waiting for them.

Since their first meeting over a year ago, Niccolò had encountered Bishop Soderini perhaps half a dozen times, enough to sense the outlines of his companion's character. Like his brother, Francesco Soderini was a serious man with a forceful demeanour. However, where Piero impressed by force of intellect and a sharp intolerance of fools, Francesco was a model of inscrutable and affable charm, quick to deploy the honeyed words of diplomacy to achieve his aims. Niccolò was curious to find out what might lay below this urbane surface.

As they jogged along, the bishop entertained him with witty and amusing anecdotes of the latest doings at the French court, interspersed with acute observations on Florentine and French policy. The churchman had been in Florence for only a few days, having just returned from a long embassy to the court of King Louis XII, where he and Luca degli Albizzi had achieved the signal success of finalising the treaty of friendship for which Niccolò's efforts had laid the foundations. Despite having had only a few days to recover from his journey home, he seemed as fresh as if he had spent the whole of the last few months at his country villa.

The morning having passed thus pleasantly, they stopped at the little town of Pontassieve. After a brief courtesy call on an awestruck local priest who would have been less astonished at the appearance of an angel in his garden than he was at the unexpected arrival of a bishop, they decided to have an impromptu alfresco lunch beside the river. They had barely settled themselves, wine, cheese and bread laid on a spare saddlecloth between them, when the priest came scrambling breathlessly down the bank, accompanied by another of his brethren who showed signs of having endured a hard ride.

'Signori, I am glad you are still here,' the priest said, breathless. 'Father Andrea here has some news that you must hear.'

The bishop looked up at them both, his hands shading his eyes from the sun, an annoyed look on his face. He was something of an epicure and did not

171

appreciate having his meals, even a repast as simple as this one, interrupted without good cause.

But the news that Father Andrea had for them soon dispelled his annoyance. 'Your Grace, I bear grave news—the army of Duke Valentino has taken Urbino!'

The envoys scrambled to their feet, their picnic forgotten.

'What? How can that be so? We were told Borgia is in Forlì.' The bishop's confusion was complete.

Father Andrea's story tumbled out incoherently. He was a priest, not a military strategist, so it took a little while before they could piece it together.

Guidobaldo da Montefeltro, the young Duke of Urbino, had apparently agreed to allow one of Valentino's armies to pass through his state, ostensibly on its way to attack Camerino, yet another of the Romagna's unruly principalities. Guidobaldo was a faithful ally of the pope and had no reason to suspect treachery. Apparently he had gone off to enjoy a feast in the park of a monastery not far from his city. Mid-meal, he was brought the news that, far from passing through his territory, Cesare's army was converging on Urbino itself, and was just twenty miles away. The duke had fled in despair, abandoning his city to the marauder. More than this, the priest could not tell them.

'This makes no sense,' the cardinal said, watching the departing back of the priest. 'Urbino has never been part of the papal domain'

'But it does control the passes between the Romagna and Tuscany.'

'Which means he could block our trade routes to the Adriatic.' The cardinal might have been a churchman, but like every Florentine he understood trade.

'Or worse,' Niccolò said. 'First Piombino, then Arezzo, and now Urbino. He is surrounding us, eminence, picking off one strategic point after another.'

The cardinal climbed up onto his mount and kicked it into motion. 'I used to think this Borgia was nothing, just another warlord with pretensions, but I am beginning to think you are right about him, Niccolò.'

Though the bishop had barely rested since his return from France, Niccolò was astounded at his energy as they resumed their journey with a new sense of urgency. Each day they were up early and, with their little retinue, trotting along the dusty summer roads to make as much distance as they could before the midday halt. Much of the time on the road and at their overnight halts was spent in discussing the implications of the news they had heard at Pontessieve, the mission before them, what Borgia might want from Florence, what they might be able to concede, and what they could not.

'No doubt Valentino will want his money,' the bishop said as, on their second evening, they sat down to dinner—a veritable feast provided by the monastery whose hospitality Soderini's status had easily procured; travelling like this was a far cry from Niccolò's previous forlorn and penniless mission in France. 'It is a pity that the Signoria seems to be determined not to pay him.'

The money to which Soderini referred was the first instalment of the thirty-six thousand ducats annually which his brother had negotiated the previous year as the fee for Borgia's nominal services as a *condottiero*. Not that it was really a fee since the number of lances that Borgia was supposed to provide for this vast sum was derisory. It could, Niccolò thought sourly, better be described as a piece of extortion. Even so, it had been formally and solemnly agreed and subsequently ratified by the Signoria. The problem was, as usual, that the Signoria that had ratified it had been replaced a few months later by another, who then proceeded to temporise in the face of Borgia's demands for payment.

'They are being even more reckless than usual, if you ask me,' Niccolò said bluntly. 'This is a dangerous and ruthless man, and to renege on the agreement will only enrage him.'

'Pass me that capon, will you? Yes, you are right of course,' Soderini said as he delicately separated flesh from the bones of the bird on his plate, 'but the state of the treasury continues to be a problem. And we do have the protection of King Louis to fall back on.'

'For so long as it lasts. The French have got what they wanted, now that Naples is theirs. And the king does seem to be extraordinarily fond of Borgia. We need to hope that the king and d'Amboise continue to see an expanded Borgia state in central Italy as a threat to their interests.'

173

'Oh, I think you impressed that point on the good cardinal.' Soderini smiled. 'He spoke several times of your conversations with him when I was in Rouen.'

Niccolò smiled in return, then frowned as he remembered something else. 'I was told, in Tours, I think it was, that the pope is not entirely enthusiastic about his son's adventures and ambitions and that he may well prefer that Valentino not disturb too much the balance of power in Italy, beyond his obvious interest in the Romagna. Perhaps it is the pope that we should be applying to, rather than France.'

'Perhaps. Florence needs help from wherever she can get it, Niccolò.' The bishop said. 'Now, I was promised custards by that scoundrel in the kitchen. Be a good fellow, will you, and go and remind these villainous monks that their guests are hungry!'

Late in the afternoon of the following day, they rounded a bend in the road and beheld the splendours of the city of Urbino. As the rays of the setting sun washed its ramparts, it looked like a vision from the age of the troubadours, walls and towers seeming to grow out of the rocky eminence that made it all but impregnable, flags and banners snapping in the breeze from the minaret-like towers of the grand ducal palazzo that crowned the summit.

When they arrived at the city gates, their credentials ensured that they were conducted swiftly through the town's central piazza and up the hill to the palazzo entrance. As they went, Niccolò looked about him for signs of the new regime. Puzzlingly, there were few. Apart from the soldiers of their escort, there seemed to be almost no other signs of military occupation and the residents of the city were going about their normal business, although they were careful to stand aside as the escort passed and he saw one or two hastily-suppressed looks of anger. But otherwise, they might as easily have been visiting the old duke, rather than his confidently arrogant replacement.

The palazzo, when they arrived, was every bit as magnificent as its reputation. Built around a regular courtyard and arched double loggia, inside it was sumptuously decorated and painted with brilliantly coloured frescos. Conducted up a broad flight of stairs, they were deposited in the guest apartments on the western side of the building, overlooking a pleasant little garden. Everywhere they went, the signs and marks of the Montefeltro family were evident—their coat of arms emblazoned above doors and their eagle emblem repeated over and over along the cornices.

Duke Valentino, they were told, was not at present in the palazzo, but would be returning soon. Perhaps, the deferential major-domo suggested, they might care to refresh themselves, and he would ensure that they were summoned as soon as his excellency returned. This they proceeded to do, re-joining each other from their separate rooms to partake in the small mountain of food and drink that was piled on a side table.

Now that the moment had arrived for them to beard the lion in his den, Niccolò felt an unfamiliar sensation of nervousness in the bottom of his stomach, which he did his best to assuage by tearing into the food and downing several glasses of wine with a gusto uncharacteristic of him. Soderini looked on, amused.

Their anticipation was blunted when, after more than an hour of waiting, there was still no sign of a summons to meet with the duke. The sound of hooves ringing on cobbles in the courtyard below drew them to the windows, where they were just in time to see half a dozen men disappear into the entrance door opposite, leaving their grooms to deal with the blown and lathered horses. Presumably, this was Cesare Borgia returning to the palazzo, and they returned to their seats, confident that the major-domo would appear soon and conduct them into his presence.

More time went by. Niccolò had by now calmed his nerves and propped himself in a chair against the wall, only half-awake. Bishop Soderini, more conscious of his dignity and importance, was less sanguine, and began pacing up and down, muttering his annoyance under his breath.

Eventually, an amused Niccolò couldn't help himself. 'Come on, Ser Francesco, settle yourself down. He is just playing games with us, that's all. Cardinal d'Amboise used to do this to me all the time. You'll wear out your shoes, going back and forth like that.'

The bishop looked startled at Niccolò's use of his first name, then let out his own gentle laugh. 'No doubt you're right. It's an old trick, one I've used myself before now. Let's see if they have a pack of cards somewhere and we'll find a more amusing way to fill our time until his high and bloody mightiness decides to see us.'

So it was that the major-domo, when he finally appeared with his summons a little before midnight, appeared startled to find the two Florentine ambassadors deeply engaged in their cards, so much so that they made *him* wait for ten minutes until they had finished their game.

Conducted up through a series of interconnecting anterooms, all shrouded in darkness save for a single candle in each, they found themselves at the door of the ducal audience chamber. At a gesture from their guide, they entered a large room that was almost entirely in darkness, save for the wavering light emitted by a single large candle. Between them and the light, they could make out a marble table, behind which sat a dimly-apprehended figure, utterly still and seemingly waiting for them. A black-clad arm beckoned them into the room and the major-domo quietly departed, the click of the door as it closed sounding as sharp as a gunshot in the silence.

'Welcome to Urbino, signori,' Duke Valentino said, his voice a surprisingly alluring light tenor. 'I am sorry to have kept you waiting, but I am sure you will understand the press of business.'

Even close up, it was hard to make out his features in the stygian darkness, but Niccolò's immediate thought was that he was as comely as his reputation had said. Unblemished ivory skin spoke of youthful vigour and his face was regular of feature, the nose long and straight, and the jaw beneath its close-trimmed black beard strong and angular. Eyes black as coals, unblinking and imperturbable, gave no hint what was going on behind them.

As he reached across and poured himself a glass of wine, the candlelight flashed on the French order of Saint-Michel that hung from a gold chain around his neck over a simple black doublet, his only adornment other than the rings on his fingers. Making no offer of wine to his guests, he sat back in his seat, appraising them. Niccolò, returning his gaze, sensed a reined-in energy, trembling to be released at any moment into furious action, like one of the leopards that it was said the duke kept for hunting.

'How is your brother, My Lord Bishop?' Valentino asked finally. 'I had thought that Florence might send him to me again since we are known to each other and have had dealings before.'

Since it was Piero who had negotiated the treaty at Campo di Forni that Florence had so cavalierly refused to honour, this opening gambit was more than a friendly enquiry after an acquaintance; it was an immediate reminder of the Duke's main grievance.

'As far as I know, my brother is very well, Your Excellency.' Soderini was unperturbed. 'He is presently at the court of King Louis, so I have not heard from him for a while.'

Return of serve, Niccolò thought. *We are talking to your master, the bishop is saying, so be careful.*

The Duke's laugh was ironic. 'Ah, that ever-moving court. I know what it is like to follow King Louis around from town to town. As do you, Signor Machiavelli, eh?'

This startled Niccolò. Borgia had obviously done his homework. 'It can indeed be wearisome,' was all he said, resisting the urge to expand on the subject.

Borgia cocked his head on one side and regarded him with that chilling, empty black stare. 'They told me that you were a most eloquent ambassador, Signor Machiavelli. How wrong they seem to have been.' He turned his gaze back to Soderini. 'Well, My Lord Bishop, shall we get down to it? I must formally demand that Florence immediately pay me the first instalment of the fee for my services that I agreed with your brother months ago, and which your Signoria has been refusing me.'

This the two envoys had anticipated, and Bishop Soderini replied with some asperity. 'Excellency, as you well know, the treaty does not stipulate any particular payment schedule and certainly it makes no provision for any immediate payment of an instalment. As we have advised in our letters to Your Excellency, our treasury is for the moment exhausted, and it will be many months before we are in a position to make the required payments.'

'If it ever is,' Valentino shot back impatiently. 'You entered into this agreement in good faith and if you could not pay you should not have agreed to it.'

'Even so, as I have said, we will meet all our obligations when we can and in full accordance with the provisions of our treaty.' Soderini said, holding Borgia's gaze across the table.

'No, no, that will not do. If you will not abide by the terms of this treaty, how can I trust you? How do I know that you are not holding back this money in order to build up your arms to attack me?'

177

This time, Soderini looked shocked. 'My Lord, Florence has ever protested her friendship for you and your father the pope—'

'Words, that's all you Florentines ever offer me. Well, saying is one thing, doing is another.' The voice was still soft, but there was a hard edge to it now. 'You protest your friendship, but in truth you are at best neutral, waiting to see whether I will prevail before committing yourselves. But as you see, I am now master of Urbino and Lord of the Romagna, not just some mercenary captain. And I will be greater still.

'So, it is time you got your arses off the fence and decided to join me. What I want from you is a new agreement, a treaty that binds Florence in alliance with me, as lord of the Romagna.'

'The Signoria would consider such a proposal,' Soderini said, thoughtfully. 'Though I doubt they will do so while your troops are camped on Florentine soil, outside Arezzo.'

'That is your fault; a case of old sins casting long shadows. Vitellozzo Vitelli hates Florence for the reasons that you know and is simply acting according to his nature.'

'Yet, My Lord Duke, they are your soldiers, your cannon,' Niccolò observed.

Borgia's brows narrowed in irritation. 'Vitelli and Baglioni proceeded entirely on their own initiative, without my knowledge or consent.'

Interesting, Niccolò thought, *perhaps, behind the bravado and bluster, this duke is not quite as sure of himself as he wants us to think, his army not entirely under control.* 'Yet whether you unleashed them or no, you have it in your power to call them to heel, do you not? As I am sure the King of France would wish you to do so.'

'And what, Messer Secretary, makes you think you know King Louis' intentions? Because you had an audience or two with him, all the while hiding behind the skirts of Georges d'Amboise? Whereas I know his mind well. We are like brothers and, as brothers, we help each other in every way.' Borgia stared at him, hard and unblinking, then turned back to the bishop. 'Whatever your honeyed words, I know that your city is not well disposed towards me. At the first opportunity, you will abandon me like an assassin, then seek to make trouble for me with the king and the pope. Which is why I must have a treaty.'

'Excellency, you are mistaken. The Signoria holds you in the greatest esteem.' Soderini's tone was soothing. 'All we wish is to ensure that there is harmony between us.'

Borgia leaned menacingly forward in his chair, his voice hardening again. 'I have no love for this government of yours, which changes its mind like the wind and reneges on its promises at a whim. I cannot trust it.' He showed his teeth in a mirthless smile. 'In fact, I think if you don't change it, I will have to change it for you.'

Soderini drew in a sharp breath. Their system of government had its flaws, but the suggestion that Borgia might overthrow it by force of arms was a flagrant insult. And though he had not used the name, it was obvious to Niccolò that the change he would impose would be the return of Piero de' Medici. 'My Lord Duke, we are quite satisfied with our government in Florence and see no reason to alter it,' the bishop said, stiff with indignation. 'In any case, it is no one's business but our own to decide how we are governed.'

Once again Borgia subjected them to a silent stare. His next words, which, when they came, had the ring of finality. 'Enough of this. Let me be plain. Florence must decide—are you my friend or my enemy? If you will not give me a treaty, you reject the hand of friendship and the consequences should be obvious. Vitellozzo might have acted without my approval at Arezzo, but he did do me one favour—he has demonstrated I can take your cities away with ease at any time I wish. Ponder that when you scribble your despatches. Now, goodnight to you both. We will talk further tomorrow.'

As if he had been listening at some hidden spyhole, which he probably had been, the major-domo appeared once again at the door and conducted them back to their apartments in the eerie quiet of the early hours of the morning.

Niccolò tossed his hat onto a side table, dropped into a chair, and poured them both wine. 'He's bluffing. He knows King Louis will never allow him to control any more of our territory than he has already seized, so instead, he wants to turn us into a client-state, cowed into submission and unable to stop him moving his soldiers around Tuscany as he pleases.'

179

'It's a shrewd gamble, though. We don't have an army to resist him and he knows that, so we have little choice but to invite the fox into the hen-house.'

'And with him, the Medici,' Niccolò concurred, grimly. 'Oh, not immediately, but once he has his knife at our throats, he will insist on making good the threat he made tonight.'

'Was he behind the rebellion at Arezzo, do you think?'

'No, I suspect Vitellozzo really did move without authority. He's an actor, this duke, and a good one. But I think that his irritation when I suggested he could call off his dogs was real enough. I am not at all sure he is completely in control of Vitellozzo and Baglioni.'

Soderini, pouring the wine down his throat in one gulp and reaching for the flask to pour a second one, nodded in agreement. 'You may be right, Niccolò. It can be no simple matter for him to impose his will on men who have been used to ruling their own petty kingdoms and commanding their own armies, even if they now style themselves merely as his captains.'

'A wolf may shed its pelt, but it is still a wolf. Their move on Arezzo might have been these particular wolves showing their teeth, warning Borgia that they can turn and rend him if they choose to.'

'But by God, he does not lack confidence, this duke, and no doubt he has their measure.' The bishop shook his head as if he could not quite believe his own conclusions. 'He moves like lighting, arriving at each new place before anyone even knows he has left the old. Nothing seems to daunt him and he makes each victory seem easy. A formidable general indeed!'

Niccolò was a little taken aback by this unexpected paean to their adversary's skills. Though he too had been a little unnerved by their first encounter with Cesare Borgia, he sensed that the duke's success owed as much to good fortune as to his skills. Yet it could not be denied that this young man— how old was he? Just twenty-six?—had achieved an extraordinary coup when he had, with frightening ruthlessness, seized Urbino, and with it, effective control of the Romagna. Niccolò felt more than a little admiring, particularly when he contrasted Borgia with the vacillating and uncertain leaders with whom his state was burdened.

With these thoughts rattling around in his brain, he retired to his chamber to jot down a few notes of their meeting that would go into his despatch the following day (under the bishop's name, of course),

> *This lord is of such splendid and magnificent bearing and, in war, so decisive, that there is nothing so daunting that it does not seem to him a small matter. And, for the sake of glory and in order to secure his state, he never rests, nor does he know weariness or fear. He arrives at one place before one hears he has left the other, he treats his soldiers well, he has acquired the best men in Italy, all of which, in addition to his eternal good fortune, makes him formidable and victorious.*

Was this too effusive? Perhaps, though he was all but quoting the very words that Francesco Soderini had used earlier in the evening as he'd pondered the remarkable achievements of the duke. Let them stand. If the bishop wanted to change them, he could.

Chapter 17—An Encounter in Urbino

Urbino, June 1502

No summons came the following morning, so they decided that it was too pleasant a day to waste inside and went instead for a stroll through the city. Niccolò was curious about this place where the deposed duke's father, the renowned *condottiero* Federigo da Montefeltro, had spent the preposterous sum of two hundred thousand ducats creating his palace and various other buildings in his hilltop stronghold, transforming it into a centre of art and culture that was at odds with his fearsome military reputation.

There were still few signs of military occupation as they wandered down the long, evenly paved main street that led towards the central piazza. Apparently, Valentino had bivouacked the bulk of his army a few miles away, outside the town of Fermignano, retaining only the soldiers of his personal bodyguard in the city itself. This was a remarkably self-confident thing to do, especially since the deposed Duke Guidobaldo was far from unpopular there.

From behind, the petulant lowing of overburdened oxen and the clatter of wheels warned them to jump aside just in time to allow the passage of a long convoy of wagons, piled high with furniture and brocades, marble statuary and gilt-framed paintings. When it had passed, they found themselves looking at two young men whose passage along the street, in the opposite direction, had similarly been interrupted. One, a fleshy-faced youth whose upper lip was decorated with a wisp of a moustache and whose auburn hair was showing the early signs of incipient baldness, was vaguely familiar to Niccolò. As the pair crossed the street towards them, he searched his mind for a name, an exercise that was cut short by a jovial introduction shouted at them from the middle of the road.

'My Lord Bishop, Signor Machiavelli, well met! No, I can see you don't recognise us. I am Paolo Orsini and this is my cousin, Giulio.'

Two of Borgia's captains, Niccolò remembered. Partisans of the Medici and therefore enemies of the current Florentine regime. Mild-seeming though both appeared—Giulio was a slighter, narrower and younger version of his cousin—they were from a family of tough and ruthless *condottieri* with a blood-soaked history of intrigue and feud. Still, they seemed friendly enough, and one of the lessons that Niccolò had learned in France was that information could be had from any source, even those whose motives might seem hostile. Bishop Soderini appeared to be of the same mind, so they fell into step, agreeing to walk down into the city's main piazza to find a tavern.

'Where are the wagons going?' Niccolò asked as they walked.

Paolo Orsini's grin was piratical. 'My Lord Cesare thinks that the treasures of Urbino will be safer in his care at Cesena,' he said. 'That's the fifth convoy in three days. At this rate, the palace will be empty by the end of the week.'

Niccolò exchanged a glance with Soderini. The splendours of the ducal palazzo of Urbino were legendary. Federico da Montefeltro had acquired a vast collection of paintings and sculptures, and manuscripts to fill his library, which was said to be one of the best in the world. It was nonsense to suggest that all this would be safer at Cesena, a border fortress town, than here in one of the most impregnable cities in Italy. What Borgia was doing could more accurately be described as looting. But just then it was politic to ignore that crime. 'Why Cesena?' he asked, all innocence.

'It's to be the duke's new capital for the Romagna,' said the younger Orsini cousin. 'He has installed Ramiro da Lorqua as his governor there to start setting up a permanent government. Do you know him? Bloody character; you wouldn't want to cross him.'

That, coming from an Orsini, was a chilling assessment.

They arrived in the piazza and found a small tavern which, to the bishop's delight, served not only good wine but a reasonable array of meats and cheeses as well. As they settled in, Niccolò watched their two new acquaintances with some scepticism. He remembered from somewhere that Paolo was nicknamed 'Madonna' Orsini by his troops, apparently because he was unsteady under pressure. And there was something devious about Giulio. He was, Niccolò's whirring mind told him, the brother of Cardinal Giambattista Orsini, one of the most duplicitous men then wearing a cardinal's robes. Their presence in the street and their apparent friendliness was, he thought, not accidental.

'We know why you are in Urbino,' Paolo said abruptly, signalling rather crudely that they had had enough of polite chit-chat.

'Oh, indeed?' Francesco Soderini looked unperturbed, seemingly more interested in dissecting an orange than listening to the man on the other side of the table.

'Naturally. Everyone in Urbino knows that My Lord Cesare summoned emissaries from Florence so that he could give you a piece of his mind. I wouldn't want your job.'

'The duke was courtesy itself last night,' the bishop said, his attention still on the orange. 'We do have some matters to debate and resolve, that is true, but we are allies, are we not? These are disagreements between friends, nothing more.'

Bravo, Niccolò thought. The bishop's unflappable demeanour was clearly disconcerting to the Orsini lads, who exchanged somewhat mystified looks before the younger man tried again. 'Allies today, My Lord Bishop, it is true. But alliances do not last forever. If Duke Valentino wished to move against Florence, who is to stop him?'

'The King of France, presumably. Do we not also enjoy his favour and support? He would not be pleased to find his Italian confederates at each other's throats.'

'But surely you know,' Giulio smiled, 'that King Louis knew of Vitellozzo's plan to foment rebellion in your city of Arezzo and did nothing about it?'

Not true, Niccolò thought. He was more than ever convinced that Vitellozzo's moves had taken Borgia by surprise, so the possibility that the King of France was in on it seemed remote.

'Oh, Louis won't abandon you publicly,' Giulio went on, a crafty smile creeping across his face. 'His honour would not permit that. But if, let's say, he advanced slowly, very, very slowly, from Milan, he could allow us enough time to do whatever we wish in Tuscany. And then, when it is too late, he would cry all the tears of regret he wanted.'

'And bring Piero de' Medici with him, no doubt.' Niccolò laughed. 'I'm afraid it doesn't seem all that likely to me.'

Paolo Orsini seemed annoyed by his casual dismissal. A flush rose to his cheeks as he leaned confidentially across the table. 'On the contrary, Signor Machiavelli, the plans are already laid.' He looked around in such a

184

melodramatic way to check that there was no one in earshot that Niccolò was hard put not to laugh even harder. 'And as you know, My Lord Cesare can move very quickly when he wishes to. You would be well advised to consider this seriously.'

'So he can and so we will.' Bishop Soderini was bland. 'Time and events will tell, anyway, whether our faith in the King of France is misplaced or not. But tell me my friends, what is the latest news from Rome?'

Thus unwillingly diverted, the two Orsini talked for a little about the latest gossip from the papal court, before abruptly announcing that their duty called.

'It was a pack of lies, of course,' Niccolò said, once they were safely out of earshot. 'Neither Louis nor Cardinal d'Amboise will ever countenance Valentino controlling both the Romagna and Tuscany. If I am sure of nothing else in the world, I am sure of that.'

Soderini nodded. 'They were set on us deliberately. Cesare wants to send us a message and try to bluff us into thinking that he has already cooked our goose with the French.'

'Not a bad plan, but he might have chosen a more believable couple of accomplices!'

Their summons back into the presence of Valentino himself finally came that evening, long after the sun had set. This time, Borgia received them in the wood-panelled study that had once belonged to Federigo da Montefeltro, the brilliant frescoes of ancient writers and contemporary prelates illuminated by dozens of candles, a complete contrast to the darkness of their previous encounter.

The duke seemed to be in no mood for pleasantries. His expression was stern, and his eyes had an unfocused quality about them, as if only a small part of his mind was paying attention to his visitors, while the rest was busily calculating.

'Well, gentlemen,' he said eventually, 'I hope you have considered carefully everything I said yesterday. I mean Florence no harm, but I must know whether you will be with me or against me.'

'Excellency,' Niccolò replied, improperly forestalling his superior, 'we have sent urgent messengers to Florence communicating your requests. Even if they

185

were equipped with the winged heels of Hermes, they could not have returned with an answer in so short a time.'

'Are you telling me that the great Republic of Florence sent me a bishop and a senior secretary, but neglected to give you the authority to conclude anything?' The duke's sarcasm cut like a lash. 'Despite your great status, it seems you are no more than messengers!'

'My Lord Duke, you asked our Signoria to send you emissaries so that you could advise us of your wishes. You have done so and we have communicated them to our government.' Soderini was as calm and unruffled as if he were responding to a polite request to pass the sauce at the dinner table. 'Naturally, we could have had no instructions to respond to demands that had not as yet been made. But I do not doubt that once the Signoria has considered the issue, we will be provided with all the authority necessary to conclude whatever arrangements seem to meet our mutual interests.'

Borgia eyed them. The corners of his mouth turned down and his lower lip thrust petulantly outwards. 'As I said yesterday, I do not trust this government of yours. Mere promises will no longer suffice. I want you to pay me the money you have promised and I want a formal agreement between our two states allowing my armies to quarter themselves as needed on Tuscan soil. You can have four days, not an hour more, to get your answer from that spineless bunch of shopkeepers you call your Signoria.'

With which they were dismissed. Afterwards, back in their quarters, Niccolò again voiced the obvious. 'More bluff. He hopes to extract our submission in one form or another before Louis can intervene.'

'But why so urgent? It will take a miracle to get the Signoria to decide what to do and get an answer back to us in four days!'

The sudden change of tempo had puzzled Niccolò too. Did Borgia know something they did not? 'I wonder... could it be that he is more worried about his security than he wants us to think? Perhaps he doesn't have these captains of his fully under his control and fears that his authority over them would be undermined even further if the French order him to leave us alone. So if he can make Louis believe that we have allied with him voluntarily, the king's intervention will be forestalled. And with both Florence and France behind him, even Vitellozzo would not dare to raise the flag of rebellion.'

The theory tumbled out of his brain pell-mell, the words forming seconds behind the thoughts, but as he spoke, the conviction grew that he was right.

Soderini was less sure. 'It would be a colossal gamble to take,' he said doubtfully. 'He must know that the Signoria will choke on the implications of his demands and delay out of sheer fright.'

'Yet this man has demonstrated that he is a bold gambler, has he not? And the Signoria's fright could just as easily lead to panic and from there to capitulation.'

That logic seemed to convince the bishop, who became brisk. 'That, at least, we must prevent. I think that we should write a despatch conveying the duke's demands, as is our duty, but rather than entrusting it to a courier, I think you should take it personally to Florence and give them the benefit of your advice.'

So the following morning a bleary-eyed Niccolò climbed once again into the saddle and set off for Florence. Arriving, he had just handed the reins of his horse to an attendant and was crossing the courtyard of the Palazzo della Signoria when he was intercepted by an agitated Marcello Adriani. 'Thank heaven you are here, Niccolò, they are all in an uproar.'

'They', of course, were the Signoria. His and Soderini's first despatch from Urbino had, it seemed, caused panic and shock among the priors, and Adriani was having great trouble calming them down. Nor was the current gonfaloniere, Francesco Taddei, all that much help; a worthy but indolent man, he was at the end of his two-month term and had lost what little authority he had ever possessed.

Niccolò's eyewitness account, rendered swiftly and precisely, did at least settle their nerves, as did his recommended course of action.

'Signori,' he told them, wryly aware of the irony of the words about to come out of the mouth of one who had frequently chafed at the dilatory habits of the Florentine government, 'our best course of action is delay. Tell Duke Valentino that, as much as we are eager to have him as a friend, it seems inadvisable to conclude anything until the pope and the king have both been consulted. He can hardly object to that. He is trying to gull us. Let us call his bluff.'

Thus poor Francesco Soderini was condemned to some uncomfortable weeks of temporising while yet more urgent appeals were sent off to France. Afterwards, when he had finally returned from Urbino, the bishop told him that he had been in fear of his life, so enraged was Borgia at this, as he saw it, pusillanimous response from the Florentines.

But for Duke Valentino, the game was up. When French couriers arrived and ordered him to leave Florence alone and to take measures to get Vitellozzo Vitelli out of Arezzo, he had little choice but to comply.

What neither Machiavelli nor Bishop Soderini had known that morning when they'd sat in the tavern sparring with the Orsini cousins was that a detachment of the French army was leaving that morning towards Arezzo. Incredibly, the two *condottieri* stubbornly refused to loosen their grip on the town even after the French arrived and set up camp. It was only when Borgia threatened to attack Vitellozzo's home base of Città di Castello that they finally and grudgingly withdrew.

All this Niccolò found out later when, Arezzo having finally been quietened and returned to Florentine rule, reports started coming in from the Florentine loyalists there. Vitellozzo Vitelli, it was said, had departed in a rage, shouting dire imprecations against Florence—nothing new there—and against his erstwhile master, Duke Cesare Borgia. That might not bode well for the duke in the future. He commanded a formidable force, but it was still an army of made up of mercenary troops, led by men who were powerful, dangerous, and unpredictable. It was like driving a chariot pulled by tigers and leopards—it might be a magnificent spectacle to watch, but it took consummate skill to prevent the wild animals from turning on each other or their driver.

*

But that month most of Niccolò's attention was taken up by domestic affairs, the most important of which was the birth of his first child, a daughter that Marietta had, in that generosity of spirit that he had come to love in her, called Primerana, an echo of the name of Niccolò's deceased elder sister. The pregnancy had been trouble-free and the birth quick and easy.

'So like you, my dear,' he said with a smile, as he watched her cradling the baby girl in her arms, 'brisk and efficient.'

He had, over the year they had been married, come to value his wife's character, something that had been all but unknown to him on their wedding day. Efficient she certainly was, taking command of the household and reducing it to obedience and order with a smiling ruthlessness that would have done any general in the field proud. Ruefully, he recognised how much the domestic routines of their household had fallen into disarray in the interregnum between Primavera's death and Marietta's accession as its mistress.

She had a good head for business, too, that went far beyond the prosaic concerns of domestic budgeting and expenditure. Increasingly, he found himself deferring to her good judgement in the management of their properties and the farm, with the result that, for the first time in years, he found himself to be relatively prosperous. All in all, he could congratulate himself on his choice of a wife.

Pleasant though the tranquillity of his domestic life was, inevitably the demands of his job soon intruded. In September, the War Committee sent him to Arezzo for a few days, as their representative to the French army that was still encamped outside the city. His tasks were simple enough—mostly administrative issues to do with the provisioning of the soldiers—and soon completed. Then, when he returned to Florence, he had barely finished writing his report when his attention was focused on political developments that would have a profound effect on the city's governance.

Ever since that wintry meeting back at the beginning of 1501, the little cabal of senior patricians had been working away at various proposals to reform the Florentine government. They had tried and failed to establish a form of senate that would balance the unwieldy authority of the Great Council, which would not brook any diminution of its power, however divided it might be on almost every other issue.

Then they had proposed that the two-month term of the gonfaloniere be increased to three or five years so that the state could at least have some permanence in its titular figureheads. Niccolò Zati, a member of the War Committee, took that idea one step further and suggested that Florence imitate the Venetians and appoint the gonfaloniere for life, like their Doge.

These ideas had rumbled around, never really being resolved, until this latest Borgia crisis had come along.

189

'Now's the time, Niccolò,' Luca degli Albizzi told him one afternoon late in August, bailing him up in the Hall of the Lilies after a meeting of the Signoria. 'Even the most unreconstructed of the populists are beginning to be disenchanted with a government that runs around clucking like hens who've just seen their first fox every time there's a crisis. Zati's idea of a lifetime gonfaloniere is slowly taking hold. The Mediceans like it, just as I said they would, and the rest of the *ottimati* are with us. We just need to get the Savonarolan rump and we will have a majority.'

'Why don't you remind them that Savonarola himself wanted a Doge?'

'Did he? I don't remember that,' Albizzi said, puzzled.

'That's because he didn't, not in any of his sermons, anyway.' Niccolò allowed an imp-like grin to invade his face. 'But it *is* in his deposition before he was executed. His last testament, so to speak.'

Albizzi was dubious. 'Extracted under duress, though.'

'They won't know that. As far as the Savonarolans are concerned, every word of the master is gospel.'

In the end, that was the argument which swayed those populists who still cleaved to the teachings of their prophet Savonarola, and finally procured a majority in the Great Council. A month later, the elections were held. There were three competitors—an elder from the populist party, a judge and the recently returned ambassador to France, Piero Soderini. After three ballots, the latter was elected, to the general satisfaction of everybody.

Well, almost everybody—Bernardo Rucellai, an outspoken leader of the *ottimati* and a long-time enemy of Soderini, stormed out of the assembly and announced he was withdrawing entirely from public life. Even so, the new gonfaloniere was roundly congratulated by everyone else, including Niccolò Machiavelli. But, these pleasantries exchanged, Soderini turned straight to business. 'You have seen the latest despatches from Milan?'

'Yes. It appears that Duke Valentino continues to be in high favour with King Louis.'

That was an understatement. The King of France was in Milan, assembling yet another army with which, it was openly said, he intended to take the rest of the kingdom of Naples from his erstwhile Spanish allies. The Florentine

190

ambassadors there had reported that Cesare Borgia had appeared all unheralded at court. He must, Niccolò thought, have taken horse the very day Bishop Soderini had departed Urbino.

'Well, all his enemies have found their way to Milan, like iron filings to a lodestone, so no doubt he felt he had no choice but to make sure his position with Louis is secure.' The solemn face of the gonfaloniere was split by a sardonic grin. 'I would have given a hundred florins to see the look on the faces of Bentivoglio, Montefeltro and the rest when Louis took Cesare into his private chamber, embracing him like the prodigal son.'

Niccolò smiled too at that image. 'He spent a lot of time closeted with Georges d'Amboise as well, according to the reports.'

'Not surprising. The cardinal wants to be pope one day and I expect that d'Amboise would like to keep the favour of the various Borgia allies in the college of cardinals. And now Valentino is back in Rome, no doubt plotting his next moves. Where do you think he will go next?'

Niccolò had been asking himself that same question ever since they had received this latest batch of news from Milan and Rome; now, he frowned with concentration as he rehearsed his thinking out loud.

'With the conquest of Urbino, he has achieved his supposed aim of subjugating the main principalities of the Romagna. Except for Bologna, of course, which is securely held by Giovanni Bentivoglio; he's as tough and bloody as the rest of them, but he does seem to have the affection of his people, so he would be a tough nut to crack.'

'King Louis has made it clear that Bologna is under his protection, and that Borgia is not to attack Bentivoglio,' Soderini pointed out.

'True, though how much value can we place on that? You know Louis and d'Amboise, Ser Piero: if they can see an advantage to France in abandoning any of us, they will do so in a blink of an eye. We must assume that, one way or another, Bologna will end up under Borgia's thumb. It is what happens after that which scares me the most.' He paused for the gonfaloniere;s reaction; when Soderini nodded encouragement he plunged on. 'Alfonso d'Este is married to Borgia's sister Lucrezia, which ties Ferrara to him by bonds of family affection. King Louis insisted that Borgia bury his old enmity against Francesco Gonzaga, and enter into a formal alliance with Mantua. And

Pandolfo Petrucci, down in Siena, is providing Borgia with soldiers and guns; though he is ostensibly our ally, that act suggests his loyalties are, shall we say, flexible. So when you look at the map...'

'We are surrounded.' Soderini finished the thought for him. 'Bologna is the last piece in the puzzle. I see what you mean. And since most of our own mercenaries have always come from the Romagna or from Siena, we would be at Borgia's mercy. With only the king of France to restrain him.'

Both men let that thought settle into the silence.

'I think we are going to need to have someone keep a close eye on this aggressive young man.' Soderini finally said. 'You did a good job negotiating with king Louis to keep Borgia at bay, and we need you to perform the same trick with Valentino himself. As soon as we can find an excuse, I want to send you to join his court as a fully accredited ambassador. Will you do that for me?'

Niccolò agreed instantly, though he was both flattered and a little apprehensive. For the first time, he was to be sent on a major diplomatic mission not as the junior partner, but as the sole and senior representative of the government of Florence. And he was going to be doing so at the court of the greatest threat the republic had ever faced.

Chapter 18—Into the Lair of the Beast

Florence, October 1502

'And so My Lord Paolo asks that you respond to him with the utmost haste, so that he may convey your lordship's views to his friends when they meet at Magione.'

The guarded looks that the members of the Committee of War exchanged with each other could barely disguise their astonishment at the message they had just heard from a herald who had arrived that morning bearing a letter from, of all people, Paolo Orsini, the *condottiero* whom Niccolò and Francesco Soderini had encountered in the piazza in Urbino. The burden of the message was that the Orsini cousins, fearing that Duke Valentino was about to turn on them, had decided to detach themselves from his service. In this, they were to be joined by Vitellozzo Vitelli, Oliverotto da Fermo, and the Lord of Perugia, Gianpaolo Baglioni, all senior Borgia captains, in a council of war at the fortress of Magione, near Lake Trasimeno. Guidobaldo Montefeltro, the ousted duke of Urbino, had also accepted an invitation to attend.

Even more astonishing than the fact of this conspiracy was the request, conveyed orally for the sake of secrecy, that Florence should herself send a representative to this meeting, no doubt with the aim of inveigling the republic into joining their alliance against the Borgias.

The courier was dismissed with the promise of a prompt answer so that the ten could debate his message privately. At first, there was some appetite for entertaining the Orsini proposal, with Niccolò's old colleague from Pisa, Luca degli Albizzi, leading the charge.

'If this insurrection gains pace, it might give us a real chance to finally get rid of Borgia,' he said, slapping his hand on the table. 'A rebellion by the Orsini would be one thing, but Baglioni and Vitellozzo, and Oliverotto are all in on it. They are Borgia's most senior mercenary captains. What's more, if what that fellow said is true and they have persuaded Guidobaldo da Montefeltro to come to Magione, Borgia will be facing a powerful rebellion.'

'When Giovanni Bentivoglio hears the news from Rome, if he hasn't already, no doubt he will make his way to Magione, too.' That observation came from Pierfrancesco Tosinghi, who had replaced Niccolò at the court of

France, and who had arrived in Florence the day before bearing the extraordinary news that Cesare Borgia had extracted from a besotted King Louis an agreement that he would not interfere if Borgia chose to attack Bologna. The agreement was supposedly secret, but Pope Alexander, in one of his more garrulous moments, had let the details slip. Quite why Louis had given in to Borgia's demand was a mystery, though it was speculated that the French were preparing to go to war with Spain once again, and that the agreement was the price of papal support.

'Still, that is a lot of ifs,' Gonfaloniere Soderini cautioned. 'Guidobaldo might still be popular with his people, but he has no troops to speak of. And the others are petty warlords whose arrogance is greater than their actual power. Only Bentivoglio has real substance, of the lot of them.'

'And what if their rebellion fails?' put in Filippo Carducci, a greying and permanently gloomy aristocrat. 'What then?'

'We should be no worse off, surely?' Albizzi said, looking around the table for support. 'At the very least, Borgia will be distracted for months, and even if he does succeed in putting the rebellion down, we can rely upon the support of King Louis, can we not? The treaty specifically forbids any move against our interests by Borgia.'

'What are Louis' guarantees really worth, Luca?' Carducci was scornful. 'A king who abandons Bologna with such ease can hardly be relied upon to keep his word to us.'

Niccolò, listening impassively to the debate, silently agreed with Carducci. It might suit the French king to keep Borgia on a tight leash for now, but so long as he needed the pope's support, that could change in an instant. And his experience at the French court had taught him one certainty—the king and his chief minister d'Amboise would act upon what they saw as their interest and nothing else.

'Filippo is right, Luca, I think we should be wary.' Gonfaloniere Soderini was judicious, folding his hands on the table in front of him. 'These *condottieri*, however fearsome their military reputations, are for the most part petty warlords with unstable loyalties and limited political skills. How can we trust someone like Paolo Orsini? Or, more to the point, Vitellozzo Vitelli, who hates us with every fibre of his being?'

194

'And whether we can trust King Louis or no, we are bound in treaty with him, and that makes Borgia our ally too, whether we want him or not,' Tosinghi agreed. 'If we are seen to condone this rebellion, all the good work that Machiavelli and your brother and I have done to secure French support will be undone.'

'Very true,' Soderini said. 'We must, I think, send this emissary on his way with a negative answer. We should also make sure that Borgia knows we have done so. To that end, I propose we send Secretary Machiavelli to advise him accordingly.'

There was no dissent, and after some discussion a broad commission was drafted that required him to communicate to Borgia the undying friendship of Florence, while at the same time avoiding any definite commitment beyond general protestations of affection. In short, the same old temporising strategy that Florence always seemed to pull out of the drawer when faced with a challenge!

'You are a little hard, my friend,' the gonfaloniere said when Niccolò expressed his concern at being sent off again on yet another toothless mission. 'You know we have little alternative. It is true you are being asked, once more, to offer nothing, but we don't know how this rebellion will evolve. It may succeed, in which case our problem is solved.'

'And if it fails?'

'If it fails and Borgia remains in control of the Romagna, we can negotiate an alliance then.'

'That seems to be something of a gamble, Ser Piero.'

'It is.' Soderini's expression was sombre. 'Niccolò, I can't emphasise enough the importance of this mission to the future of Florence. We must walk a tightrope here. This Duke Valentino is capable of destroying us if he is permitted to continue to grow in strength, but we do not have the soldiers or generals capable of defeating him. And even if we did, we cannot move against him without offending the King of France. So we must wait upon events, then shape our course accordingly.

'I recommended you for this mission because I know we can depend on you to ensure that we are well informed of the Borgia's actions and intentions. But

I need you to do more than that. You must befriend this beast if you can and do everything to keep him away from our borders. Buy us time that we can use to build up our strength.'

Niccolò accepted the realities and nodded his agreement. Yet as he walked home, he thought that Florence would get better terms in any negotiation for an alliance now, while Borgia was weakened, than after he had beaten off the rebels and emerged even stronger. Were the positions reversed, he felt reasonably sure that Borgia would have assessed the risks and made his throw of the dice, not chosen to prevaricate until the wheel of fortune had turned.

Marietta, when he found her supervising the kitchen maids at the Machiavelli house in Oltrarno, was in an unusually truculent mood. 'How long will you be away this time Niccolò? You know I hate it when you go away.'

'Not for long—seven, eight days at the most. I will be back before you know I've gone!' He hoped it was not a lie. It was possible he could go to Imola, where the Borgia court now was, deliver his messages and learn enough to report back to the Signoria in that time, but the experience of France was still in his mind—he knew the capacity of his political masters to string him along while they delayed and debated.

'Look, you'll have plenty of company—Monna Alessandra and Monna Agostanza—and I'll ask Biagio to call in as well to make sure you have the most up to date news of me. How's that?' He cupped her chin in his hand and smiled down at her, hoping he had reassured her. Biagio's new wife Alessandra was a jolly woman with an earthy sense of humour whose company Marietta had enjoyed from the day they had been introduced and Agostanza della Valle, the wife of Chancellor Adriani's secretary, was a practical, no-nonsense sort who could be relied on to keep Marietta's head, which was prone to flights of anxiety, firmly on the ground. Between them, he hoped his wife would be sufficiently well-entertained that she would barely miss him.

*

The Signoria allowed him sufficient funds to employ two servants for the duration of his mission, with horses for each and a pack-horse to carry his baggage. The younger of the two was Luca, a boy of fifteen who usually worked on the farm at Sant' Andrea, and who was excited to be travelling as Niccolò's groom, responsible for looking after the horses and baggage. The other was Antonio Giacomini, an intelligent youngster from a good but

196

impoverished Florentine family, who would serve as Niccolò's servant and secretary.

He had hoped that they would make it as far as Firenzuola by evening, but one of the horses threw a shoe and they were delayed for several hours while Luca found a blacksmith. In the end, they only made it to the post-house at Scarperia just as the sun was setting. The following morning, Niccolò was seized with a sudden and inexplicable desire to get going to his destination as fast as was humanly possible. Travelling with the packhorse would probably mean another night on the road, so he decided to commandeer a post-horse and set off alone, instructing the two yawning youngsters to follow on as soon as they could.

It was a hard fifty-mile ride up through the mountains, along the pass carved in the hills by the Santerno River, and finally down into the vast Po River plain. By the time the red-brown walls of Imola were in sight, it was late in the afternoon, and close to six in the evening when he was finally allowed through the gates by an efficient and suspicious guard who took some persuading that his credential documents were valid. His dusty appearance and the absence of any servants probably contributed to the man's scepticism.

Despite the lateness of the hour, the city was bustling as he picked his way down a narrow street, heading towards the city's central piazza and the stables where, the guard had informed him, post-horses were usually housed and fed until they were needed again. Having disposed of his horse and negotiated with the stable-owner the rent of a room above its courtyard for the night, he set off on foot in the direction of the Rocca Sforzesca, the fortress that stood, like a key in a lock, on the south-western corner of the city.

He emerged from the deep shadows of the city's streets into a broad expanse of ground, swept clear of obstacles to provide an unimpeded field of fire for archers and crossbowmen stationed on the crenellated walls and four massive drum towers of the castle that confronted him across a moat that could only be crossed at a heavily defended causeway. It was a formidable stronghold indeed.

After another verbal wrangle with the castle guards, he was finally admitted through the main gates and into the courtyard of the fortress, where he stopped for a minute, trying to orientate himself. As he looked around, he was struck by the martial efficiency of the place. Officers and soldiers moved purposefully across the courtyard; a courier dashed past him, his horse's flank already heaving with exertion as he headed for the gate; in the far corner of the courtyard, a small company of soldiers was drilling with their pikes, practising over and over a series of complicated evolutions accompanied by growls and shouts; and in the other corner, half a dozen horses stamped and snorted, awaiting the attention of the blacksmith, from whose workshop there emerged the clang of hammer on iron and a roar from the furnace as an apprentice pumped the bellows.

It was from amid this bewildering cacophony that he heard a surprisingly familiar voice call out. 'Niccolò Machiavelli! Good God, man, what brings you here?'

The voice belonged to Alessandro Spannochi, the young banker upon whom he had last laid eyes in Tours, getting on for two years ago. They embraced and held each other at arm's length for inspection. Alessandro had not changed at all, and his infectious smile communicated more clearly than any words his delight at this unexpected encounter.

'I'm here as Florentine envoy to Duke Valentino,' he said as they disengaged. 'Come to talk about safe-conducts for our merchants through the Romagna.'

Spannochi's fine black eyebrows arched. 'Really? That's all they have sent you for? Florence must be brimming with talented secretaries if they can spare you for such a trivial task!'

Niccolò shrugged his shoulders and laughed. 'Well, there might be a few other things to talk about. But what brings you here, my friend? I thought you were going back to Rome after your time in France?'

'Oh, so I was, and did. But the holy father wanted someone he could trust to look after all the gold he has been sending north to feed My Lord Cesare's campaigns, so he made the duke take me as his treasurer. Cesare wasn't entirely thrilled with the arrangement, but he and I get along well enough so, in the end, he didn't complain too much. Come on, let me take you to him… unless you want to get changed and refreshed first?'

Niccolò became aware that he was still in his riding clothes and dusty as any Arab. But there was no point in wasting time on changing into new clothes, even if he had had any with him. 'No, not to worry Alessandro, all my spare clothes are with my servants anyway and they are at least half a day behind me. Besides, the duke doesn't seem to me to be one to stand much on ceremony.'

'Ah, I forgot. You met him in Urbino, didn't you? Yes, I'm sure you are right.'

They had crossed the courtyard and were ascending a broad flight of stairs that led from the lower loggia of the residence into its interior. As they climbed up, they were almost knocked over by a couple of officers coming down, feathered helmets bobbing and polished cuirasses flashing in the sun, muttering their impatience as they shouldered their way past.

'Damn soldiers,' Alessandro said, scowling his annoyance. 'They get so puffed up with their self-importance at the merest whiff of a crisis.'

'Crisis?' Niccolò pounced.

His innocent air fooled Spannochi not at all. 'Come on, you know what has been going on. The uprising in San Leo, that's what has brought you here hot-foot and breathless to see the duke, isn't it?'

This was the first he had heard of any rebellion in the little town of San Leo in the duchy of Urbino, whose fortress guarded the road to Rimini. Was this the beginning of the revolt of Borgia's captains? Niccolò kept those thoughts to himself and schooled his features into blandness. 'Well, you will admit it is something of a development, but though I love you as a brother, I am afraid I can't say much more about my instructions.'

Spannochi laughed. 'Same old Niccolò. Discreet as they come.'

They arrived at an ornate door that led into an anteroom. Alessandro sent a footman to tell the duke that he had a guest and gestured to a seat. 'I must go, I'm afraid—my desk is groaning with paperwork. I expect Cesare won't keep you waiting long. Come and find me tomorrow when you've rested and we'll talk some more.'

He didn't have to wait long. Barely ten minutes after the treasurer had left, the footman was back and conducting him into a well-proportioned room with three tall windows that overlooked the courtyard. Despite the chilly air outside, the shutters were open, admitting the shouts and clashes from the martial activity below. The room was simply furnished—a settle and a couple of chairs

199

grouped around an empty fireplace, a few chests and shelves, some well-worn but expensive carpets in the floor, and that was it.

In the middle stood a big table, its surface covered with papers. A black hat, decorated with a single enormous ruby, was perched on one corner. Sitting behind the desk was Cesare Borgia, his head bent over a document, pen poised to affix his signature. The pen came down, the document was signed with a flourish and handed to the footman who was hovering at his shoulder in anticipation. 'To Michelotto Corella by the fastest horse available.'

The boy nodded and ran from the room as Borgia focused his attention on his visitor. He seemed uncertain as to what expression he wanted to put on his face. First frowning displeasure, then puzzled curiosity, before he finally settled on a kind of smiling, sardonic bonhomie. 'Welcome, Signor Machiavelli, the silent secretary of Florence! I am glad to see you here, though hopefully you will have more lines to speak than you had in Urbino.'

Niccolò smiled warily, wondering which version of Cesare Borgia was he going to get today. 'My Lord Duke, in Urbino, I was present as secretary to Bishop Soderini, there to witness and advise in private. He would not have appreciated me upstaging him in his negotiations with you.'

Borgia rose from the desk and walked over to the window. He stood looking down at the activity in the courtyard for a few moments, before turning back to Machiavelli, a glint of humour in his eyes. 'No, I suppose not. Bishop Soderini is a very dignified man—though his dignity fled when I promised I would throw him into the deepest dungeon in Urbino if he didn't give me a straight answer. I hope *you* will give me some straight answers, Machiavelli.'

'That depends, My Lord, on what the questions are.'

'Let us start with why you are here; that should be straightforward enough.'

Niccolò launched into the small formal speech he had prepared, outlining the ostensible reasons for his mission to Imola, expressing Florence's sincerest thanks for Duke Valentino's assistance in arranging for the return of some merchandise that had been stolen from Florentine merchants in Urbino and asking him to agree to provide a safe-conduct covering the passage of merchants travelling through the duke's new domains of the Romagna.

Borgia, his arms folded across his chest, listened courteously throughout, saying nothing until Niccolò finally came to a halt. He broke the silence with three mocking handclaps. 'Bravo, Signor Machiavelli. I can understand why you sped across the mountains and dragged yourself into my presence still dusty from the road to deliver such an important message. I am grateful that Florence took the trouble, but if there is nothing else, go and see Spannochi about your safe-conducts. I have much to do…'

The Niccolò Machiavelli who had departed to France all those months ago might have been disconcerted at such a brusque dismissal, but since then, he had stared down kings and cardinals and was not intimidated. He decided that a little bluff of his own was in order. 'Naturally, My Lord, I would not want to keep you. No doubt the defection of the Orsini will be exercising your mind.'

'What do you know of the Orsini?' Borgia's brows drew together.

'That they and others of your captains are conspiring against you, that they plan to draw into their conspiracy Giovanni Bentivoglio and Guidobaldo Montefeltro, and that they have attempted to recruit the support of my republic in their schemes. But I am sure you are already aware of all this.'

'All the worms you mentioned are meeting at Magione, that I know.' With a flick of a ringed and manicured hand, Borgia dismissed them. 'But their approach to Florence, that does surprise me. I trust that your Signoria treated their petition with the contempt it deserves.'

'Excellency, the Signoria declined their invitation most speedily,' Niccolò said, allowing himself an ironic smile. 'Further, Gonfaloniere Soderini enjoined me to express on behalf of the Signoria their affection for you, bound as we all are in obedience to the holy father and in friendship with the King of France, all of whose friends we regard as allies.'

He got a long, considering look as his reward for that little speech, followed by a genuinely amused laugh. 'Bravo again, Machiavelli. I almost believe you. Well, you may tell your masters I am grateful for their support. I have ever wanted Florence's friendship, and if I haven't managed to obtain it, that is due to the malice of others. Come, let's sit.'

Even walking the few feet to the fireplace, Borgia moved with the grace and power of one of his hunting leopards. Dropping himself into one corner of the settle, he stretched out the long and muscular legs encased in fine black hose and black knee-length boots and picked up a small bell from a side-table to summon the footman, who was given orders to bring wine and food. Niccolò sat in a chair opposite and waited, wondering what would come next, unable to read what was going on behind the handsome dark countenance.

'Your Signoria does not trust my motives,' Borgia said, breaking the silence.

Deciding not to take the bait, Niccolò said nothing, keeping an expression of polite interest on his face.

'I am not much in the habit of justifying myself,' Borgia went on, 'but I can see that you will not take me at my word when I say that I am a friend of Florence, so let me explain some things to you so that you can better understand my position.'

'My Lord Duke, I am here to listen and to learn so that I might better inform the Signoria.'

'Then listen carefully,' Borgia resumed, his eyes locked on Niccolò's. 'I have all this trouble only because I defended the interests of Florence against Vitellozzo Vitelli.'

Despite his best efforts to school his face into immobility, something of his incredulity at this statement must have shown, causing a flicker of irritation to cross Borgia's face. Then he started speaking again, quickly this time, the words tumbling over each other. 'I see you don't believe me. But it is true. After I took Rimini and Pesaro and Faenza, Vitellozzo was after me to turn on Florence. I refused because His Holiness the Pope had instructed me not to do so. Then, when I announced that decision to his captains, he threw himself at my feet, begging me to change my mind. It was pathetic—he was weeping like a woman with frustration when I refused him. He even swore he would do no violence to your towns and cities.

'I didn't really believe him, but he kept on at me and eventually I agreed to let him take an army into Florentine territory, with two strict instructions: that he should not molest your towns, and on no account was he to even talk about the return of your Medici outcasts.

'Of course he disobeyed and decided he would create the disturbances at Arezzo to drag me into conflict with your Signoria. I told him I'd fight him if he caused you any trouble. And eventually, I had to drag him away from

Arezzo, which he wanted to add to his possessions. It is that action, in defence of Florence, that turned him against me.'

More likely, Niccolò thought, Borgia acted only when he realised that, with French troops eyeing Vitellozzo's soldiers across the gap between their camps and King Louis' orders ringing in his ears, his bluff had failed. 'And the Orsini?' he asked, deliberately ignoring the points that Borgia seemed so keen to make.

'I have no idea what caused those two maggots to turn on me.' Borgia's expression was bland; if he was irritated by Niccolò's evasion, he wasn't about to show it. 'Perhaps some malcontents have been spreading rumours that I intended to deprive them of their possessions.'

Or perhaps they had simply realised that if Borgia could turn against Vitellozzo, one of his most senior captains, he might just as easily turn against them. This thought, too, he kept to himself.

'Anyway, if they and the other bankrupts gathered at Magione ever get up the courage to attack me, they will prove themselves to be even greater fools than I suppose them to be. While the pope is alive and the King of France is in Italy, I am sustained by a fire that all the water the Orsini can command could not quench.'

Niccolò was surprised that Borgia was prepared to be so open about the twin pillars upon which his future depended—the pope's money and the king's soldiers. But his strength was also his weakness: he wasn't as free an agent as he wanted to seem.

'The Signoria will be relieved to hear that you are confident of success,' he said. 'And at least you still hold Urbino, though I heard something about a disturbance there when I arrived...'

'Oh, Urbino is lost, at least for now.' Again, the surprising candour. 'The loss of San Leo makes that an inevitability. But I know how to win it back again when the time is right.'

The gaze that Borgia now turned on Machiavelli was chilling, implacable. 'You know, when I took Urbino, I did so in three days without hurting a hair on anyone's head. What is more, I left many of its principal citizens in the public offices of the state. My clemency has been repaid by treachery since it was one of those very citizens who raised the rebellion at the San Leo fortress. That is not a mistake I shall repeat.'

Abruptly, he stood, and courtesy dictated that Niccolò follow suit. The duke walked over to the desk, picked up a paper and looked at it, then made his way to one of the windows, where he stood looking down into the now-silent courtyard.

'Messer Machiavelli,' Borgia finally said, turning back to his guest, with the fading light behind him and his face in shadow. 'Let me put a proposition to you. Now that the Orsini and Vitellozzo and the rest have shown themselves to be my enemies and your republic has repudiated them, I believe I am in a better position to enter into a more formal arrangement with Florence.'

'What kind of arrangement do you have in mind, excellency?'

'A treaty, let us say. For our mutual support and defence. And an appointment as captain-general of the Florentine forces, so that we may better coordinate our military efforts.' Borgia raised one ringed and beautifully manicured hand to forestall the expected temporising answer. 'Messer Machiavelli, your republic should decide now whether you want such an arrangement, for who knows what the future might bring? Though I have every intention of bringing these rebellious dogs to heel, fortune is a fickle mistress, and circumstances may force me, with the greatest reluctance, into some kind of agreement with them. And that cannot be to Florence's benefit.'

It was the same demand he had made in Urbino, but this time dressed in more modest clothing. There was none of the threatening bluster that had so disturbed the Florentines and none of the urgency, just the hint that they would be better doing a deal now than later.

What Borgia said was true, as far as it went. Vitellozzo's hostility to Florence was unlikely ever to be satisfied by anything less than the destruction of the city and the Orsini family ties to the Medici made it inevitable they would never agree to any treaty that did not re-establish that family in control of the political levers of the republic. But in making the crude and barely credible threat that he might make peace with his rebels, men who he could not trust and who would turn against him again at a whim, he showed he was more desperate than he appeared to secure his western flank.

'Excellency,' Niccolò said automatically, even as this analysis formulated itself in his brain, 'my government has instructed me to convey its support and most earnest expressions of friendship but has not given me any authority to go beyond that. Naturally, I will convey your request to the Signoria and recommend that they give the matter the most serious consideration. I flatter myself that my words will carry some weight, but of course, I must await their further instructions.'

'Messer Secretary, I am sure your words carry a great deal of weight.' Borgia's irony was heavy. 'Now if you will excuse me I have much to do.'

To Niccolò's surprise, the duke hooked a hand through his arm and walked him to the door, his stern expression giving way to a friendly grin. 'I have enjoyed our little talk, Messer Machiavelli. I sense you have reservations, but believe me I have not an ounce of doubt I will prevail in this little struggle. Good day to you and we will meet again soon.'

As he left and made his way out of the fortress in the direction of his lodgings, he felt he had begun to understand a little more of the mystery behind this extraordinary young man's success. That he was a general of considerable skill and boundless energy was evident. But Niccolò also felt the tug of the man's charisma: he was capable of considerable charm and at times displayed a disarming self-awareness.

And yet, when he sat down in his seedy temporary lodgings to write his despatch describing all that had occurred, he still felt that much of the duke's confidence was just bravado. Despite his every effort to appear unperturbed by the treachery of his most senior captains, he was more than a little rattled. His rapid talk, full of self-justification, his unsubtle attempts to blackmail Florence into an alliance with him, his reiteration of the support he believed he had from pope and king, all suggested a man who was nowhere near as sure of himself as he wanted everyone to believe.

He would write to the gonfaloniere and the Signoria, reporting everything that Borgia had said and everything he had asked for, but he would also recommend that they hasten slowly. Florence needed that time to see whether this rebellion would flower into full-blown insurrection and bring Duke Valentino down. And time to build up her defences in case it was the duke who emerged victorious.

Chapter 19—Valentino in Crisis

Imola, October 1502

'Niccolò, I hope your servants turn up soon. Your coat looks as if it is ready to walk away all by itself!'

It was true, he thought, holding his arms out and inspecting sleeves that, like his hose and boots, were squalid with mud from the road, which no amount of brushing had been able to get out. He needed a change of clothes and the services of a good laundrywoman, that was certain.

His dismay must have shown on his face, for Alessandro Spannochi let out a short laugh as he settled himself behind the desk that dominated the little cell that had been allocated to him as an office. Behind, a large window opened onto the castle courtyard, through which weak October morning sunlight was streaming. He waved Niccolò to the chair opposite. 'Never mind, we aren't standing on ceremony today. How was the duke last night?'

'Confident. Cheerful. Charming, even. Still making demands, even though he virtually admitted that he had lost Urbino.'

Spannochi nodded. 'He has. He sent orders yesterday to Ugo de Cardona to break camp and withdraw from the duchy. But he's not discouraged at all. He has messengers flying in every direction and we are sending money with them to mobilise his forces. Michelotto Corella has been sent to join Cardona with a thousand infantry, Rafaello dei Pazzi is riding post to Milan to recruit among the Gascons stationed there, we have someone raising soldiers among the Swiss, and we expect to get another six thousand or so militia from within the Romagna. All we need is enough time to get them here.'

Niccolò nodded at this recitation, mentally committing each fact to memory for the despatch he would write that evening. Alessandro's frankness was of course deliberate, intended to reinforce the idea that Borgia had everything under control, but that didn't make the information any less useful.

'Well, he is nothing if not energetic, your duke.' Niccolò laughed. 'Now, about these safe-conducts…'

A few hours later, Luca and Antonio arrived with the packhorse and found their way to his temporary lodgings above the stables, having ridden as hard as they could to catch up. They spent the afternoon dealing with the stabling of the horses and finding their way to the new and more suitable accommodation he had arranged that morning—two rooms on the top floor of a decent house that stood in the shadow of the city's cathedral. It was owned by a candle-maker, whose workshop facing onto the street on the ground floor produced a reek of tallow that permeated the whole building. But their rooms looked out onto the Piazza del Duomo on one side and a small garden on the other, and they were light and spacious. Compared with some of the fleapits he had experienced on his previous diplomatic travels, this was luxury.

It was another small luxury to be able to change his attire and send Luca off to get his riding clothes laundered. A bath completed his inventory of indulgences for the day and, by late afternoon, he felt clean and fit to be seen in the world for the first time in days. He was sitting at a small table at the window that overlooked the piazza, puzzling out the first draft of his despatch for the day, when Antonio came crashing through the door, out of breath from having climbed three flights of stairs. 'I'm sorry to disturb, master, but the duke is below, asking to see you!'

'What? Here?' Niccolò was completely taken aback then, recovering himself, he did his best to regain his dignity in the boy's eyes. 'Tell His Excellency that I shall be down directly. Go on, go!'

Antonio vanished and Niccolò hunted for his hat, buttoned up his doublet and draped a newly-laundered robe over his shoulders before following him at a more measured pace.

Sure enough, Borgia was standing at the bottom of the stairs, waiting impatiently for him with hands on hips. 'Ah, Messer Secretary. Come, it's a fine day. Let us walk.'

The candle-maker and his wife stood stammering to one side as they swept out, no doubt as bemused as he at this sudden apparition. Outside, a couple of bodyguards in the yellow and red Borgia livery fell into step behind them as they walked across the piazza in front of the massive façade of the cathedral. Niccolò was conscious of the glances sent their way by those they passed, some surreptitious, others gawping outright. Borgia, clearly used to such scrutiny, paid no attention.

207

'I have had news, Machiavelli, that will interest you.' He snapped his fingers and one of the soldiers handed him a document, which he passed across to Niccolò, stopping so he could unfold the stiff pages and read.

The letter was from Monseigneur d'Arles, the pope's wily ambassador to King Louis, and its essence was that the king had given explicit orders for the despatch of significant numbers of troops to his well-beloved Duke of Valentinois.

'As you see, I am not without friends.' Borgia prompted, when Niccolò said nothing.

'That is evident, excellency. But the king says that he makes this army available to you solely for the purpose of attacking Bologna.'

A wolfish grin appeared beneath the beard. 'True. But my enemies don't know that, do they?'

Borgia began walking again, down the long street that led back to the Rocca, all the while keeping up a triumphant monologue. 'I tell you, Vitelli and the Orsini and the others could not have chosen a worse time to declare against me. Before too long, I will have enough soldiers of my own gathered to crush this rebellion of theirs and, with the addition of King Louis' soldiers and the money that comes every day from Rome, I will certainly prevail. Tell your Signoria that when you write to them again.'

'I will, of course, excellency. I am sure they will be as pleased as I am to hear your news.'

They reached the open ground in front of the Rocca. Borgia came to a halt and, gesturing to his two attendants to draw back, he turned to Machiavelli, crossed his arms across his chest and regarded him. 'Messer Secretary, I am sharing this news with you so that you are fully aware of my situation and can advise your Signoria accordingly. You are here, I know, to spy on me. But I have no objection to that. In fact, I will make a point of informing you whenever I can of any developments of importance, so that your government will see that I have nothing to hide from them'

Niccolò nodded, wondering where this conversation was headed, and whether he was being duped in some way he did not yet apprehend.

'For example, you should know I have despatched, secretly, an envoy to Paolo Orsini, suggesting that if he returns to his obedience, he will be rewarded both by myself and the holy father.'

That was a shrewd move. Indecisive, flabby-minded 'Madonna' Orsini was probably the weakest link among the conspirators.

Something of his appreciation for the shrewdness of this manoeuvre must have shown in his face, for Borgia grinned like a schoolboy. 'I see you understand me, Machiavelli. All right. Spannochi and Geraldini are waiting for me in the council chamber, so I must go. Have a good afternoon, Messer Secretary.'

He strolled off, followed by his two guards, leaving Machiavelli standing on the grass, one hand holding his hat and the other rubbing his chin in thought. Crafting that night's despatch would be a more interesting exercise than he had anticipated.

*

'We have good news from every quarter!'

It was Cesare Borgia's usual late hour for giving audiences, but this time the three-windowed room above the fortress courtyard was crowded with people—Alessandro Spannochi, all smiling youthful energy, Agapito Geraldini, Borgia's dour and grey chief secretary, and half a dozen other minor functionaries. They were all crowding around an excited Duke Cesare Borgia, his usual sober black contrasting with the bright plumage of his entourage.

'Don Ugo and Don Michelotto have routed the rebels in battle and sacked their towns of Pergola and Fossombrone.' the duke said, holding above his head like a trophy the despatch that had just been delivered by a breathless courier. 'And better still, God has stricken that cur Vitellozzo with a fever. I tell you, an evil star reigns over all those who have rebelled against us!'

A ragged cheer broke out from his courtiers and Borgia called for wine to be brought in celebration.

As the servants bustled about and the room began to buzz with general conversation, Borgia sauntered over to where Niccolò stood by the window, a little aloof from the others. 'So what do you think, Niccolò? Will your Signoria back me now?'

Machiavelli was startled by the duke's familiar use of his first name and felt a little flush of satisfaction at being singled out. He was also conscious that he was now the object of the gaze, curious and suspicious, of everyone else in the room. 'My Lord, you are to be congratulated indeed. Fortune seems to be favouring you at last.'

'Fortune! She is a harlot who is best tamed by a strong man between her legs.' Borgia laughed and threw an arm around Machiavelli's shoulders. 'Come on, man, don't look so glum!'

Niccolò was more nervous than anything else, for he had disagreeable news to convey to the duke. In his despatches that morning he had received the news that the Signoria had declined Borgia's demand that he be given a contract to command the Florentine forces.

He waited for an explosion, but to his surprise, Borgia just laughed. 'I am disappointed, Machiavelli, but it doesn't matter all that much. I proposed it merely as a matter of convenience. And the alliance? Have they refused that too?'

'No, excellency. Though I recommended that the Signoria consider your proposal favourably, I am advised that they have decided to refer the question to King Louis, for his guidance.'

That did bring a frown to Borgia's brow. Niccolò braced himself, but was again surprised.

'Hmm. I don't doubt what Louis will say.' The duke was mild, though his eyes narrowed. Then he shrugged, dismissing the whole question. 'Keep pressing them, Messer Secretary. Remind them that we have enemies in common. Vitellozzo, the Orsini and their Medici in-laws, not to mention Venice. An alliance between us makes sense. When we have dealt with this rebellion and put down all these little petty warlords, your security will be enhanced by having a peaceful Romagna that is bound in alliance with you.'

All of these arguments had already occurred to Niccolò, but he saw no point in saying so. 'Of course, I will do so. And I know Gonfaloniere Soderini is also determined to find an accommodation between our states. But I fear the Signoria will not make any decision until they know King Louis' views.'

'Your government does seem to have some difficulty knowing its own mind, Machiavelli.' That was tart.

'You should see it from my side,' Niccolò said drily. His words had the intended effect of making Borgia laugh.

'Well, in the meantime, there is some other news that you and your Signoria should know which might help them make up their minds. This damned conspiracy is falling apart. You remember I wrote to Paolo Orsini? Well, both Vitellozzo *and* Orsini have sent me secret messages, separately protesting their loyalty to me. You watch, before long they will crawl back to me on their bellies, begging to be let back in.'

Borgia left him to re-join his celebrating staff and, not long after, Niccolò made his farewells. Back in his lodgings, he discarded his robe and hat, sent a sleepy Antonio to find some wine and a little bread and cheese, and sat down to begin the task of composing a despatch, ready for the courier in the morning.

The facts of the evening's events were easy enough to recount, and he did so with his usual economy. But by now he knew that the gonfaloniere and the Signoria also expected him to offer some guidance as to their significance, and that caused him to pause, absentmindedly stroking his cheek with the quill of the pen.

While the news that had so excited Borgia was indeed important, it was hardly so momentous as to justify his elation this evening. That the rebels were protesting their loyalty meant nothing, and he doubted that Borgia was taking them seriously either. As for Vitellozzo's illness, while it was no doubt gratifying, it would hardly stop the rebellion in its tracks.

Even the biggest item was not as significant as it seemed. Borgia had been furious when he was told, a few days ago, that Ugo di Cardona and Michelotto Corella, two of his most experienced Spanish captains, had disobeyed his orders to withdraw towards Rimini and instead had declared their intention to attack the relatively weak forces holding Fossombrone and Pergola. No doubt he was relieved that they had succeeded, and of course it would boost morale among Valentino's remaining loyal troops, but neither place was so strategically important and neither fight so conclusive that the outcome of this struggle was placed beyond doubt.

So in short Cesare Borgia was once again employing bluff and bluster to disguise the fact that his fortunes remained in the balance. Which also explained his equanimity in the face of the disappointing news from Florence: he still needed Florentine friendship while matters were uncertain, and so he was not going to give offence just now.

He began writing again, this time on a separate sheet of paper which he would later rewrite in code.

> *Since King Louis is infatuated of Duke Valentino, he will most likely insist that we support the duke in all his enterprises. It would be to our advantage if our ambassadors to the French court are able to delay as much as possible to bring our suit before the king and his ministers, so that we can see how matters play out in the Romagna and elsewhere. I will endeavour meantime to plumb the duke's intentions, the better to advise your lordships.*

By the time he had finished and coded everything that needed to be hidden from prying eyes, it was close to midnight. It had been a long day, and he found himself yawning with exhaustion. Settling back into his chair, his eyes closed into a sleep from which he was only roused by a startled Antonio the next morning.

*

The troop of soldiers arriving from Milan made a brave sight as they marched across the courtyard of the Rocca Sforzesca, banners snapping in the cold October breeze, drummers beating out a relentless tattoo, the late afternoon sun glinting off halberds. Their captain, splendidly mounted on a black horse trotted ahead and, halting in front of Cesare Borgia and his assembled officers, drew his sword in salute.

'Welcome, Lodovico!' the duke shouted, throwing his arms wide.

The captain slipped off his horse and embraced Borgia. They talked quietly for a few minutes, then the captain saluted once again and strutted off to organise the billeting of his troop. Turning, the duke caught Niccolò's eye. He had been loitering under the long loggia that lined one side of the great courtyard, at something of a loose end.

'Whenever I look around, Machiavelli, there you are, watching everything with that damned secret smile on your face.' Borgia's greeting was playful. 'Come up; I have ten minutes, so we can talk.'

Upstairs, in the familiar apartments, Borgia was in an expansive mood, pouring wine for them both. 'As you see, our strength grows day by day. Those were the first of the troops coming from Milan. The Swiss arrived yesterday and we have more soldiers coming in from the Romagna and Siena tomorrow. Have you had any reply from your Signoria?'

Niccolò had come to recognise the sudden change of subject as a typical Borgia tactic to try and put him off-balance. 'I can say no more than I already have, excellency—the Signoria is interested in your proposition, but we are awaiting word from our embassy to the court of King Louis.'

'No doubt you will get your reply from Louis soon enough. I know him and I am more sure than death itself that he will insist upon your support for me. In the meantime, it would be a show of good faith if your Signoria were to order some troops to make a demonstration in the direction of Citta del Castello, a small force only, enough to show the rebels you are on my side. Can I rely on you to press that proposal with them?'

It seemed to be a simple thing to ask, and though Florentine forces were few and thinly spread, such a demonstration was not beyond their powers. He told Borgia he would indeed convey his request to the Signoria in his despatch that very night.

'Good.' Borgia, perched on the edge of his desk, arms crossed in his usual self-confident attitude, looked at Niccolò in silence, as if considering what he wanted to say next. Then, without warning, he drew his sword from its scabbard. In spite of himself, Niccolò flinched at the sound, causing a bark of laughter from the duke. 'Don't worry, Machiavelli, you are in no danger!' Somehow, despite the amused tone, the words didn't seem all that reassuring. 'Come here, I want to show you something.'

Borgia reversed the sword and lifted it so that Niccolò could see the words engraved just below the pommel. *Caesar aut nihil*—Caesar or nothing. 'I chose this motto because I want the world to understand I am not just another *condottiero*, a sword for hire to the highest bidder. I want to make something greater here in the Romagna, a real state that is well-governed and prosperous, not a lawless wilderness where every citizen lives in fear of the nearest petty warlord with a castle and a few soldiers.'

That was a surprising statement, but Niccolò could not leave it unchallenged.

'If that is your objective, excellency, why do you continue to allow Ramiro da Lorqua to terrorise your people without hindrance?' His tone was deliberately blunt. Da Lorqua was one of Borgia's longest-standing lieutenants, who he had appointed as governor-general of the Romagna, where he had set to work in a savage programme of pacification. 'I don't suppose that they think there is much difference between your garrisons and those of their previous masters.'

Borgia slid his sword back into its scabbard, frowning: was he used to getting blunt advice like this?

'Perhaps you are right, Machiavelli,' he said slowly, as if thinking out loud. 'Da Lorqua may have been over-zealous; I had been thinking of demoting him anyway, and replacing him with Antonio Sansovino. What do you think of that idea?'

'The jurist?' It was Niccolò's turn to frown. 'He is well respected and incorruptible, so it is said. Yes, an excellent appointment, I would think. And you would demonstrate that anyone, even your closest associates, can be made or broken as you decide.'

'I see that you understand me,' Borgia smiled, sliding the sword back into its sheath. 'One of the things I like about you is that I never have to explain anything twice. Why don't you leave the employ of that shopkeeper-republic of yours and join me?'

Borgia laughed even harder as Niccolò sputtered and choked on his wine at this suggestion. 'Excellency, I am honoured,' he said when he had recovered himself, 'but I am Florentine through and through, and could not consider any other allegiance.'

'I employ other Florentines on my staff, my chief military engineer for one. And they find life in my employment profitable.'

'Even so, My Lord...' Niccolò trailed into silence, though he held Borgia's gaze in a mute challenge.

'I see that you are immovable.' The duke waved a hand to dismiss the subject. 'Well, your loyalty is to be commended and I will not trouble you again with any such suggestions. Still, perhaps you might advise me now and then when you think doing so does not conflict with your duty to Florence.'

Niccolò bowed his head in acknowledgement. Over the past year, he had grown used to a certain amount of flattery as his influence in the councils of government grew, and he had thought himself immune to its effects. He was surprised by the little glow of pride he felt now, even though he was perfectly aware of Borgia's motives.

'I have heard that Paolo Orsini is coming here to seek terms for reconciliation with Your Excellency,' he said, deciding to test a little the limits of this new intimacy to confirm something that Spannochi had accidentally let slip that morning.

'The Orsini, da Fermo, Baglioni. What an unsavoury crew they are.' Borgia's vehemence was unexpected; hitherto his attitude had always been cool contempt. 'As for Vitellozzo, he has never done anything that showed him to be a man of either courage or honour. All he is fit for is to devastate the defenceless countryside and practice treason.'

Niccolò could hardly disagree with Borgia's characterisation of his former captains. Oliverotto da Fermo, for instance—a small-town despot, he had murdered all his relatives, having invited them to a banquet in a scene reminiscent of a Greek tragedy. Then there was Gianpaolo Baglioni, the tyrant of Perugia, a vicious and cowardly man whose path to power was similarly littered with homicides. The sleazy Orsini cousins, whom Niccolò had met in Urbino, were matched by their uncle, Cardinal Giambattista Orsini, a man of a thousand tricks.

'At least they are now out in the open,' he said, hoping to coax more. 'You know what you are facing.'

'True, though the more I know of them, the less I make of them. Without me to lead them, they are nothing. They have realised that, and no doubt Paolo will be coming here to beg that they should all be returned to my service.'

215

So the rumour was true. 'And you will accept them?'

'We will see. It all depends...' Did Borgia not want to answer Niccolò's question? Or was he genuinely uncertain of his course? Either way, it wouldn't hurt to fan the flames of suspicion between them.

'Since you asked me to offer my advice, excellency, it is this—do not trust any of them. A wolf may shed its pelt, but it is still a wolf. They may pretend friendship, but I believe they will continue to scheme and plot against you unless you show them they cannot prevail against your strength.'

Borgia stopped pacing and propped himself against the windowsill, arms crossed, considering. 'You are mistaken in your metaphor—these men are not wolves with teeth that might rend me, they are but monkeys dressed in silk and they will dance to any tune I care to play.' The low voice dripped with contempt. 'But don't worry, Niccolò. When these captains of mine come back to the fold, I assure you they will be treated as they deserve.'

Whatever that might mean, Niccolò thought.

Later that evening, he settled down to compile his usual daily despatch. Having recounted as accurately as he could recollect the details of his conversations that day, he decided to add a few words to recommend what course of action the Signoria should, in his opinion, adopt.

> *If you judge it advisable to comply with the duke's request to send a force in the direction of Città del Castello, do so without making it known publicly and without compromising yourselves. In that case, you ought to send some regular troops towards the borders, hold reviews, pretending that you fear an attack from that direction...*

Niccolò's pen came to a halt as he stopped to think about what he was writing. Though he was fulfilling his promise to Borgia, as secretary to the War Committee he knew, probably better than anyone else in the republic, that the forces that Florence could call on were few and ill-trained. But Borgia didn't need to know that.

216

You could raise yourselves still more in the duke's estimation by representing the number as double what they really are for the duke will not be able to get reliable information to the contrary.

He smiled to himself as he went through the familiar routine of heating wax to seal his letter. Perhaps he too was learning something of the art of bluff.

Chapter 20—The Lion at Bay

Imola, October 1502

Niccolò sensed the changed atmosphere the moment he entered the courtyard of the Rocca. He had become used to seeing messengers coming and going, but this was the first time he had seen half a dozen of them leaving at once, jostling each other as they pounded through the gatehouse.

Crossing the courtyard, he noticed that there seemed to be an extra urgency in the way that the soldiers and their officers moved and their usual cheerful chattering arrogance had been replaced by a silent grimness. One party of Gascons were huddled in a corner having a spirited argument that was abruptly ended by the barked orders of their officer. The soldiers subsided into a mutinous muttering that brought back memories of the camp before Pisa.

'What has happened, Alessandro?' he asked as he sat down across from the treasurer in his little office. 'They are going about down there as if the devil himself had descended among them.'

'Here are your safe-conducts.' Spannochi slid a sheaf of documents across the desk; the ostensible reason for their meeting that day. The treasurer's expression became serious. 'Cesare doesn't want anyone to know, but we have had a serious setback. Corella and Moncada have managed to get themselves defeated at somewhere called Calmazzo, not far from Fossombrone. Moncada has been captured, Michelotto Corella wounded... though he did make it back into Fossombrone, at least. We also received word this morning that Oliverotto da Fermo has retaken Camerino and Guidobaldo da Montefeltro has returned to Urbino. In short, disaster.'

A disaster it might have been, but Spannochi seemed remarkably calm. 'Don't worry, Niccolò, Cesare has it all in hand. I've seen him in crises like this before. He's magnificent, cool and calm. Messengers have been sent off in every direction with instructions for his soldiers and we have plenty of money to hire more armies if we need to. All will be well, I promise you.'

This was all meant to be reassuring, no doubt. But by Niccolò's reckoning, the duke's forces were still nowhere near sufficient to repulse a determined attack by the rebels. No doubt Borgia knew that well enough, which was why

218

he was continuing to try to separate his opponents from each other with promises of their safety if they came back to him.

Scratching his head in perplexity, he took leave of Alessandro Spannochi and made his way down the stairs and across the courtyard to the gatehouse, deep in thought and all but oblivious to his surroundings, already composing that night's despatch in his head.

A week passed with little additional news, though there was much coming and going of troops and messengers. One afternoon, he was crossing the bridge that connected the Rocca with the town when he had to squeeze to one side to avoid a squadron of cavalry clattering their way into the castle, barely avoiding being pitched into the muddy and weed-filled waters of the moat below. Cursing under his breath, he straightened his robes and set off again, only to trip over a complicated-looking contraption that was leaning up against the bridge wall.

'Watch out, you idiot! That's a delicate machine you are stomping on.' The shout came from a handsome, curly-haired youth standing at the city end of the bridge, his arms filled with a pile of books. Next to him, another man stood, presenting a broad back to Niccolò as he peered through the aperture of some kind of instrument mounted atop a tripod.

At the boy's cry, he turned in annoyance to see what had occasioned it, the frown on his square, vigorous face clearing as he assessed the situation. 'Hush, Salai, don't you know who this is? Messer Machiavelli, I must apologise for my young man's impudence. I am afraid he can't help himself; he's a born troublemaker. But he keeps me amused, so I keep him.'

Niccolò, never one to stand on his dignity, laughed at this little speech. 'Never mind, my wife always tells me I am a clumsy oaf. But you have the advantage of me since you seem to know my name while I am ignorant of yours.'

'Oh, everyone in Imola knows that Niccolò Machiavelli is here as the Florentine envoy. I am Leonardo di Ser Piero da Vinci. Currently employed as the duke's military engineer.'

Niccolò looked with new interest at this man, famous throughout Italy as a painter and engineer. He was probably about fifty years of age, though his strongly made frame was as athletic as anyone half his age and there was no

219

trace of grey in the abundant brown hair that sprang in waves from his head. His face, clean-shaven and squarely handsome, carried the lines and seams of life's experience, and his eyes, as sharp and inquisitive as Niccolò's own, nevertheless had a kindly quality, as though he had seen and comprehended all the world's sadness and all its joy.

'Then well-met, Messer da Vinci. It is always pleasant to hear a Tuscan accent at this polyglot court.' Niccolò stopped, considering. 'But I see you are busy. Perhaps we can meet again later when you are not detained by duty?'

'No, no, we are all but done here,' the artist said. 'Just let me complete one or two observations, then Salai can take everything back to the fortress while we find somewhere more congenial to talk.'

He watched, fascinated, as da Vinci set to work, measuring angles and calling out numbers to his young assistant, who rather sulkily jotted them down, all the while shooting resentful looks at Niccolò, to which he returned a pleasant smile that disguised a suppressed urge to laugh out loud. Eventually, the mysterious tasks were complete, and an openly mutinous Salai was despatched laden with notebooks, tripod and the device over which Niccolò had tripped—a wheeled contraption that Leonardo called a hodometer, used for the precise measurement of distances.

Da Vinci had not missed the young man's odd behaviour, which he tried to explain as they made their way through the narrow streets of the town in the general direction of the piazza. 'He does get jealous, I'm afraid, whenever I meet someone new. It can be troublesome, but he is at heart a good boy, and loyal.'

Niccolò allowed that to pass without comment, though some suspicions formed in his mind.

A few minutes of companionably silent walking found them crossing the big square and into a small and discreet tavern, popular with the silk traders whose stalls occupied the nearby arcade below the Palazzo Riario. Niccolò had made a point of frequenting the place as a source of gossip and rumour and he was by now well known to the proprietor, who gave him a vociferous, back-slapping welcome, then conducted them to a little booth at the back of the place where it was less noisy. In a few moments, a jug of wine and a platter of bread and cured meats were deposited on their table with a clatter and a flourish by a buxom young serving-girl, who flashed a big and cheeky grin at Niccolò before disappearing back into the throng, much to da Vinci's amusement.

'So how does an artist so well-known as Leonardo da Vinci come to be employed as a military man?' He asked the question light-heartedly but was genuinely curious as to how the painter, who was famous throughout Italy, had found himself in a fortress city on the borders of the Romagna, serving Cesare Borgia.

Da Vinci's scowling response was a surprise. 'Cesare. He has been chasing me since before I left Milan, writing me letter after letter begging me to join him. I didn't want to, but you know how persuasive he can be.' He frowned as if considering how much he was prepared to say. 'I would have been resisting him still, but those damned Servite monks at Santissima Annunziata got me into trouble with the authorities in Florence and I had no choice but to leave.'

'What kind of trouble?' Niccolò thought he knew the answer.

'One of the interfering busybodies found me in bed with Salai.' Da Vinci's eyes were defiant as he made this bald proclamation, with no hint of shame or regret, just anger.

'And denounced you to the Officers of the Night, I suppose?' The Office of the Night was a branch of the Florentine judiciary whose sole function was to identify and prosecute sinners against the city's anti-sodomy laws. In theory, sodomy was a capital crime, the penalty death by burning. In practice, offenders were rarely subjected to this extreme punishment, suffering instead little more than a few nights in the cells. Even so, the penalties became much harsher for second and third offences, so being reported to the authorities was not a trivial matter.

Niccolò had been infatuated with his share of boys in his youth; fleeting affairs that meant little to him beyond immediate sexual gratification. In this, he was no different from most other young Florentines and, by the time he'd finished with the Studio, those juvenile obsessions had slipped away behind him and he had discovered the delights of sexual commerce with girls. But he had never felt the moral repugnance towards sodomy that the church taught so obsessively (and hypocritically, for the sins committed between the brothers in their monasteries was legendary) nor could he censure those like Leonardo who had never emerged from the chrysalis of youthful passions and remained devoted to their own sex. He had met a few such men over the years, had even

221

intervened once in a case that had been brought before the Office of the Night, taking some pleasure in cheating the night police of their quarry.

He felt sorry for da Vinci, who had to live in constant fear of denunciation and whose life had been upended because of his affection for a handsome youth. Perhaps something could be done about that, but he kept that thought to himself, instead trying to put his new acquaintance at ease with a wry joke. 'That boy does seem to cause you grief. I hope he is good in bed!'

Leonardo looked at him, startled, then his face dissolved into relieved laughter. 'I like your sense of humour, Messer Machiavelli. Salai *is* trouble, that is for certain, but his physical charms aside, he has been loyal to me. Anyway, as I was saying, we had to go somewhere, so I finally decided that I would accept the duke's invitation. He has been indulgent—he allowed me to take my time, just asked me to do a survey of his fortresses on the way here, and eventually, I found myself attached to the army of Michelotto da Corella.'

This piqued Niccolò's interest, for he had not yet heard any first-hand reports from anyone who had been with the ill-fated armies of Corella and Moncada. 'You were at Fossombrone?'

Da Vinci's face clouded with the memory. 'That is an experience I hope never to have again. Michelotto is an evil bastard—Borgia's strangler-in-chief. When we took Fossombrone, he just let his soldiers loose. It is not a big place—you could hear the screams of the women as they were being raped from every corner of the town. There was blood everywhere and you didn't dare look cross-eyed at any of the soldiers for fear they would run you through. I tell you, Machiavelli, it was every nightmare you've ever had rolled into one.'

'And Calmazzo?'

'A bloody rout. The rebel army wasn't much, just a few hundred strong, but they surprised us, and Corella and Moncada quarrelled with each other over tactics. Their orders confused the troops, who broke in no time and before we knew it, everyone ran away, dropping their arms as they went.' He shuddered at the memory. 'All I could think of as I ran with the rest of them was that God was punishing us for the massacre at Fossombrone. Anyway, we barely got through the gates of the fortress ahead of the enemy. That was when it was discovered that Moncada wasn't with us—he had been injured and captured by the rebels. I hope they treat him with respect; he is a decent man, not like Corella.'

222

Niccolò had heard much the same, though all things were relative when you considered the crew of cut-throats with whom Borgia surrounded himself. 'But you are here now, safe and sound.'

'Yes, I am, a little shaken up but otherwise none the worse for wear and happy to be back working on something constructive again. Cesare wants me to complete a survey of the town and fortress and to give him recommendations as to how the defences of both can be improved.'

'A task that is a long way from painting.'

'Ah well, I am done with painting. It takes too long.' Thus the most innovative artist that Florence had ever produced dismissed his achievements, in favour of his new obsessions. 'Mathematics and science, engineering, hydraulics, those are the things that interest me these days. Real things, of brick and earth and wood and metal, useful things.'

'For a man with such interests, the duke must be a congenial employer.'

'He is indulgent, as I said.' Da Vinci shrugged, downing his glass of wine and waving to the serving-girl for another jug. 'He asks me to make maps and plans for his fortifications, devise machines for war, all of which I do willingly, in exchange for a certain amount of freedom to investigate the other subjects that interest me.'

'But you are his chief military engineer. I imagine he would expect you to attend his war-councils and give him advice, as he does his other captains. That must take up some time?'

Da Vinci sent him a sharp look. 'He confides in me, yes, if that is what you are asking, as he does in others. He is not an easy man to know, mind you, very secretive. What is it that you want of me, Messer Machiavelli?'

'Just this—when you can, tell me anything that might be of use to Florence, what Borgia is thinking, what is said in his councils that might affect Florentine interests, rumours you hear, that sort of thing.'

Da Vinci focused his attention on his newly-refilled wine glass, rolling it back and forth in his hands so that a little of the red liquid slopped onto the table. When he looked up, his eyebrows were arched in a question. 'I might do such a thing for you personally, Niccolò. You seem to be a man I could trust. But Florence has done little to endear herself to me lately.'

223

'That is understandable. Perhaps I can do something that might raise your standing in Florence just a little. Denunciations made to the Office of the Night are not easily expunged from the records, but I might be able to arrange for such a thing to happen.'

Da Vinci's laugh was a mirthless bark. 'The last time such an intervention had to be made on my behalf, it was the Magnificent Lorenzo who did the meddling. I am lucky to know so many powerful men, am I not? You have a bargain, Messer Machiavelli.' The artist's hand shot across the table and gripped Niccolò's in a powerful shake.

'I am no Lorenzo de' Medici, my friend, just a middling public servant. But I promise I will do everything I can to ensure that your record with the state is as white as virgin snow.'

Their bargain sealed, they sat and talked for a little longer, da Vinci wistfully recalling his days working in Milan for Duke Ludovico Sforza, Niccolò telling stories from his time trailing the French court. They said nothing more to each other about the agreement they had struck until, leaving the tavern and walking out into the late afternoon sun, da Vinci took Niccolò by the sleeve and steered him into the shade of one of the arcades of the Palazzo Riario.

'I'll tell you the one thing Borgia is worried about right now,' he said, his voice low and conspiratorial. 'So far, the rebels have been slow to follow up their advantages, the victory at Calmazzo and so on. He is mortally afraid they will combine and descend on him before he has got the reinforcements he is waiting for from France and his own lands here in the Romagna.'

Having delivered himself of this intelligence, da Vinci turned and walked off to return to his workshop, where young Salai would no doubt be sulking, leaving Niccolò to contemplate his last words, which the artist had no doubt intended as a demonstration of his bona fides.

Back at his lodgings, Niccolò found a pleasant surprise waiting. Antonio had laid out on his bed the contents of a parcel that must have arrived while he was out. It was an elegant new doublet that Marietta had sent to him, accompanied by a bolt of velvet cloth that he could have made into a new robe. Given the threadbare state to which his clothes had been reduced by the constant wear and tear of travelling, both were very welcome indeed. Even more welcome were the letters from Biagio and Agostino that had accompanied the clothes.

Biagio's letter was, as always, full of office gossip and scurrilous jokes at the expense of Antonio della Valle. They had worn each other out, it seemed, and their feud had shifted from a spitting high melodrama into a minor key, a game of silly pranks and name-calling that nevertheless had Niccolò (and no doubt the rest of the chancellery) in stitches of laughter. Agostino, too, was mostly concerned with office politics, though his letter was written in his elegant Latin and filled with the sly erudite references that Niccolò always found hugely enjoyable. Both men lamented his absence, Biagio in his usual clinging way, Agostino more concerned with the problems of managing the politics of Florence.

More worrying was the veiled suggestion in Agostino's letter that there were those in the body politic of Florence who were resentful of Niccolò's position and sought to undermine him, even though he remained in favour with the gonfaloniere and Signoria.

Then there was his wife. It seemed that she had been making a great fuss about the fact that he had been away for more than the eight days he had so rashly promised, sending her brother Lanciolino to pester Biagio and others in the chancellery. He frowned in irritation. He had only been gone for ten days. With a little spurt of self-righteousness, he told himself that her complaint was a little premature. Still, there was not much he could do about it except to ask Biagio to soothe her as best he could. And perhaps he would write to Antonio della Valle and ask him to send his wife Agostanza around to the Machiavelli house to explain how the world worked and make her duty plain.

*

The next morning, Niccolò was summoned to the duke's presence at an uncharacteristically early hour by a particularly peremptory young page. Following the boy through the deserted streets, one part of his mind was preoccupied with the many possible reasons for his summons, the other registering the change in the weather that late October had brought—there was no warmth left in the sun, the skies were a dull and depressing grey, and the chill wind blew the leaves to and fro in little eddies and washed them up in piles against the doorsteps. He shivered and pulled his robe more closely about his narrow frame.

Contrary to all the foreboding that had built up on the short walk to the Rocca, Borgia seemed to be in a cheerful mood, smiling and beckoning him across the room. The smile had more than a hint of mischief about it, the reasons for which became clear as he handed Niccolò a document and bade him read it while the duke stood, arms crossed on his chest in his usual stance, toes tapping with impatience as he anticipated Secretary Machiavelli's reaction.

The letter, from Monseigneur d'Arles at the French court in Milan, informed the duke that the Florentine ambassadors had presented themselves to deliver their appeal to King Louis for direction as to how to deal with Borgia. Apparently, the king had quite forcefully told the Florentines that they should do everything they could to support the duke. So that was the end of that ploy.

Borgia could barely wait for him to finish reading. 'You see, Machiavelli? I told you that Louis would support me and tell your ambassadors to do the same. Now, you must write to your Signoria and tell them to send me ten squadrons of cavalry.'

He wanted to argue, but this letter left him exposed, conveying as it did events of which his political masters had not seen fit to inform him. He could only nod and await the next demand.

'And tell them—again—that I am ready to form a firm alliance with Florence, which is in accord with the expressed will of the king, and which, if they are sensible, they will now make haste to conclude..'

This encounter set the pattern for the next few days. Niccolò found himself summoned to the ducal apartments in the Rocca at all hours of the day and night and, at each meeting, he was treated to some demonstration of his growing strength—a letter from King Louis to the Venetian Republic supporting Borgia's campaign in the Romagna, a report that French soldiers were expected any moment–followed by renewed demands of one kind or another on Florence. Niccolò did his best to parry each stroke as skilfully as he could, telling Borgia over and over again that Florence wanted nothing more than peace and friendship with him.

'He really does think he has gained the upper hand,' Leonardo da Vinci told him one afternoon when, exhausted after a particularly long session with the duke, he had dropped by the artist's little workshop in a secluded corner of the Rocca. 'The rebels seem to be paralysed. Have you ever seen a rabbit confronted by an angry snake? That kind of paralysis. While they are sitting around shitting themselves with fear, he has been busy garrisoning castles and strong points.'

'But I also heard that rebel troops are at Doccia, just three miles from here.'

'And at Castel San Piero. But these are minor places. Borgia holds Cesena, Forlì, Faenza and Imola as secure as you like, and they are the heart of his dukedom.'

'I see your plan of Imola is almost completed,' Niccolò said, changing the subject. The map in question was lying on the table, an extraordinarily precise view of the city as if from the perspective of a bird. He had never seen anything like this, a thing of both utility and beauty.

'I am rather pleased with it,' Leonardo said, joining Niccolò at the table. 'It is a new science, making these kinds of maps. One has to combine exact measurements with the imagination to be able to see what it would look like if one were hovering far above, like a hawk. I find the combination of mathematics and aesthetics pleasing.'

Something else struck Niccolò about the map. 'The Rocca doesn't look like that. Did your imagination get carried away?'

'No, no.' Leonardo laughed. 'They are proposed improvements to the fortifications. I do have to earn my keep occasionally, you know.'

That evening, Niccolò began to wonder whether *he* was earning his keep on this mission. What was he doing here? The minor matters which were his ostensible reason for being in Imola, had long been settled. As usual, he had no authority to negotiate anything, particularly now that Borgia had made his main demands clear, and he felt his presence was redundant. He missed his wife and little daughter and, of course, the family business affairs were being sadly neglected. On an impulse, he added a codicil to his despatch, asking to be relieved of his position and brought home.

The reply came a few days later in the form of a kindly personal letter from Piero Soderini. The gonfaloniere expressed his sympathy with Niccolò's feelings, but told him, firmly and politely, that he was needed where he was, and that his duty was to remain with Duke Valentino until he was recalled. Soderini added a few flattering words to say that the Signoria had come to find his reports invaluable, and daily commended him for his work.

It seemed he was not to be released just yet.

Chapter 21—An Uneasy Peace

Imola, October to December 1502

Winter's darkness had descended on the Rocca as Niccolò, having concluded an audience with the duke during which Borgia had seemed unusually on edge, hurried across the courtyard, a cloak pulled close against the wind and one hand clamped onto his hat to prevent it flying away. A glance at the sky told him that a storm was on its way, and he was anxious to get back to his lodgings before the heavens opened.

He was a few yards from the gatehouse when a horse and rider erupted from the darkness of its arch and cantered to a halt. Its rider, in the livery of one of Borgia's couriers, slid off the horse's back and, staggering slightly as he landed, turned his face towards where Niccolò stood, waiting to pass.

That face was the familiar jowly countenance of Paolo Orsini, whom he had last seen in Urbino, and Niccolò could not stop himself from laughing at the absurdity of the encounter. 'Well, Signor Paolo, is this to be your new profession? A courier?'

Orsini pouted, no doubt completely put out that his ruse, such as it was, should be so easily penetrated. 'I am here for confidential consultations with Cesare,' he spluttered, 'so some disguise was necessary. So that I could pass through the countryside unrecognised.'

'Oh? Are you going to make peace with him, then?'

'That is my business, and not yours, Messer Secretary. Now, if you will excuse me...' Orsini bounded off in the direction of the palace, leaving his horse to be led away by a groom who had met him at the gate. The rebel conspirator was obviously expected, which explained why Borgia had been so restless. And Orsini could only be there because the rebels had decided to sue for peace.

They were pathetic. Having bloodied Borgia's nose, they'd had the upper hand for weeks. All they had to do was to press him hard, and they would have had a good chance of bringing him down. Instead, they vacillated, making half-hearted jabs at him while he built up his strength. And now, if Orsini really

229

was here to negotiate a peace agreement, they seemed to have lost their nerve entirely.

A spatter of rain recalled him to the moment and he hurried off, exchanging pleasantries with the guards, with whom he was by now on familiar terms, and made his way across the moat into the relative shelter of the town's narrow streets. Still, he only just managed to avoid a drenching, and his cloak was steaming when he took it off and draped it before the fire that Luca had lit in his room. Pouring himself wine, he sat at his table and pulled pen and paper towards him in readiness for his usual evening routine of writing up the events of the day.

*

It was as if the sudden and clandestine arrival of Paolo Orsini had turned off a tap. In the following days Niccolò, who had spoken with the duke almost every day since he had arrived, found himself unable to get admittance to Cesare Borgia's presence. It was all done with great politeness, but the refusals were nevertheless adamant. His excellency was engaged with his ministers, or he was seeing no one that day, or he was about to leave on some unspecified journey. The duke was little seen outside his apartments and the life of the fortress and town seemed to go on without his involvement.

Rumours swirled and settled for a moment before taking flight again. The silk merchants in the little tavern near the piazza said that traders coming in from Urbino had reported that Duke Guidobaldo, now settled back into the ducal palace, was assembling an army to attack Valentino. Vitellozzo Vitelli was said to be sick again, suffering from the French disease, that mysterious pox that had come into Italy with the French armies. Another rumour held that Valentino was himself about to leave and march… somewhere. Yet, though messengers came and went on their furious errands, there was little sign that the army that had gathered so painstakingly around Imola was going anywhere.

'I can't imagine that Guidobaldo will stir far from Urbino, now he has recovered it,' he said to Leonardo one afternoon. They had contrived to escape from the city and, it being an unusually pleasant day for October, were sitting on a grassy bank of the river Santerno a little outside the town, where the road to Faenza crossed a rickety-looking wooden bridge. Leonardo was sketching the scene in one of his little notebooks, while Niccolò idly tossed a stone from hand to hand.

230

'I think Borgia would agree with you. He calls him "the boy", and says he is nothing like his father.'

'He's not. About the only thing he has in common with old Frederico is a love of art and music.' Niccolò moodily skimmed the stone across the sluggish surface of the water, watching it skip a couple of times before sinking. 'So what is Cesare waiting for? Surely his army is big enough by now to deal with the rebels.'

'He's still waiting for the French soldiers to arrive, I think. They have been taking an age to get here.' Leonardo closed his notebook and put his lump of charcoal into a pocket. 'By the way, do you know Tommaso Spinelli?'

'Spinelli? Giovanni Bentivoglio's man, who pretends he just a courier? What about him? Last I heard he was in Bologna.'

'He's not: I ran into him in the duke's anteroom this morning,' Leonardo said. 'He's usually as tight-lipped as a priest in the confessional, but for some reason he was quite chatty today. I don't think he meant to, but he let slip that Bentivoglio is preparing to abandon the rebellion altogether.'

'You bastard,' Niccolò said without rancour. 'That really is priceless news. You could have told me sooner.'

Leonardo laughed, and glanced towards the city. 'Always keep the best until last. Spinelli also told me that Bentivoglio wants Cesare to assure him that he will not be attacked and for that promise to be guaranteed by the King of France.'

'Is that all?' Niccolò laughed. 'No doubt Cesare will make whatever promises he thinks he must, but whether he will actually get a formal guarantee from Louis or d'Amboise, that is another thing entirely. And why would Bentivoglio trust the word of the French, since they have thrown him to the Borgia wolf once already?'

'How would I know, Niccolò?' Leonardo said irritably. 'I am just an artist and engineer. The motivations of these rascals is well beyond my understanding. All I can do, in return for my freedom, is to report what I hear.'

Niccolò didn't miss the oblique little protest, which made him feel guilty, for though he had written secretly to Gonfaloniere Soderini to ask him to investigate the case and get Leonardo's record expunged, so far there had been

231

no reply. 'Don't worry, my friend,' he said, raising his hands in a placatory gesture. 'I am sure I will get word any day now. Piero is probably just being thorough and making sure that all the right paperwork is done before writing back to me.'

'I am not in much of a position to bargain, am I?' Leonardo was sour. 'I must get back. I left Salai alone at the workshop, mixing up plaster. He will be bored by now and that is never a good thing with him.'

Not for the first time, Niccolò wondered what Leonardo saw in the admittedly handsome but endlessly troublesome Salai. But then he was the first to admit that while he could easily see through the wiles and political strategy of statesmen, he was frequently dumbfounded by the more prosaic impulses of his fellow men. For a few moments he contemplated Leonardo's broad back as he made his way up the bank and onto the muddy and rutted road into town, and then turned back to face the river. The gentle play of sunlight on the brown surface and the whisper of the breeze through the reeds that lined the riverbank soothed his agitated mind and allowed him to think.

It seemed obvious that Borgia was playing for time, waiting for the last of his soldiers to turn up, steadily amassing all the material that an army needed to make war—gunpowder and saltpetre, cannons and cannonballs, supplies of swords and pikes and halberds, food stores for the march, horses and wagons to carry it all. Enough to crush this rebellion if he were so minded.

Meanwhile he was playing his adversaries off against each other, splitting them up. That was why Paolo Orsini was making clandestine visits, and Giovanni Bentivoglio was sending his trusted adviser to Imola. Negotiating with them all would also take time, and keep them off balance. It was a clever strategy.

Another thought sent a chill down his back. What if Borgia was genuine in dangling the possibility of a renewed alliance with these treacherous captains of his? Could it be that he had promised them that, having reconciled and combined their forces, they would turn on some third party? A common enemy that could furnish them with sufficient plunder that their greed would overcome their distrust of each other, and their mutual fear of Borgia? And of course, of all the states in northern Italy, poorly-defended Florence was the easiest target for such a venture. That idea would certainly appeal to Vitellozzo and Orsini, and probably Baglioni as well.

But would King Louis allow Borgia to go in that direction? So far, he had kept his word and warned Borgia off from any such move; then again, there was the example of Bologna, which the French had abandoned without a backward glance. The future of his city might once again hang by the slender thread of the French king's whim.

Perhaps that was why Borgia was suddenly inaccessible to him. Maybe the king had privily agreed to turn a blind eye to such a scheme and Borgia didn't want him to have any hint of it. Getting to his feet and following the footsteps of his fellow Florentine back towards the walls and gates of Imola, he realised that he would need a lot more of Leonardo's help to find out what was going on.

*

Weeks went by, October became November, and still Niccolò was unable to get time alone with Borgia, though he did see him at a distance from time to time, either in the palace or marching across the courtyard of the Rocca accompanied by the usual gaggle of officers and civilian underlings. Leonardo had disappeared into the bowels of the fortress, working on some project or another, so he was left to try and sniff out from his other sources whatever clues he could about what was going on.

One of those sources was Alessandro Spannochi. Niccolò had finally received from his Florentine bankers a draft for a loan of forty ducats, not a huge sum, but enough to keep him in funds when added to his salary, and he had arranged to meet with the banker to have the draft converted to cash.

'Here you are, my friend.' Alessandro pushed the small pile of coins across his desk and watched complacently as Niccolò put them away in his purse. 'If I can be of service again, you must let me know.'

Niccolò nodded his thanks, doing his best to hide the embarrassment he felt at having to resort to private loans in order to meet the considerable expenses of his mission. The Signoria, of course, promised to reimburse him eventually, but he thought he would probably be retired on his farm by the time they got around to honouring their promises.

Private business completed, he thought he might as well attempt to do some public business as well.

'So tell me, Sandro, what do you hear?'

'Nico, you're a crafty devil, asking me tricky questions like that.' Alessandro chuckled. 'You won't trap me with your cleverness!' Niccolò just waited, one eyebrow raised. 'Actually, there is some news I can give you. You know that we have been negotiating with the rebels?'

'Everyone does. Messengers have been going in and out of here every day for weeks.'

'Yes, but what everyone doesn't know is that Cesare has agreed to the main heads of the treaty with the rebels. The Orsini and Vitellozzo are to provide hostages and they are obligated to join their forces with ours to recover Urbino. In return, they will be given a full pardon by the pope and their services will be engaged on the same terms they had before.'

'Well, that was easy. You must work on your defences, my friend, lest you give up all your state secrets. Let me try you with another—I also heard that Cesare is considering making a separate agreement with Giovanni Bentivoglio.'

'That fact is obviously not as closely held as it should be,' Alessandro said, though he didn't seem at all put out. 'But there's no harm in confirming it since you already know. Yes, Cesare will make peace with him, we are just haggling over the price.'

'Forgive me, Sandro, but I am dizzied by these changes of direction. After all, it was not so long ago that the duke was planning a campaign to attack Bologna.'

Spannochi shrugged. 'It's simple enough, Niccolò. Cesare just has come to believe that it will serve his purposes better to have Bentivoglio as a friend, rather than to drive him out of Bologna and be left in possession of territory he might well struggle to hold.'

That made sense, though it was unexpected. Perhaps Borgia was learning that statecraft might produce more long-lasting results than violent conquest. Or it could simply be that his position was weaker than he was trying to make out.

'And the others? The Orsini and Vitellozzo? They will learn of this negotiation of Cesare's soon enough, I expect. How will you justify it to them,

234

dealing separately with Bentivoglio while at the same time negotiating a peace treaty that is supposed to embrace them all?'

'Oh, that's easy enough.' Alessandro's laughter was merry. 'We'll just tell them that King Louis insisted on it!'

Niccolò smiled at the audacity of the lie, though he had little doubt that the conspirators would believe every word.

'If he didn't have to, Cesare wouldn't deal with any of them,' Alessandro went on, resuming a more serious expression. 'Thinks they are simpletons. He can't bear to hear Vitellozzo's name, you know. Calls him a venomous serpent and wishes he had never entered into negotiations with him. But he does have to keep some relations with the Orsini because when the pope dies, he will need their support in Rome.'

'When the pope dies? But the Holy Father is in robust good health, from everything that one hears from Rome.'

'So he is. But he is also seventy years old, and has immoderate habits. Cesare knows he can't last forever, and so he has to think about the future, after his father is dead.'

Niccolò thought about that. Papal support gave Borgia two advantages: legitimacy, as the captain-general of the papal armies, and the money that flowed from the papal treasury. So if and when his father died, he would have to find some way to secure both. To do that, he would have to ensure that the next pope was someone who would be favourable to him: hence his caution with the Orsini, who controlled a bloc of votes in the college of cardinals. Niccolò was beginning to see the outlines of the Borgia strategy.

'And he can't rely on France forever,' he mused, trying to draw more out of Borgia's young treasurer. 'King Louis and the cardinal will follow their own interests, which won't always coincide with those of the duke.'

'That goes without saying. For now, the French are omnipotent in Italy, but that will not always be so. I told you that Cesare plans for everything, and this is no exception. For example, he has written to the pope asking him to secure a cardinal's hat for Francesco Gonzaga's brother, and has proposed to marry his little daughter to Francesco's son, so as to tie Mantua more closely to him.'

That was another surprise, for Borgia had been dragooned into a pact with the Marquis of Mantua only at the behest of King Louis; this suggested he now wanted to make a temporary alliance of convenience into something more permanent.

'And his sister Lucrezia is already married to the heir of the Duke of Ferrara, he is being paid a subsidy by the Venetians, and he is supported by King Louis, who rules Lombardy. So he will have alliances of one kind or another with every power in the north of Italy, and if he can make peace with Bentivoglio he will have Bologna in his pocket as well. Very neat.' Niccolò folded his arms across his chest, pleased with himself.

'Bravo, my friend. Cesare's objective is to make sure that, before his father dies, he has a secure and well-governed state that is protected by friendly relations with all its neighbours. That is why getting a treaty with Florence is so important to him. You must admit, too, that such an arrangement has some advantages for you.'

Spannochi's attempt to seem guileless almost made Niccolò laugh out loud. 'Perhaps, but it should also be obvious to you why we could not ever appoint Duke Valentino as captain of our armies. The experience of Italy in the last ten years tells me one thing—alliances between princes are best maintained by arms. Only the power of arms can enforce the observance of the terms of any treaty. However rich she is, Florence is weak as a military power. So what security could we have if three fourths or more of our troops are under the control of the duke? How then would we ensure that the terms of any treaty are enforced?'

Spannochi laughed. 'Why do you think that Cesare was so relaxed when you told him he couldn't have that particular plum? He never thought the Signoria would bite. But he still wants the alliance.'

'He may well get it,' Niccolò said, gathering up his papers and preparing to leave. 'But if you will allow me one more observation: though Duke Cesare's intentions may be honourable, he has a history that does not inspire confidence. The Florentine Signoria may seem indecisive, but it is made up of prudent men who are too cautious to open themselves to deception. They will want to see more evidence that the duke's actions are consistent with his promises before they will commit.'

236

The younger man's easy-going smile was undisturbed as he embraced Niccolò in farewell. 'No doubt they will be guided by your sage advice, my friend. Now, enough of all this seriousness. Are you going to Clara's tonight?'

Clara's was a discreet little brothel hidden away in the north-west quarter of Imola that Niccolò had been in the habit of frequenting as a distraction from the frustrations of his mission. Surprised that Alessandro knew that he went there, he nodded cautiously, prompting his young friend to clap his hands and give a little yelp of pleasure.

'Good. I'll meet you there: Clara is throwing a private drinking party out the back to show off some of her new girls. I'm sure she won't mind if you come as my guest.'

It was much later that night when Niccolò, arriving back at his lodgings with a buzzing head and unsteady feet, settled down to compose his daily despatch. Absentmindedly cutting a new quill, his thoughts went back to his conversation that morning. Alessandro's frankness had been quite deliberate, of that he was sure, probably at his master's instruction.

Which meant that the duke wanted the Florentine government to believe that Borgia's strategy was changing. The suggestion that he was planning for whatever would happen after the death of his father was startling enough. But he also seemed to have recognised that an aggressive campaign of conquest against all his neighbours was, for now, beyond his powers, even with the king and pope behind him. Borgia could, of course, just be bluffing again, and would return to his plundering ways when he felt that he had sufficient strength once more.

Of one thing Niccolò was now certain: Borgia would prevail against his rebels. They would be seduced or cowed into submission, or he would defeat them in the field. And Florence would have to come to terms with the reality of a strong, well-armed neighbour in the Romagna.

*

The note, delivered to his room by the breathlessly curious youngest son of the candle-maker, seemed at first sight to be gibberish, merely scratched markings scrawled across the page. But Niccolò recognised it instantly as Leonardo's ingenious private code. He wrote back-to-front so that what looked like nonsense was easily intelligible when held up to a mirror. The artist had demonstrated the technique one afternoon in his workshop, to his guest's astonishment.

'I have become so adept at using this method,' he had said gleefully, 'that I can write my notes as quickly and easily as you write your despatches.'

Smiling as he recalled Leonardo's child-like enthusiasm, he rummaged among the items on his table for a small looking-glass and held the note up against it so that its contents became clear. It was brief enough.

Come to the workshop in one hour and Salai will bring you to me. I have news that can only be shared in private.

Salai, when he arrived at the workshop door, was as truculent as ever, muttering under his breath that Niccolò was to follow him close behind. This proved to be unexpectedly challenging, as the young man sped down dark streets and through tiny alleys at a pace which Niccolò found hard to match. Salai was, he realised, playing a childish game, one which Niccolò was determined not to allow him to win. Even so, he was breathless when, to Salai's obvious disappointment, they arrived at a house somewhere in the back streets of Imola.

A knock brought Leonardo to the door. 'Salai made you run, did he?' Leonardo laughed, watching Niccolò's ill-disguised attempt to get his breath back. Salai stood by, an insolent grin on his face getting the better of his attempt to feign innocence. 'One day, young man, your impudence will land you in gaol. Now go and get us some wine.'

'Next time, you might send a more sedate messenger,' Niccolò puffed. 'Now, what was it that was so important that I had to half-kill myself getting here?'

'The treaty with the rebels has been signed and sealed at last.'

'I knew that.' Niccolò was terse, in no mood to submit to Leonardo's teasing. 'Alessandro told me this morning.'

'But I bet he didn't tell you the terms.'

'No-one knows them, or so he said. Apparently only Borgia and Geraldini know what they are.'

238

'Yes. Geraldini has the only copy.' He picked up his big leather satchel, worn almost through in places from prolonged use, fished inside and pulled out a sheaf of papers, putting them down with a flourish on the table for Niccolò to inspect. 'And here it is.'

Niccolò's jaw dropped, and Leonardo's cheeky grin grew even wider. 'I filched it from his desk. He is supposed to be away for a day or two, but I can't risk him coming back early, so you'll have to copy it out now, before you leave.'

Niccolò nodded, only half-hearing him. It wouldn't take long to copy, for it was a brief document. The confederates were to be re-engaged, in exchange for pardons, and it was agreed they would let bygones be bygones. Interestingly, these simple provisions were hedged about with requirements for hostages and the like, that suggested that all of the parties to the agreement were mired in mistrust and suspicion.

He read it again, more slowly, looking for the matter of most importance to him, and was relieved to confirm his first impression: there was nothing in the treaty to suggest that Borgia and his newly-reconciled captains were planning any kind of assault on Florence or any of her Tuscan possessions. In fact, it confirmed that the immediate objective for their combined military action was to be the recapture of Urbino.

'Well done, Leonardo, my friend. Well done indeed, this is a real coup. I will send Antonio off to Florence first thing tomorrow with the copy in his saddlebags.'

As he set to work copying out the text of the treaty, half of Niccolò's mind was busy assessing the situation. With the treaty agreed and ratified and an agreement with Bologna no doubt not far away, Borgia was well on the way to neutralising his former enemies. French and Swiss soldiers had been arriving all week and it was believed the rest would be in Imola in a few days. That left only the hapless Montefeltro of Urbino to deal with.

His task completed, he made ready to go, folding the papers into his doublet for safety. He was at the door when he recollected another piece of news, one of great importance to Leonardo. 'I am sorry, I almost forgot—Ser Piero wrote to me privately yesterday and said that he has your case with the Office of the Night well in hand and that you should not fret as to its outcome. He added some warm words of praise for your assistance to me so far.'

'I truly do not know what to say. Except thank you.' The slow smile that invaded Leonardo's usually stern visage was the best reward Niccolò could have had, for he had come to like this big and gentle man a great deal over the last month.

Chapter 22—A Frustrated Diplomat

Imola, November 1502

It was infuriating. After all his diligence in reporting everything he had learned and everything he thought, some in the Signoria were displeased with him because he had not written anything for a few days. One of Biagio's letters had hinted as much, but it was galling to have their unhappiness expressed directly in a terse note included with the other more routine correspondence. It was not his fault. He had given his precious despatches to an idiot of a messenger who, unfamiliar with the route, had managed to get himself lost on the way back to Florence.

To this was added the frustration that he had little new to tell them. Since sending off the treaty, his every attempt to get an audience with Borgia had been rebuffed, and his other sources—Agapito, Spannochi, even Leonardo—seemed unable or unwilling to give him any other news.

Abandoning his usual caution, he allowed some of his annoyance to find its way into his latest missive.

> *Please bear in mind that matters here cannot be guessed at. You must understand that we have to do here with a prince who governs by himself, and to avoid writing mere fancies one must study matters well. Thus time passes, which I do my best to spend advantageously.*

Was that too sharp? Perhaps, but it was time that these critics of his were given a lesson in the realities with which he was dealing. His pen moved purposefully across the paper and, before long, he had covered three pages with his observations, sarcastically reminding them of everything he had already communicated. At the end, he added some trivial observations about the price of wheat in Imola and the of spices in Venice, as if to say, *You see, I neglect nothing in my reporting to you!* Sealing it up, he felt a cathartic pleasure. If they wouldn't recall him—something he was beginning to long for—they could put up with his impertinences.

The days went past, November was drawing to a close without any audience with the duke, and he was forced to rely on the rumours that circulated among the silk merchants and in the taverns to pad out his reports back to Florence and forestall any further complaints from the Signoria. He was at least a little reassured by several kind and encouraging letters from Piero Soderini, who urged him to stay at his post and told him that his despatches were being well-received.

Other letters from Florence were less comforting. His wife, according to Biagio, was still complaining about the length of his absence (she now had some justification, he had to admit) and had gone to stay with her sister so as not to be alone. The Signoria and the Great Council, notwithstanding their repeated expressions of confidence in him, seemed unable to bring themselves to vote the necessary appropriations to reimburse his expenses, making it necessary for him, again, to go cap in hand looking for loans. He thanked God for Biagio, who was tireless on his behalf, if a little peevish in his letters. And Totto seemed to be getting along with things, making a good fist of managing the farm and the other family business concerns while he was away.

To make matters worse, for the first time in his life, his health was poor. The onset of cold weather, the drafts that whistled through the poorly-made shutters of his room, the burden of overwork and his generally melancholy frame of mind all combined to weaken his frame. He developed a persistent cough and was stricken by a bout of fever that sent him scurrying off to bed for a day or two, tended by the faithful Antonio and the candle-maker's wife, whose efficient matronly care eventually restored him enough so he was at least able to resume his work. But the fever had left him weakened and the cough worse.

One evening, driven by a need for some company other than that of his two servants, Niccolò made his way to Leonardo's lodgings, bringing a meagre meal of cheese and bread, cold meat and a flask of wine. There he found the artist deeply engrossed in sketching Salai, who was sitting in the corner of the room in front of the fire, restringing his lute. The young man had a sweet tenor voice and had occasionally entertained them with simple peasant songs that he had learned as a child in his village.

Niccolò found something comforting about this little domestic scene and he settled himself on a stool and watched Leonardo work for a while, the strong face furrowed in concentration and the big hands ceaselessly moving as he wielded the charcoal. After a little while, he looked up, almost as if he had noticed Niccolò for the first time. 'Now you see me at my true vocation, friend Niccolò.'

'I thought you had given it up.'

'Painting, yes, though I will go back to it before long. I just needed a break, I think.'

Niccolò picked up a sketch that was lying on the table, a drawing of a kind of conical platform that seemed to have wheels so that it could be moved. He held it up to Leonardo, his brow raised in a silent query.

'I draw those things to satisfy Cesare.' The artist laughed. 'He always wants new ways of making war, so I let my imagination go to work. I am half afraid he will try and build some of them. Take that one, for example. He insisted I should make him a set of more detailed plans so that his workshops could try and make it.'

'It looks horribly lethal. What are these, cannons?' Niccolò pointed at the barrels that protruded all around the circumference of the cone's base.

'If they can ever build it, it would be a horrifying thing.' The smile turned sly. 'They might be able to construct it, but they'll never be able to make it work because I've hidden a few little traps they will never be able to figure out.'

Now it was Niccolò's turn to laugh. He could imagine the frustrated carpenters and armourers and the wrath of Cesare Borgia. Leonardo had told him once that he hated war and was working for Borgia only out of necessity, as Niccolò well knew.

'It's just an intellectual exercise, Niccolò,' Leonardo said, reading his thoughts. 'I can't imagine them ever being used. Pass that bloody wine flask, would you? Before Salai gets to it and downs the lot.'

The youth grimaced, poked his tongue out at the artist, and, this mute protest done, went back to strumming his lute and absent-mindedly humming a tune.

'The deal with the rebels seems to be common knowledge,' Niccolò said, tearing apart some bread and dipping it in a small bowl of olive oil. 'The silk traders were all nattering about it this morning.'

243

'So much for it being a secret.' Leonardo poured wine for them both. 'By the way, I overheard Spannochi grousing to Geraldini about the cost of buying off Giovanni Bentivoglio: apparently, he is to be paid a subsidy of nine thousand ducats a year.'

Niccolò whistled. 'I'm not surprised Alessandro is complaining. So, that just leaves Guidobaldo da Montefeltro, in Urbino. He must be feeling very uncomfortable, now all his co-conspirators seem to have reached an accommodation with Valentino.'

'Just a matter of time, I would say.' Leonardo shrugged; he had little interest in the fate of the young duke of Urbino. 'Now, if you look under that pile of papers there, you'll find a sketch of something really interesting…'

Niccolò listened with only half his mind as Leonardo launched into his explanation of a system he had devised to lift water from a well by pumping air into the bottom. The other half was busy evaluating what he had just been told.

With Orsini, Vitellozzo, Baglioni and the rest all neutralised, Bologna bought off, and Urbino isolated, the pattern of things was becoming clearer. But as he finally made his way back to his own lodgings through the cold night, he reflected that the biggest question of all was still unanswered: where was Borgia going to strike next? Once he had secured Urbino, would he then turn on Florence? Only the duke himself was likely to give him an answer to that question, and Niccolò resolved to seek an audience once more.

To his surprise, his request for an audience when he lodged it with Agapito Geraldini the following morning was met with an instant approval.

'His excellency had been planning to send for you anyway, Machiavelli.' The secretary was, as usual, sourly disapproving of his Florentine counterpart; quite why he so had excited the man's antipathy was something that Niccolò had never been able to fathom. 'But he is in Faenza, won't be back until this afternoon, so you will have to wait until then.'

Though he arrived promptly at the appointed hour, it was no surprise to be kept waiting in the anteroom while various officials came and went; the sun was setting by the time he was finally admitted.

244

For the first time since Niccolò had arrived in Imola, Borgia looked tired. The handsome face was pale, there were dark smudges under the eyes, and two deep frown lines seemed to have etched themselves between his eyebrows. His skin, moreover, was blotched beneath the surface. Niccolò wondered again about the rumour that Borgia had contracted the French pox; one of the symptoms of the disease was this kind of skin condition. But it was just as likely that he was simply exhausted from the continual strain of trying to outwit his foes.

Nevertheless, his mood seemed cheerful enough. 'I am sorry, Messer Secretary, that I have not been able to see you for some time. We have been busy, eh Michelotto?'

With a shock, Niccolò realised that they were not alone in the room, the winter's evening gloom only slightly relieved by the uneven, flickering light from half a dozen candles placed here and there. Emerging from the shadows, the tall and lean figure of Michelotto da Corella came over and casually draped itself over one of the empty chairs in front of the low fire that was burning in the fireplace, a mocking smile on the dark unshaven face. This was the first time that Niccolò had laid eyes on Borgia's closest henchman, the Spaniard who, it was said, had strangled the duke's brother-in-law at his orders. Niccolò found it easy to believe that this impassive man with the fathomless dark eyes was a cold-blooded killer.

'Don't mind me, signor,' he said, his voice a gentle purr, 'just pretend I'm not here.'

Easier said than done, Niccolò thought, turning back to an equally amused Borgia.

'Excellency, it is true I have missed our regular chats,' he said, still unsettled by the saturnine presence behind him, 'but your servants have been generous in keeping me abreast of most matters of importance.' It was hardly true, but he wasn't going to give Borgia the satisfaction of knowing how frustrating it was to have been frozen out.

'Just as well: we must keep you in credit with the gonfaloniere and the Signoria, eh?' the duke grinned. 'And what of the treaty with Florence that I asked for? Can I assume that, since you have not come running to my door begging to be let in with good news, that your government is still

245

procrastinating? Even after King Louis has directed them to assist me in every way?'

Niccolò's silence was an eloquent answer to that barrage of questions.

'Never mind, Messer Secretary. Don't trouble yourself about it. I am not sure I can trust your double-dealing Signoria anyway.'

Niccolò felt as though the temperature in the room had suddenly dropped. 'Excellency? I don't understand.'

'No? Then let me enlighten you. When Paolo Orsini was last here, he told me that your damnable Signoria had sent two envoys to him to propose that if he would undertake to serve Florence in their war against Pisa, they would make would make him captain of their forces. The same position they deny me. He says he declined their offer, even though there was nothing to stop him from accepting it. What do you say to that?'

The idea that Florence would employ Paolo Orsini in any capacity was ridiculous, though Niccolò resisted the urge to say so, instead drawing a breath and looking the duke steadily in the eye.

'Excellency, did Signor Paolo give you the names of the two Florentine envoys?'

'No, he did not.'

'And did he show you their letters of credence? Or any other paper to prove their bona fides?'

'Of course not. He's not a complete fool,' Borgia said impatiently.

'And, excellency, has Signor Paolo ever told you any lies before now?'

There was a moment of disbelieving silence, and then Borgia laughed and clapped his hands. 'Ah, you have me there, Niccolò. Signor Paolo has told me plenty of lies. All right, I believe you.' Another pause, and the duke's smile became a little coy. 'I should have seen through Orsini's stupid little gambit right from the start, shouldn't I? Perhaps you should tell your government that I did, so there are no misunderstandings.'

'Of course, excellency. The avoidance of misunderstanding is a diplomat's chief responsibility.'

'Good. Then let us see what else we can do to improve their understanding of the way things stand here.' He began ticking items off on his fingers. 'Matters are settled with Giovanni Bentivoglio to secure Bologna. The treaty with the Orsini, Vitellozzo, Baglioni and the rest of them is now done. Every day my army grows in strength. The Swiss are up to their full complement and the last of the French will arrive within days.'

'And what, might I ask Your Excellency, do you propose to do with this army now you no longer need it to put down your rebels?'

'I haven't decided yet. Perhaps I will retake Urbino first and then we will see. Perhaps, if your Signoria were to engage me to do so, I might take Pisa for you. What do you think of that idea?'

Niccolò, keeping his voice even, decided not to take the bait. 'I think, Excellency, that you have no intention whatever of telling me what your real plans are. But if I were Vitellozzo or Gianpaolo Baglioni, I would be watching my back.'

'What do you think, Michelotto, shall we fall on Vitellozzo and rend him?'

'I'm shocked that the secretary should suggest we might attack our colleagues, so newly returned to the fold.' The voice coming from the shadows was a mocking drawl. 'But you know me, Cesare, I'm just a simple soldier. If you command me to tear Vitellozzo limb from bloody limb, I shall happily do so and not lose a second's sleep.'

'And I should like nothing better than to give you that command. Vitellozzo will never be anything other than a snake and his only talent is to plot treason. But, as you say, he and the others are about to be bound in friendship with me once again, so I suppose I must hold my hand.' That was accompanied by a theatrical sigh and turned down lips that would have been a credit to any fairground clown.

A quiet knock on the door admitted an apologetic servant who handed the duke a paper and retreated. Borgia's levity evaporated as he opened and read the note. Switching to his native Catalan, he directed a few swift sentences at

247

his faithful retainer, who unfolded his length from the chair in which he had been sprawled and made his way to the door.

'God, I've had enough of being cooped up in here,' Borgia broke the silence. 'Let's walk.'

Borgia stood abruptly and led Niccolò out and up onto the battlements of the Rocca. The sun had by now completely disappeared, and all that could be seen of the houses and palaces of Imola were shadows and silhouettes, punctured here and there by glimmers of light from those few windows that were opened to let in a little of the chilly night air.

The appearance of the duke on the wall-walk did not seem to disturb the soldiers who were interspersed on sentry duty at various points along its length, making Niccolò think that this was one of his favoured places to escape from the cares of the council chamber.

'It is a pity you Florentines won't engage me, Niccolò. Imagine what we could do together. It would be a great thing to be known as the general who finally brought Pisa to its duty.' Borgia's face was alight with enthusiasm as he no doubt pictured himself riding in triumph through the Pisan streets. 'And then we should turn on Lucca. That is a fine morsel for a gourmand.'

They came to one of the four immense drum towers that pierced the walls of the fortress, necessitating a stop and a few moments of soldierly banter with the sentries on duty there, which gave Niccolò a moment to formulate his reply.

'My government would indeed dearly love to reduce Pisa,' he said carefully as they resumed their pacing. 'But you must know that the Signoria will be reluctant to engage you as captain-general of our forces. We have not had a happy experience with mercenary commanders. Think of Paolo Vitelli. With that history, why would we put our heads in a noose by giving the command of all our forces to a neighbouring power?'

Niccolò waited for an angry tirade, but instead, there was a short silence. 'You don't trust me.' The words were spoken softly; a simple statement of fact and an implicit question.

'My Lord, you have given us little reason to trust you. You have made war up and down the Romagna, marched across our territory and threatened our

248

allies. Who could feel safe knowing that his neighbour is an ever-hungry lion, for whom he might be the next meal?'

'I take your point.' The even white teeth showed for a moment in a mirthless smile, no doubt enjoying the comparison. 'But Niccolò, Florence should trust me, for I will be a better neighbour than those you now have. Pandolfo, in Siena? The treacherous Lucchese? All these petty tyrants in the Romagna?'

'True enough, excellency. Though we do not put our faith in any of them, except insofar as they have demonstrated that they can be trusted.'

They came to another tower, but instead of going in, Borgia came to a halt and turned to look out across the battlements to the silent town beyond. A chilly breeze swirled up around the tower and Niccolò pulled his cloak tighter around his body. The duke, he noticed, was still clad for the indoors but showed no sign of feeling the cold.

'So it all turns on this question of trust.' Borgia's voice was musing, as though the question was of mere academic interest to him. 'How then, might your countrymen be persuaded to attribute this quality to me?'

'Excellency, to date you have acted like any warlord and so they judge you as a warlord. But if you proved yourself a good governor, as skilled in the arts of peace as you are in those of war, I think they might begin to see you differently.'

'But have I not done so?' Borgia was impatient. 'I dismissed da Lorqua, did I not, when it was obvious he was oppressing the people of the Romagna? I have appointed Sansovino to bring uniform justice to my domains, and I have imposed laws that are respected and enforced impartially. I have made alliances with Bologna, and Ferrara, and Mantua. Is all that not enough to prove my serious intent?'

'All this is true, and I have explained your policies in my despatches, on several occasions.' Niccolò felt no need to say that the Signoria's cautious procrastination also had largely been at his own urging.

'It doesn't matter,' the duke said, waving his hand to dismiss the subject. 'They will come to it sooner or later. Though the longer they wait, the more the terms will favour me. By the way, you should know that Urbino is mine again. A detachment of Orsini's troops chased Guidobaldo out two days ago.'

Niccolò guessed that news was in the note Borgia had just been given; he felt sorry for poor Guidobaldo da Montefeltro, the only half-decent member of the gang of assassins who had met at Magione, cut out as expertly as a clever sheepdog detaches a ewe from the flock, and sent once more on the bitter road to exile. It was the last pillar to fall, and the rebellion was, in effect, at an end.

'Cat got your tongue, Niccolò?' The duke laughed, breaking into his thoughts.

'You have brought me to that rare condition, Excellency.' Niccolò matched the mercurial duke's mood. 'You have given me much to think upon when I advise my government, but I promise I will do my best to represent your position faithfully.'

'Which is all I ask. You're turning blue. Let's get out of the cold.'

That conversation went around and around in his mind over the next few days. As he had promised, his formal despatch conveyed the details accurately and dispassionately. But he went further in a private coded note to the gonfaloniere.

> Duke Valentino is now secure in his dominions. He shows some signs that he wishes to be a good and just ruler of the Romagna, for which he is to be commended. But it is not clear that his territorial ambitions have been entirely sated, and he must therefore still be seen to be a danger to Florence. It is now my opinion that my lords of the Signoria should enter into a formal treaty with the duke, as he has so often asked us to do, though we will not get as good terms as we might have achieved before his recent successes.
> I beg of you, Ser Piero, to prevail upon the Signoria to send an ambassador as soon as may be, empowered to negotiate a treaty. I can do little more here, except observe, report and wherever I can nudge the duke's intentions away from Florence.

The courier had barely left Imola when the city was closed in by a snowstorm that was to last four days, blanketing everything in thick swirling snow driven

250

by bitter winds that penetrated every crack in the walls of his lodging, and caused him to once again fall ill with fever. By the time he had returned to his senses, Borgia and his entire army, by then amounting to some twelve thousand men and twenty cannons, had disappeared.

*

Flurries of snow, much reduced by a wind turned fitful, eddied around the strangely empty town and citadel. The townspeople, having emerged from their houses as the storm abated, walked about in a daze. Duke Valentino, his army and his court had been at the centre of their lives for more than three months, enriching some of them, making many of them poorer as the army consumed everything down to the very stones, and now that they were all gone the city of Imola seemed to be inhabited by ghosts as well as the living.

Once he had ascertained that the army was headed to Cesena, Niccolò was on fire to get packed and on his way. Even so, it was mid-morning, perfunctory farewells having been made to the candle-maker and his family before they were on the road. By the late afternoon of the following day, they were approaching Cesena along roads clogged with soldiers and their camp-followers.

Most of Borgia's army had, it seemed, halted outside the city walls, each contingent—French, Swiss, Gascons, the newly-trained local Romagnese militia—strung out in their separate camps along the road. In the bitingly cold wind under a grey sky that threatened to disgorge a freezing downpour any minute, even the toughest of the soldiers looked miserable, huddled around fires between their thin-walled tents and pavilions. It all struck Niccolò as being odd. They were well past the normal campaigning season and an army such as this would expect to go into snug and warm winter quarters. That suggested that Cesare Borgia did not intend for his army to stay there for long.

The road wound past a vast frowning fortress standing high above the city on a great rock, its escarpment cleared of trees and vegetation. Once inside the town walls, it was as crowded and noisy as Imola had been empty and silent. Finding somewhere for them to stay was a tiresome process, but eventually, he found good rooms overlooking the Piazza Maggiore directly opposite the former gubernatorial palace that was now Cesare Borgia's residence.

Having sent Antonio off to try and establish the whereabouts of Leonardo da Vinci, he wrapped himself in a thick blanket, settled back into the one big

251

chair in his room, a jug of mulled wine on the table at his side, and began to think. What, he wondered for the thousandth time, were the duke's intentions? That question would be the only one of interest to the Signoria, and he had no answer. He had heard rumours and speculation, of course, so the best he could do was to commit what he had picked up to paper and hope it would be sufficient to satisfy his masters.

Antonio's search for Leonardo proved fruitless—neither the artist nor Salai was anywhere to be seen. As far as Niccolò knew, Leonardo had marched south with the main body of the army, so he had to be here somewhere, perhaps up in the fortress, whose forbidding gatehouse had even daunted the otherwise enterprising young Antonio. Thanking the boy and sending him off to find a courier to take his despatch to Florence, Niccolò decided he had had enough of it all and that he would have a few days of rest to recover his health. When he was at Imola, he had asked Biagio to find him a copy of Plutarch's *Lives of the Illustrious Greeks and Romans*, a favourite text in his father's old library. With many grumbles, his friend had obliged, and the book had reached him just before he had set out from Imola.

Sipping the bowls of hot chicken broth that Antonio had got their landlady to prepare, Niccolò spent the next two days quietly reading and making notes, disappearing into the ancient world in search of exemplars who could help him make sense of his present-day challenges, and particularly the enigma of Duke Valentino. So many of them—Marius, Sulla, Caesar his namesake—seemed both to be loved by Fortune and to possess the ruthlessness and unscrupulousness to seize the right moment to act. Cesare had those qualities too and with them, he had been able to build his successes on his version of the goddess Fortuna, the twin foundations of papal money and French military support.

At other times he seemed more like Crassus or Pompey, warlords who had to please their soldiers more than their people to sustain their own position. Like them, Borgia often seemed unable to rein his captains in, allowing them to oppress the countries through which they passed, and only able to keep them happy with lavish gifts of money.

For any prince to have true security, it seemed to Niccolò, he would have to make sure the foundation of his state was deeply anchored in the goodwill and support of the mass of the people. Perhaps Borgia knew this. Certainly, that conversation on the windswept battlements at Imola had demonstrated he was at least aware of the need for proper administration and sound justice. The problem was that he lacked patience for the hard work that such a programme required, though appointing Sansovino was a good move, provided he was allowed to do his work unmolested.

These reflections kept him entertained between bouts of sleep through the long, cold days and into the nights, until on the third morning, he finally felt his strength had returned sufficiently to dress and get out of the house. Threading his way through the jostling crowds in the piazza, the familiar guards admitted him with a genial nod to the gate of the palazzo that lodged Borgia and his court. Up a flight of stairs, he found himself in a large antechamber, where a crowd of people, members of Borgia's entourage and diplomats like himself, had gathered outside the room the duke had appropriated for his presence chamber.

Wandering from person to person, group to chattering group, he listened, talked and made jokes in a routine now so practised that it was all but unconscious. He was entertaining the Venetian envoy with a particularly long and absurd tale that had just wound its tortuous way to an improbably foolish ending when the doors to the ducal chamber crashed open, and a group of officers emerged and marched as a body across the room, their faces red with indignation. As they passed, he recognised them as the captains of the companies of French soldiery that King Louis had sent to Borgia, ostensibly for the purpose of attacking Bologna.

Behind them, half a dozen of Borgia's other officers emerged into an antechamber that was now buzzing with astonished comment, among whom Niccolò was delighted to recognise the face of Leonardo da Vinci, give his head the tiniest of tosses, to which Niccolò raised an eyebrow in response. By this barely detectable method of semaphore, they arranged to meet later in the day.

The duke himself was, it seemed, unavailable for Niccolò or anyone else, so after half an hour of desultory chat with various courtiers, he returned to his lodgings on the other side of the piazza, where he was unsurprised to find a message telling him where the artist could be found and assigning a time to meet. A few minutes later, he was knocking on the door of an undistinguished house near the cathedral. Admitted by a grubby boy with a shock of black hair that stuck out in all directions, he was taken upstairs to a small room, occupied only by Leonardo.

'You look as if you could do with a month's feeding,' the artist said after they had embraced.

'You try living on gruel for a few weeks and see what it does for you. I had a fever, that's all. Where have you been? I was beginning to think you had disappeared altogether.'

'I do have military duties, you know.' Leonardo undermined his attempt at tartness with a crooked smile. 'There was the movement of the cannon to be supervised, then Cesare had me running about surveying the fortress walls. All very routine. None of which you care about in the least, I suppose. You just want to know what happened this afternoon.'

Niccolò laughed. 'You see right through me. Well, what did happen?'

'It was the damnedest thing. One minute we are talking about the usual army matters—you know, provisioning, allocation of camp duties, that kind of thing—when the French just burst out that they had had enough of being insulted and attacked by the Romagnese wherever they went and they had resolved to write to the king to be relieved of their duty and return to Milan.

'The duke seemed at first to be dumbfounded, but then he grew angry and told them they had brought this mistreatment on themselves by their careless treatment of his subjects, which he resented since it undermined his policy of ruling the Romagna justly. You should have seen the look on their faces! They just about turned purple with indignation.

'Then Cesare confounded them even further. He said that they need not write to King Louis, for he was dismissing them here and now, and they could go back to Milan as soon as the orders could be prepared and issued to them, two or three days at most.'

Niccolò's astonishment could not have been more complete. Why would he dismiss them so cavalierly? It was true that their brutish behaviour had damaged his relations with the local people, but the French cavalry and infantry amounted to perhaps a third of his strength; a lot to send away without a backward glance.

'There is something else you should know.' Leonardo was thoroughly enjoying his coup. 'Spannochi said to me on the way out that it was all just play-acting. Cesare had already decided to send the French off.'

254

'Why would he do that?' Niccolò was bewildered; then he noticed the look on his friend's face. 'Of course, you know the answer to that question too.'

Leonardo's grin grew even wider. 'Because the pope is threatening to cut off the supply of money if he doesn't curb his expenses.'

That was startling news. Was Alexander's patience and willingness to bankroll his son's enterprises coming to an end? Or was the old man just tugging on the reins to make sure Cesare knew who was master? Either way, it was a reminder just how dependant Borgia still was on the church's money.

'So whatever he plans to do next, he can do it without the French.' Niccolò said, half to himself. 'What do you think, Leo?'

'Niccolò, you know as well as I that this is one of the most secretive men in Italy. He gives no clue in general councils what he plans to do. Michelotto might know what he plans, but I am certain no one else does.'

'Well, it will be Christmas soon and I should think he will want to be back in Rome by then, so I expect that before long we will all know what he intends.'

Chapter 23—Showdown

An expression of surprise still on its round-cheeked, black-bearded face, the severed head stared sightlessly from the pike upon which it had been placed. Below, the stocky body to which it had once been attached lay propped against a well, fully clothed in rich velvet and silk, a scarlet cloak about its shoulders, kidskin gloves on its hands. Nearby, surrounded by a pool of rust-coloured congealed blood, was a simple execution block and an axe. The whole scene seemed to have been contrived with some care, as if the executioners, having carried out their bloody task, had wanted their handiwork to be revealed to maximum theatrical effect in the pearly light of a foggy dawn. This they had certainly achieved.

'Who is it?' Niccolò asked, having shouldered his way through to the front of the murmuring crowd that had gathered around the corpse.

'Ramiro da Lorqua,' the man standing next to him said, then spat, 'and he got what was coming to him if you ask me.'

It was a sentiment Niccolò could understand easily enough; clearly, da Lorqua's depredations had not been forgotten. What puzzled Niccolò as he made his way back through the crowd in the direction of his lodgings, was why he had been executed now, months after he had been demoted. Such an execution could only have been carried out on Borgia's order. But what message was he trying to send? And to whom?

Back in his room, a shaken Antonio was laying out a simple breakfast of cheese, eggs, oil and bread. Not that Niccolò felt in the least bit hungry after what he had just seen. Instead, he went over to the window and watched the crowd slowly disperse.

The quiet was interrupted by the noisy arrival of Leonardo da Vinci, who came pounding up the stairs calling his name at the top of his voice. 'There you are! Hello, Antonio. Pour me some wine, would you? There's a good lad.'

He came across and joined Niccolò at the window, where they could see the scene in the piazza. The crowd had gone and the usually busy square was deserted, leaving the grisly little display forlorn and abandoned in its centre. It felt as though Borgia's demonstration, if that was what it was, had fallen flat, leaving behind a population that was at once shocked and resentful.

Leonardo, after one glance, turned away, a look of disgust on his face. 'God, what an awful sight. Michelotto told me what they'd done to him, but even so, I wasn't prepared for it.' He lapsed into silence.

'Michelotto?' Niccolò prompted.

Leonardo's face cleared, seeming to make a conscious effort to banish from his mind the sight that had so obviously distressed him. 'Yes. He told me this morning that Cesare had ordered him to be executed. There was some kind of trial yesterday but I don't think it was exactly regular.'

'Why? Wasn't da Lorqua one of his closest allies?'

'He was in a fury. It seems that da Lorqua was conspiring with Vitellozzo and da Fermo to have him murdered! Orsini is in on it too. Da Lorqua confessed everything when they interrogated him. I don't think they want anyone to know about the conspiracy just yet, but Michelotto was so furious he couldn't keep it to himself.'

That wasn't surprising. It must have been a terrible shock to discover that this man, a member of Borgia's inner circle of Spaniards, was conspiring with his worst enemies in yet another attempt at a coup.

'There's something else,' Leonardo said. 'Borgia left early this morning with a troop of his cavalry on the road to Rimini. And the army followed a couple of hours later.'

'Towards Rimini? Why?'

'Michelotto was a bit cagey about that, but he told me that Oliverotto da Fermo has offered to take Senigallia for the duke. The others, Vitellozzo and Orsini, are going to take their armies there too. They are trying to prove their loyalty to the duke, Michelotto said.'

Niccolò frowned. Senigallia was a small but important coastal town just a few hours' march south of Rimini. It was a fiefdom of the della Rovere family, whose exiled head, Cardinal Giuliano della Rovere, was one of the pope's bitterest enemies. Once Cesare's troublesome and treacherous bunch of mercenary captains had taken the town, they would all be there together, but unaware that their new plot to betray Duke Valentino had been revealed by their doomed co-conspirator. And Borgia would be at the head of the army he had been so determinedly building up over the last months. The conclusion was obvious: he was planning to confront and deal with his rebels, one way or another.

It was now close to the middle of the day. The army had been on the march for several hours and would likely make it to Rimini by nightfall. If he hurried, he might catch up with them there. 'Antonio, get me a horse quickly and pack my travelling bag with the essentials; you know what I will need. You and Luca can follow on with the rest of our gear later.' The youth scurried off. 'What about you, Leonardo?'

'The artillery train is at Rimini so I may as well ride with you.'

An hour later, they were on their way, following the Via Emilia from Cesena towards the coast along roads muddied by the passage of one of Borgia's infantry contingents just a few hours before. Eight miles south of Cesena, they crossed a little stream which, a small sign nailed to the bridge proclaimed, was called the Rubicon. What, Niccolò wondered as they clattered across the wooden bridge, had Borgia thought when he had crossed the same stream earlier that morning? Had the new Italian Caesar felt that his die was cast, that there was no going back, as there had been no going back for his ancient namesake when he had crossed this same river to march on Rome fifteen hundred years before?

That afternoon, they reached Rimini, where they found the army, some twelve thousand men by Leonardo's estimate, encamped outside the town. The duke and his entourage were holed up in the Castel Sismondo, the fortress on the edge of the town and, they were curtly informed, were seeing no one. Leonardo had responsibilities to attend to, looking after the small train of guns that accompanied the army, so Niccolò was left to his own devices to find lodging for the night.

*

If Senigallia was Borgia's objective, he didn't seem in any great rush to get there. From Rimini, the army ambled its way down the coast, a sparkling Adriatic on their left and the bulk of Monte Titano, the city of San Marino spilling down its slopes, on their right. Niccolò trailed along some way behind the soldiers and the guns with the small train of cooks, servants, clerks, farriers,

258

armourers and carpenters whose services kept the army fed and its equipment in good order. They were congenial company and made him welcome that night when they bivouacked outside the city of Pesaro but were no more able than the birds on the trees to enlighten him as to what the Cesare Borgia's plans might be.

The next morning, they marched the few miles to the little town of Fano and there they stopped.

Niccolò was happy to see Leonardo making his way through the bustle of the camp, his eyes searching everywhere for the Florentine emissary. Having found each other, they decided to walk down to the seashore so they could talk.

'Cesare has had word that Oliverotto da Fermo and Paolo Orsini have taken Senigallia, though Doria is still holding out in the fort.'

The town was known to be weakly held, so its capture was no surprise. The fortress, on the other hand, was altogether more formidable and was commanded by a renowned Genovese *condottiero*, Andrea Doria. 'And Vitellozzo? Where is he?'

'Due to arrive in Senigallia tomorrow, I'm told.'

'So then he will have all his chickens in the coop. It only remains for the fox to sneak in and devour them all.'

'You do love a metaphor, my friend.' Leonardo grinned. 'But if you are right and Cesare plans some kind of revenge on them, none of them seems to suspect anything.'

It wasn't entirely surprising, though. This was a particularly close-mouthed court and at its head was a skilled dissembler devoted to secrecy. Niccolò himself would never have been able to guess what was going on if he hadn't had help from Leonardo. Still, suspicious or not, they would be surrounded by their own soldiers and bodyguards so he couldn't see how Borgia could do them any harm without provoking a full-scale battle. When he retired for the night he was no closer to understanding what the duke was about than he had been that morning.

The following day was the last of the year 1502 and, at dawn, the camp stirred into activity. Tents were dismantled and stowed away, campfires extinguished and cooking utensils stowed, straps checked and tightened, and horses led into the traces of their wagons. A fine mist from the sea obscured the view ahead, where the soldiers were also preparing to march the twelve or thirteen miles down the road to Senigallia.

Niccolò had mounted his horse and was waiting to move off when a messenger came down the long column, calling out his name. 'The duke sent me to escort you to join the van of the army,' the breathless youngster said, once he had located his quarry.

Slightly mystified, Niccolò followed the boy past the cannons and the cavalry and the infantry and deposited him with the little mounted leadership group at the head of the column. Borgia, wearing chain mail and a gleaming breastplate, was buried in conversation with Michelotto Corella. After a few moments, Corella spurred his horse into movement and rode off. Borgia, looking around, spotted Niccolò and waved him over.

'Well, Messer Secretary, you have managed to keep up with us, I see!' Borgia seemed to be in a high-spirited mood. 'I won't have much time to talk today but stay nearby and you will see something, I promise you, that you will remember for the rest of your days.'

With that, Niccolò was dismissed, and the duke stood in his stirrups to wave the army into motion. Four hours later, with the town and fortress of Senigallia clearly visible a mile or so ahead, a small squadron of cavalry appeared coming up the road towards them. At their head rode a group of three men, one of whom Niccolò recognised as the familiar pudgy form of Paolo Orsini. The others he had never met but recognised from their descriptions. The man riding next to Orsini was tall, red-headed, with a mournful-looking face scarred by the pox—Vitellozzo Vitelli, brother of the executed Paolo and Florence's mortal enemy. Just a little behind came Oliverotto da Fermo, narrow-boned, bearded, and broken-nosed, watching everything with shifty, suspicious eyes.

Dismounting, the little party approached Borgia, their caps in their hands. Paolo Orsini smiled as though he didn't have a care in the world, but Vitellozzo's pock-marked face was white with tension. Niccolò realised that this was the first time that he and Borgia had come face to face since the rebellion had begun.

The duke sat and stared down at them. Then, sliding gracefully off his horse, grasped Vitellozzo's hands and took him in a smiling embrace, muttering something in his ear that seemed to have the effect of banishing his apprehensions. Paolo was given a more familiar slap on the back; a gesture of comradeship between two soldiers. 'Paolo, Vitellozzo, Oliverotto, welcome. You have done well, all of you. Senigallia is ours and all we have to do is winkle that Genoese bastard out of the fort.'

He stood back, hands on hips, and regarded them. 'Where have you disposed your troops, my friends?' he said, his voice even and friendly.

The four captains exchanged looks with each other, as if uncertain as to who should respond.

'Camped along the shore to the south of the city, awaiting your orders, Cesare,' Vitellozzo said.

'Then let us march!'

The contingent of Oliverotto's army that had accompanied the three *condottieri* were despatched to their place in the cavalcade, immediately behind Borgia's personal bodyguard, and the column set off. Niccolò, from his place in the middle of the bodyguard, was too far away to hear what the little group around the duke were saying above the sound of hooves and jingling harnesses, but they appeared to be chatting easily among themselves, as though they had never had a disagreement in their lives. Now and then a laugh floated back, and Niccolò supposed that they were reminiscing about past campaigns, as old comrades do.

Senigallia was a small town, its walls surrounded on every side by water, with a river on two sides that fed a moat on the other two. The only way in was by crossing a bridge across the moat, which then led to street bisecting a cluster of houses hemmed in between the moat and the town's main gate. It was towards this bridge that an advance guard of cavalry headed, followed by a contingent of Borgia's Swiss and Gascon infantry. All this was done without a single order from the duke or his officers, as though it had all been carefully prearranged.

Borgia kicked his horse into motion and headed towards the bridge, accompanied by Vitellozzo, Orsini and da Fermo, all of whom had fallen silent. Left behind, Niccolò found himself riding in the middle of Borgia's personal guard, smartly turned out in their red and yellow livery. Their captain, a grizzled middle-aged soldier, leaned across and lightly grasped his arm, his grin revealing gapped and yellowed teeth. 'Don't you worry, Messer

Machiavelli. His excellency has told us to make sure you are kept safe. You just stay with us.'

This struck Niccolò as an odd thing to say if they were simply making a ceremonial entry into a conquered town. Nevertheless, he was grateful for what the officer clearly meant as reassurance and managed a nod and a weak laugh in response.

They crossed the bridge over the moat and passed between two rows of the cavalry advance-guard, now deployed on either side of the road, their lances at an angle to make a ceremonial tunnel leading to the massive stone gatehouse, the entrance to the city itself. To his right, Niccolò could see the rest of the rebel army, drawn up in little clusters between the houses to his right, behind the wall of cavalry. With a start, he realised that they had now been neatly separated from their leaders.

Looking up as the cavalcade moved out of the sun and into the coolness of the gatehouse arch, he met the impassive gaze of soldiers in the Borgia uniform; more of Borgia's soldiers lined the gatehouse tunnel. Niccolò frowned: how had Borgia's troops taken control of the entrance to a city that was ostensibly being held by Oliverotto's army?

Emerging into the sunshine, he was startled by the creak and thud of the gates shutting behind him. Twisting in his saddle, he saw the bodyguard of Oliverotto's men that had accompanied the erstwhile rebels milling around in confusion. One of Borgia's sergeants rode up and barked a few words of command; after a moment of hesitation, the soldiers formed up and began to move forward once more.

Turning his attention back to the front of the column, Niccolò realised that the leadership group had moved too far ahead to hear what was going on behind them, what with the noise coming from the townspeople who leaned cheering from their windows, and the tramp of Borgia's bodyguard.

The column rode on, and then halted before the open gates of a palazzo, where Borgia dismounted.

'Come, gentlemen, we have much to discuss.' He turned towards the palazzo, as if entirely confident they would follow him. When they did not, he turned back, giving them a quizzical smile. 'What's the matter? Afraid for your safety?'

'Of course not, Cesare,' Paolo Orsini said, though his voice sounded irresolute. 'It's just that we have duties to attend to with our army.'

'They can wait, I am sure, for a half-hour or so.' He laughed. 'I give you my word. You are perfectly safe. Come on, get down, you're giving me a crick in the neck.'

Though obviously reluctant, a refusal would have meant open conflict, and so they dismounted and followed the duke through the door, leaving Niccolò stranded in the middle of the bodyguard who were clustered on one side of the street. Oliverotto da Fermo's guard stood to on the opposite side.

Half an hour went past, with nothing happening. Then the gate of the palazzo swung open again and out came Borgia, mounted and accompanied by one of his officers. Orders were shouted for da Fermo's bodyguard to go back and join the rest of their comrades, waiting outside the walls in the village. They hesitated for a moment, and then marched off down the street. Borgia watched for a few minutes then, with a gesture, sent his own bodyguard after them, Niccolò perforce being carried along in their midst.

At the still-locked city gates, they caught up with da Fermo's escort, now completely confused and frightened. Disembodied shouts and screams were coming from beyond the gates, accompanied by the scrape and clash of steel. From the battlements above, the guards in Borgia livery looked on impassively as the soldiers below hammered frantically at the gates.

What happened next drove the breath from Niccolò's body. To his astonishment and horror, Borgia's bodyguard drew swords and lowered halberds, and methodically set about slaughtering the terrified young men before them, stonily ignoring their desperate pleas for mercy as they dropped their weapons. Nauseated by the metallic reek of blood and the sight of corpses twisted in the agony of their death-throes, Niccolò fought down the bile that rose into his throat.

The bodyguard's captain, sitting placidly on his horse, grunted his satisfaction. 'That's that done. Now let's see what's happening outside.'

What was happening outside, when the gates were at last swung open, was pure mayhem. While Niccolò had been inside the city, the rest of Borgia's advance guard of a thousand or so men had poured across the bridge and set to work destroying the rest of da Oliverotto da Fermo's force, left leaderless among the houses of the village. Worse, blood lust had taken over and they were beginning to rampage through the streets and alleyways, indiscriminately killing both enemy soldiers and townspeople alike. As Niccolò watched, smoke began to rise from one of the houses that had been set on fire. It was clear that the troops were out of control and would soon be pillaging everything in sight.

The grizzled captain of Borgia's bodyguard, though unmoved by the bloodshed, nevertheless seemed unhappy at the breach of discipline, muttering his displeasure under his breath.

'Captain, I cannot believe that the duke intended this,' Niccolò said, trying to put an authority into his voice that he didn't feel. 'Surely he must be told what is happening?'

The captain looked sideways at him and nodded. 'You're right. Cesare said they were to be disarmed only. Jacopo, go and tell the duke what is going on.'

The soldier thus detailed trotted off back into the city, leaving the rest of the bodyguard to wait and watch. They didn't have to do so for long. Hardly ten minutes had gone by before Borgia emerged and rode over to join them. The dark eyes shone as brightly as the polished armour in which he was clad, and the smile was triumphant. 'So, Messer Secretary, it is done. The vipers have been trapped and are under lock and key. As we speak, the rest of their armies are being disarmed and the safety and security of the Romagna is preserved.'

'And this? Is this how you will rule your domains in the future?' Niccolò was surprised by the vehemence of his own anger, prompted partly by the sickening sight before him, and partly by a sense of betrayal: he had begun to think that Cesare Borgia had the makings of a wise and just prince, yet here he was gloating over a dastardly act of treachery as vile as any committed by his enemies.

The object of his fury was unperturbed. 'You are too sentimental, Machiavelli. Do you think I ordered this out of simple revenge? What do you take me for? No, this is a small price to pay to secure peace in the Romagna. From this day on, I will no longer have to rely on the uncertain loyalty of mercenary captains and their armies for my security.' Borgia turned his attention back to the chaotic scene in the streets, just as an anguished scream ascended from the general noise of mayhem. '. Still, we can't allow it to go on for too long, else they will forget discipline entirely.'

He flicked his reins to get his horse into motion and, followed by the rest of the bodyguard, trotted off to begin restoring order, leaving Niccolò to watch as he disappeared into the pandemonium. Eventually, he turned his horse and rode glumly back into the town, accompanied by a single soldier who had been detailed to escort him and help him find somewhere to sleep for the night.

*

'I have been planning for this day for months, Niccolò, even before you and Bishop Soderini came to see me in June. I knew something was boiling in the pan back then and I was sorely tempted to tell you what I planned to do about it. But my father always says that trust in great enterprises should never be lightly given, and he is right. I couldn't trust anyone with the secret, not even him, until everything was in place.'

It was two hours after sunset and Borgia was in the highest of spirits, exulting in his success that day, and pouring out all his pent-up excitement, mixed with self-justifications, to his sole audience, Florentine emissary Niccolò Machiavelli. It was odd, he thought, this excitability. He had noticed it before whenever Borgia was trying to be persuasive, as if he was afraid that if he stopped talking his listeners would see through his arguments.

Borgia poured them both wine and hurried on. 'They should have attacked me when I was at my weakest but I knew they couldn't trust each other. So all I had to do was sow the seeds of discord by treating with each of them separately. Bentivoglio, Montefeltro, Orsini, all of them fell for it. While they were dithering, all the while looking over their shoulders and wondering which of their number had done a separate deal, they gave me the time I needed to build up my strength.'

Borgia sat contemplating the wine in his glass, savouring his triumph. When he looked up, his expression was thoughtful. 'But you know Niccolò, fools though they are, I might still have been prepared to make peace with them all.'

Niccolò was astonished, and his face showed it.

'Oh, don't mistake me—I originally intended to destroy them all. But it seemed to me that, their teeth having been drawn, if I could unite them behind me, they would be useful in the future. I do have to rule the Romagna, after all, and for that, I need loyal governors. So they had entered into binding agreements with me and I would have been willing to give them a chance to prove their fidelity. I remembered, you see, our little talk about trust back in Imola, and how it has to be earned.'

'And then you learned from da Lorqua that they intended to betray you.'

If Borgia was surprised that Niccolò knew the source of his information, he didn't show it. 'It was the worst blow, Niccolò, I think I have ever suffered. Not that these vipers could not be trusted; that was no surprise, but the fact that one of my oldest companions should have been drawn into it, that was terrible. I heard it from his own lips, you know. They intended to kill me, either on the road somewhere or here in Senigallia. That damned Genoese was in on it as well.'

'Doria, you mean?' Niccolò was puzzled. Andrea Doria, the *condottiero* who had been in command of Senigallia's fortress, had held out until late that afternoon when he had seen which way the tide was flowing and surrendered. How was he involved in this sordid conspiracy?

'Da Fermo said that Doria refused to surrender the castle to anyone except me. But it was a ruse. They planned to shoot me with a crossbow bolt when I rode in to take possession of the fortress. I only found that out when we put Doria to the question. I tell you, there never was a more evil assembly of men than these conspirators. They deserve the end they will surely get.'

As he said the last words, Borgia looked up at the ceiling, and Niccolò realised that they must be incarcerated somewhere above them, awaiting their fate. None of them would be alive by the morning, of that he was sure, though he left the thought unspoken. 'I will make sure, excellency, that the Signoria is fully informed of the events of today and that they understand the justice of your actions completely.'

'These men are enemies of Florence too, and of the King of France. We should all rejoice at the destruction of their plots.' Borgia was imperious. 'But my task is not yet complete. I intend to bring Città del Castello and Perugia to obedience. Then I will reduce the Orsini castles in the Lazio, as my father has commanded me to do. I expect your Signoria to join me in this enterprise and to send some troops.'

Seizing control of Vitellozzo's base of Città del Castello would be easy enough, given that he had the city's master in his cells and Vitellozzo was not much loved there anyway. Perugia, where Gianpaolo Baglioni ruled and where he had had the good fortune (or good sense?) to be recovering from illness while his co-conspirators were being rounded up in Senigallia might be a tougher nut to crack. The Orsini fortresses were further south, around Rome, and proceeding against them would require a longer-term strategy, given the power of the wily cardinal who stood at the head of the clan.

'So you see, Niccolò, nothing now stands in my way. You must tell your masters that. And remind them that they promised me troops; there will be benefits for them if they now join me in finishing this campaign and joining with me in alliance.'

Making his farewells, Niccolò murmured some gently neutral words; the Florentine Signoria would no doubt be even warier of allying themselves with a man who had proved himself such a ruthless dissembler. But he promised to faithfully communicate the request anyway.

Within its walls, Senigallia was quiet as he went to his lodgings. Outside, in the houses between the town and the moat, occasional shrill cries and screams could be heard, reminding Niccolò just how tenuous Borgia's hold on his troops still was. But that thought did not find its way into his despatch that night, which told of a triumphant Valentino, now undisputed master of the Romagna and of Urbino, a man who had mastered the greatest crisis of his career, who now stood like a colossus dominating northern Italy and who was capable of doing anything.

And he was just twenty-seven years old.

Chapter 24—Niccolò Relieved

The Romagna—January 1503

As Niccolò had suspected, while he had been chatting with Cesare Borgia, Vitellozzo Vitelli and Oliverotto da Fermo were awaiting their fate, locked in the room where they had been surprised and arrested. By midnight both were dead, strangled by Michelotto Corella, Duke Valentino looking on.

All this Niccolò heard the following morning from Alessandro Spannochi, who had himself been given the story by a gloating Borgia. Perhaps not entirely by chance, Niccolò and Alessandro were lodged in the same house, whose occupants had been summarily bundled out to make way for the officers of the Borgia court. A blazing fire and the thick cloaks they both wore could not entirely keep out the cold as they breakfasted on hard cheese and bread, washed down with ale.

'They didn't show much courage at the end, according to Cesare,' Alessandro said. 'Vitellozzo begged to be sent off to the pope, wanting an indulgence for his many sins. You can imagine what the duke's reaction was to *that*. Oliverotto da Fermo was even worse—weeping and wailing, blaming everything on Vitellozzo.'

Niccolò couldn't feel much pity for either of them; both had been savage murderers in their time and if they had been the executioners instead of the victims, he didn't doubt they would have been at least as cruel. 'What about Paolo Orsini?'

'Still under guard. I don't know what Cesare is going to do about him.'

Probably he was hesitating because the Orsini family, though weakened, were still powerful in Rome. The family's head, Cardinal Giambattista Orsini, might be in prison but his influence reached deep into the Roman establishment and could not be ignored.

Leonardo da Vinci's mood, when Niccolò caught up with him, was far less cheerful. He had been travelling with the artillery train, which moved even more slowly than the footsoldiers and cavalry. So he had only arrived in Senigallia late in the afternoon, when Borgia's soldiers had been running wild, pillaging and raping. Leonardo was still profoundly disturbed by the

268

recollection of the things he had seen, trembling with emotion as he talked. 'It was horrible, just horrible, worse than Fossombrone. Blood everywhere, corpses with their entrails hanging out and the carrion birds already picking at them, women and children sitting crying on their doorsteps. The soldiers were no better than beasts. Awful.'

'It's distressing, I know,' Niccolò said, pouring wine. 'But I am afraid that is what war looks like.'

He knew how inadequate his words must seem, how little comfort they offered to his friend. In truth, Niccolò had been equally appalled by the scenes outside the city which had so disturbed Leonardo, but he had forced himself to keep his emotions hidden in front of the soldiery. It was only after he'd got safely to his lodgings that the reaction had overtaken him and he had quietly thrown up in the laneway behind the house. Da Vinci, on the other hand, seemed to be completely unmanned by the experience. For the first time, Niccolò understood just how unworldly the artist was.

'If that is what war is like, then I want no more of it. Oh, I'm not a complete fool, Niccolò, I know that war and death go together, but there is a difference between a battlefield and what we both saw yesterday, don't you think? Anyway, I want to get as far away from it as I can!'

'That's going to be a little hard to achieve for Cesare Borgia's military engineer.' Niccolò tried to sound light-hearted, but his joke just made da Vinci even gloomier. 'Look, Leo, you will have to be practical about this. If you want to get away, you'll have to think up a strategy. If you just leave without his permission, he'll send his cavalry after you and haul you back. You're under contract, after all. He might release you if you ask him, but he'll be reluctant about it and you don't want him as an enemy.'

'I thought you were the clever one with this sort of thing. You must have *some* ideas.'

Actually, there was one possibility. While he was sure that Borgia would turn down any request from Leonardo himself, a request from Piero Soderini would be more difficult to refuse. So all Niccolò had to do was to convince Soderini that Florence needed an experienced military engineer. But he didn't want to get Leonardo's hopes up until he had a better idea as to what reception his proposal might get. 'Let me think about it, Leonardo. I promise nothing,

269

but there might be a way of getting you away from the army and back to Florence. Meanwhile, do and say nothing to Borgia of your disenchantment.'

It was a small enough hope, but it cheered the artist up and, before long, he was back to his old self, talking with his usual volubility about the myriad of subjects that seemed to interest him. For Niccolò, it was like being back in the Studio, listening to a learned scholar delivering a philosophical oration, except that Leonardo's mind seemed to be inhabited by five professors at once, so wide were his interests—mathematics, engineering, natural phenomena, architecture, painting—and so erudite his understanding of each. Thus for a refreshing hour or two, Niccolò was able to forget the prosaic and practical concerns of statecraft and diplomacy and bathe in the innocent purity of his friend's thoughts.

*

It might have been expected in the depths of a cruel and freezing winter that the army would go into winter quarters. But the duke had other plans and, within days, the army was on the march, bundled up against a bitter wind under grey skies that threatened sleet, heading south-west. Leonardo returned to his position of duty with the guns and Niccolò found himself among his old friends in the baggage train. It was in their company that he and his two young servants plodded their way from town to town—first Conrinaldo then Sassoferrato, Gualdo and finally Torgiano, where the army was at last halted for a rest after a week on the road.

Here, a courier was waiting for him with a packet of letters from Florence, containing the very welcome news that the Piero Soderini had finally decided to appoint Jacopo Salviati, a former gonfaloniere and a member of the current Signoria, as a fully accredited ambassador to the court of Duke Valentino, authorised to negotiate the treaty that Borgia had so insistently been demanding.

While the rest of the army bivouacked around the little town, the duke had installed himself in a small villa on the outskirts, overlooking the banks of the Tiber. It was here that Niccolò found him, pacing up and down the villa's main salon, accompanied by Secretary Geraldini, to whom he was issuing a stream of instructions. He waited deferentially just out of earshot until Borgia noticed him and waved him over. The secretary withdrew, bobbing his head to Niccolò with the slightest hint of mockery.

'Agapito doesn't seem to like you very much.'

'We serve different masters, excellency, that is all,' Niccolò said with a shrug. 'Some degree of animosity is to be expected.'

Borgia chuckled and moved to a chair that was set before the fireplace, gesturing for Niccolò to occupy its twin. The duke studied the crackling fire for a few moments, absently playing with the ring on his index finger. This was the first time that Niccolò had laid eyes on Borgia since Senigallia. Though in outward appearance he was much the same, the euphoric mood of that interview was gone, replaced by the calm self-possession of a man who knew his own power.

'I have had letters from Florence at last, excellency,' Niccolò said, breaking the silence.

Borgia nodded; he would have been informed that a courier had arrived as he was told of everything that happened in the army. 'And did they bring good news, these letters?'

'Florence is sending a new ambassador. Signor Jacopo Salviati, a respected member of the Signoria. I understand he is empowered to negotiate a treaty with Your Excellency, though their lordships have not confided to me the full scope of his commission.'

'Well, we shall find all that out when he arrives,' the duke said, with surprising indifference. 'Did the Signoria say anything about the troops I asked for? Are they coming too?'

'They wrote that Florence is ready to send its soldiers whenever they should be needed.'

'Excellent, excellent. Though they may not be required after all. I had word this morning that Città del Castello has surrendered and Gianpaolo Baglioni has fled Perugia; the city will be ours within days. And then I will restore both places to the authority of the pope.'

Niccolò thought about that. Both cities were in Umbria, their respective lords held their fiefs directly from the pope, and neither had ever been part of the Romagna, so returning them to papal authority was logical enough. But perhaps Borgia was making a mistake.

271

'His holiness will no doubt be grateful. But if I may ask, excellency, why do you not appoint your own military governors to these places? Surely that will make them more secure?'

Borgia shook his head impatiently. 'The pope will choose men who I recommend, who will be grateful to me even beyond his reign.'

Niccolò wondered where Borgia going to find such paragons of gratitude and loyalty; certainly not among the ambitious men of Italy. But on the principle that one should never interrupt one's foe when he is making an error, he kept that thought to himself. 'Of course, Pope Alexander may live for many years yet.'

'He is over seventy, he eats and drinks too much, and he sleeps but poorly. Other than that, he is in good health! If you knew my father, you would know that he is nigh-on unstoppable.' Borgia's laugh was complacent. 'But none of us can know when God will call him, so it is a contingency that I have prepared for. Between the papal treasury and the loyalty of the Spanish cardinals, I am confident I can ensure that the conclave will choose a successor who will be amenable to me.'

'Which is why Paolo Orsini still lives, I assume?'

'You are very perceptive, Niccolò. Yes, Paolo is on his way to Rome, where we have prepared a cell in Castel Sant'Angelo not too far from that treacherous uncle of his, Cardinal Giambattista. But you are right, I must proceed carefully in case I need the Orsini votes.'

A page slipped into the room and came across to whisper something in the duke's ear, prompting a look of irritation and a dismissive wave of his hand. 'Tell them they can wait. Niccolò, what do you hear of the French king's intentions?'

There had been a lengthy item on that subject in a letter he had received that morning from Piero Soderini. He felt that no harm would be done by sharing its contents. 'In Florence, it is believed the king will tear up his agreement with the Spanish and invade Naples as soon as the spring weather arrives. He expects all his Italian allies to support him, of course.'

'My intelligence is the same. Which gives me just enough time to deal with Siena.'

'Siena?' Niccolò was confused. The Republic of Siena lay to the south-west of Florence and had long been her rival for territory and influence in Tuscany. But both were under the nominal protection of the King of France and therefore allies of sorts. For the last few years, Siena had been ruled by a wily *condottiero*, Pandolfo Petrucci, known to be tough and ruthless, but popular at home.

'Why else did you think I am keeping my army together through the winter? I must have Pandolfo out of his seat before Louis demands that I join his invasion.'

'Excellency, I am perplexed. On what grounds do you want to attack Pandolfo? How has he offended you?'

'Because he was involved with the late conspiracy and must be punished accordingly.'

This was news to Niccolò. He knew that Pandolfo had provided some mercenaries to Borgia, and now he remembered Alessandro Spannochi telling him that Pandolfo had been invited to the conference at Senigallia; he had never arrived, apparently because he was ill. Perhaps the illness was a convenient excuse for a guilty man, but something didn't add up. From what he knew of Pandolfo, he was far too cautious to get involved with such a hare-brained scheme as the late conspiracy.

For now, though, he decided to accept Borgia at face value. 'I cannot say what the attitude of the Florentine Signoria would be towards any move against Siena, though I imagine they would be concerned at the prospect of your soldiers attacking a neighbouring state,' he said. 'And neither does it seem likely that King Louis would approve such an assault.'

'Who said anything about *attacking* Siena?' Borgia was arch, a conjurer about to pull an unexpected card from the pack. 'I wish merely to detach Pandolfo from the city, to be placed in my care. The Sienese may then choose whoever they like to replace him. Louis will not care; he is allied with the Sienese Republic, not whichever mercenary happens to control it today.'

That was sophistry on a grand scale, which King Louis and Charles d'Amboise would see through in an instant. But Borgia's reputation for speed and unpredictability might well scare the burghers of Siena into giving up their master before the French king's interdiction could arrive. Niccolò found himself involuntarily admiring the audacity of Borgia's gamble.

'Excellency, it is a bold plan, and I understand your desire to bring Pandolfo to justice if he is indeed guilty of participating in the conspiracy. But I beg you think of the effect this could have on your relations with your other allies, not to mention the treaty negotiations that Ambassador Salviati is ready to commence.'

'Your advice is noted, Niccolò.' The formal words hung in the air like a full-stop; clearly that subject was closed, and Niccolò made to stand, taking this as his dismissal. But Borgia waved him back to his seat.

'Indulge me a moment more, my friend,' he said, then stopped and frowned as if he was not sure how he wanted to proceed. When he did speak, it was in a musing, uncharacteristically hesitant way. 'Consider my position: I am now secure in my possessions in the Romagna, I control Urbino, and as Captain-General of the Church I am virtual master of the rest of the pope's domains. My armies can strike wherever I wish, whenever I wish. And yet...'

'And yet your security still depends on the pope's health and the king's goodwill.' Niccolò's blunt assessment seemed to go to the heart of what was bothering Borgia, whose face cleared into a broad smile.

'No-one talks to me the way you do, Machiavelli. Everyone else tip-toes around and talks behind their hands. Yes, you are right, that is the question I wrestle with day and night.' Another pause, and a quizzical tilt of the ducal head. 'So, Messer Secretary, advise me.'

That was unexpected, and it took Niccolò a moment or two to think how he should respond, as all the great exemplars from his wide reading appeared one after the other in his mind, Was the man in front of him another Augustus? Or merely a Sulla?

'Excellency, it seems to me that you have an opportunity in these next few years to create a principality that will withstand all the buffets of time and circumstance, that can stand strong even without the props of king Louis and the papal treasury. But to do so, you must abandon the arts of war and embrace those of peace.'

Borgia said nothing, but his eyes, coolly appraising, encouraged Niccolò to continue.

'You have begun, I think, to see the wisdom of alliances, with Bentivoglio, with Mantua and Ferrara. That is well done. But alliances in Italy can be flimsy things, and your allies will abandon you if they can see advantage in doing so. They will be deterred by your armies, of course, but armies are not sustained by themselves: you must pay them and arm them, for which you need taxes. And for that you need a populace who can pay those taxes, and better yet do so willingly.'

That caused Borgia to laugh. 'Surely there is no such population in the world, let alone Italy! But you intrigue me: go on.'

'My Lord Duke, you have already started down the path that will furnish you with the security you need. When you appointed Antonio Sansovino as president of the Romagna, you made it clear that you intended to rule justly in your new domains. And from everything I have heard, he has begun well.' Suddenly Niccolò found the ideas and words tumbling out of his brain faster than his tongue could give them shape. 'But Sansovino cannot work alone: recruit additional judges to assist him. Place his authority above that of your military governors. Get the laws codified and make justice available to everyone. Oh, and make sure that local laws and customs in your cities and towns are respected. Leave local administration in the hands of local officials, for they will be more readily respected than anyone appointed from outside...'

'Stop, Machiavelli, for heaven's sake,' Borgia said, throwing his hands in the air and laughing. 'I am exhausted even thinking about your programme.'

Niccolò felt himself blushing, slightly embarrassed that he had allowed himself to get so carried away. But he had one final point to make.

'Excellency, I know much of this must seem like mere administration to you, but I tell you from experience that this is what good governance looks like. And when your neighbours, Florence included, come to understand that your country is justly ruled, that you are a serious prince, they will respect your word when you give it in alliance.'

'Trust. That is an expensive commodity that too often evaporates like the mist at the coming of dawn. But what you say is true, and I will ponder your advice.' Borgia stopped, and frowned. 'What I most need is time: when you have worked out how to manufacture more of that, you must let me know. Well, I look forward to engaging with Signor Salviati on these subjects. And you must be looking forward to returning to home to your family.'

'I do miss them, it is true,' Niccolò said, surprising himself with the truth of the words. 'Though I am not sure I want to confront my wife—she thought I was going away for just a few days!'

'Just another diplomatic challenge for you, Niccolò. Think of it that way.'

A door opened and the same page entered, an enquiring look on his face. Borgia nodded at him, then turned back to Niccolò. 'My servants need my attention, apparently. But before they come, I wanted to say that I will miss your presence at my court. I know you were sent to spy on me and your masters will judge best how successful you were at that, but I have also benefitted from your advice from time to time and have learned to respect your judgement. You are a rare man, Niccolò, intelligent and loyal. Go with God.'

It was a surprising and emotional moment for Niccolò, made more satisfactory by the look on the face of Agapito Geradini as the secretary came into the room to behold his master embracing the Florentine emissary.

*

'Well, Machiavelli,' Jacopo Salviati said, stamping the mud off his boots, 'Soderini told me I should listen to what you have to say, so here I am. Though I will take my own counsel as to how best to proceed, understand that.'

It was hardly an encouraging start and Niccolò resisted with difficulty an impulse to show the new ambassador straight back out into the street and take horse for Florence that night. Instead, he had summoned up his usual reserves of professional courtesy and, having settled him in front of a roaring fire and offered him mulled wine, he set about giving Salviati as honest and forthright an appraisal of the situation as he could.

That situation was full of peril for Florence. If Borgia succeeded in his gambit, he would no doubt ensure that Pandolfo Petrucci was replaced by a puppet of his own choosing and Florence would be surrounded by potential enemies—Borgia and his allies on three sides and a stubborn Pisa on the other. Urgent action would be needed if they were to counter the threat.

'So you see,' Niccolò concluded, 'Borgia is throwing the dice once again, hoping that he can bluff Pandolfo out of Siena before the pope and the king yank him away from his quarry.'

'We won't get much joy from the French. Louis is more interested in Naples at the moment, so our ambassadors say.' Salviati, never an optimistic man, seemed to be particularly gloomy this afternoon. 'All he wants to do is throw the Spanish out and install himself there as king.'

'But he still has to get to Naples and for that he will need the goodwill of his Italian allies, and of the pope. And he won't want Borgia's army tied up besieging Siena. We should write to him by the fastest couriers and ensure that he knows what Borgia's intentions are.'

'Yes, I suppose so.' Salviati sounded bored with the subject. He was, Niccolò recalled, a man with a reputation for arrogance, though he had little to be arrogant about other than his aristocratic pedigree.

'In the meantime, Ser Jacopo, I would advise you to progress slowly with your negotiations for the treaty. It will buy us time and Borgia will at least feel some restraint if he thinks we might oppose him outright,' Niccolò pressed on. 'Our other avenue is the pope. Alessandro Spannochi told me the other day that Alexander is fit to be tied—he wants his son busy reducing the Orsini fortresses in the Lazio, not attacking Siena.'

'Spannochi? Who is he?'

'Borgia's treasurer, but he is also close to the pope. His family are the Borgia bankers. You should take care to cultivate him and also Agapito Geraldini, Borgia's secretary.'

At the suggestion he consult with such people, Salviati looked as shocked as if Niccolò had suggested he listen to the advice of his horse, which, he was beginning to suspect, might have more sense than its owner. 'Anyway,' he hurried on, 'let's hope that parental authority will finally prevail.'

'If Alexander's relationship with Borgia is anything like mine with my son, that's not much of a hope at all,' the ambassador said, gesturing for young Antonio, hovering nearby, to refill his goblet.

The moment of levity passed and Salviati's face returned to its habitual expression of drooping gloom. 'Can he be trusted, this man? Half the Signoria thinks we can, but the other half of us don't.'

'Trusted? No. Borgia follows his self-interest above all else. I think that, once he has dealt with Siena, he will turn on us and will try the same trick—if he cannot defeat us by arms, he will try and cow us into submission. That is why we must look to Rome and Milan to bind him.'

'Yes, yes, I think I have that point.' Salviati was testy.

'Even if we succeed in countering this particular stratagem, we will have to live with Duke Valentino as a neighbour, and a powerful one at that. Which may not be an entirely bad thing.'

'What? Are you mad, Machiavelli? He is like a ravening beast!'

'Hear me out, Ser Jacopo. I have spent many months observing this man and he has many good qualities. He is decisive and determined, he plans well and he knows how to make the best of his good luck. He understands statecraft, and his plans for the future of the Romagna are well thought through. His weaknesses are that he is impatient and he is a gambler. Rather than take the long road, he will instead risk everything on a single throw.

'Yet, provided we can restrain him, it seems to me that having a settled and prosperous state to our east and south would be better than the lawlessness we have become used to. And I have done everything I can to persuade him to go down a more pacific path.'

He might as well have saved his breath. Salviati just grunted and stared at him as if afraid that he might start foaming at the mouth. 'You can tell all that to Soderini and the rest when you get back to Florence if you like. I am here to do just one job, get this damned treaty agreed, then go home myself,' he said, as if completing this task would take less effort than ordering a good dinner. Then he seemed to remember something else. 'By the way, in my verbal instructions, I have been directed to request that the duke release Leonardo da Vinci from his service as a special favour to the gonfaloniere so he can return to Florence to help in the campaign against Pisa. You wouldn't know anything about that, would you?'

278

'Not much.' Niccolò was bland. 'Leonardo asked me to see whether his services might be of use to the republic, that's all. He's had enough of trailing about after the army and wants to spend some time back home.'

Salviati's sharp look suggested that he either thought or knew there was more to it than that, but Niccolò wasn't much inclined to satisfy his curiosity. It was important that Borgia should see Leonardo's release as a favour he could do for Piero Soderini, one of the few Florentines he respected. He was gratified that the gonfaloniere had seen fit to act on Niccolò's unsupported recommendation, which had been conveyed verbally by young Antonio, sent to Florence in the absence of any other reliable messenger. Leonardo would, of course, be in transports of excitement at the news when eventually he got it.

In the event, Niccolò was denied the pleasure of telling his friend in person, for Leonardo had been sent off on a surveying mission by the duke and did not return before Niccolò began the long ride home. All he could do was to leave a note at his deserted lodgings, telling him the glad tidings and suggesting they meet again when he eventually made it back to Florence. With that duty done, he and his remaining servant, faithful young Luca, climbed into their saddles and set off.

Half an hour later, having climbed a barren hillside, the road was about to enter a patch of trees. Niccolò stopped his little cavalcade and turned in his saddle to take a last look at the army in whose company he had travelled for the previous three months. In the valley below, the encampment was spread out like an infestation around the little walled town. Wisps of smoke rose from the fires and the distant mutter of camp-noise drifted up to where he sat. It had been a hard and exhausting few months, and he was keen to get home to his wife and daughter. But he also knew that part of him would miss this life, despite its hardships.

Drawing in a deep breath that was almost a sigh, he turned and kicked his horse into motion to start the long ride home.

Part Four—Triumph and Fall

Chapter 25—Valentino Triumphant

He had expected that Marietta would greet him with a basketful of reproaches, which he had to acknowledge would not be entirely unjustifiable. From the letters he had received from Biagio and his other friends, he knew she had been lonely and impatient every day for his return, so he had readied himself for tears and anger. But when he finally arrived at the Santo Spirito house, leaving his horse in Luca's care, she surprised him with a welcoming smile, a warm embrace and no hint of disaffection.

Bemused, he followed her upstairs for the ritual inspection of their daughter, sleeping peacefully and oblivious to the return of her father. Disposing of his heavy travelling cloak in its accustomed cupboard and throwing his hat onto the stand next to the door, he went back down to the first-floor parlour, where Marietta had mulled wine waiting for him in front of the fire.

It was only then that she hinted at her displeasure with an ironic arching of her eyebrows. 'That was a long eight days, wouldn't you say? I was beginning to think I would forget your face, you were gone so long.'

'This face? Surely it's not that easy to forget.' His attempt at humour won him the tiniest twitch of a smile at the corners of her mouth, though the rest of her expression was still stern. 'But I am sorry, my dear, that you were left alone for so long. I might have been exaggerating a bit when I said I expected to be away for a few days, but I really didn't think I would be travelling for as long as I was. Duty—'

'Oh, I know, duty. That's what Biagio kept saying, you were just doing your duty, and there was no help for it. But you could have written.'

Niccolò sighed. He knew this had been her chief complaint, made over and over to Biagio and Agostino and anyone else who might listen.

He crossed his hands on his chest in a little gesture of submission. 'Marietta, you are right, of course. I meant to write more often, I really did. But I was so busy during the day and at night I had to deal with all my despatches and all the other letters I had to read and send, but *mea culpa*, I am guilty as charged.'

She looked at him as if deciding whether she had made her point and weighing the sincerity of his apologies. Evidently deciding in the affirmative on both questions, she changed the subject. 'Well, you are home now and that's all that matters. Anyway, you mustn't think I was moping all the time. Monna Agostanza and Monna Alessandra were wonderful, coming around almost every day to see how I was getting on and to help with the baby. And you'll be pleased to know that the household is finally running as it should and that all the winter repairs you wanted to do at the farm are well underway.'

As she talked, he was impressed in spite of himself. Far from pining away in his absence, she had continued with some vigour the program of improvements to the household routines and the management of the farm that she had devised in the early days of their marriage. Totto had provided some help, although he was increasingly busy with his own interests in trade. But essentially, it was all her own work. It was in the evenings, mostly, that she had felt alone and abandoned when she no longer had servants and shopping lists and tradespeople to distract her. She confessed it was true she had run off to stay with her brother for a little while, but it wasn't for all that long. Biagio had, it seemed, been exaggerating somewhat her unhappiness.

*

Walking into the chancellery room the next morning, he was greeted with the usual vulgar jokes from Biagio and Casavecchia, and with insouciant, languorous irony by Agostino Vespucci. It seemed that everyone was happy to see him and they made a great show of escorting him to the big chair behind his desk, as if they were enthroning a returning general. They all wanted to know about his experiences—what was Cesare Borgia really like? What was the style of his court? What had *really* happened at Senigallia? How was Florence seen by Borgia and his courtiers? Which town had the best whores? Entertaining them with a series of stories, only mildly exaggerated, he eventually got them back to work and settled down to begin tackling the papers that had been piled on his desk, awaiting his return.

He had been working for barely half an hour when a note from Piero Soderini requested his presence whenever he should be at leisure. When he arrived at the gonfaloniere's austere suite of apartments on the opposite side of the palazzo, he found Soderini bent over his desk writing, a task he abandoned the moment Niccolò walked into the room. 'The prodigal has returned! I am very glad to have you back, my young friend. Your despatches over the last few months have been helpful, but we've missed your advice in council. Have a seat.'

'Regrettably, I have not yet found a way of being in two places at once, Ser Piero.' Niccolò laughed. 'But I too am glad to be back. As is my wife.'

'I'm sure she is. It can be hard on them, the service that the state demands of us. And hard on us to be without them.' He frowned, his words prompting an unpleasant memory. 'They criticized me, you know, when I moved my wife in here with me. Said that I was breaking the rule that requires both priors and the gonfaloniere to reside alone in the palazzo for the duration of their time in office. Ridiculous. All very well when the gonfaloniere was elected for two months, but they can hardly expect me to do without conjugal comfort for the rest of my life!'

'Ah, that was what I missed when I was away, the high-minded and noble Florentine Republic in all its glory.'

The gentle raillery had the desired effect—Soderini's face creased into laughter. 'It wasn't the most elevating debate that the Great Council has ever had, I grant you. Now, let us get on with serious business. This arrived this morning.'

Unusually, the despatch that Soderini passed across the desk to him had not been routed first through the chancellery. Making a mental note to find out why, he skimmed quickly through the contents, which were sensational. The citizens of Siena, having been bombarded with a series of written tirades from Duke Valentino, had regrettably decided that they would have to surrender their popular leader, Pandolfo Petrucci.

'So Borgia's bluff worked. Pandolfo has fled Siena.' He looked up. 'I must confess I am a little surprised. I thought the duke's hand was weaker than that, and that Pandolfo would see through it.'

'At least he was wily enough to evade Borgia's soldiers and make it to Lucca. He is no friend of ours, but I am not sure I relish the idea of Cesare Borgia on our southern borders in his stead.'

'Borgia won't stay near Siena for very long, I shouldn't think. The pope will want him to turn south and deal with the Orsini and Colonna castles down in the Lazio.'

'Let us hope you are right; you usually are. But we can't go on for much longer like this. You know the situation—Pisa blocks our access to the sea in the west, so trade in that direction is at a standstill, and Borgia stands in our way to the east. As a result, the treasury is empty. We have no money to hire a new army and we are dependent on the goodwill of King Louis for our security.'

'Which might be withdrawn at any time.'

'Quite so. Well, we need to do something to change things. I want to make a formal speech to the Signoria, outlining the problems and asking them to support me in a new effort to raise the necessary funds so we can build up our own forces and make another attempt on Pisa, this time without foreign help. And I would like you to write it for me.'

This Niccolò approved of wholeheartedly. One of the things he had observed in the Romagna was that Borgia's military strength relied on a core of hardened Spanish veterans, augmented by the militia he had raised from within his dominions, recruited, trained and armed by him, and loyal to him alone. It was the mercenary captains who had deserted him, while the Spanish and the militia had stayed loyal. Florence, he was more than ever convinced, needed a similarly loyal army if it was to preserve its independence.

While he was working on this new assignment, one of his predictions came true. Cesare Borgia, heeding at last the demands of his father, turned away from Siena and marched south. One by one, the Orsini castellans abandoned their castles and fled before him. Then, inexplicably, he stopped at Viterbo, set up a siege of the fortress of Ceri, and then left his army to it, returning to Rome for Carnival, the riotous celebrations that marked the beginning of Lent.

Niccolò noted all this in a corner of his mind. The rest was fully engaged in constructing the speech that Piero Soderini planned to give to the Signoria as soon as it was ready. He put aside most of his regular duties or delegated them to Agostino, Biagio and Casavecchia, and retreated to his study in the Santo Spirito house, where he could work in silence all day and often late into the night. Within a fortnight, he had finished..

Soderini, reviewing the ten pages covered with Niccolò's neat script, was enthusiastic. 'Well done, Niccolò, well done indeed. Your arguments for raising our own armies are very thorough.'

'And the taxation proposals? How do you think they will go down?' Niccolò had been particularly anxious about that particular aspect of the speech.

'Well, you do have a sense of humour, I must say,' the gonfaloniere chuckled. 'Taxing the clergy to pay for an army to ward off the pope's own son, that is ingenious. Don't worry. The Signoria will, I am sure, approve that idea in the blink of an eye.'

So it proved: the meeting was brief and amazingly unanimous. When it was over, Niccolò remained behind as the priors departed for their apartments in twos and threes, chattering cheerfully as men do when they feel they have done something worthwhile.

'That went well, Niccolò,' Soderini said, gathering up his papers. 'For once, I think we might have achieved that rarity in Florentine politics—unanimity and resolution. No small thanks to you, my friend.'

Niccolò bobbed his head in modest acknowledgement of the compliment.

'By the way,' the gonfaloniere went on, 'my brother wrote to me yesterday to say that King Louis has ordered Borgia to hand the city back to Pandolfo Petrucci.'

'I am not surprised. Louis wants Borgia and his troops for his campaign against Naples, not charging about Tuscany. If he thought he could persuade the pope to let his son go, he would have Valentino back up in Milan now.'

'I'm sure.' Soderini said absently, picking up a paper from the pile on the table. 'Cesare has agreed to my request to release Leonardo da Vinci from his service, though he was reluctant. You persuaded me that he is worth the risk of offending Borgia, but for the life of me, I don't know what we actually have for him to do. It's not as if we have any military campaigns that require the services of an engineer.'

'But we will, Ser Piero. We both know it is vital we finally recover Pisa if we are ever to revive our trade routes to the west. Leonardo has some powerful ideas that could make that campaign a success.'

'Such as?'

Niccolò frowned. He and Leonardo had talked of many things during those cold nights on the road, including some of the military projects he had planned

287

to undertake for Borgia. One in particular had stuck in his mind and, over the weeks and months that had followed, he found that he could not get it out of his head. But he feared the gonfaloniere would find it outlandish. Still, he had come this far.

'Leonardo thinks we could divert the Arno and thereby cut the Pisans off from being resupplied from the coast. He planned something similar for Borgia in the Val di Chiana.'

'Like Lucca in '34, you mean? I'm not sure I want to repeat that disaster.'

Everyone knew that piece of history, when the Florentines, besieging Lucca, had tried to divert the Sercio to flood the city. The Lucchese had simply sortied out one night and re-diverted it so that it washed out the Florentine camp instead, drowning the workmen and soldiers.

'And I wouldn't recommend such a project, Ser Piero, if I didn't think that Leonardo has the engineering and mathematical skills to do it. We should at least let him draw up some plans.'

Soderini considered him, then nodded, turning towards the door. 'We can't do anything at Pisa until we have raised a new army anyway. But yes, let's see what he can do.'

*

Leonardo arrived in Florence a fortnight later, accompanied by Salai, to take up Niccolò's offer of temporary accommodation until he could find himself more permanent lodgings. His appearance was much as it had been when Niccolò had last seen him, fussing over some cannon in the siege train of Borgia's army, though he was pleased to see that haunted look had gone from his eyes. His face was also now decorated with a straggly beard.

'It makes me look more like a philosopher, don't you think?' the artist said after they had exchanged embraces.

Niccolò, for whom the daily wrangle with the razor was a sacred ritual, thought it made him look unkempt more than anything else. But he hadn't the heart to say so. 'You certainly look more mature; that will be helpful when you are trying to persuade the Signoria of the merits of your various projects.'

Frown lines appeared on the strong brow. 'Niccolò, I appreciate you getting me this position, I truly do, but we must talk about what it entails. You know how I feel about war.'

'I do, my friend. But let's not talk about all that now. Come on and meet Marietta.'

His wife immediately took to Leonardo, who had a kind of old-world courtesy about him that she found irresistibly charming. More surprisingly, she seemed to adore young Salai—they were of a similar age, and she was soon giggling and joining in with his arch little jokes, revealing yet another unsuspected side of herself to her bemused husband.

Not that she was in any way fooled by the façade that Leonardo maintained, that the boy was merely his assistant. 'I assume they are lovers,' she said, the moment they were safely out of earshot.

Niccolò almost choked on the fig he was eating. 'Marietta! Be careful what you say. The Office of the Night is still powerful, you know, even if they spend more time warning than arresting people these days.'

'Niccolò Machiavelli, do you think I am a complete fool? Of course I'm not going to go bruiting it about to all and sundry. If your friend Leonardo wants to pretend Salai is his "assistant" I won't betray him. And I like Salai. He makes me laugh.'

'So I noticed. Never mind, it'll be our secret to keep. By the way, I have to go away again.'

The happy and conspiratorial grin was replaced instantly by a pout. Niccolò threw his hands in the air to forestall the inevitable outburst. 'I am sorry, my love, but you are going to have to get used to these absences of mine. The Signoria trusts me and it is a mark of great honour that they send me on these missions. Were I a wealthier man or our family more ancient, I could refuse, but as things stand I have little choice but to go where and when they bid me.'

They weren't new arguments, nor was it the first time they had talked about it since he had returned, but this time she seemed to accept the inevitability of it. 'Where to this time? And for how long?'

'Just to Siena. And I really will be back in a few days—I am being sent with a message, no more.'

289

She took his hands and gently placed them on her belly. 'Perhaps this will give you another reason to hurry back to me.'

It took him a few moments of confusion before he understood what she was saying. Then, in pure giddy joy, he picked her up and swung her around two or three times until, laughing, she begged him to stop. Bending down, he put his ear on her stomach. 'What's that? You want to be called Bernardo when you come out? Well, I'm sure that can be arranged.'

'And if it is a girl?' Marietta asked, still breathless.

'It won't be,' Niccolò said with certainty. 'Primerana needs a brother, so that is that. And I promise I will hurry back.'

This time he was not forsworn. His mission to Siena was a simple matter of soothing the jittery nerves of Pandolfo Petrucci, newly reinstalled in the Palazzo Pubblico. Ironically, the cause of those nerves was Niccolò's plan to raise money by taxing the clergy, which had necessitated negotiations with Pope Alexander. Pandolfo, hearing that Florence had sent a delegation to Rome, had jumped to the conclusion he was about to be stabbed in the back. Niccolò was back in Florence within a week, having calmed the old *condottiero* down and reassured him that betrayal was the last thing on the Signoria's mind.

He returned to another problem. Piero Soderini had turned from sceptic to enthusiast for the idea of diverting the Arno, the idea that Niccolò had so casually floated several months before and was keen to see some plans drawn up. The difficulty was that Leonardo was now reluctant to do anything in the military line if he could avoid it. 'You know how I feel about war, Niccolò. How can you ask me to design a plan that will just result in destruction and death?'

'Because that is what we told Valentino we needed you for!' Niccolò immediately regretted allowing his exasperation to get the better of him and tried to soften his tone. 'Look, we must win this war against Pisa if we are to have prosperity again. It has already cost too much in lives and treasure and will cost many more unless we can find a way to bring it to an end swiftly, and you can help do that. Besides, it's not as if we want to divert the Arno to drown the enemy army, we just want to cut them off from the sea so they can't be resupplied. Your project will cause no lives to be lost directly and will save many others indirectly.'

In the end, it was the last argument that swayed da Vinci, and he reluctantly got to work on putting together the required plans. Typically, though, once he had started the whole project became an obsession and, by the time it was finished, it was a masterpiece of its kind, pages of detailed drawings and estimates. Presented triumphantly to a newly confident Signoria, it was approved and the funds allocated in record time to enable the project to begin.

Work had started on the project under the watchful but impotent eyes of the Pisan soldiers lining the walls of the city, when the political climate, which had been relatively benign for most of the year, began to look threatening again. That the French began their assault on the Spanish-occupied half of the kingdom of Naples surprised no one, but this time the all-conquering French seemed to have met their match. By the time the heat of August was beating down upon the Italian peninsula, the Spanish captain Gonsalvo da Cordoba had driven them out of their half of the kingdom, leaving them with a bare toehold in the port-town of Gaeta.

Further north, Cesare Borgia had succeeded in taking the fortress of Ceri and was progressively attacking the remaining Orsini castles, and Cesare Borgia, Duke of Valentinois and the Romagna, was now the leading prince in Italy.

'The tyrants who used to rule every city of the papal states are now dead or in exile,' Niccolò told the Signoria. 'Only Bologna is not yet under direct Borgia control, though Giovanni Bentivoglio is in alliance with him. The Orsini and the Colonna, and all the other clans who have plagued pope after pope, are subdued. King Louis dare not offend either Valentino or the pope if he is going to take his army south through their states to relieve Gaeta, and the Borgia army is still encamped at Perugia under Michelotto Corella's command, waiting for instructions. In short, no power in Italy is in a position to constrain him.'

'But King Louis also needs *our* goodwill if he wants to march through Tuscany on his way south,' Soderini objected. 'Still, I take your point. We cannot rely on the French to check Borgia, for now at least, and perhaps not ever if this setback in Naples turns into a full-scale defeat for French arms. I think it behoves us to bring our soldiers on the Arno back to Florence, at least until we know where the wind will blow.'

Which meant the end of the Arno scheme project for now. Niccolò's disappointment was not shared by Leonardo da Vinci, who shrugged his

291

shoulders in acceptance. He was, in any case, more excited by a new assignment Niccolò had procured for him—the painting of a monumental picture to decorate one wall of the Hall of the Five Hundred, the vast chamber on the first floor of the Palazzo della Signoria that had been created to hold meetings of the Great Council. The subject, which Niccolò had suggested, was the battle of Anghiari, which had been fought sixty years before between Florence and Milan.

Agostino Vespucci was recruited to write a detailed history of the battle from which Leonardo could draw his images and as a sort of overall supervisor of the project; he and Leonardo soon became fast friends. Niccolò, dragged to the workshop to view the work in progress, found himself caught up in their enthusiasm. And indeed, from what he saw of the sketches and drawings strewn across tables and benches and pinned on walls, Leonardo was about to create something extraordinary, a fresco that would rival his famed *Last Supper*. What he also saw was Leonardo's horror of the inhuman emotions that war unleashed, the rage and the terror, and the sad desperation. Exchanging looks with his friend across the table, he realised that working on the painting was cathartic for him, and for Niccolò that made the whole project particularly worthwhile.

War, real war, was also imminent in the world outside the peace of Leonardo's workshop. In early August, the French army once again began the long and wearying march south through Tuscany and the papal states, aiming to relieve the beleaguered forces cooped up in Gaeta, and Italy prepared itself for another bloody summer.

Then, in the third week of the month, news came like a thunderbolt from a summer sky—Rodrigo Borgia, Pope Alexander VI, was dead.

Chapter 26—The Wheel of Fortune Turns

Florence, August 1503

The pope's death had been a shock, not so much because it was completely unexpected—he was seventy-one years old after all, and it had been an exceptionally hot summer, conditions always conducive to outbreaks of sickness in Rome—but because of the speed of it. He had fallen ill on August twelfth, a week after he and Valentino attended a dinner party at the home of Cardinal Adriano da Corneto. By the seventeenth he was dead.

It was curious that Cesare should have contracted the same illness at the same time. Naturally, the rumour was that they had been poisoned; a possibility quickly ruled out when Cardinal Adriano himself was stricken with fever. But poison or no, Cesare was sufficiently conscious to be able to order the ever-faithful Michelotto to ransack the papal apartments on the floor below and remove the treasure that was hidden in a secret chamber behind the pope's bed. After that, he lapsed back into feverish incoherence.

These were the bald facts contained in that first hurried report from Rome. As he read it, Niccolò knew this was a disaster for Cesare Borgia. His father's death he would, of course, have anticipated and prepared for. But it seemed doubtful he would have planned for the possibility that he would be so incapacitated as to be unable to direct events in the aftermath of the papal demise.

More couriers came in over the following days, horses lathered and clothes coated in grime kicked up from the dusty high summer roads. The news they brought was of an empire beginning to fall apart. First to go was Urbino, which received its returning Duke Guidobaldo with rapture at the end of August. Then in rapid succession, the *condottieri* who had variously served and betrayed Duke Cesare reacquired their cities of Pesaro, Rimini, Piombino, Perugia and Città del Castello.

Yet the cities at the heart of the Romagna held firm, the towns where Cesare Borgia's name had come to mean good government and prosperity. Cesena stoutly resisted an assault by the ever-opportunistic Venetians. Not that they had a monopoly on cynicism, for after only a short and gleeful debate, the Florentine Signoria had backed the efforts of Ottaviano Riario, the *condottiero* son of Caterina Sforza, to recover his patrimony of Imola, Forlì and Faenza. Florentine excitement was extinguished, however, when the news came that Riario had been thoroughly and bloodily repulsed, the citizens of all three towns declaring their undying allegiance to Duke Valentino.

Then King Louis once again came the rescue of his much-favoured young friend and announced that any state attacking Cesare's dominions would be considered to be making war on France. In one of the most rapid decisions Niccolò had ever seen it make, the Signoria withdrew its support for Riario and proclaimed its support for the continued rule of Cesare Borgia. Venice, too, beat a hasty retreat.

The dead pope having been buried in macabre and grotesque circumstances as his bloated body was stuffed into a coffin too small for him, it was necessary for a papal conclave to gather and elect a successor. Francesco Soderini, now a cardinal since his elevation at the hands of the late pope in May, hurried south to attend. At the end of September, the name of the new pope was proclaimed in all the churches of Europe—Pius III, formerly Cardinal Francesco Piccolomini of Siena.

'Why did they pick him?' Niccolò asked Luca degli Albizzi, newly returned from Rome, where he had been attending to family business. 'He's worthy enough, I grant you, and the right age, sixty-four, but his health is famously poor. I can't imagine he will last long.'

'You mean you can't see through it? You're losing your touch, Machiavelli!' Albizzi's grin grew even wider when his little joke was rewarded with a scowl. 'Here is how it worked, according to Cardinal Soderini. The conclave was hopelessly split between the Spaniards, who wanted to elect Borgia's candidate, Cardinal Vera, and the French, who wanted your old friend Georges d'Amboise. The Italians, as usual, sat in the middle, waiting to see who would offer them what.'

'And Giuliano della Rovere? Where was he in this?'

'Good question. Now you're back on form, Niccolò.' Albizzi laughed. 'Since he returned from exile last month, della Rovere has been agitating for his own candidacy, telling everyone that he was the natural compromise between the Spanish and the French.'

'Which of course would be the worst possible outcome for Cesare Borgia.' Della Rovere had been the sworn enemy of the Borgias ever since the cardinals chose Rodrigo Borgia over him in 1492. Having failed to win the papacy, he went into exile and had spent best part of the last ten years railing against Pope Alexander.

'Exactly. Anyway, Soderini told me that once they were in conclave, none of the factions was able to muster the necessary two-thirds majority and, in the end, the Spanish and the French combined to choose Piccolomini as a compromise. Anyone other than della Rovere.'

Who must have been furious to have been denied the papacy for a second time by the Borgia faction. Of course, if the new pope expired soon, the chess pieces would end up back where they had started; both sides would no doubt be hoping that they could strengthen their support in the meantime.

'Where was Cesare all this time? Still holed up in the fortress at Nepi?' Borgia had retired there to recover from his illness.

'So far as anyone knows, yes. He has the most remarkable spy network, you know. He seems to know everything that happens in Rome almost before the event.'

'That at least is no surprise. With all the gold he ransacked from his father's treasury, he can afford to make sure he is well informed.' Niccolò frowned, thinking. 'The key thing is that Pius owes his election to Borgia's Spanish cardinals, so Cesare more or less has the new pope in his pocket.'

Which was exactly the position that Borgia had told him he wanted to be in, that last time they had met. Silently, Niccolò applauded the political and strategic skills of his old adversary, who had managed under extraordinary circumstances to wrest a future from the wreckage of his father's death.

'One more thing,' Albizzi said. 'Just before I left, it was announced that Cesare Borgia was to be restored to his position as captain-general of the papal armies. What is more, Pius has sent messages to the Venetians and Baglioni in Perugia demanding they desist from harassing Borgia's possessions in the Romagna. It rather looks as though Borgia is back in the saddle.'

'For as long as Pope Pius lives.' Niccolò replied thoughtfully. 'After that, he will have to play the whole game again.'

Neither of them realised at the time just how soon Niccolò's prediction would come true. Just twenty-six days after he had been elected, the shortest papacy in history ended when Pope Pius III died as the result of an ulcer in his leg. The cardinals once again prepared to gather in conclave to choose a successor, and the Florentine Signoria, anxious to have first-hand reports on the events that were about to unfold, despatched to Rome their most reliable observer, Niccolò Machiavelli.

*

The first thing Niccolò thought as he greeted his old colleague Francesco Soderini was that he had put on weight since his elevation to cardinal, a condition that seemed to have reached epidemic proportions in Rome if the sample of well-fed priests, deacons, bishops and cardinals he had passed in the streets on his way into the city was anything to go by.

'Welcome to the Eternal City, Niccolò. Awful place, isn't it?'

'It does seem a little... dilapidated,' Niccolò replied.

He had been disappointed by his first sight of Rome. Looking down from the heights of Monte Mario, he saw a town that occupied only a tiny portion of the famous city of antiquity, jammed into a bend of the Tiber and spilling across into the district around the Vatican known as the Borgo. The rest of the area, still enclosed by the vast Aurelian walls snaking around the fabled seven hills, was almost entirely farmland or open wasteland, within which the ancient monuments, triumphal arches, baths and basilicas stood like stranded monsters. The city itself was, for the most part, a filthy, overgrown village of cheap and ramshackle houses overlooking muddy streets through which gangs of ragged children roamed, and pigs and other livestock rooted among the rubbish piled in the corners.

Amid the squalor, the palazzi of the bishops and cardinals and the local grandees stood in stark contrast; a permanent reminder of the wealth of the church flung in the faces of a resentful population. Francesco Soderini's house, in whose main salon they were now sitting, was a fine but relatively modest building on the busy Via Sant' Angelo, midway between the forbidding bulk of the Castel Sant' Angelo in one direction and the Vatican Palace in the other. Niccolò's lodgings, rented for ten carlini per day, were in a hostelry not far away, and he had hurried here to meet with the cardinal as soon as he had unpacked and settled horses and servants.

'A good place to invest, though,' the cardinal said comfortably, his fingers dancing above a bowl of fruit, from which he plucked a perfectly ripe fig. 'I've bought quite a lot of property here that is yielding excellent rents. Let us get to business—what are your instructions from the Signoria?'

'To watch and report, mostly. And to do what I can to further Florentine interests, in conjunction with yourself, of course.'

The cardinal bobbed his head in acknowledgement. 'Good. It will be a great help to have you here. I can look after things in the conclave, but you have more freedom to ferret about and find out what is going on outside.'

'And what *is* the situation at present?'

'More like an eastern bazaar than a papal conclave, there are so many promises of money going around.' Soderini's mouth turned down in distaste. 'Borgia has the eleven Spanish cardinals in his pocket, so everyone is trooping up to the Castel Sant' Angelo, making offers and trying to find out what he will do with his votes. The French will be pledged to Cardinal d'Amboise, of course. And as usual, the Italians are in the middle, waiting to see who offers what.'

'And Giuliano della Rovere? I suppose he will be supported by the Italians?'

'The good Cardinal San Pietro in Vincola is going around promising everything to everyone, so desperate is he to be elected this time. You know Johannes Burchard, Alexander's master of ceremonies?' Niccolò nodded, though he only knew of him by reputation. 'Well, he told me that della Rovere met with Cesare and all his cardinals at the Vatican last week, and promised to confirm Borgia in all his possessions and reappoint him as captain-general of the papal armies in return for his support in the conclave.'

'So even if della Rovere is elected, Cesare will be back in power once again?' Niccolò had to admire the shrewdness with which Borgia played the limited cards he held in his hand.

'Though one imagines the new pope might be somewhat less indulgent than the old,' Soderini said dryly. 'I've known Giuliano for many years and I think he would be a difficult man for Valentino to manipulate. But his election is not necessarily certain. My colleagues often express one opinion before a conclave and act entirely differently once they have been shut up in the Sistine Chapel. So we will have to see.'

But in the end, there was not long to wait and this time the outcome was a surprise to no one. It was nearly midnight a few days later when, sitting up late in his lodgings writing despatches, one of Cardinal della Rovere's servants arrived accompanied by no less than twenty soldiers, disturbed the entire hostelry with his banging on the doors, and told him that his master had been elected pope after one of the shortest conclaves in history.

'And what name will Cardinal della Rovere take?'

'He has let it be known that he will be called Pope Julius, the second of that name.'

Which in itself said something about the new pope: only a man of supreme self-belief and towering ego would take a name that was virtually the same as his own Christian name, instead of picking from the pantheon of long-honoured papal cognomens available.

Cardinal Soderini, when they met a few days later, was enthusiastic. 'It was all but unanimous in the end, Niccolò. And a good outcome for Florence, I think. He has a temper, it is true, and can be inflexible, but he is also a true pastor to the holy church and will, I think, place the church's interests over his own.'

Unlike the late Pope Alexander, Niccolò thought. But he also thought that Julius might find himself more hemmed in than he wanted to be once it became apparent that the many promises he had made conflicted with each other.

'The duke at least seems satisfied with the result,' Soderini went on. 'As we speak, he is moving himself and his fifty retainers from the Castel Sant' Angelo to the Vatican Palace, at the invitation of the new pope.'

'What are his next moves likely to be, do you think?'

'He has two hundred thousand ducats or more banked with the Genoese, so it is thought he might go there, before joining Michelotto Corella and the rest of his army. But I imagine he will not want to leave Rome until the pope has been crowned and his position as captain-general confirmed, as he was promised. That will give him the authority he needs to launch a new campaign to recover the Romagna.'

298

'A strategy that relies upon Pope Julius keeping his promises,' Niccolò said dryly.

'Why would he not?' Soderini seemed taken aback by the very suggestion.

'Forgive me, eminence, but the hatred that the former Cardinal della Rovere has for both Cesare and his father is well known. And I doubt he will easily forget that he endured ten years of exile under Alexander VI. He might well come to think that Borgia running around the Romagna with an army, building up his state again, will be a lot less biddable than Borgia fed on hope and kept close at hand here in Rome.'

'All that may be true, but I think you are underestimating the integrity of this pope. Julius would find it difficult to break his promise, once given.'

'Yet he has made many so promises, eminence, that some of them must be broken in the end.' Niccolò hesitated, wondering if he had gone too far. 'No, Borgia is foolish if he believes that the word of others, even that of the pope, is to be relied upon any more than his own, which has been given in bad faith often enough.'

Though Cardinal Soderini still did not seem convinced, this last point did at least give him pause. 'Time alone will tell, Niccolò. In the meantime, put all that in your despatch and the Signoria can chew it all over while we await events.'

*

Niccolò's introduction to the pontiff-elect came two days later when he presented himself at the Vatican to formally offer the congratulations of the Florentine Republic on his election. At sixty-nine years of age, Giuliano della Rovere had an air of vigour about him that suggested a man of many fewer years, his fingers tapping restlessly on the arm of his chair as he listened to Niccolò's looping diplomatic phrases expressing the pleasure of the Signoria and the general joy of the population of Florence at the great event.

When he had finished, the new pope's long, manicured fingers combed the luxuriant white beard for a few moments as he contemplated the Florentine emissary. 'We thank your Signoria for their kindness, Signor Machiavelli, and reciprocate with our affection towards the Republic of Florence, upon whose support we have ever relied.' The voice was deep, clear and determined. 'We also owe a debt to His Eminence, the Cardinal of Volterra, who was, in great measure, instrumental in our elevation. You may be sure the interests of your republic will ever be in my mind.'

With which the pope-elect offered his hand to be kissed, and the interview was over.

*

'The Venetians have invaded the Romagna!' Niccolò announced rather breathlessly, having pushed past the startled the doorman and charged up the stairs to where the cardinal was working in his study. 'The city of Imola has fallen, though the Rocca remains in Borgia's hands, Forlì has finally abandoned the duke and risen in revolt, and Faenza is under siege.'

'Sit down, Niccolò; you'll have a seizure. Now, where did you hear that news?'

'One of Francesco del Bene's couriers.' He slid gratefully into a chair and handed over a packet of papers; while Soderini read quickly through its contents, Niccolò continued talking. 'I doubt that anyone else in Rome has this news as yet. The courier rode post from Florence and told me that as far as he knew no others had yet left when he rode out.'

The cardinal looked up and nodded. 'We should tell the pope at once. But as the official Florentine emissary to his holiness, you should take it to him; I must be seen to be independent of the secular government of Florence as much as possible.' He picked up a bell to summon a retainer. 'Let me send a messenger first to clear the way and make sure you are sent straight into His Holiness. You know how tedious the papal bureaucrats can be otherwise.'

An hour later, Niccolò was being into the surprised presence of the pope. 'Signor Machiavelli, I had not expected to see you again so soon. I trust you do not come to bring me evil news?'

'Whether good or evil I cannot tell, Your Holiness, but my news is, I think, important and comes directly from Florence, outrunning all others.'

The pope listened politely as he detailed the contents of his despatch that morning. At the end, his reaction was surprisingly tranquil. 'We thank you, my son, for sharing this intelligence, but I see no cause for alarm. The Venetians have proven to be my good friends over the years. I can only suppose they

300

have launched this attack in ignorance of my election. Once it is known, they will surely desist.'

'And if they do not, holiness?' The sharp drawing of breath among the courtiers surrounding the papal throne told Niccolò that his bluntness was on the edge of impertinence. 'I do not mean to be disrespectful, but Florence views this incursion into the Romagna with deep concern and we would not want our security to depend entirely upon Venetian goodwill towards Your Holiness.'

'I understand, Messer Machiavelli, why your Signoria might be concerned.' The pope's voice was still amiable. 'But I believe that I know the Serenissima well enough to trust that they will withdraw when word gets to Venice that I have been elected.'

'You trust them enough to risk losing all of your key cities in the Romagna which Duke Valentino secured for the papacy at such cost to the papal treasury?'

The slap of the pope's hand on the arm of his throne echoed through the room. His eyes blazed dangerously, and his voice rose a pitch. 'Enough, Messer Machiavelli! I have said that I expect the Venetian government will desist and I have every confidence that they will.' The flash of anger passed, and he raised a placating hand. 'But in deference to the concerns of your government, we will cause letters to be sent to the Doge to remind him that the Romagna is papal territory, lest he should have forgotten.'

With which Niccolò had to be satisfied. It was clear that the pope was not ready to offend the Venetians, whose cardinals had voted in a bloc for him in the conclave and to whom he had promised who knew what in return.

As the door closed behind him, he found himself face to face with the saturnine visage of one of the most powerful prelates in Italy, Cardinal Asciano Sforza. Younger brother of the ill-fated Duke Ludovico of Milan, Sforza was vice-chancellor of the church, and had been a competitor for the papal throne in each of the last two conclaves, at which he had controlled a sizeable bloc of votes. He was accompanied by Cardinal Sanseverino, who, in his late twenties, was one of the youngest members of the curia. The two had obviously been deep in conversation before Niccolò startled them with his sudden appearance from the papal throne room.

301

'Machiavelli, isn't it?' Sforza said in a deep and booming baritone that emerged from a corpulent frame luxuriously swathed in red silk. 'You've just come from the pope, I assume. What has he said to make you look as if the heavens are about to fall?'

Niccolò hastily bent to kiss the casually offered episcopal ring and, straightening, relayed the news as economically as possible, all the while watching the face of this cardinal who had a reputation for wily shrewdness and vaulting ambition.

He was relieved that Sforza at least seemed to be taking the news as seriously as Niccolò thought it deserved, though his younger companion was airily dismissive. 'Surely, Asciano, anything that discomfits Borgia is to be applauded! Besides, this is a matter that affects Tuscany more than the papacy. Perhaps Messer Machiavelli here is more concerned that the Venetians will attack them next?'

'Your Eminence,' Niccolò addressed Asciano, pointedly ignoring Sanseverino, 'it is not a matter just for Tuscany, but for the security of the church in Italy. If you allow Venice to extend its territory into the Romagna, the pope will end up being nothing more than the chaplain of the Venetians, something that anyone who might one day aspire to the papal tiara ought not to countenance.'

A small smile appeared on Sforza's face. Though his last two candidacies had failed, Sforza was young enough to hope that his chance might yet come. 'He does have a point, Federico,' he said, still smiling. 'Very well, Messer Machiavelli, we will see what we can do to encourage His Holiness to understand the gravity of the situation.'

As the two churchmen were ushered into the pontifical apartments, Niccolò remembered that the one person for whom his news was most important, Duke Valentino, was also lodged in the Vatican. Enquiring of a page the duke's whereabouts, he threaded his way through the labyrinth of corridors and anterooms, and eventually presented himself at the duke's door, where Borgia's long-serving secretary, Agapito Geraldini, greeted him with his usual wintry reserve before ushering him into the ducal presence.

Niccolò was shocked by the appearance of the man who rose from his desk and came across the room to greet him. Though he still moved with the same leonine grace, he seemed to have aged a decade. His olive complexion had acquired a yellowish tinge and was stretched tight over the bones of his face. The once-powerful frame seemed shrunken under the rich black doublet and his hand shook as he extended it in greeting. But the black, impenetrable eyes were the same, as was the beguiling voice.

'Well, well, my friend, you find me in reduced circumstances.' As he gestured Niccolò to a seat, Borgia was assailed by a fit of coughing which he did his best to smother with a fist. A handkerchief appeared from somewhere in his doublet and he dabbed at his lips as he sat down. 'My health, as you see, has not yet quite recovered, though I am much improved from the worst. It was the last thing I expected, you know, to be struck down with illness at the same time my father died. I planned for every other contingency, but not for that.'

'Fortune is sometimes capricious, excellency, and chooses to throw those who ride her just when they are in the last turn of the race.'

That brought a wry smile to the stricken man's face. 'Your analogy is apt, as usual. I promise you I will be mounted again and very soon! But tell me what brings you to my door hot-foot and with, so Agapito tells me, urgent news?'

'Urgent indeed, but it is news that I fear will not be to your liking. The Serenissima has invaded the Romagna. The city of Imola is lost to you, though the Rocca still holds out in your favour. The Venetians have also attacked Forlì and Faenza. Our despatch said that they were resisting, but for all I know both places may have fallen by now.'

There was silence, and what colour remained in Borgia's face drained away as he comprehended the significance of what he had just been told and calculated its implications. 'How certain is this?' he asked softly.

'The courier arrived this morning and the despatches were attested by the Florentine Signoria. It is certain.'

'And Pope Julius? What action is he taking?'

'None that I am yet aware of, though I and others are seeking to persuade him that this Venetian attack is as much a danger to him as it is to Florence.'

'Pope Julius is new to the game, but I expect he will learn its rules soon enough. As for the Venetians, they are like a pack of hyenas, feeding on the carcass left behind from the lion's kill. That is their nature and one cannot

303

expect them to behave any differently.' Borgia frowned and his voice began to rise in pitch and volume. 'You Florentines are hardly any better. Your damned Signoria say they are my friends, but they backed that puling boy, Ottaviano Riario, and his bitch of a mother in his schemes against me, before King Louis terrified them into changing their minds. You think I didn't know? Well, they will see soon enough what a mistake they've made in not dealing honestly with me.'

Niccolò said nothing; in truth, he was unsurprised that Borgia was aware of the Signoria's pathetically ill-considered manoeuvres, and he was a little ashamed on their behalf for the half-hearted way they had gone about trying to exploit the situation.

Borgia pressed on, sensing Niccolò's hesitation. 'If you Florentines had given me the alliance I asked for, a real alliance, not that meaningless treaty your ambassador Salviati foisted on me, with its endless excuses about lack of money and the like, none of this would have happened. Together, we could have secured all these cities against the Venetians and none of them would have been threatened. You know, whatever honeyed words they used, I think you Florentines have always been my enemy.'

A violent, hacking coughing fit brought this tirade to a momentary halt. When it was over, the duke glared at him, and then resumed, his tone savagely sarcastic. 'Well, Niccolò, nothing to say? No sweet words of balm for me? I will tell you this—I am not done yet. When the pope confirms me in my offices, I will be back and I will sweep all my enemies away. And I will so manage matters that your republic will come to regret that it did not ally with me when it could. In fact, I think I will turn everything else I have over to the Venetians and throw in my lot with them. Then your republic will be ruined and it will be my turn to laugh.'

Would Borgia do such a thing? Niccolò couldn't be sure. After all, the Venetians had once before dangled before the duke an appointment as captain-general of their armies, complete with a palazzo in Venice, so it wasn't impossible. Whether they would still want him now his power base was so reduced might be another question. Then there was the position of the French in all this. 'The French king—'

'The French king! I would not count on Louis to pluck your chestnuts from the fire. He is too busy with Naples and he will be too distracted to give you any help.'

This was probably true, but Niccolò saw no point in saying so; Borgia was now well launched into his rant, and there was little he could do except listen in silence. As the words tumbled urgently over each other, almost to the point of incoherence, he did his best with murmured monosyllables and placatory gestures to soothe a man who seemed to verge on being completely deranged.

But eventually the storm blew itself out, and Borgia came rambling to a halt. An odd expression came over his face, puzzled, almost as if he had only just heard himself speaking.

'Ah, Niccolò.' Out of nowhere, the old charming smile was back. 'You must forgive me. These are trying times for me and I lose my temper too easily. We are men of the world, you and I, and we understand each other, do we not? I know your masters are afraid of me. But you must tell them that my only desire is to rule the Romagna for the pope as wisely and well as I can and that I am no threat to them.'

'Excellency, I will, of course, convey your words faithfully,' Niccolò said carefully. Then, on an impulse, he added, 'If I may venture a word of advice, My Lord, it is this—do not trust the word of this pope.'

'Why not?' Borgia seemed genuinely surprised. 'Giuliano della Rovere has a reputation as a man who keeps his word, and he owes his election to me.'

'Excellency, that the pope will wish to keep his promises to you, I have no doubt. But you know he has made so many undertakings to so many others, some of them your enemies, that he may find it expedient to break his promises to you.'

There was silence, then the duke rose to his feet, signalling that the interview was over. 'I appreciate your advice, Niccolò, but I fear you see shadows where there are none. The pope and I are in perfect accord and I am certain he will keep his word.'

It seemed a startlingly naïve thing to say for a man who had himself broken his word so many times to so many people, and he said as much to Francesco Soderini and Georges d'Amboise when he joined them at supper in the

Soderini palazzo. The Cardinal of Rouen had changed little since Niccolò had last seen him in Tours, apart from a few new lines etched across the broad forehead, and he had greeted Machiavelli with affection. 'You have had a busy day of it, young man. Come and join us. I don't know where you found your cook, Francesco, but this stuffed pork is excellent.'

Cardinal Soderini inclined his head in acknowledgement of this compliment as a servant pulled a chair back from the table for Niccolò, who suddenly realised that he had not eaten all day and was ravenous.

'So our young duke was in a less than charitable mood, eh?' d'Amboise continued. 'Well, perhaps the time has come for him to learn that God never yet allowed any sin to go unpunished and he certainly will not allow those of Cesare Borgia to pass.'

'Will the pope keep his word, do you think, Your Eminence?'

'I am sure we will find out tomorrow at Julius's first consistory meeting. If he intends to confirm Borgia as captain-general of the church, he will do so then.'

'And if he does not, Georges?' Soderini asked. 'What then?'

'Anything may happen. Borgia has been gathering troops to go back to the Romagna, but without the formal authority of the pope behind him, regaining his territory will be much more difficult, even if Julius allows him to go. If he does not, then he will have to raise an army himself.' The French cardinal paused and smiled sardonically. 'Or perhaps he will hand the whole province over to France.'

The two Florentines exchanged glances under the amused eyes of d'Amboise.

'Better to have the Romagna in French hands than Venetian,' Soderini said, though with little conviction. 'Mind you, I expect you will have your hands full until the campaign against Naples has concluded.'

'Which it soon will be, Francesco, if the generals are to be believed.' D'Amboise was complacent.

The conversation turned to other topics, which Niccolò attended with half of his mind, the other half busily evaluating the prospects for the brilliant, violent, moody man he had left earlier that afternoon. They were not good.

Chapter 27—A Roman Farce

Rome, November 1503

It was a pleasantly sunny, cool November afternoon and Niccolò was on his way back to the cardinal's palazzo after a day spent sightseeing. Earlier that morning he had abandoned his half-finished despatches and decided to give himself a small holiday, wandering across the Tiber into the maze of narrow streets that criss-crossed central Rome, seeming to run in every direction at once. A small crowd of ragged children seemed to appear from nowhere to follow him around, filthy arms stretched out from ragged sleeved in search of alms; only the unexpected appearance of the Watch sent them scurrying away down alleys and into the doors of nearby houses.

He had expected to behold with wonder the monuments of the ancient world, but instead had been invaded by ever more melancholy thoughts as he went from the jumbled ruins of the Forum, now populated mostly by sheep, to the empty, echoing brick shells that was all that remained of the ancient bath complexes. Even the Colosseum seemed dejected, its lower tiers half-buried and the rest of its arches festooned with shrubs and weeds, moss and flowers. Only the Pantheon, now reconsecrated as the basilica of St Mary and the Martyrs, was able to inspire awe and wonder; gazing around its dome, Niccolò could understand how it had inspired Filippo Brunelleschi to come up with a design for the construction of the great dome of Florence's cathedral.

The sense of sadness at Rome's decline from the greatest city in the world to a drab half-empty village stayed with him as he joined the chattering throng of pilgrims and priests crossing the bridge across a muddy and sluggish Tiber towards the vast and forbidding drum of the Castel Sant'Angelo. Dodging around a vast litter conveying some pampered prince of the church towards the Vatican, he headed up the Via Alessandrina towards cardinal Soderini's fine palazzo.

'I know, Niccolò. It's a shock at first when you realise how much has been lost, how many buildings have been stripped of their marble and their statues so they are barely recognisable,' Francesco Soderini said as they began an early dinner. 'Mind you, the political unrest, the endless feuds between the Orsini, the Colonna, the Barberini and the rest doesn't much help. Pope after pope has pledged to build a new Rome, but they have all ended up spending most of their time just making sure of their own survival.'

The dinner and the conversation moved on, and they were deep in a discussion of the works of the Roman historian Sallust when they were interrupted by the cardinal's chamberlain, who handed him a note.

'Ah. Well, well.' Looking up from the paper, he met Niccolò's expectant gaze. 'The consistory, it appears, has decided not to renew Valentino's commission as captain-general. If friend Borgia was angry the other day, he will be fit to be tied after he gets this news.'

'Then I'm glad it's not me who has to deliver it to him; I could only stand one such tirade in a week.'

'Yes, I think you've earned a reprieve. But give it a day or two, then go to see him and try to find out what his intentions are now.'

But, as unpredictable as ever, Cesare Borgia surprised him when Niccolò presented himself at the ducal apartments two days later. It was almost as if, by taking this decision, the consistory had relieved him of one of his burdens and, far from being downcast, he was positively ebullient. 'I don't need this false title, Niccolò. Don't you see? Without it, I am free to recover my cities beholden to no one. Michelotto is mustering troops for me as I speak.'

'And the pope has agreed to this enterprise?' Niccolò was startled. 'Given you leave to depart?'

'Not yet, but he says he will. He has finally come to understand it is not in his interests for the Venetians to make themselves masters of the Romagna.'

Niccolò could hardly disagree, having made the same point to the pope only a few days ago.

'My friend,' Borgia went on, 'it is surely time now for your Signoria to support me. If they help me now, once I am established back in my dukedom they can count on my friendship; tell them that.'

'I will, Your Excellency, of course.'

'There is something else. I need a safe-conduct from Florence for myself and my army so that we can go across Tuscany from La Spezia. Without it, I can

309

do nothing. Can you arrange that? Agapito will give you the formal letter to send with your despatches.'

Niccolò nodded and, shortly thereafter, took his leave, a little bemused.

'Do you think the pope will really allow him to go?' he asked Cardinal Soderini when they met at the end of the day to compare notes. 'It seems naïve, to say the least.'

'Julius doesn't know his own mind. One day he rails against Borgia, the next he offers him the use of the papal galleys to transport his household and his troops to join Corella at La Spezia. He doesn't have an army that could expel the Venetians from the Romagna, so instead he hopes that Borgia might do it for him, even though he doesn't trust him.'

'In all honesty, eminence, it seems to me that both the pope and the duke are deluded; Borgia has at most a few hundred men mustered with Corella at La Spezia, not enough to reconquer the Romagna without serious reinforcements.'

'True enough.' The cardinal shrugged. 'We will just have to wait and see what happens; in the meantime we may as well send Borgia's request for a safe conduct off to Florence and see what they say.'

Over the next fortnight the situation in Rome became almost comical. Pope Julius finally made up his mind, and told Duke Valentino that he could embark for La Spezia with his blessing and support. Borgia then succumbed to an uncharacteristic bout of irresolution, one day making preparations to leave, the next cancelling them and withdrawing to his apartments in solitude. Finally the duke and his entourage, accompanied by a strong force of five hundred infantrymen, departed Rome and went to Ostia, there to board the galleys Julius had provided. The sigh of relief could almost be heard echoing off the walls of the Vatican.

But then the comedy descended into farce as the pope had yet another attack of indecision.

Niccolò and Cardinal Soderini were playing cards late in the evening when a messenger arrived at the palazzo with a summons for Soderini to the papal bedchamber. Returning an hour later, the cardinal was both perplexed and annoyed. 'He wants me to go down to Ostia. Apparently, he hasn't been able to sleep for worrying about the state of things in the Romagna and wants me to try and persuade Cesare to hand over the fortresses at Imola and Forlì.'

'Persuade?'

'He meant demand. But with promises to restore them to him in the future.'

'And if Borgia does not give them up?'

'His Holiness was silent on the question,' Soderini said with some asperity.

There was no chance that Borgia would comply. These fortresses were the last shreds of his possessions in the Romagna after all his other cities and castles had been taken by the Venetians, seized by popular uprisings, or taken back by his former mercenary captains. Without them he would have no bases from which to even attempt a reconstruction of his former state. And so it proved: within days the duke had been arrested and returned to the city, accompanied by an exhausted Cardinal Soderini.

'I have never seen a man so reduced,' he said when he came back to the palazzo, where Niccolò was waiting for him at a supper-table groaning with food and drink. 'When he realised his last hope had gone, he broke down, weeping and crying out against the perfidy of the pope.'

'Then he will be even more distressed when he learns the latest news—Michelotto Corella has been captured.' Niccolò had heard of this in the most dramatic fashion. He had been in the middle of an audience with Pope Julius when a messenger had arrived with a despatch announcing the arrest. The pope's savage pleasure had been something to behold.

'That is bad news for Borgia. Corella is his best general and certainly his most loyal retainer.' Soderini drained his wine-glass, grimacing as he got a mouthful of the lees. 'But the castles at Forlì and Imola won't surrender until they receive instructions from Cesare himself, accompanied by the secret passwords that will authenticate the messages, so he still has a little leverage.'

Niccolò frowned. Was the pope desperate enough or unprincipled enough to resort to torture to extract the required passwords? Borgia himself would not have hesitated were their roles reversed, but Pope Julius was of a different hue altogether.

'We shall see,' he said, rising to take his leave. 'I must go—my desk, as always, reproaches me for my neglect. Oh, I almost forgot—your eminence should congratulate me.' Niccolò was deliberately arch.

'Congratulate you?' The cardinal's frown was puzzled. 'What for?'

'I am a father once again. A boy.'

The news had come in a letter from Biagio the day before, almost a casual passing reference, '*your sprout looks like a little crow he is so dark*', and Niccolò assumed that a more formal announcement of the happy event had gone astray somewhere between Florence and Rome.

'A boy! My dear young friend, congratulations indeed!' The cardinal's enthusiasm was unfeigned, as was the embrace. 'You can't go now; we must have at least one beaker of wine to the baby's health! What are you calling him?'

'Marietta and I agreed that we would name him Bernardo, after my father.'

'Well, then, let us drink to Bernardo di Niccolò di Bernardo Machiavelli.'

In the end, it was long after midnight that he returned to his neglected desk and decided it would have to remain ignored until the morning.

*

'You should have seen the look on Georges d'Amboise's face, Niccolò! It took all the willpower I possess to keep a straight face.'

The cause of Cardinal Soderini's mirth was the news that the pope had asked—demanded—that Cesare Borgia be lodged in the Cardinal of Rouen's apartments, supposedly as a guest, but in fact under a kind of loose house arrest. Niccolò could well imagine the chagrin this had caused d'Amboise, whose scorn for the former Lord of the Romagna had become more and more vocal over recent weeks.

'When does His Eminence leave for France?' Niccolò asked.

'He is not sure himself—he's waiting for confirmation from the emperor that he will be received if he wishes to call on him on the way home. He told me

312

he has some hopes of getting Maximilian to resume talks about a treaty between the empire and France.'

'And in the meantime, he has Cesare Borgia lodged in his nest like an unwanted cuckoo chick. No wonder he is furious.' Another thought struck Niccolò. 'Will Borgia accompany him north, do you think?'

'More likely the pope will throw him into the Castel Sant'Angelo now he has the passwords for his fortresses.'

That had been the most surprising piece of news Soderini had brought back with him from his latest audience with the pope—Duke Valentino had finally given up the passwords that would be needed to get his castellans to surrender. How he had been convinced was a mystery, though evidently it had happened after a particularly emotional interview between Borgia and Guidobaldo da Montefeltro, now once again securely back in control of his Duchy of Urbino.

'He has the passwords but he doesn't yet have the castles,' Niccolò said, sceptically. 'And if I am any judge, this pope will do nothing further until he is sure they have surrendered.'

It was a prescient judgement. Two days later, shocking news came from the north. When one of Borgia's lieutenants presented himself in Cesena with Borgia's orders to hand over the keys to the Rocca at Imola, the equally devoted castellans had smelled a rat and decided that Borgia could only have surrendered the passwords under duress. Not only did they refuse to surrender, they murdered their unfortunate former colleague.

This piece of savagery almost sealed Borgia's fate. A furious pope was dissuaded with difficulty by the Spanish cardinals from throwing him into the deepest of the Castel Sant'Angelo's dungeons; instead, he was left in possession of the elegant suite of apartments that had been vacated by Cardinal d'Amboise.

Two days later, a surprised Niccolò received a politely worded note asking if he would wait upon Duke Valentino whenever it should be convenient.

The duke's appearance had changed considerably for the better. No longer sallow, the handsome bearded face shone with good health, as did the muscular body, returned to its former weight.

'Do I surprise you, Niccolò my friend?' Borgia's opening words as he came across the room were delivered in a confident, bantering tone. 'Did you expect me to be prostrate with grief or wailing at the evil turn of fate that seems to have befallen me?'

'Excellency, I had no expectations whatsoever,' Niccolò said with absolute truth.

Borgia chuckled. 'That's my Niccolò, giving nothing away. Sometimes I think you are just a blank page, waiting for history to write on you.'

'That may be so, excellency, although perhaps I will do some of the writing when I have the leisure to do so.'

There was silence as they regarded each other, like two chess players who had played out their familiar inconsequential opening gambits and were ready for the real game to start.

'I know you think I am finished,' Borgia said eventually, his voice deadly serious, 'but I am not. My friends still hold the fortresses at Forlì and Imola, and I know that the people of the Romagna would rather have me as their overlord than the tyrants I threw out, and will rise for me when I return. Then there is money, which is squirrelled away where only I can get at it. So I am not without prospects.'

'Excellency, no one who has followed your career would believe otherwise,' Niccolò replied diplomatically.

'I have another card to play yet. I have written secretly to King Louis asking that he intercede with the pope to provide me with the means to get the Romagna back. He will support me, I know, even though that bastard d'Amboise will be against me.'

'If I may be blunt, excellency, that seems a long throw. Cardinal Rouen's influence over the king is great, and the French enterprise in Italy is in considerable disarray. Louis may not be able to help you, even if he wanted to. And you would still be a prisoner.'

'Well, we shall see. But Julius won't keep me here forever.' Borgia seemed almost nonchalant. 'He will have to negotiate with me eventually if he wants my fortresses. And he will have to have them if he doesn't want to see Venice in permanent control of the Romagna. What was it you said? That he would

314

end up being mere chaplain to the Venetians? That shaft went home, they tell me.'

'I'm sorry, excellency, have I misunderstood? You are willing to surrender your last hope of winning back the Romagna?'

'No, you heard me correctly, my friend.' Borgia chuckled, enjoying Niccolò's confusion. 'If Louis refuses me, I will give the pope my Romagna fortresses in return for my freedom.'

'And then? Where will you go when you have achieved your liberty?'

'Can't you guess, Niccolò? Have your forgotten that I am half-Spanish?'

To Borgia's amusement, Niccolò was lost for words. He was reminded of a spectacular trick he had once seen when observing cavalry exercises while he'd accompanied the duke's army—a particularly acrobatic cavalryman had leapt from one speeding horse to another, without injury to himself or horse. Cesare Borgia was, it seemed, contemplating the same feat.

'You are... audacious, My Lord,' he said, allowing his tone to express his doubts more clearly than words.

'You think that Gonsalvo da Cordoba won't have me. You might be right. Since he was appointed as the Spanish governor-general in Naples, we have not always had cordial relations. But I have other friends—my brother Gioffre, certain cardinals—who will help me persuade him it is in his interests, and those of his masters in Spain, to support me.'

Niccolò could keep his face straight no longer, and he too burst into laughter. 'Your future negotiations will be, I am sure, most entertaining. I am sorry I won't be here since I am to return to Florence within days.' That news had arrived with despatches the day before.

'To your wife and a new child.' Not for the first time, Niccolò was startled by how well-informed Borgia was. 'Wherever I have turned in these last years, there you were, observing, writing your despatches, occasionally favouring me with your advice. I don't know why, but I will miss you, I think.'

Niccolò bowed his head slightly in acknowledgement of the compliment.

'Well, however fickle your masters must have seemed,' Borgia went on, 'they were no more so than the fates that have controlled my destiny. I would have followed all your advice and become a good neighbour and friend to Florence, you know, had fortune been less unkind. Imagine—the Romagna settled and ruled justly, the old warlords put down and at peace with its neighbours. That was all I wanted.'

'And control of Florence. Siena and Lucca after that. For all I know, Naples as well, and with it more or less the whole of Italy. If we are to be honest, My Lord Cesare, let us at least be completely honest.'

A ghost of the old wolf-smile was back on Valentino's face. 'And would that be such a bad thing? A united, whole Italy, able to withstand invaders like France and Spain, who use the Italian states as mere pawns in their continuous struggle for dominance? Tell me you don't agree.'

He did agree, that was the devil of it. The past greatness of Italy came when she was united enough to become master of all Europe. But Rome had acquired her empire as a republic, like Florence, not as a despotic kingdom, and though she had produced some remarkable emperors, in truth, much of the imperial period of her history had been one long, sad tale of internecine war and debilitating dynastic struggles. For Niccolò, if the price of a united Italy was the abandonment of republican ideals, that price was too much.

'Excellency, if I had thought the sinews and spirit of my republic could be preserved in such an endeavour, I would have supported you wholeheartedly and would do so in the future. But I fear that such a thing will be impossible and that we must perforce remain on opposing sides. To my regret.'

Borgia considered him gravely then embraced him. 'Farewell, my Niccolò. We will meet again, on opposite sides no doubt, but until then go with my best wishes. And watch from afar as I escape my bonds and prevail once more!'

Chapter 28—A Spanish Triumph

Florence, January 1504

'No, no, this won't do.' Niccolò was impatient and allowing his annoyance to show. 'I'm afraid you will have to go through every ledger again, Casa, until you can find the discrepancy.'

He and Filippo Casavecchia were bent over a table covered with ledgers in the little chamber usually used by the Collector of Customs, just off the courtyard of the Palazzo della Signoria. The hapless collector, a man of middle years whose face bore an etched-in expression of helpless anxiety, looked on in downcast silence, his hands turning his cap over and over. It wasn't entirely his fault that the republic's records of the duties owed and collected were in such a poor state. The system itself had long needed an overhaul and was riddled with inconsistencies and loopholes through which foreign and Florentine merchants alike slipped with practised ease. But it was equally obvious that this man was not up to the job and he was about to tell him so when they were interrupted by the loud clatter of hooves that echoed around the courtyard, accompanied by the shouted protests of the guards.

Gesturing to Casavecchia to carry on, he went out into the courtyard to find out what was going on. Most of the regular daily couriers had already been and gone, so it was unusual for one to arrive at this time of the afternoon, particularly one as mud-spattered as the young fellow who slid off his horse, staggering as he landed, as though he had been in the saddle for a long time. Recovering his balance, he looked around, seeking someone in authority just as Niccolò emerged from the collector's office.

'Ardingo! You have had a hard ride of it, from the looks of you.'

The young courier showed white teeth in a tired grin. 'The devil has been at my tail since I left Montepulciano this morning.' Fishing into his satchel, he pulled out a packet and handed it to Niccolò with a flourish. 'My orders were to give this despatch only to the gonfaloniere, but since you are his right hand, I think I will have done my duty by surrendering it to you.'

Niccolò turned the packet over in his hands. It was sealed with the familiar signet of Francesco Soderini.

The courier was almost hopping from foot to foot with an expectant look that made Niccolò laugh. 'From your face, young fellow, I would say that you know what is in this despatch. Care to enlighten me?'

'The courier from Rome said only that there has been a great battle and the French have been routed. Gaeta, they say, will fall any day.'

'Well, that *is* important news, worth riding post-haste for.' He dug into his wallet for a few coins and tossed them to the boy. 'Go and find yourself a tavern, you've earned a drink.'

Ten minutes later he was at the door of Piero Soderini's study, causing the gonfaloniere to frown at the interruption. 'Yes, Niccolò? What is it? I thought we were done for the day.'

'An urgent despatch from Cardinal Volterra, Ser Piero. The courier told me something of the news it contains, and I did not feel it should wait until tomorrow.'

He waited while Soderini broke the seal and began reading the contents. 'So, Gonsalvo da Cordoba has smashed the French army on the Garigliano in a surprise attack. The French are in full retreat and it seems likely that their garrison at Gaeta will have to surrender. My brother also says that there are more than four thousand dead, Piero de' Medici among them, drowned in the river during the fighting, apparently.'

That last was the only good news from what was otherwise a disaster, for Piero had been a lodestone for conspiracies since the day he fled Florence. Quite apart from the fact that many soldiers in Florentine employ had perished, the sheer scale of the defeat on the Garigliano meant that Gonsalvo da Cordoba could advance northwards beyond the boundaries of the Neapolitan kingdom. With no French army south of the Apennines capable of resisting them and the papal forces in disarray, Florence could easily find herself once again the target of an invasion.

None of this needed much discussion between two men who had worked together long enough to know each other's mind. Nor was Niccolò much surprised by Soderini's conclusions when they had talked matters through.

'King Louis will have to sue for peace with Spain once more. And this time he does so from a position of weakness. He may be tempted to ignore the interests of his allies and supporters if it gets him better terms with the Spanish. We must make sure he does not regard us as sacrificial lambs and remind him of our long support for him in Italy. Agreed?'

'Ambassador Valori will have a hard job ahead of him,' Niccolò nodded. He knew what would come next.

'He is a good man but he has only just arrived at the French court. I think we need your experience there alongside him; you know d'Amboise well and the king seems to respect you.'

'Of course, Ser Piero. Are you going to tell Marietta or shall I?'

Soderini's laugh echoed off the walls. 'I think I shall delegate that task to you, my friend. I'll have Marcello draw up your commission and you can leave in a day or so.'

*

'How many days this time? No, don't answer that because I won't believe you whatever you say, Niccolò Machiavelli!'

They were standing over their son's cradle, heads almost touching, as Niccolò engaged in his daily ritual of looking in on little Bernardo when he arrived home. The child was bundled up against the cold, only a tousle of black hair visible above the tightly closed eyes. Inexpertly rearranging the coverlet that cocooned the tiny body against the cold, he glanced up at his wife. 'I shall have to ask the King of France. I am sure he will hurry proceedings along just so that I can return home.'

'The King of France! The Cardinal of Rouen! Admit it, Niccolò, you would rather be travelling to some distant capital and talking to grand lords and captains-general and the like than staying here at home with your family. You have hardly been home for a month as it is.'

He threw his hands in the air. 'Peace, woman! I have no choice in the matter. The Signoria commands and I must obey.'

But she was right, of course, he admitted to himself. He loved being near the centre of power and dealing with kings and popes and cardinals. It was intoxicating in a strange way and, even now, he strained to get away, climb into his saddle and set off once more on a mission of importance to the future of the city and republic that he loved. The Signoria might command, but he was a willing servant.

He was still searching for something to say that would appease her when she started giggling. 'Niccolò, you are so transparent sometimes. You're standing there, trying to find a way of telling me that I will never understand you. Well, I do. I talk to the other wives and they tell me what their husbands say about you.'

'Which is what?' He was both curious and a little taken aback.

'That you are married to your job, that they all hang off every word you say and that the government would fall apart without you. That no one else writes despatches that are as insightful as yours.' She looked at him, head tilted and hands on hips. 'They also say that you are too sharp for your own good and one day that tongue of yours will cause you serious trouble. And that you are Piero Soderini's little hand.'

That made him laugh; in Florentine slang, to be someone's 'little hand' was to be their toady. Still, it was a relief to know that his pedestal was not entirely without cracks.

'Niccolò,' his wife said, taking his hands in hers, 'I am proud of you, proud to be your wife. Of course I miss you when you are away and you must let me tease you from time to time about it, but never think I don't understand you.'

He stood still, for once lost for words. Then, deciding that words would be pointless anyway, he bent forward and kissed her. As he did so, little Bernardino let out a little chuckle in his sleep, bringing a smile to both his parents' faces.

'I think our son approves. Shall we go and see if we can make him a little brother?'

*

'When Valori told me they were sending Monsieur Machiavelli I knew that the Florentine Signoria was worried!' Cardinal d'Amboise chuckled as Niccolò leaned forward into his practised court-bow.

320

Straightening, he glanced around at the various members of the French council of state who were gathered around the cardinal. Some were familiar faces from his previous visit to the court, like Robertet, while others were unknown to him. He could read nothing in their carefully blank faces as he replied, 'As My Lord Cardinal knows, the Signoria is always worried, but then, they have so much to be worried about.'

'You Italians are always nervous about something.' D'Amboise looked mischievously around the room. 'That is why we French have so much trouble understanding Italian politics, as I think you once told me.'

Like the ripples that emanate from a stone thrown into a pond, a small wave of laughter went from face to face as the courtiers enjoyed the moment of discomfiture for the Florentine envoy.

'Don't worry, Niccolò, recent events have not robbed us of our sense of humour. Sit.' He waved to a chair that had been set opposite him. 'How was your journey?'

'As well as can be expected at this season, eminence.' With a shrug, he dismissed the difficulties of a journey that, in the depths of winter, was as hard as any journey he had ever undertaken. 'I called at Milan—Baron de Chaumont asked me to convey his fraternal greetings. He was a gracious host while I was there and we conversed at length upon the state of things.'

De Chaumont was the cardinal's brother, Charles d'Amboise, newly appointed as governor of Milan. 'And what was my brother's assessment of matters as they stand? He is usually most perceptive.'

'He said he was confident that Gonsalvo da Cordoba would not advance with his armies beyond his present positions and, even if he did, he would soon apprehend that there is a large force in Lombardy to oppose him. He also said the king intended to double the size of his fleet and that this also would be a deterrent.'

'Which should be sufficient to relieve your Signoria of their anxieties, should it not?'

'Eminence, as I said to your brother, neither the fleet nor the troops in Lombardy will be of any use in defending Tuscany against an invasion. The true walls of Tuscany are the territories of the pope and the republic of Siena.

321

It would be far better to send a few thousand soldiers to Perugia, where they can combine with the forces of Gianpaolo Baglioni. That city is the key to defending both Tuscany and the pope.'

'Always assuming you could be sure that gentleman will not change sides.' D'Amboise laughed. 'You see, Niccolò, I do understand Italian politics a little.'

'Your Eminence is a first-class student of Italian politics and no doubt of much else.' Niccolò returned the smile. But it was time to get to the meat of his mission. 'Eminence, you know our situation. We are at war with Pisa, we are threatened from the south by the Spanish, and the allegiance of our smaller neighbours is uncertain following after the events at the Garigliano. Most are making preparations to ally themselves with the Spanish. We lost many of our troops in the battle and those who remain are scattered in the service of His Majesty.'

'We are aware of all this, Niccolò.' The cardinal's tone was patient, but Niccolò sensed that beneath the surface calm there was considerable tension and that irritation might not be far away. 'Tell me what your government wants from us.'

'Eminence, our one hope is that we can rely upon the continued support of the king and his armies in the event that we face aggression from Gonsalvo or from the Venetians, who will no doubt attack us as soon as our resources are engaged elsewhere.'

'The Venetians should stick to their fishing.' That from General Robertet, in a growl. 'If they do not, we will show them who is still master in north Italy.'

'I am sure the Signoria will find reassurance in your words, General. But a ragged coat finds little credit and the French coat is, if I may say, at least a little threadbare following the recent calamities.'

That sent another ripple around the room, this time of shock.

'Be careful, Machiavelli; you verge on insolence.' The annoyance in the cardinal's voice was now plain.

'If I have expressed myself coarsely, eminence, I hope you will forgive me. But I would not be doing my duty if I did not press upon you and upon the king the urgent need that Florence feels for a concrete expression, in the form of soldiers or war materials, of your support for our liberty and independence.'

Niccolò held his breath through the long silence that followed. He knew he was pushing the cardinal hard, but Gonfaloniere Soderini had been adamant on this point, that France must demonstrate by concrete actions that it would defend Florence in the event of an attack by the Spanish.

The cardinal hauled himself to his feet, forcing a startled Niccolò to do the same. 'Monsieur Machiavelli, come with me. The rest of you stay here.'

Leaving the rest of the councillors muttering to each other in confusion, he followed the chief minister across the large and echoing chamber into a smaller room that opened onto a balcony. A handsome desk stood below the window, covered in papers and folders. The only other furnishings in the room were a low table and two high-backed chairs set before a fireplace, where a fire stuttered in the grate. This must be the cardinal's private office.

Gesturing Niccolò to sit, the cardinal picked up a poker and attempted to coax some life from the coals. Once the flames had started to dance, he grunted and took his seat, staring into the fire.

When eventually he started talking, his tone was brisk and matter of fact. 'Our reverse along the Garigliano river was a catastrophe. We lost nearly half our army, dead or captured, and most of our artillery. The king is half-mad with grief at the losses.' He stopped, and a look of grief crossed his face, whether for the dead and wounded of France or for the state of mind of her king Niccolò could not tell. Then he seemed to focus, and went on in a strong voice. 'But it is clear that we must come to terms with the Spanish. In fact, commissioners have already been despatched with negotiating terms tucked under their arms and we hope to conclude a truce very soon. I tell you this here, in confidence, because their mission is, for the moment, being kept secret.'

The dark eyes regarded Niccolò steadily and he felt he was being asked to deduce something. 'Secret from whom? The generals? To keep their morale intact?'

'Yes, the generals, but also...'

'The king?'

The Cardinal's nod told him that his guess was correct. Which explained why d'Amboise wished to talk to him in private, for in going behind the king's back, he was committing treason. 'His Majesty is unable for the present to make a rational judgement about the best interests of France, so it falls to me as his chief minister to ensure that this defeat does not entirely destroy us in Italy. The king will, I am confident, approve everything when he has recovered himself.'

'Eminence, I appreciate the trust you are showing in confiding this news to me. Of course, I will say nothing of this until the treaty is public. But if I may speak without hair on the tongue, as we Italians say, I still fear that France might abandon us if it should be expedient in your pursuit of a peace agreement.'

'By God, you are dogged, Niccolò! What reason does the Signoria have to doubt our fidelity? Have we not always supported your independence?'

'In all things, eminence, except perhaps in the case of Duke Valentino.'

'I wish we had as much influence over that young man as you seem to think we have.' The cardinal sighed. 'He has written to us asking us to intercede with the pope and give him soldiers and arms; I think I can persuade the king to deny him; he has rather lost patience with Borgia anyway.'

And that is the end of Cesare Borgia at last, Niccolò thought. *With both pope and king withdrawing their support, he has no future in Italy.* 'The Signoria will be glad to hear that, eminence. Removing the Borgia threat will greatly increase our security. But…'

'Yes, yes, I know what you are going to say—what about the south? Look, Niccolò, I will do everything I can to ensure Florence is explicitly named as an ally of France, therefore entitled to our protection if the truce is broken. Will that be sufficient to stop your Signoria carping?'

'Your Eminence, I know of no force on earth that will bring about that result.' That got a flicker of a smile from the cardinal. 'But I will convey your goodwill to the gonfaloniere and express my certainty that the reassurances that he and the Signoria wish for will be forthcoming.'

'Good. Come, let us join the others and pretend you have just been given a thorough thrashing, for appearance's sake.'

'Like this, eminence?' Niccolò adopted his most crestfallen expression.

'You would make a fine actor, my young friend,' d'Amboise laughed as they made their way to the door.

*

It took some weeks, during which Niccolò amused himself with a round of parties and visits to the many and varied fleshpots of Lyon before the treaty was finally concluded. To his relief the terms were all he could have hoped for. Florence was named unequivocally as a friend and ally of the King of France, and it was made clear that any attack on her would be regarded as a breach of the truce to which France would respond with arms.

Niccolò lingered for another week or two in Lyon, uncharacteristically reluctant to face the rigours of the road back to Florence. Even in near-defeat, this was a glittering and powerful court and he had become fascinated by its workings. Being near the centre of things, talking every day with the cardinal, with the haughty generals and once even with the king himself, filled him with a feeling of power which was only occasionally pierced when his natural sense of the absurd whispered mockery in his ear. At such moments he told himself he was just a junior envoy from a small republic who was giving himself airs.

Even in his most extreme flights of self-importance he never forgot his duty and spent his time assiduously collecting information and gossip to put in his despatches, accompanied by his customarily pithy analysis of events, such as they were. But the truth was that there was not very much of note happening in Lyon, and there wasn't any good reason for him to remain much longer. When February turned to March, he finally mounted his horse and turned its head south towards home.

Arriving in Florence, he found himself washed by a warm breeze of approval from the gonfaloniere and the Signoria. So far as they were concerned, he had saved Florence. At the first Signoria meeting he attended, the priors stood and applauded him as one and the gonfaloniere made no secret of his pride in his younger protégé.

At that same meeting, once it got down to its proper business, the Signoria was astounded to learn of the latest developments from Rome. In a breathless despatch, Francesco Soderini reported that Cesare Borgia had disappeared! He had been under house arrest in Ostia while the pope tried to make up his mind

325

whether he was better off with Valentino under lock and key or out of the papal territories altogether when he had managed to escape and take horse. To where, no one knew; a frantic Julius had sent out search parties in every direction.

Niccolò, remembering his last conversation with Cesare Borgia, thought he had a suspicion where the duke was headed.

'He will go to Naples,' he said, enjoying the deference with which his intervention was received. 'When last I saw Duke Valentino, he hinted that he was in negotiation with Gonsalvo da Cordoba, though to what end he would not say.'

'But he and Gonsalvo have no reason to trust each other.' Antonio Delvigna was incredulous. 'In Naples he will surely be as welcome as a dog in a church!'

'Yet he is, after all, half a Spaniard,' Gonfaloniere Soderini said. 'Niccolò may well be right. We will have to wait on events and see whether this rosebud will end up flowering as a rose.'

It took a remarkably long nine days before Borgia did indeed turn up in Naples. Surprisingly, he was welcomed by the Spanish captain-general with open arms. All kinds of rumours began to circulate, and Ambassador Pandolfini reported that it was said in Naples that the duke planned to assemble a force of several thousand men, paid for by the Spanish, and sail up to Piombino. From there, he would march across Tuscany to Modena to link up with Duke Ercole of Ferrara, his sister Lucrezia's father-in-law.

This, to Niccolò, seemed fanciful. Ercole d'Este was a cautious man, and though it was said he had come to love his daughter-in-law, it did not seem likely that he would lend his support to such a risky operation, particularly once it became clear that he no longer had the support of King Louis XII. But hope always dies last and Borgia was nothing if not a gambler.

Then at the end of May, this last throw of the dice failed. Without warning, Gonsalvo arrested the duke and threw him into the dungeons of the Castel Nuovo. What his fate would be, nobody could tell, but since Gonsalvo had acted on the express command of King Ferdinand of Spain, it seemed likely that Borgia would be shipped off there before very long. Whether a worse fate would befall him was both unknown and much speculated upon.

But as one giant departed the Italian scene, another of a different character appeared in Florence.

Chapter 29—Diverting the Arno

Florence, June 1504

'My God, Niccolò, it is huge!'

Biagio's mouth was open in a great circle of wonder as they stood among the crowd that had gathered in the sunshine of the Piazza della Signoria on a late May morning for the unveiling of a new statue that was to stand in front of the entrance to the palazzo. Behind them, the Signoria, the gonfaloniere and various other dignitaries of the republic stood and sat under cover of the great loggia, but Niccolò, Biagio and Agostino had decided they wanted to get a little closer to the scene that was about to unfold and had pushed their way to the front of the throng.

In front of them was a tall wooden box perhaps twenty feet high, which workmen were busy dismantling under the amused eyes of a crowd who were happy to offer, in their cheery Florentine way, all sorts of advice. It had taken four whole days to get the thing there on rollers from the sculptor's workshop a mere quarter-mile away. And it had taken more than two years for the sculptor, the twenty-nine-year-old Michelangelo Buonarotti, to carve a discarded lump of marble into the statue of the biblical hero David that was about to be unveiled. Few people had seen the finished work, which the sculptor had worked on for the most part alone and in some secrecy. Those who had seen it promised a sensation.

Gradually, panel by panel, the statue was revealed and the chatter of the crowd diminished into silence. It was the removal of the last panel, which revealed the statue in its totality for the first time, that had prompted Biagio's startled remark. He was not alone—most of the crowd stared in awe at the enormous marble edifice, a massive recreation of David as a virile, powerful young man, sling over his shoulder, fierce gaze directed at an invisible Goliath, whom presumably he was about to slay.

'Well, it's in the right place, whatever your friend Leonardo says.' Agostino grinned with mischief; as always, any controversy, or better yet scandal, that involved the artistic community of Florence was a great source of amusement to Niccolò's colleague.

This one, though, he had not yet shared with them. 'Well, Agostino, spit it out. We know you are dying to tell us. I thought it was supposed to go up on top of the Duomo but that would obviously be an impossibility.'

'The committee of works couldn't decide where to put it so they appointed another committee to do their job for them and put da Vinci on it.'

'How very Florentine,' Biagio hooted. 'Let me guess—they split into factions?'

'So they did. Half of them wanted to put it up there, under the Loggia, and the other half wanted to put it outside the Signoria.'

'And of course Leonardo was on the losing side,' Niccolò said, unsurprised. 'Where is he, by the way?'

'He said he was too busy to come to a public spectacle like this. Apparently, the charms of Lisa del Giocondo are keeping him occupied in his studio.'

'Hell and death,' Biagio muttered under his breath, 'The speeches are starting. We'll be here for hours now.'

Niccolò, smiling, looked around. Sure enough, Gonfalonieree Soderini was on his feet, about to launch into a lofty speech about David's duel with Goliath, replete with heavy-handed analogies to the glorious republic that the new statue symbolised and represented. The address had been written by Marcello Adriani, which was a guarantee that it would be turgid, a condition that would in no way be alleviated by Piero Soderini's delivery, for the ability to deliver great oratory was not among that man's many qualities. Biagio was right—it was going to be a long morning.

'Oh, I don't think anyone will mind if we slip away as soon as Ser Piero is done,' Niccolò said.

His thoughts drifted elsewhere. For the first time in many years, he was living a contented life. Marietta had finally given up on her complaints about his absences, perhaps because she found that, with two children, her life was full enough without him, and they had settled into a domestic happiness that surprised him in its fulfilment. True, Biagio still managed to lure him from time to time to their favourite little brothel near the Ponte della Grazie, but conscious of his wife's dignity, he tried to be as discreet as possible. And the children were a source of constant delight and amusement when he was at home.

Thanks to Marietta's stewardship while he was away, assisted by the ever-faithful Totto, who had shown himself to have the business acumen that had been so conspicuously lacking in their father and was barely present in his elder brother, he was more financially comfortable than he had ever been. The farm at Sant'Andrea was prosperous, rents from their other properties came in regularly, and even the Signoria had eventually managed to come up with the long-delayed reimbursements due to him from his journeys on their behalf.

The gonfaloniere had finished delivering his oration and was congratulating the sculptor—a brawny young man with tousled black hair and an unruly beard—so it was an opportune moment for them to make their way through the crowd and back to the office upstairs in the brown stone building that loomed over its new guardian statue, gazing ferociously south towards Rome. There, the usual pile of work awaited them. Chief among the various papers and projects on Niccolò's desk were the latest reports on his newest responsibility—the project to divert the Arno, which had been Leonardo's brainchild.

It had taken all of his considerable powers of persuasion to get the gonfaloniere and then the Signoria, to agree to restart the project that had been abandoned the year before amid panic over the manoeuvrings of Cesare Borgia. There was no objection to the aims of the enterprise since the war against Pisa was once again bogged down in a stalemate, but many were sceptical of its feasibility. Leonardo's plans, though, had impressed even the most hard-headed members of the Signoria and the War Committee and, with some spirited support from Cardinal Soderini, the project had finally been approved, and Niccolò appointed to oversee it. As always, if it failed, he would wear the opprobrium of its failure, and if it succeeded, the grandees of the Signoria would doubtless claim all the credit for having the sagacity to follow his advice. Such is the nature of politics.

The first paper in the packet of reports on the project brought a frown to his forehead. 'Biagio, who is this fellow Colombino?' he called across the office.

'He's the engineer Alamanno Salviati recommended for the Arno project.'

Salviati, whose brother had replaced him at the Borgia court, was an arrogant aristocrat. Niccolò had always wondered about his loyalties, since Piero de'

330

Medici was his father-in-law, but he was one of the leaders of the *ottimati* and too powerful to ignore, as presumably had been the case in this appointment.

'Well, this Messer Colombino seems to be something of an optimist. Leonardo said the project would take more than fifty thousand man-days, but his estimate is just thirty thousand man-days.'

Biagio made his way across the room and examined the estimate that Niccolò held in his hand. 'Yes, I see. Still, Salviati says he is the best in the business, so he must know what he is doing.'

Niccolò was not so sure. He had faith in Leonardo's calculations, but the artist, preoccupied with his painting projects, had declined to get involved with the implementation of his plans, no doubt reluctant to expose himself once again to the dilemmas that his natural hatred of war and death presented him.

'Biagio, when the War Committee meets again, I'm going to ask them to appoint you as commissioner to inspect the project and report back. I need someone I can trust to keep an eye on things there.'

The works started in late August, two thousand sweating workmen labouring under a baking summer's sun to dig a great ditch and collect together the rocks that would be used to build a weir to block the river's course. Another thousand soldiers stood guard over the works to prevent any sorties by the Pisan forces watching impotently from their walls.

According to Colombino, the whole project should be completed within three weeks. Yet by mid-September, the work showed no sign of the progress that would be needed to meet his objective.

'The trouble is,' Biagio reported after one of his regular tours of inspection, 'Colombino seems to think he knows better than Leonardo. You remember that da Vinci specified that there should be a single ditch to divert the river once we have blocked it, dug deeper than the current river-bed, and that it would split into two after a mile or so?'

Niccolò nodded, a little impatiently—he knew every line and every note of the plans by heart.

'Well, Colombino has instead dug two separate ditches right from the start and both are shallower than the Arno. When I quiz him, he gets all lofty and tells me that he knows best and that I should bugger off back to my paperwork.'

331

'But that makes no sense. How can the water flow into the ditches if they are higher than the river?'

Which was precisely what happened when, a week later, the first diversion attempt was tried. Only when the Arno was in flood did the ditches catch any water at all, and most of that flowed back as soon as the river subsided.

Then nature took a disastrous hand. After a dry August and September, an autumnal storm blew across Tuscany in early October, dumping vast quantities of rain that swept away the half-built banks of the two ditches and flooded the surrounding farmland. After that, the whole project collapsed. The soldiers abandoned their posts, many of the workers deserted, and the Pisans sallied out and filled in the work that had been completed at considerable expense by the Florentines. It was, in short, a disaster.

Niccolò expected to come in for some criticism when the War Committee convened, but he was shocked when the first attack came from Alamanno Salviati, the very man who had foisted on him the engineer Colombino in the first place.

'It was on Secretary Machiavelli's recommendation and enthusiastic urging that this project was undertaken, despite the reservations of men of experience and sagacity,' Salviati said, all lofty indignation. 'It seems reasonable therefore that he should bear the responsibility for this failure.'

Niccolò, in his accustomed place at the foot of the table in the Hall of Lilies, struggled to control his features. After all he had done, all his years of hard-working and loyal service to the republic, to be subjected to such an attack for a failure that was not of his doing was galling. Of course, politics was at the heart of it, as soon became obvious.

'Alamanno, that is hardly fair,' Piero Soderini said, his voice soothing, 'Niccolò may have made the recommendations, but it is the Signoria and myself who made the decisions.'

'Decisions that resulted in the squandering of thousands of ducats, extracted from the pockets of the merchants and traders of the city. This war against Pisa, which seems to go on and on with no resolution in sight, and which is your policy, Gonfaloniere, has cost us enough.'

This produced a murmur around the table, disapproval directed against Salviati and the gonfaloniere in about equal proportions.

'That's enough, Alamanno,' Soderini said, an edge of anger in his voice. 'Recovering Pisa and, with it, our access to the sea has been the settled policy of every Signoria since Fra Savonarola.'

'Well, then, perhaps it is time for this ramshackle regime over which you preside, which makes such shamefully stupid decisions as this one on the Arno, to be dissolved in favour of the tried and true system of the past—'

'You mean you want to bring the family of your late father-in-law back into the saddle, Salviati, eh?' That interjection came from Niccolò Zati. 'Well, I for one am not going to countenance the return of the Medici anytime soon, and neither will the people, whatever you *ottimani* might want!'

The growl of anger around the table told Salviati he had gone too far. 'All right, all right,' he said, hands in the air, pretending to surrender. 'But someone must take responsibility for this fiasco and if it is not to be Machiavelli, then who?'

'Me, obviously,' Soderini said, waving a hand to calm the inevitable outburst from his supporters. 'And I shall do so when the Signoria meets this afternoon. But if you think they will ask me for the seals of my office, I expect you will be surprised. Now, we have a lot of other business, so let us move on...'

The meeting broke up not long after that, and Niccolò lingered behind to stammer his thanks to the gonfaloniere for his support.

'Nonsense, Niccolò. Salviati was after me, not you. He and his *ottimati* friends want me gone if they can, and the Medici back. Attacking you was just another way of getting to me.'

'I think he sabotaged the project, Ser Piero, deliberately.'

'That is a serious allegation to make, Niccolò. Can you prove it?'

'No, I can't. But Colombino was appointed at his recommendation and he seems to have been remarkably pig-headed in his refusal to follow da Vinci's plans.'

333

'Not everyone shares your faith in Leonardo da Vinci, Niccolò, and his plans might have failed anyway, even if they had been executed to the letter. No one can prove otherwise, can they?'

That was, of course, entirely true. But he was convinced that Salviati had known Colombino wasn't up to the job and had deliberately recommended him knowing he would mess it up in a piece of subtlety that would have been worthy of the late Pope Alexander.

It was also disturbing that Salviati had felt he could launch such an attack in the first place. For now, the gonfaloniere's authority had been sufficient to shut him up, but Niccolò had developed a finely-tuned ear for the political undercurrents of the republic and he sensed that the fragile coalition of interests that had combined to give Piero Soderini his position was beginning to fray. There were voices around the table who had stayed silent who might before now have been vociferous in their support of the gonfaloniere. It was all rather worrying.

As if to confirm his anxieties, over the weeks that followed, Niccolò suffered the opprobrium that he had often seen heaped on others who had been associated with a failure, the innuendo and whispering behind hands, the sharp comments and the withheld favours, and all the other ways in which men express their disapproval without ever saying a word. For the first time in his career, he found himself going to work with a reluctant and heavy heart.

Surprisingly, it was Marietta who cheered him up the most. 'Don't be foolish, Nico,' she said, over a miserable Christmas repast. 'The republic and everything it stands for is your whole life. If great men like Ser Piero and Monsignor Francesco are willing to stand by you, who are you to run away and throw in the towel? Such nonsense.'

When, he wondered, had Marietta become so strong in her opinions? Still, he was grateful for her bracing, no-nonsense rebuke and, of course, she was right. Deserting his post would be a betrayal of the Soderini brothers' loyalty to him.

Yet it also seemed that he would have to pay some kind of penalty, unjust though that seemed. The gonfaloniere, professing the greatest of reluctance, told him he was not to report for work to the Palazzo della Signoria until further notice.

334

'I am confused, Ser Piero,' he said, feeling the blood drain from his face and an inner trembling take command of his body. 'Am I out of a job? Or suspended?'

'Neither. Look, I just think it would be better if you are not seen around the palazzo for a while until tempers cool a little. We'll say you are taking some well-earned leave; after all, no one can say that you haven't earned it.'

'But, but...' For once, he couldn't find any words that would express the combination of fury and sadness that was threatening to overwhelm him.

'Niccolò, I need you to accept this. It will only be for a few months, then, I promise you, we will reinstate you as if nothing has happened.'

In the end, he nodded his acceptance, unable to say anything else. Making his way home through the crowded streets, he realised that Soderini, with his usual decency, was offering him what protection he could.

He had to hope that the gonfaloniere was right; his enemies would forget his supposed offences soon enough. Crossing the Ponte Vecchio, his mood lightened considerably, enough so that by the time he got home he was smiling at the thought of the chancellery being managed by the erudite, urbane, but inefficient and lazy Marcello Adriani. It wouldn't be long before they were positively begging him to come back to work!

Chapter 30—Out of Office

Florence, January 1505

Leonardo da Vinci's beard had grown from the straggly thing he had presented to Niccolò all those months ago into a fine and luxuriant mat of hair, carefully combed and powdered, and arranged to suggest to all the world that here was a true philosopher.

Not that his friend was ever likely to adopt the ragged poverty that popular imagination associated with such a calling. He was too much the popinjay for that, Niccolò knew. Had this always been his style? Or had he been influenced by Agostino? It was hard to tell. When they had first met in Imola, both had been labouring under the necessities of travel; a condition that was not conducive to displays of fashionable excess. But whatever the case, the Leonardo da Vinci, who stood working away at the portrait propped in front of him, was gorgeously dressed, the sleeves of his short doublet ballooning out above the elbow in the latest fashion, excellent woollen hose descending into patent leather boots and a black velvet hat perched on the unruly mop of hair.

Hauling himself to his feet, he stretched his arms and went over to peer across Leonardo's shoulder at the painting, a portrait of Monna Lisa, the pretty young wife of the merchant Francesco del Giocondo. He had been labouring away on it for months, in between all his other projects.

'That looks like the Val di Chiana,' Niccolò said, pointing at the background behind the portrait.

Leonardo grunted; he disliked being interrupted and usually flew into a rage when anyone did so, but he made an exception for Machiavelli. 'It could be. Could also be the upper Arno. But it isn't really anywhere, just something from my imagination.' He stopped working, stood back and flexed his fingers, all the while looking critically at the picture. 'She is devilishly difficult to paint, Niccolò. I had half a dozen sessions with her to do the preliminary drawings, but I just can't quite reproduce what I saw.'

Niccolò had never met the lady in question, but if he had, he felt sure that he would have fallen instantly in love with her. Though her whole pose was as demure as would be expected of any young Florentine matron, Leonardo had

336

given her a certain air of mystery, a hint that she had secrets that she was never going to tell. Then he chuckled, realising something.

'What's so funny?'

'I know where I've seen that smile before—in the mirror!'

Now it was Leonardo's turn to laugh. 'Yes, now you mention it. You get the same look when you're bursting to tell me something I'm not supposed to know. But on Monna Lisa's face, it is seductive. On yours, it's just infuriating.'

Though he had not intended it to, Leonardo's joke brought Niccolò's darkest thoughts to the surface. Perhaps that was why it had been so easy for Alamanno Salviati to attack him. Maybe he annoyed people more than he knew and that was why they didn't want to see his face around the Palazzo della Signoria.

'Nico, what is it?' Leonardo was solicitous; Niccolò realised that his friend had rarely seen him drop his confident mask.

'It's nothing, Leo. I am just envious of you, that's all.'

'Envious of me? You must be joking.'

'You have your vocation, your painting, your drawing, your experiments. So long as you have a patron, you can pursue them all and nobody tells you what to think, what to say. Whereas I...'

'You are temporarily out of favour, Nico, nothing more. Don't be gloomy, this will pass soon enough. You have the gonfaloniere's word on it. And then you'll be back in here moaning that your back is aching from some long ride to Siena or Perugia or somewhere, all the while grinning that grin of yours that tells me you are enjoying every minute of it.'

'And when I do, I give you leave to tell me you told me so. But in the meantime, I am bored.'

'Dear God, spare me the self-pity. Niccolò, you are one of the most intelligent and erudite men I know. Take up your pen and write something!'

Niccolò opened his mouth to reply, then stopped. Of course, da Vinci was right. Before he had become the second secretary of the Florentine Republic, all he had wanted to do was to contribute something to Italian literature. Now was his chance.

And he knew what he would do. 'An epic poem,' he told Leonardo a few days later. 'Chronicling the events of the last ten years. Everything that has happened since the end of the Medici.'

'That seems... ambitious.' Leonardo's response was less excited than Niccolò had expected. 'A lot has happened in the last ten years, not a lot of it all that poetic. But if anyone can do it, I am sure you can!'

Leonardo's scepticism turned out to be justified. Niccolò spent every spare hour he had working on it, either in Florence or on the farm at Sant' Andrea. By early February he had finished it, and Agostino had arranged for it to be published. His friends professed to have enjoyed it, which was gratifying, and even Marcello Adriani found grounds to praise *Il Primo Decenale*, as he called it. But Niccolò knew he was no Dante; the poetry was workmanlike, no more, and, as Leonardo had suggested, fitting the convoluted events of the last ten years into the formal demands of the poetic structure had proven challenging. Still, all in all, he thought it had been a worthwhile effort and it had at least stopped him brooding on his idle state.

The end of the year came and went, and still Niccolò received no official reinstatement, though he was encouraged when he got a letter from Cardinal Francesco Soderini, who told him that his brother was quietly doing everything he could to get him back to the Palazzo della Signoria. And Biagio called by now and then and kept him up to date with the state of affairs in the chancellery, where Marcello Adriani was, as Niccolò had expected, proving a less than efficient leader. Biagio's old feud with Antonio della Valle had broken out again, though in muted tones, and he kept Niccolò amused with his stories of della Valle's supposed shortcomings.

It was early February, when winter's claws had begun to recede and there was the slightest hint of spring's softness in the air, that he arrived at the Grapes, a small tavern near Santa Croce that he and Biagio favoured since it was a discreet distance away from the centre of the city. He was surprised to see his old colleague accompanied by a stranger, sitting in a booth at the back of the room.

'Niccolò, over here!' Biagio was as ebullient as ever. 'I've just been to see my banker and I'm in funds for once, so the first round is on me.'

'That is good of you Biagio. I can't remember the last time you bought wine without having your arm twisted first.' Niccolò laughed, turning an enquiring eye towards the stranger.

'This is Tommaso Cremuello,' Biagio said. 'He is one of Francesco Frescobaldi's clerks.'

The short, powerfully built young man sitting next to Biagio reminded Niccolò of a bullock. Close-set bright black eyes were separated by a large and bulbous nose above a small mouth and dimpled chin. Niccolò, sliding onto the bench opposite, sensed a kind of tightly-wound energy beneath the composed expression and eyes that regarded him with polite and intelligent interest.

'Pleased to meet you, Tommaso. Have you been with the Frescobaldi for long? I don't remember ever seeing you in his household.' Francesco Frescobaldi was a banker, one of many with whom Niccolò had dealt with over the years on the business of the Signoria.

'Only for two months, Messer Machiavelli.' His voice was low and pleasant and his Italian grammatically perfect but oddly accented.

'Tommaso fought at the Battle of Garigliano, Niccolò,' Biagio said as the wine and food arrived at their table. 'Signor Frescobaldi found him on the streets of Florence, half-starving, and took him in.'

'Uncharacteristically benevolent, for a banker.'

'You mean he has flesh and blood in his heart, instead of stone?' the young man said, matching Niccolò's ironic tone. 'I think rather that Signor Frescobaldi has an eye for an investment—he recognised that I had sufficient education to be of use to him, and I was going cheap.'

'Yet you are built like a labourer.'

'My father is a blacksmith; I have inherited his build. But not, thank God, any aptitude for his trade.'

'Ah. And where does your father ply this trade of his? Not in Italy, I would guess.'

'No, for fortune's breath has blown me half across the continent. I am English, Messer Machiavelli. My name is Thomas Cromwell, which Italians find impossible to pronounce, so I have become Tommaso Cremuello, which is as near as your tongue can get.' He seemed to think this amusing.

'*Tommaso* was engaged with Andrea del Corte's company,' Biagio said, comically emphasising the Italian pronunciation, to Niccolò's amusement; he probably thought that the Englishman had been insulting the Italian language in some obscure way.

'Del Corte I know of. He is a condottiero, is he not, originally from somewhere in the Romagna? I forget where. Arezzo?'

'Citta di Castello. He was a protégé of Vitellozzo Vitelli.'

'Ah. So tell me about the battle. When I was in Lyon, I heard several accounts from the French generals who were there, but something tells me that their stories were not entirely, shall we say, reliable. And please, *Thomas*,' he made a face at Biagio, 'call me Niccolò, else we will be here all day.'

Cromwell laughed merrily at the byplay between the two Italians. 'Hardly surprising you heard mixed stories, since they were so comprehensively beaten! Let me tell you what I saw...'

For the next half an hour, Cromwell told the story of the battle from his perspective, how the defending Norman crossbowmen had been surprised and unprepared when the Spanish troops had crossed the Garigliano river in the early hours of the morning. Then they'd fled in panic. Running into an advancing force of French cavalry, the rabble had caused sufficient confusion that they too turned and retreated. The regular French infantry eventually mounted what proved to be a hopeless defence, soon overrun by the Spanish.

'By the end of the day, the French army was in full retreat, abandoning their sick and wounded, cannons, everything.'

'And you? What happened to you?'

'I was separated from my comrades somehow. I didn't know the roads or even where to head for. I hid in a barn for a day or two, then just started walking. Eventually, I found my way here to Florence, where Signor Frescobaldi rescued me from the streets.'

Niccolò could not imagine the hardships that this phlegmatic young man had endured travelling on foot across Tuscany in the middle of winter. He was obviously uncommonly tough. He also had opinions, which he proceeded to expound as more drinks and food arrived at the table.

'I do not understand the way you fight wars here in Italy,' he said when the tavern-keeper had gone, 'this over-reliance on mercenaries, men paid to fight for you. Their captains and officers seem more concerned with manoeuvring than with fighting. They would rather march and counter-march, entrench and encamp, anything to make sure they keep their precious soldiers unharmed while making sure that they get paid every last ducat for their efforts. And they will change masters without scruple for any small amount of gold. While I was on the Garigliano, all the talk in the camp was that del Corte was seriously considering going across to the Spanish, if he didn't quit the fight entirely.'

Niccolò nodded; ever since the fiasco at Pisa that had led to the execution of Paolo Vitelli five years before, he had observed the same thing over and over again. The rebellion of the Swiss and Gascons at Pisa, the ceaseless treachery of Cesare Borgia's supposed allies, the endless threats of the condottiere that were nominally in the employ of Florence to tear up their contracts unless they were given more gold. Yet this was the way war was waged in Italy; until the French came, there had never been any such thing as a professional army, permanently employed by the state for its defence. Such an idea seemed both too expensive and too dangerous—better by far to pay what the *condottiere* demanded and hope for the best.

'They order these things differently in England, do they not?' Biagio was determined not to be excluded.

'Yes. Our soldiers come from our soil. Every countryman in England must be trained in the use of the longbow and are bound to give military service if their lord demands it. And we fight under our commanders, not under foreigners.'

And you have been using those soldiers to fight each other for the last thirty years, Niccolò thought, *until your present King Henry finally ended it.* Still, there was something useful there.

'Duke Valentino tried something of the kind,' he said, half to himself. Borgia's Romagnese militia had proven to be his most loyal and capable troops right to the end. 'Thomas, if your duties at the Frescobaldi banking house permit and you are willing, would you like to assist us, Biagio and I, to prepare

341

a memorandum for the Signoria on the subject of militia armies? How they should be recruited, trained, maintained and deployed.'

Cromwell's agreement was instant and enthusiastic. Over the following weeks, the three of them met whenever they could to work on their report. When it was finished, he sent it privately to the gonfaloniere, with a polite request that he be received in the Palazzo della Signoria to discuss it.

A few days later, he was summoned by a short note in Piero Soderini's hand.

'This is excellent work, Niccolò,' he said as soon as Machiavelli arrived at the door of his study. 'Come in, sit down. Everything you say here is right, and your proposals for the recruitment and training of a militia are entirely sensible. But I am afraid that your report will have to stay here, in my office, at least for now.'

Niccolò was shocked. He had been expecting that Soderini would immediately take the report to the Signoria, with calls for action. 'Why, Ser Piero? I don't understand. If we are bold and adopt this plan, we can rid ourselves of these mercenary captains forever.'

'Because I would risk splitting the Signoria if I did what you ask. A good third of the Great Council want to depose me as it is; they think I am setting myself up as a dictator, and if I supported a proposal such as this, they would think I am doing so to create my own private army. So I dare not.'

'Then why did you call me here, excellency?' Niccolò was bitter. 'You could have told me all that in a letter or sent a messenger.'

'Calm down, Niccolò. When the time is right, I promise you I will pull your report out of the drawer and we will prosecute the case together. But I do have good news for you. Marcello Adriani is sick with a fever, so we need you back at the chancellery. Permanently. My enemies have realised that trying to bring me down by getting rid of you is not going to work, and my supporters have been loud in demanding that you be reinstated. We need your skills, my young friend, more than ever.'

When he walked into the chancellery half an hour later, he was treated to a standing ovation from his colleagues, who then proceeded to crowd around his desk and compete with each other to thump him violently on the back and welcome him back to work.

Biagio, when Niccolò found a quiet moment to tell him that the fruits of their labour had fallen on fallow ground, was phlegmatic. 'If the gonfaloniere says he will take it to the Signoria when the time is right, I'm sure he will. As long as you are back with us, I don't care'

Within a month, he was on the road again, first on a mission to the Giovanni Francesco Gonzaga, the Marquis of Mantua, and then back down to Siena, where the alliance with Pandolfo Petrucci needed some shoring-up. When he got back, Biagio told him that young Thomas Cromwell had left Florence, bound for Flanders, then presumably his native England. Niccolò had become fond of the young man and was disappointed he had not had an opportunity to say goodbye.

By then, winter was on its way and Niccolò, happily busy dealing with the never-ending press of business that found its way to his desk, had all but forgotten the militia report. Though the siege of Pisa dragged on, everywhere else the Florentine frontiers were peaceful, and so there had been no occasion when Piero Soderini had felt the time was right to discuss it with the Signoria. But then Niccolò was sent off to inspect the army at Pisa, and everything changed.

*

'It's hopeless, Ser Piero. These mercenaries just decide when and where they will fight, and when it all gets too hard, they sit down in camp and eat and drink all the supplies we have sent them, or march off home.'

Niccolò had arrived back in Florence late that afternoon, spattered in mud from the road and in a furious frame of mind, having ridden all day from Pisa, which had been under siege until that morning, when Gianpaolo Baglioni had seen fit to disband his army and send them home to their various territories for the winter. Frustratingly, the Pisan walls had been breached in two places just a few days before by the Florentine artillery, and the Florentine forces were still sufficiently strong to have made another attack entirely feasible. But instead, the troops had literally sat down in camp and refused to budge until Baglioni had finally given in and discharged them, over Niccolò's furious protests.

Gonfaloniere Soderini's face drained of colour when Niccolò told him what had happened, and he slumped into his chair. Baglioni had been Soderini's appointment, over considerable opposition, and he would bear the

343

responsibility for the fiasco. 'They will crucify me,' he said bitterly. 'And they would probably be right to do so. I should never have trusted Baglioni.'

Privately, Machiavelli agreed—Gianpaolo Baglioni was, after all, one of those fickle captains who had joined the conspiracy against Cesare Borgia, though he had been wily enough to stay away from that fateful rendezvous in Senigallia. But it was the Florentine system of relying on mercenaries that was really at fault, and maybe this disaster was an opportunity.

'Perhaps, Ser Piero, it is time to talk again about my militia proposal,' he said. 'We cannot just go on pouring money into the pockets of these *condottieri* and watching them fail us time after time. That money would be better spent recruiting, arming and training our soldiers. At least they would be loyal to Florence, not to their own pockets.'

Soderini was reluctant but resigned. 'It would seem we don't have any other choice. Even the *ottimati* must see that, though they will raise their usual cries about the danger of arming urban mobs.'

This was the argument that had always been raised against forming a militia—that an aroused, armed populace would be far more dangerous than the street-gangs Savonarola had inspired. It was not an unreasonable fear, but Niccolò had an answer. 'What if we restricted recruitment to the countryside? The towns and villages outside Florence. That would minimise the risks, wouldn't it?'

'Not without risk, though. There are plenty of trouble-makers in the country. Some of them among our aristocratic friends, when I come to think of it.'

'Is there anything in this life that is without risk, Ser Piero?'

'True enough.' Then the gonfaloniere came to a decision. 'Your proposal would work, I think. All right, let's take it to tomorrow's meeting of the Signoria. I will have to give them the news then anyway, but at least this offers them a plan.'

Niccolò was surprisingly nervous when the nine priors gathered the next day in their usual venue, the blue and gold magnificence of the Hall of the Lilies, so named after the *fleur-de-lis* emblems that seemed to cover every spare inch of the walls. It was mid-afternoon and the room was illuminated by a watery winter light that came through the three tall windows, through which he could see the dome of the cathedral seeming to float above the roof-tops of the city. In the middle of the room, the Signoria was seated around a long table, with Niccolò in his accustomed place next to the throne-like chair of the gonfaloniere.

Piero Soderini appeared from the direction of his apartments, and everyone shuffled to their feet; the gonfaloniere waved informally for them to be seated and called the meeting to order. A few routine matters took half an hour to deal with, and then Soderini began his report on the events at Pisa. He didn't get very far before he was interrupted.

'Will we never learn our lesson?' Francesco Taddei had a naturally ruddy complexion, but now he was almost glowing with indignation. 'Time after time we entrust our fortunes to these mercenary captains, and always they let us down.'

'What else should we expect, when we appoint people like Baglioni?' Alamanno Salviati said, glaring at an impassive Piero Soderini. 'I told you he wasn't to be trusted, Soderini, but you wouldn't listen.'

'That's all very well, Alamanno, but it seems to me that it wouldn't have much mattered which *condottiero* we gave the job to, they are all as untrustworthy as each other.' This came from Luca degli Albizzi, always a staunch supporter of the gonfaloniere. 'Besides, from what Piero said, the whole thing started when the soldiers themselves decided to sit down and demand to be allowed to go home.'

The discussion went round and round, various priors lining up behind either Salviati or Albizzi, until Soderini, who had remained silent throughout, finally raised his hand to stop the debate.

'I think we have heard everyone's views,' he said, allowing himself a little irony. 'Now let me offer you mine. First, let me remind the Signoria that we appointed Gianpaolo Baglioni after a full debate of this body; I recommended him, it is true, but we all voted on the final decision. However, you are correct in saying that our problems stem as much from the system we have always used in military affairs as from any particular appointment. This we must address, and I have therefore asked Secretary Machiavelli to prepare a report and proposal to do so.'

At a gesture from the gonfaloniere, Niccolò stood and began speaking, his voice a little uncertain at first, but growing firmer as he went along. The priors listened in silence, though their attitudes were written on their faces, either patient encouragement or surly scepticism; as far as he could see, the room was split fifty-fifty between the two.

'And so, my lords,' he concluded after fifteen minutes, 'it is my recommendation that the Republic of Florence should, indeed must, set about recruiting a militia army of men who can be called out to defend their homes and our state in times of need, trained and paid for their service from our treasury. Only thus can we free ourselves of the risk we take every time we engage a *condottiero* and his mercenary soldiers to do our fighting for us.'

He sat down and waited for the inevitable storm.

'Before we debate this proposal, I should make it clear that it has my full support,' Soderini said quietly. 'Niccolò is right: there is no other way that I can see to give Florence the military strength we need if we are to hold our many enemies at bay, and ensure that our own objectives can be achieved without relying on foreigners. Now, let us hear your views.'

'This is just another of Machiavelli's mad ideas,' Salviati wasted no time going on the attack. 'Just like the Arno fiasco. It will cost a fortune, and worse we will have an armed peasantry to deal with the next time there is a famine or some disturbance in the city. Do you want to see Savonarolan mobs in the streets again, this time armed and trained to kill?'

'Nonsense, Alamanno,' Albizzi shot back. 'Niccolò just made it clear that the cost of paying to train a militia who are only called out when they are needed will be much cheaper than paying a permanent army, as the Venetians do, and certainly cheaper than all the gold we waste paying mercenaries who will not fight.'

'And the militia will be recruited from the countryside, will it not?' Niccolò Zati looked tentatively around the room, a nervous look on his face; though a supporter of the gonfaloniere, he was, Machiavelli knew, afraid of the bullying, blustering Alamanno Salviati. 'So surely you exaggerate when you talk of Savonarolan mobs?'

The discussion went on, back and forth between the two camps, until eventually Soderini called a halt and asked for a vote. Half a dozen hands shot up in favour of the proposal; Salviati and two priors who had been loud in their opposition sat with their arms folded in truculent disapproval. The gonfaloniere declared the proposal approved in a deadpan voice. Then Salviati raised his hand to speak.

'Gonfaloniere, the Signoria has made its decision, which of course I respect. But if I may make a suggestion: since this entire idea seems to have originated in the brain of Secretary Machiavelli, he should be appointed to ensure that it is implemented satisfactorily.'

The table broke into a hum of comment. Soderini allowed it to run for a moment, and then raised his hand once more. 'That seems reasonable, Alamanno, so unless Secretary Machiavelli has an objection?' Niccolò nodded his agreement. 'Good, then let it be so decided. Let us all pray for his success.'

'Of course,' Salviati's smile was that of a particularly cunning vixen who imagines she has trapped her quarry. 'And should the whole idea fail, at least we will know who to blame.'

Chapter 31—Niccolò's Militia

Tuscany, January 1505

The main piazza at Borgo San Lorenzo was much like that of every other town of any significance in Tuscany. A handsome but modest church, dedicated of course to San Lorenzo, stood on one corner; at its other end, the town hall stood as the symbol of temporal authority, the place where the local magistrates met and the podestà dispensed justice. Usually, the square between these two buildings was occupied by a daily market where life's necessities, meat, vegetables, olive oil, livestock, were bought and sold. But this morning the market had been temporarily suspended so the town's mayor could address his citizens on the subject of the new laws for the formation of a national militia.

Standing alongside the mayor, Niccolò sensed a mixture of annoyance and curiosity from the crowd. Annoyed at being delayed from what they saw as the critically important and practical business of selling the product of their labour and buying the means for their future production, curious at this new demand from the metropolitan government fifteen miles away in Florence. Niccolò was used to such ambivalence after visiting half a dozen towns over the last couple of months as he travelled around Tuscany getting his recruiting drive underway. Imperturbable, he waited for the mayor to finish his remarks, fairly sure that he knew how this would go.

'…and if someone is conscripted who seems unsuitable to serve because of infirmity or who has other legitimate reasons for exemption, he will have one month to appeal.' The mayor's wooden delivery of the written text came to an end and he reverted to his more natural style of speaking. 'Well, that's it, lads. I know every man in San Lorenzo will do his duty. If you have any questions, ask them of Signor Machiavelli here, who has been sent to us by the Signoria to get everyone registered. I am sure he will explain anything that is not clear.'

Niccolò motioned for his two assistants to come forward and start setting up a trestle-table where they would enter names and ages in the big ledgers they carried for this purpose. As they did so, he addressed the crowd, which was already showing signs it wanted to disperse as quickly as possible.

'Citizens of Borgo San Lorenzo, for hundreds of years, wars in Italy have been fought between mercenary armies, paid for by taxes levied on the

348

common and the wealthy citizens of Tuscany alike. Those soldiers were supposed to give a fair return for what we paid them, fighting for us when we needed to defend our liberty and our homeland. But we have learned to our cost that these *condottieri* are, in truth, little more than brigands, more interested in filling their bellies than fighting, better at pillaging than combat, lusting after gold more than glory.

'Well, the Signoria, in its wisdom, has decided that this must stop. There must be a better way. In ancient times men fought for their own land, for their own country. Indeed, in many countries outside Italy, they do so today. Why should Italians not be capable of doing the same? So the Signoria has decided that the time has come for us to create our own army, a citizen-militia that can be called out in time of need to fight our enemies and preserve the republic that guarantees your liberties.'

He stopped and let his eyes travel across the faces in front of him, stopping here and there to lock his gaze on an individual, a farmer, a labourer, a tradesman. His expression had been stern and unyielding, but now he smiled, lifted his shoulders and turned his palms outwards.

'Well, that's the official statement done.' There was a nervous giggle from someone in the crowd. 'But look, lads, you know how it is. For decades armies have trampled across your fields, killed your sheep, and stolen your precious winter stores. Your women have been molested, or worse. Every time there is a war in north Italy, it is you who suffer, usually at the hands of the very soldiers that we in Florence have engaged to protect our country.

'You would be right to say that the Signoria are bloody slow learners, and that's fair enough. The truth is that they have been scared. Scared of you, and what you might do if you are given arms and training. Well, I think they are wrong. I think that it is our country's enemies who will be scared when they confront an army made up of the fine peasants of Tuscany, fighting for their own land. No, not scared, they will be absolutely terrified!'

That got a few more smiles out of them, and he knew he had said enough. He clapped his hands once and then rested them on his hips.

'Today, we begin. As the mayor has just told you, our first step is simple—to register the names of every able-bodied man between the ages of fifteen and fifty in this town and the surrounding countryside. After that, we will arm you, train you and make you into fine fighting-men!'

349

Niccolò had made this speech a dozen times and he knew what would happen next. They would not cheer or throw their caps in the air—these were country people, like the men he employed on his farm at Sant'Andrea in Percussina, phlegmatic and stolid, not given to displays of emotion. But if he had pitched his remarks right, they would nod to each other and murmur their agreement, mixed in with low-voiced questions and the occasional joke. Then they would come forward in ones and twos and start giving their names to the two clerks sitting behind the table.

Which is exactly what happened in Borgo San Lorenzo that sunny January morning. By early afternoon, they had registered a hundred and fifty names. Niccolò was satisfied, but the mayor, on being told the total, frowned. 'There should be at least two hundred men eligible, by my guess,' he said. 'Something is holding them back.'

Frowning, Niccolò went over to a little knot of men who had just been recruited and stood chatting among themselves. As he approached, they fell silent, curious as to what he might want of them now.

He offered them his broadest smile. 'Well done, men. This is the fifth town I have visited this month and this is by far the biggest turn-out that we have had.' An out-and-out lie, but it served its purpose—the men began to smile and look a little pleased with this praise from such an important Florentine official. 'But tell me, are there others that we can recruit to the cause? Men who aren't in town today or who might be reluctant to sign up? So that Borgo San Lorenzo will be a shining example to the rest of Tuscany.'

Eyes exchanged looks that conveyed hidden messages and greasy caps turned nervously in dirty hands. Eventually one of them, a young man of about twenty or so, summoned up the courage to look him in the eye. 'Every man of the district who is of any worth is in town today, signor. But not everyone is as willing as we are to approach your clerks.'

'Oh? Why not? Are they afraid that they will lose too much time from their work when we start drilling? Is that it?' Niccolò simulated puzzlement rather than annoyance.

'No, signor, it's not that. At least I don't think so. It's taxes, mostly.'

That genuinely puzzled him. 'Taxes? How so?'

'Well, several men told me this morning that they wouldn't be joining your militia because when they give you their names they will also have to tell you what their property is and the next thing you know, Florence will be levying new taxes on us.'

That one he hadn't heard before, although he told himself he shouldn't be surprised. Probably the only other Florentine officials these people had ever met were the tax-gatherers. 'I see. Thank you for being honest, young man. What is your name?'

'Biagio, excellency.'

'Biagio!' Niccolò laughed. 'A fine name; you share it with one of my best friends. Well, Biagio, and the rest of you, do me a favour. Go among your fellow-citizens and tell them from me that the only questions we are asking are each man's name and his age, nothing else. I don't have much time for the tax assessors either, and I'm certainly not going to do their work for them. I'll tell you what: if fifty more men sign up by the end of the day, I will set up a barrel of wine in the piazza for the enjoyment of everyone. How does that sound?'

It sounded very well, from the alacrity with which young Biagio and his friends set off into the back streets of the town. By the end of the day, he had his extra fifty recruits and more and was satisfied with his day's work.

Not everywhere was as straightforward. The habit of disobedience to any authority except that of their local magistrates made recruiting difficult in some places; in others, ancient feuds like the one he had encountered in Castrocaro years before had to be settled before he could make any progress. He found that it took every trick and wile that he had learned in years of diplomacy at foreign courts to convince these stubborn countrymen of his. But these were the exceptions; in most places he and his little team of recruiters were received with an open mind by the magistrates and the people, who in their common-sense, practical way, seemed to perceive the necessity for a militia with greater clarity than their leaders in Florence.

By the end of January, he was back in the Palazzo della Signoria, exhausted but happy, and dealing with the mound of paperwork that had piled up in his absence. Having worked his way through the regular correspondence, he turned to the small pile of letters that he had put aside relating to the militia recruitment campaign. He allowed himself a little inner sigh, for he knew that

351

almost all of them would contain some kind of special pleading from men wanting to be excused their obligations.

The first letter was exactly that. It was addressed to him 'as a brother' (the superscription brought a wry smile to his face) by none other than Alamanno Salviati, the patrician who had been so adamantly opposed to the militia proposal in the first place. It had been hand-delivered the day before by one Antonio di Giusto, who had no doubt wanted to place it personally into the secretary's hands and plead his case directly. Giusto seemed to be a client of Salviati's, whose letter went on to say that poor Antonio was, because of his age, not suited to military service, and that as his son was needed to run the family cobbler's business, the names of both should be removed from the lists of citizens who could be called up for military service. Should he accede to this request, he, Alamanno Salviati, professed himself 'most ready to do whatever you please' in return. The patent insincerity of that offer left Niccolò shaking his head.

He was belaboured every day with such demands. Some were genuine and moved him to leniency, but most were like this one, citing nothing more than the 'great inconvenience' that a cobbler's business in... where was it again? Castellina di Chianti? would suffer if either father or son were to be absented from it to serve the republic. It was one of the many ways that aristocrats like Salviati went about sabotaging the whole militia programme.

Well, the good citizens of Castellina would just have to be inconvenienced. It would greatly offend Alamanno Salviati, no doubt, but Niccolò's relationship with him was probably already beyond being repaired, no matter what honeyed words he used in the reply he now set about crafting. He did his best to be diplomatic, but could not resist a gentle dig, hinting that perhaps Salviati might in future save his efforts for worthier causes.

'We just cannot tolerate bribery or special favours for those who can persuade some aristocrat to intervene in their favour,' he told Piero Soderini later that day. 'We have to get the people's trust, and we will only get it if they perceive that everyone is being treated fairly.'

'I fear you are too idealistic Niccolò. You know these great men of ours derive most of their power from their ability to do deals on behalf of those they regard as their clients. By turning down the likes of Alamanno, you are issuing them a challenge they won't like.'

352

'Yet what else can I do, Ser Piero? If I am to lead these people, simple peasants as they are, I must give them an example of the kind of fair dealing they can expect when they are under arms on our behalf. We are asking them to fight for us, after all.'

'Calm down Niccolò, I am on your side, remember!' The gonfaloniere laughed and threw his arms into the air in mock-surrender, then his face settled back to its more habitual serious expression. 'I will do my best to smooth Alamanno's feathers, but you know how the *ottimani* are, they don't give up even the slightest authority without a fight. For now, you are winning, but please, just be a little judicious when you choose which aristocrat you are going to offend next, I beg you.'

It was, he had to concede, good advice, and he did his best to apply it. Despite these petty irritations, recruitment and training proceeded apace and, by early February, he felt it was time to show off what his little army of sheepherders, woodcutters and farmers could do. He sent out orders to his captains to prepare their troops for a display of their martial spirit in Florence. Now these doubters would see what might be possible.

Standing with the gonfaloniere and other members of the Signoria on the platform of the Loggia, Niccolò could barely control his nerves as the four hundred recruits marched into the piazza. They looked magnificent in their uniform white doublets, red and white hose, white caps and shining breastplates, each contingent led by their own constable who was decked out in even more finery and carried the battalion staff and insignia. Marching evenly across the flagstones, on a series of commands they shouldered their arms, stamped their feet, and came to a halt facing the Loggia.

Niccolò scanned the line of faces in front of him, the many faces of Tuscany, some old, some very young, weather-beaten and sunburned, but all of them solemn and proud to be showing these effete Florentine city folk what they, mere peasants, could do. The spectators on the Loggia and the onlookers gathered in the piazza seemed to hold their collective breath too, struck by the beauty of the scene in front of them. Then the tension broke and a low buzz of comment started up, instantly stilled when a trumpeter issued a blast and the gonfaloniere rose to make his speech.

Soderini's remarks were brief and graceful, complimenting the men on their appearance and discipline and telling them that they were true patriots who

353

future generations of Florentines would look back on with pride, saying that this was the day upon which the future freedom and independence of Florence and Tuscany was ensured. Then the drums rattled once more and the troop went through a series of marches and counter-marches across the piazza, before disappearing from whence they had come, leaving behind a happily chattering crowd.

Up on the Loggia, various members of the Signoria and his colleagues from the chancellery crowded excitedly around Niccolò, congratulating him on his achievement, telling him how they had always known it would be a success and claiming some of the credit for themselves in ways that were so egregious that he could not help laughing.

'Let us not get carried away, my lords! What you saw was a mere parade, such as any party of *condottieri* could mount at a moment's notice. We have yet to see them fight, though I am certain they will acquit themselves honourably when the time comes.'

Still, he was the man of the hour and, at least for the moment, the voices of his critics were stilled. There was a long way to go with the militia, but he was proud of what he had accomplished so far and he continued to spend a good part of his days on militia business.

By mid-summer, they were ready to be tested in the field, albeit in a limited capacity, supporting the mercenary arming that continued the siege of Pisa. In a series of small skirmishes, they acquitted themselves well, and the Signoria professed themselves satisfied that Niccolò's limited experiment was a success, so much so that the Great Council was prevailed upon to approve a new body to expand and oversee the new force. Niccolò, naturally, was appointed as its secretary.

Secretary to the War Committee, secretary to the Committee of Militia, second secretary of the Chancellery of the Florentine Republic. Machiavelli had gathered together all the strings of the republic's foreign policy into his own hands and, at the end of 1506, he was probably the most important man in Florence next to the gonfaloniere.

Chapter 32—A Despatch from Spain

Florence, April 1507

It was just before dawn and the Casa Machiavelli was still draped in the deep folds of night-time's silence. Niccolò quietly splashed water on his face, afraid to wake anyone else in the still-sleeping household. Lifting a candle high, he inspected his reflection in the small looking-glass that hung on the wall. He needed a shave, but otherwise, the narrow-boned, dark-eyed visage that regarded him with its habitual mocking half-smile was much the same as it had looked when he was twenty, and a student. About the only thing that had changed in the last dozen years was the arrival of the flecks of grey that peppered his short-cropped black hair.

The sudden clangour of bells from the nearby church of the monastery of Santo Spirito shattered the silence and told him that, by the monks' reckoning at least, the day had officially begun. Crossing the room, he pushed open the shutters of a window; sure enough, the first of the morning's sun had found its way into the deep canyon of the street, casting slanting shadows across the paving stones. Leaning out, he watched as a cart lumbered by, its driver singing softly as though he too was reluctant to disturb the morning's peace.

Retrieving his doublet and long pleated tabard from their clothes hooks, he finished dressing for the day with his customary practised efficiency. On the way to the door, he picked up hat and satchel from where he had dropped them last night on his return from Siena, took a last look around the familiar room, and made his way towards the stairs that would take him down to the street, pausing outside the bedroom door to satisfy himself that his wife was still fast asleep. Twenty minutes later he was being waved through by the yawning guards who stood at the entrance to the Piazza della Signoria.

Before going upstairs, he stopped, as he often did, to gaze at Leonardo's great fresco depicting the Battle of Anghiari which adorned one wall of the enormous hall where the Great Council met. Da Vinci had finished the middle section, a wonder of sinuous movement, so lifelike that Niccolò could almost hear the whinnying of the horses and the whistle of the swords cutting through the air, but after that, he'd seemed reluctant to complete the rest of the work. Perhaps it brought back the screams of the dying soldiers and townspeople in Fossombrone and Senigallia. But finish it he must, since the Signoria had paid him for it, and no doubt he would do so when he came back from Milan, where he was finishing a painting for Charles d'Amboise, the cardinal's brother.

A few minutes later, he was settled at his desk in the chancellery. Niccolò loved the quiet of these first hours of the morning, when he had the office all to himself. It gave him a chance to get a look at the correspondence that had arrived while he was away, read the various intelligence and diplomatic reports, and compose replies to the more difficult letters. Absorbed in his work, he was startled when another peal of church bells interrupted the silence, telling him that he had already been at work for two hours. Stretching cramped fingers, he rose and went across to one of the windows that overlooked the piazza below, propping himself on the windowsill to take in the familiar view across the piazza, by now full of people going about the day's business.

Idly, he tried to imagine what the vast marble-clad mass of the city's basilica, the Cathedral of Santa Maria del Fiore, must have looked like before Filippo Brunelleschi had been given the task of building that preposterous dome, nearly ninety years before. It must have been odd, and a standing reproach to the city—a project it had started but had no idea how to finish. No wonder old Cosimo de' Medici had been so keen to fund its completion as a symbol of his and Florence's wealth and power.

The sound of familiar voices coming from the Hall of the Lilies next door gave him a moment's warning, and he turned just as Agostino and Biagio crashed into the room, leaving the door banging on its hinges behind them.

'You're back, Niccolò!'

Niccolò raised an eyebrow. 'It does rather seem so,' he said, unable to restrain his laughter as Biagio made his way across the room and embraced him in a bear-hug, followed by formal kisses on each cheek. 'Missed me, have you?'

'You know he always misses you, whether you are away for a day or a month,' Agostino drawled. 'Even Marietta doesn't fret as much as Biagio whenever you are out of his sight.'

Biagio half-heartedly raised his middle finger in Agostino's direction, lifting his shoulders in a shrug presumably intended to communicate indifference.

'These days Marietta is only too happy to see the back of me, if only so that she can get on with organising the household without my interference.'

That got a laugh from both of them. His wife had finally decided that complaining and moping whenever Niccolò was away would get her nowhere, and had instead developed a sturdily independent outlook on life which was only disturbed when her husband came home and attempted to impose his ideas on her domain. Matters weren't helped by the fact that he was as incompetent in the domestic arena as he was proficient when it came to managing the politics of the complex, overlapping and irrational system of committees and councils that was the government of Florence. Small wonder that Biagio—and Agostino, too, if the truth be known—missed him more than his wife did.

Agostino retreated to his table at the far end of the room near the door, and Biagio settled at his desk next to Machiavelli's, carelessly dropping a sealed packet on the edge of the table. Niccolò waited patiently while Biagio busied himself with sharpening a new quill.

'What's that?' Niccolò asked, gesturing to the unopened package.

His concentration interrupted, Biagio looked up with a frown of irritation. 'Oh, I forgot. The despatches from Spain. I ran into the courier on the way in this morning.'

'No doubt you would have remembered to give them to me before the day is out,' Niccolò said drily and reached across to pick up the hefty packet. When the seal was broken, half a dozen documents fell onto his desk, one of which was a long despatch from the Florentine ambassador at Zaragoza, the capital of the Kingdom of Aragon. His eyes flicked past the opening salutations and the routine complaints about the Signoria's stinginess with money (God knew he had written enough pleas of this sort himself over the years) to get to the meat.

The first few items were straightforward enough—reports on conversations with King Ferdinand's ministers and with the king himself, matters that could be easily summarised into a memorandum for the Signoria. But it was the last item that stopped him in his tracks with a startled grunt loud enough to prompt his colleagues to look up from their work.

'What's the matter?' Biagio asked.

'Valentino. It seems that he's dead.'

'How did he die?' Agostino broke the silence. 'The last we heard, he was in prison, was he not?'

'It says here he that escaped from the castle at La Mota, wherever that is, in October last year, and fled to the court of Navarre. King Juan is brother to his wife, you'll remember. For some reason, none of our agents in Zaragoza saw fit to report it at the time. Anyway, the king received Borgia with open arms, appointed him to lead his armies and sent him off to put down a rebellion.' Machiavelli consulted the report again. 'It seems he was killed in a skirmish of some kind while besieging a rebel fortress. His horse bolted while he was chasing a group of rebel soldiers, and he was trapped in a canyon, alone.'

The report also said that Borgia's body had been found naked, stripped of weapons, armour, jewellery and clothes. It seemed a particularly tawdry end for a life that had been lived with such zest and courage. In his imagination, Niccolò could see Cesare roaring defiance at his attackers as he faced his last moments, no doubt believing until the last blow was struck that he would somehow escape, as he had so often before. But death was one trap even he could not escape.

'An obscure end to a tempestuous life.' Biagio said, an edge of contempt in his voice.

'He deserved a better end, Biagio.' Niccolò was sharp. 'Yes, he caused us a great deal of trouble, and he was ruthless and unpredictable, but he might have become a great man had fate been more kind.'

He didn't miss the look of surprise that Biagio and Agostino shared at this pronouncement, but any chance to explain what he meant was lost as Filippo Casavecchia and the rest of the chancellery clerks arrived in a flurry of shouted greetings.

Once everyone had settled down, Niccolò picked up the packet of despatches and made his way across to the other side of the building, where the priors had their apartments, where he found Piero Soderini at work in his study. Nodding his visitor to a seat, the gonfaloniere listened calmly as Niccolò read the despatch from Spain.

358

'A sad end, one that he didn't deserve.' Soderini unknowingly echoed Niccolò's own sentiments. 'I always thought that Cesare would one day mature into a capable ruler of the Romagna, someone we could live with. But he was too mercurial, too unstable for our ever-cautious Signoria to trust him.'

'Oh, he wanted a lot more than just the Romagna, Ser Piero. He once hinted that he wanted to be the war leader for all of Italy, to throw out the French and the Spanish, and to make us one country.'

'Yes, I remember you saying as much in one of your despatches. Well, it might have been a brave and laudable aim, but I can't ever see it happening, can you? Italy united into one kingdom? Not in my lifetime, and probably not in yours.'

Niccolò had to admit the truth of that, though it was sad that it should be so. Cesare had been right about one thing, though: Italy, united or not, could have no peace until the foreigners who fought endlessly over her territory were chased back to their own borders.

A brisk Piero Soderini recalled him to the day's business. 'Enough on that subject: just make sure that you include a note about Borgia in your daily summary for the Signoria. Now, what did you write back to the Imperial ambassador about his demand for the return of his damned horses? I don't want to get into a quarrel with him but...'

It was late in the afternoon when he returned to the chancellery, having gone from Soderini's study to a formal meeting of the Committee of Militia, which had lasted until the middle of the afternoon; after that several other members of the Signoria each wanted some of his time, either in their apartments or in hurried corridor conversations.

By now, the chancellery office was filled with its full complement of a dozen officials. Other than a few nods as he crossed the room to his desk, they barely noticed his arrival as they worked diligently to get through the day's load of correspondence, ledger entries, meeting minutes and reports. This was as it should be; he had worked hard and long to bring the chancellery to this state of efficiency.

His desk carried its usual freight of paperwork that had been awaiting his attention since mid-morning and, before long, he too was hard at work reading, assessing, scribbling and writing, dealing with the letters and reports that were

359

reserved for his attention alone. Soon he was deep in what Agostino had once laughingly called his 'working trance', oblivious to everything and everyone. An hour went by in this state, and then he suddenly became aware that the end of the working day had arrived, signalled by the rising hum of conversation and the rustling of papers being placed back in their pigeonholes and folders.

'Ugolino has invited everyone to a party at Martina's house,' Biagio had obviously been waiting for him to realise that everyone was packing up for the day. 'Casa and Rafaello and Agostino are all going; she is going to have music and dancers there, and some of her friends. Come on, it will cheer you up.'

Martina was Ugolino Martelli's mistress, a courtesan of spectacular beauty. Quite how Ugolino, a man with few physical charms and little wealth, had managed to snare such a catch was something of a mystery to his colleagues in the chancellery. Her parties were usually riotous. It was tempting. 'Maybe later, Biagio. I want to finish up my report on Siena, then there is the notaries' work to be reviewed. I'll be here for a while.'

Biagio shrugged. 'All right, no need to say trot to a good horse. It's your loss.'

'More likely it will be your loss unless your usual luck at cards changes. Go on, I'll see you later, I promise.'

Niccolò settled back into his chair and watched, an affectionate smile on his face, as the cheerful, chattering group left. He had known most of them since they had studied together; they were friends as much as they were colleagues and subordinates, and usually, he would not have hesitated to join them for what promised to be an entertaining evening. But he had been accompanied all day by a small cloud of melancholy, and he didn't feel like laughing and singing and making up the improbable stories that always amused his friends.

It was hard to believe that Cesare was dead. Throughout his career, he had shown an uncanny ability to extricate himself from the most parlous situations; Niccolò had never been entirely persuaded that another resurrection was impossible and thought he might still come back to Italy to pursue his magnificent, impossible dreams, and he didn't doubt that Cesare himself had believed he had a future in Italy right up until the end.

What, he wondered, would Leonardo da Vinci make of the news when he heard it? The painter was living in Milan with Salai, having been summoned there to complete a painting that he had started long ago for Ludovico Sforza, but abandoned when he fled Milan after Sforza's regime fell. He would probably just say good riddance; in the years he had spent in Florence, Leonardo had never once spoken to Niccolò or anyone else, not even Agostino, about his time with the duke. It was as if he had decided to bury those memories forever.

A large coffer stood next to his desk, used for filing documents that he referred to regularly. Unlocking it with a large key that always hung from his belt, he opened the lid rummaged around inside until he found a smaller box, also locked, which he lifted out and placed in the centre of the desk. In the centre of the box lid there was a small metal plate engraved with a single word: 'Valentino'. Over the years, Niccolò had collected together memorabilia from his various encounters with Cesare Borgia and put them away in this little chest. It contained copies of his despatches, handwritten notes of one kind or another, receipts for expenses incurred on government business, sketches and rough plans of towns and fortifications.

The first document that he saw when he opened the box made him smile. There, right on top, was a diagram of the parade order for the militia for that day almost a year ago when they had first appeared before the public, detailing in coloured blocks and lines where each unit was to stand and what manoeuvres it was to complete. Leonardo had drawn it up for him, with his usual flair for detail and precision; his little contribution, along with the designs for the militia uniforms, to Niccolò's triumph.

One day, when he had some leisure, he would sort through all these bits of paper and write something to memorialise the life of Cesare Borgia. Having witnessed every stage of that remarkable young man's career, he was in a unique position to undertake such a project. But such a task would require the investment of many hours of his time, something that was impossible for the moment, and so he placed the copy he had made of that morning's despatch into the box, locked it and returned it to its place in the coffer.

Picking up the first of the letters that was waiting for his attention, he stared blankly at it for a few moments, then put it down with a sigh. He just wasn't in the mood to concentrate, and he decided that it could all wait until tomorrow. Maybe Biagio was right, spending the evening with his friends would shake off his melancholy. Picking up his hat, he made his way to the door, took a last look around, and left.

361

Chapter 33 – Niccolò's Triumph

Pisa, September 1508

From his vantage point on a small hillock, Niccolò watched as two dozen men worked to drive a pile into the bed of the River Arno. At the shouted command of the overseer, they hauled the great stone weight of the piledriver to the top of its enclosing frame, stamping their feet and chanting a scurrilous little ditty that made Niccolò smile. After a moment's hesitation, a shout from the overseer sent the weight dropping with a hiss and a loud bang onto the top of the pile. The workers, their naked torsos gleaming with sweat under the autumnal sun, walked chattering back to their starting positions, ready to begin the whole operation again.

This was the last of the three rows of fifteen piles that the team had driven into the muddy bottom of the river, just a few miles from its mouth. The next stage would involve binding the elaborate barrier together with iron bands, just below the level of the water, so that the Pisans would not be able to dismantle the completed barricade. Designed to prevent any shipping from getting up the river to deliver supplies to the beleaguered city, it was just one element in a comprehensive strategy that he had urged on Piero Soderini over a year ago to bring the never-ending siege of Pisa to an end by comprehensively laying waste to the city's sources of supply. Crops were to be destroyed or confiscated, livestock slaughtered, and every possible way of getting the means of carrying on the war into the city interdicted.

At first Soderini had been dubious. 'If we press Pisa too hard and reduce them to utter desperation, we risk rousing support for them from elsewhere in Italy, which will be hard to counter. And then there is France: Louis is already complaining that our siege is too brutal, though he has stopped short of absolutely forbidding it.'

Quite why King Louis should have suddenly developed this new compassion for the fate of the Pisans was something of a mystery, but Niccolò wasn't going to let that argument stop him.

'Ser Piero, we have tried everything else, and we have failed. The time has come for ruthlessness; it is obvious that the Pisans won't surrender until we have our boots on their neck.' This unaccustomed ferocity startled the gonfaloniere, and Niccolò softened his tone a little. 'You know I have always questioned the wisdom of this war. But if we believe it is a just war, a necessary war, then we should do whatever is necessary to win it. We can be generous when we are victorious.'

Soderini had eventually been convinced, and, as was his way once he had decided something, he prosecuted the case with vigour in the Signoria. The strategy had eventually been approved, though not without opposition, and with the proviso that Secretary Machiavelli be despatched to get things going. And so here he was on the riverbank, supervising the construction of the barrage that would stop supplies getting to Pisa from the sea.

Not that there was a great deal of supervising to be done just at the moment: the overseer had the construction team well in hand, and having made sure that troops were placed in a cordon around the works to ensure their safety from any unexpected Pisan sally, he had for the moment nothing to do except sit on this grassy slope and watch, alone with his thoughts while he enjoyed an impromptu picnic of boiled eggs and bread, washed down with a flask of wine from his own vineyards at Sant'Andrea.

It had been an exhausting year and a half since Cesare Borgia had died in Spain. He had been back and forth to Siena several times, and then had been despatched to the court of Emperor Maximilian, who was threatening to come down into Italy and assert his claim to overlordship of Lombardy; since that duchy was still held by the French, such a move would have meant another war that the Florentines could ill afford. He went to the imperial court in the mountain city of Bozen in the company of Francesco Vettori, a young patrician who had been appointed as the senior ambassador. Niccolò did not know him well before this mission, but he turned out to be a cheerful and optimistic fellow with a sharp wit, and by the time their mission ended six months later, they had become fast friends.

He had been back barely a month before the Signoria sent him here. Since then he had been frantically busy, reviewing the militia infantry, sending out men to search for pockets of enemy troops who rumour said had slipped out of the city into the mountains, arranging furloughs for those militiamen who were urgently needed at home as the silkworm harvest approached, and dealing with the usual stream of correspondence from the government in Florence.

363

It was a demanding life, but as he sat watching the piledriver ascend ready for another blow, he realised that he was probably as happy as he had ever been. Florence wasn't far away, so he could get back and see his wife and family regularly, and though the work was very different from his diplomatic postings it was just as challenging and absorbing. Oddly, he felt he had a real talent for the military life; occasionally he wondered where this taste for soldiering had come from, and the only answer that he could come up with was that it must have rubbed off from all those months spent with Cesare Borgia and his army.

Thinking of Borgia reminded him of something else. Before Niccolò went off to the imperial court, Piero Soderini had made the extraordinary proposal that Florence should appoint Michelotto Corella, Borgia's old henchman, as captain of the new militia army. Corella had been handed over to Florence after his capture by the pope's army, and was languishing in prison there.

'Well it's convenient, I suppose, that we have him in our prison.' Niccolò didn't quite know what to think of the idea when the gonfaloniere first broached it with him. 'But do you think the Signoria will approve? Borgia's former lieutenant?'

'They'd better.' Soderini was pugnacious. 'Think about it, Niccolò: we need someone who has a military reputation that will frighten anyone who comes up against your new army. He will do that.'

'He certainly frightened me every time I had anything to do with him. And he did prove himself to be bone loyal to Cesare. Still, I think you will have a devil of a job to persuade the Signoria to take him on.'

Niccolò had never made a more accurate prediction: the debate over the matter was bruising, both in the Signoria and in the War Committee. But Soderini had finally got his way, and Michelotto was released from prison and sent off to take command of the militia army.

But something strange had happened to this fearsome mercenary captain: he had become something of an old woman. As secretary to the Militia Committee, Niccolò was his nominal superior, and over the two years that Michelotto was in the job he had been bombarded with endless letters explaining away every little incident that might tarnish his reputation, whining about every perceived slight, and referring every decision that was not routine up the command chain. Clearly without Borgia to wield the whip, he was out of his depth, and eventually the Florentines decided they could do without him and terminated his contract. He went back to Milan where, Niccolò had read in a despatch from that city some days ago, he was murdered by person or persons unknown.

His thoughts were interrupted by the overseer who, having climbed the little hill, saluted and announced that the last blow of the hammer had secured the final pile. Dismissing him and the crew with the promise of an extra wine ration for their efforts, he got to his feet and brushed the breadcrumbs off the front of his doublet. Climbing into the saddle, he kicked his horse into motion, back along the road that would lead to Pisa, an hour's ride away if he kept up a steady trot.

Settling himself into the familiar riding rhythm, his thoughts grew darker, as Pisa and the confrontation he would be facing when he got there grew nearer. A few days ago a civilian commissioner had been appointed whose task was to oversee the military men carrying out the siege. Niccolò had always understood that his own appointment was to be temporary in nature, and that he would eventually be superseded by a more senior permanent commissioner. After all, he had many duties back in Florence that could not be neglected forever. But he had been startled when he learned that the new commissioner was to be Alamanno Salviati. It was expected that he would arrive to take up his new appointment that day and would be in the camp by the time Niccolò arrived back there.

Alamanno and Niccolò had never got on since the patrician's instrumental part in his fall from grace after the Arno fiasco. Since then, he had opposed everything that Soderini had ever proposed, and as Niccolò was now widely seen as the gonfaloniere's right hand man, he too was a target of Alamanno's enmity. Ruefully, he remembered the letter requesting an exemption from service in the militia on behalf of one of his clients that he had turned down; on the surface Alamanno had accepted the verdict calmly enough, but there was a glint in his eye the next time he and Niccolò met that suggested he would not forget the slight.

Arriving at the sprawling, noisy Florentine camp just out of bowshot range of the walls of the city, Niccolò handed his horse off to a groom and went straight to the rickety structure, half tent and half shack, that served as the militia headquarters. As he had expected, Alamanno Salviati was there waiting for him, accompanied by a couple of junior aides; the three of them were bent over a map that covered half the table in the centre of the room.

'Ah, Niccolò, there you are.' Salviati was all bonhomie, though the smile decorating the lower half of his face didn't quite seem to reach his eyes. 'They told me you were off inspecting some siege-works or another. A pity you weren't here to meet me. But duty calls, I suppose.'

Niccolò inclined his head. 'We were driving the last pile into the barrage across the river mouth today, so I wanted to make sure it went well. But my apologies, Ser Alamanno, for my absence, necessary though it was.'

Salviati waved that away, gesturing for a servant to bring wine. A few broken veins on his nose and the slightest of pot bellies betrayed the fact that he was a habitually heavy drinker, though otherwise he looked lean and fit. Startlingly blue eyes regarded Niccolò over the rim of his glass, somehow contriving to seem both bland and calculating.

'I want to talk to you about my new strategy, Machiavelli.'

'New strategy? Has the Signoria and the gonfaloniere decided to abandon the old?'

'No, no. We will continue to press the Pisans as hard as we can, squeeze their supplies, and devastate their hinterlands. But I have a ploy that will bring this siege to an end even more quickly, if we apply a little intelligence to the task.'

Niccolò didn't much like the inference that intelligence had been missing from their efforts so far, but he did no more than raise his eyebrows in a silent and respectful query. Salviati gestured to one of the young officers to explain.

'We have arranged to release a prisoner, one Alfonso del Mutolo, who has been held in the Stinche for over a year. He has told us that if we return him to Pisa, he will open a gate for us, at an appointed time.'

Niccolò frowned. 'And what surety do we have for his honesty? What if he betrays us?'

'He won't.' Salviati was brusque. 'I have interviewed him myself and I am satisfied that he is honest. He is motivated, he says, by a desire to bring this war to an end.'

That Niccolò doubted. The one thing that Florence ought to have learned by now was that the long years of war and siege had bred a fanatical determination among the Pisans to resist. Why would this Mutolo prove to be any different? But he had little choice other than to accept Salviati's authority. And at least the core strategy to reduce the enemy's supplies from the countryside was still intact. If this stratagem worked, all well and good, but if not, at least they were not going to take their boot off the Pisan neck.

A few days later, Alfonso del Mutolo arrived, accompanied by a dozen other Pisan prisoners who were to be released to make it all seem like a legitimate show of clemency on the part of Florence. Niccolò was astonished when the big, burly son of a blacksmith separated himself from the rest of the group and came over to talk openly to Salviati and his officers. Why would he do such a thing, in front of his countrymen, if he was dealing with the Florentines honestly? Again, Niccolò could smell a large and hairy rat.

It only took a week for him to be proven right. The assault against the gate that Mutolo was supposed to open for them ended in disaster as, instead of admitting them they turned their artillery on the attackers, causing great carnage. It was all watched from the city walls by Mutolo and his compatriots, clearly visible against the late afternoon light.

'Not a word, Machiavelli,' Salviati said as they watched the wounded stragglers come back into the camp. 'I didn't really think it would work either, but it was worth a try.'

Niccolò was staggered by the hypocrisy of this lie, and he could not restrain himself. 'Was it worth the lives of a dozen valuable men, Ser Alamanno? This debacle was entirely predictable to anyone who has an ounce of sense!'

Salviati's glare was eloquent: Niccolò had gone too far. 'I think your usefulness here is ended, Machiavelli. I would be obliged if you returned to Florence immediately.'

'Are you relieving me, Ser Alamanno?' Niccolò knew well that Salviati did not have the authority to take that step.

'No, but I am sick of the sight of your face. Take yourself home for some leave, and let me get on with this damned siege without you looking over my shoulder every few minutes, counselling caution and despair.'

None of that was fair criticism, but Niccolò had little choice but to comply with his superior's demand. Back in Florence the next day, Biagio was blunt.

'If you're not careful, Niccolò, you'll find yourself out of office again. You know what these powerful men are like: they must always be right, and one must show respect for them, even if they are idiots.'

It was good counsel, underlined by Piero Soderini when Niccolò met him to report on the events at Pisa. 'I never thought it would work either, but Alamanno insisted. And he is too powerful to snub these days, something you would do well to keep in mind, my friend.'

'I suspect it is too late for me to ever repair my relationship with either of the Salviati brothers,' Niccolò said with a shrug. 'I fear for the future, though, with people like Alamanno in charge of important operations like the siege. These great gentlemen of ours find it all too easy to fall back on old habits, trying to buy the Pisans off, or trick them into surrender so as to avoid the hard work that will be necessary if we are to win this war.'

'We have no choice, Niccolò, except to work with the material we have to hand. Don't fret: I am determined to make sure that we apply the greatest possible rigour to the siege, no matter what Alamanno's inclinations might be.'

The gonfaloniere stayed true to his word, and over the next nine months the Florentine army slowly strangled Pisa, emptying the countryside all around of supplies and driving more and more of the peasantry to take refuge in the city itself, thereby putting even more pressure on dwindling food supplies. Signs began to emerge that there were cracks in Pisan resolve, tentative feelers appearing to suggest that some kind of peace might be possible. Niccolò himself was despatched to Piombino to respond to one such proposal; no peace agreement came out of that encounter, but Niccolò, talking to the various members of the Pisan delegation, was convinced that their final surrender could not be long delayed.

The end, when it came, was swift. In May, news came that there had been a great battle between the French and the Venetians at a place called Agnadello. The Venetians had been soundly beaten, and as a consequence were no longer in a position to provide financial and material support to their allies in Pisa. That was the last nail in the Pisan coffin, and early in June Pisa finally surrendered itself into Florentine hands, unconditionally. The Signoria was jubilant on receiving the news, and debate immediately began on what terms should be enforced against the defeated city.

'Wring their necks, I say,' was the blunt sentiment expressed by Luca degli Albizzi, supported by nods around the table. 'This bloody war has cost a fortune, and we must make them pay for it.'

Niccolò, at his usual place next to the gonfaloniere, was appalled at such short-sightedness. His glance at Piero Soderini, eyebrows raised, was enough to prompt the gonfaloniere to hold up his hand for silence.

'Thank you, Luca, for your opinion, expressed as pithily as ever.' That got a laugh from the table. 'But I would also like to hear Secretary Machiavelli's views on the subject. After all, it was his policy that won us this great victory.'

Niccolò was used by now to being asked for his views in council, but he also noted that not everyone in the room was happy that he had been asked to speak on this occasion, judging from the frowns he spotted here and there.

'Thank you, Ser Piero. Much as I esteem Signor d'Albizzi's opinion, I must disagree. Now is the time for magnanimity, not vengeance. Let us remember that Pisa has had a long and proud history, and they have resisted us to the point of utter exhaustion. But their pride is, I put to you, not by any means extinguished. The lesson of Rome and Carthage should guide us, for the Romans understood that the only way they could really defeat a proud enemy was to terminate their very existence by reducing Carthage to rubble. Can we honestly say that we have the means, or the will, to do the same to Pisa? To kill all their leaders and force their population into cowering subservience?'

His words and his passion had the desired effect. The doubting frowns had become thoughtful, and there were nods here and there. 'So, my lords, it seems to me that if we cannot crush Pisa, we should embrace her. Offer the most clement terms possible, raise the Pisans up from their prostration, and they will become our partners and our greatest bulwark in the west. Let justice secure our victory.'

When the silence stretched after he had finished speaking, he began to wonder if he had, after all, misread the mood of the men sitting around the table. But then his old comrade Luca degli Albizzi clapped his hands.

369

'Niccolò, your eloquence silences me,' he grinned. 'I am vanquished and entirely converted to your point of view. Signori, let us follow the secretary's excellent advice in this matter.'

When, just a week later, the Pisan representatives gathered with the Florentine Signoria and the War Committee to ratify the peace, Niccolò was among them. Walking through the streets of Pisa with Biagio and Marcello Adriani and the rest of the Florentine delegation, he was astonished and saddened by the devastation that he saw about him. Once-fine buildings were dilapidated, their windows boarded over and the paint flaking from the walls, rubbish was piled in every corner, and the silent sad-eyed people who watched them pass were terribly thin and clad in rags. Niccolò wanted to cry out to them, to reassure them that things would get better now that this long bloodletting between neighbours was over.

At least the terms of the treaty were as moderate as he could have hoped for, and there was some prospect for a prosperous peace between the two cities.

'This is your victory as much as it is anyone's, Niccolò,' Adriani said quietly as they waited for their turn to affix their signatures to the document that lay on the table in the middle of the room. 'Whatever Alamanno might say.'

Predictably, Alamanno Salviati had not stopped bragging that it was 'his' militia and 'his' cavalry who had done all the work to bring this day about, even though he had in fact proved to be a lazy and disinterested commissioner whose interventions in the military sphere had if anything prolonged the siege unnecessarily. Watching as a gorgeously attired Alamanno signed the treaty with a theatrical flourish, Niccolò allowed himself a small grimace of distaste.

'God help Florence if he and his other *ottimati* friends ever succeed in their plots to bring down the gonfaloniere. The Medici will be back in no time.'

'Be careful, Niccolò,' Adriani said, putting a cautionary hand on his arm. 'A braggart and poseur he may be, but Alamanno Salviati and his brother are both crafty and vindictive. And you are an easy target for them: you are close to Piero, and if you will forgive me for saying so, you do not guard your tongue as rigorously as you ought.'

'Biagio said much the same thing,' Niccolò said, smiling. 'And you are both right. I will do my best, I promise, to mend my fences with both of the Salviati.

370

Now, it looks as though all the great men have finished, and it's our turn.' He gestured and bowed extravagantly. 'After you, My Lord Chancellor!'

Turning to follow Adriani to signature table, he intercepted a look of utter contempt on Salviati's face. With an inner sigh, he realised then that whatever attempts he might make to win the patrician over would be doomed to failure. Oh well, what would be would be.

Chapter 34 – The End of the Republic

Blois, July 1510

There really could not be, Niccolò thought, a more pleasant place to be in summer than the valley of the Loire. He was standing at one of the half-dozen tall windows that lined the audience chamber of the royal chateau of Blois, enjoying an expansive view across golden fields that merged into the cool green forests that ascended the slopes of the hills beyond. Blazing from a cloudless azure sky, the beams of a westering sun intensified the colours and deepened the shadows of the landscape; just below the window, a lone palace gardener who had been busy among the flower-beds straightened and stretched an aching back, taking a brief moment of respite from his labour to look out across the same view that Niccolò was enjoying. That was Leonardo's skill, he mused, to be able to capture such an instant in his brain and then reproduce it on canvas.

Pleasant though it was to stand here enjoying the view, it could not seduce his mind for long from the reason he had been sent once again on the long journey across the Alps to find the peripatetic court of King Louis. Florence had enjoyed a rare year of peace after the surrender of Pisa, but such a state could not persist for long in Italy, and it had been disturbed by a bellicose Pope Julius, who a few weeks ago had raised the banner of a crusade to 'throw the barbarians out of Italy'. Everyone, Niccolò included, had been astonished at the papal volte-face, abandoning his old friendship with France.

A door clicked open, startling him out of his reverie. Turning, he swept off his hat and made a court bow towards the tall angular figure of Florimond Robertet, King Louis' chief counsellor since the death of Cardinal d'Amboise two months ago.

'Welcome to Blois, Signor Machiavelli! I hope they have found you comfortable rooms?' Robertet's jovial greeting was delivered in perfectly accented Italian.

'They have indeed. Much improved on my accommodation when I was last here.'

Robertet frowned, thinking. 'God, that seems so long ago. Fifteen hundred, was it? With that other fellow, della Casa?'

'Your memory is excellent, signor. Though Francesco grew ill and had to go off to Paris, leaving me to deal with Cardinal d'Amboise and the king by myself.'

'God rest the cardinal's soul,' Robertet said, crossing himself. 'We all miss him, not least the king. Now, before he arrives, tell me the meat of your mission here.'

'As always: to reassure the king that Florence remains his devoted ally, and that we have not been seduced by the pope.'

'Well I am glad to hear that the Florentine Signoria at least does not believe we are barbarians.' Robertet said, a thin smile on his face. 'But I fear that this pope's bellicosity can only lead us into war.'

'*Papa Terribile*, they are calling him. He seems to like nothing better than climbing into his armour and marching off to fight someone. He fancies himself as the arbiter of power in Italy, I think.' Caution stopped him speaking as he tried to gauge the temperament of the Frenchman, a man he did not understand as well as he had the late cardinal. Seeing nothing but a polite interest in Robertet's face, he decided to continue. 'Florence, as you know monsieur, is only now beginning to recover from the rigours of our war against Pisa, and the last thing that we wish to see is a resumption of warfare in north Italy. The Signoria has therefore charged me to assist in any way that I can to help reconcile the king with the pope...'

Whatever Robertet's response to that might have been was cut off when the door opened again, a major-domo entered and, with a thump of his staff on the parquetry floor, announced the arrival of His Catholic Majesty King Louis XII. Niccolò was shocked by the king's appearance as he walked across the room, his hand extended in greeting. He had lost weight, his face was sallow, and his gait was shuffling. Close up, the dark eyes had lost none of their intensity, but his forehead was etched with deep furrows and there were streaks of grey threading the long hair.

'Welcome back to our court, Machiavelli. The late cardinal held you in high esteem, and I was heartened to learn that Florence had sent you as her emissary.'

'Your Majesty is kind.' Niccolò switched to French. 'Cardinal Soderini and his brother the gonfaloniere charged me to convey their sadness and condolences on the death of the cardinal, a true friend to Florence.'

'As we are ourselves. And with this new trouble with the pope, now is the time for your Signoria to reciprocate that friendship.'

Once Niccolò had reassured the king on that point with a florid and flattering prepared speech, Louis seemed to relax a little, gesturing for them all to be seated and calling for wine. 'Secretary Machiavelli, I have no desire, none, to find myself at war with the pope. But I will not allow him to molest my possessions in Italy.'

'Perhaps, Majesty, Monsieur Machiavelli may be able to help us,' Robertet interjected before Niccolò could respond to the king. 'He mentioned Cardinal Soderini: perhaps the cardinal's interests and resources could be engaged to help mediate between ourselves and the pope?'

Niccolò was somewhat dubious about that proposition, for he knew (though perhaps Robertet did not) that Francesco Soderini's influence with Pope Julius was waning. More and more, the pope was leaning on another cardinal, Giovanni de' Medici, the late Piero's brother, for all his advice on Florentine and Italian affairs. Nevertheless, he said that he would raise the subject with the cardinal and see what could be done.

'We will be grateful if you can achieve something, Machiavelli,' the king said, rising. 'I promise you this: if the pope makes any demonstration of affection towards me, be it only the length of my fingernail, I will go the length of my arm to meet him.'

So for the next month Niccolò did everything he possibly could to find a way of mediating between king and pope, with letter after letter going back and forth between Blois, Florence and Rome. But it was to no avail; as Niccolò had feared, the pope was no longer listening to Cardinal Soderini. Worse, with Giovanni de' Medici whispering in the other ear, the attempt at mediation had just made Julius even more hostile to Florence.

'Nothing will convince this pope to desist except a good thrashing,' a frustrated Robertet told him, reminding Niccolò that the urbane courtier had a martial past. 'And if he's not careful, we will give him one.'

374

Niccolò left France with a strong sense of foreboding. Another war in Italy would be disastrous for Florence. More worryingly, her colours were now firmly nailed to the French mast, which gave them little room to change tack should the French be defeated. Niccolò had seen for himself that Louis was not the man he once was, and after the Garigliano the possibility of a setback on the field of battle for the French did not seem so far-fetched.

Yet peace, of a sort, held for another year. King Louis came up with another scheme: he would convoke a rebel council of the church, at which he would denounce the present pope and declare him deposed. He was convinced, so one of Robertet's private letters told him, that he could succeed if he could recruit the king of England and the emperor to his cause.

To Niccolò, the plan seemed mad, and caused even more difficulties for Florence when Louis announced that the venue for his council would be Pisa, of all places. The Signoria sent him to that city with instructions to try to persuade the king to call the whole thing off, a forlorn hope that earned him several uncomfortable interviews with Louis and his advisers; eventually he managed to convince the king to move the council to Milan. But it was too late. Julius was not in a forgiving mood, and in October 1511 he formed the so-called Holy League, recruiting both Venice and Ferdinand of Spain to his cause. Though there had been no fighting that year, it ended with an ominous sense that war could not be long delayed.

When it came the following summer, it went very badly for the French. They lost Lombardy, leaving the pope dominant in northern Italy. Still reeling from that news, Florentines were even more dismayed when they heard that a huge Spanish army was moving towards them. In short order, an embassy of arrogant Spaniards arrived to demand that Florence abandon her alliance with France and pay a huge tribute of thirty thousand ducats.

'We should accept, Ser Piero,' Niccolò urged the gonfaloniere after a shocked Signoria had broken up without making any decision. 'What the Spanish are asking is outrageous, I know, but we must face facts. The French are finished in Italy now, so we no longer have any obligations to King Louis. In the same circumstances he would have abandoned us without a backward glance. At least we would preserve the republic.'

'While exchanging one foreign master for another.' Soderini said tiredly. 'And I don't know about you, but I would trust King Ferdinand even less than

I do Louis. No, let us trust to the fine army you have given us to prevail against the invader.'

Niccolò could hardly argue with that, though he worried that his militia, however fine they seemed to Soderini, were not going to be a match for the massive army of Spanish regulars who were now outside Prato, only fourteen miles down the Arno valley. And then there had been a bitter dispute about strategy, Niccolò advocating that the bulk of the militia be sent to defend Prato so as to buy time to build up there defences here in Florence. But he had been overruled, and in the end it had been decided to keep most of the militia close at hand.

His worst fears were eclipsed by the next bulletin that came in from Prato. The Spanish army had swept aside the small force posted there and proceeded to sack the city. Four thousand or more of the city's citizens had been put to the sword and the streets had become slippery with their blood. Panic seized the citizens of Florence who were so noisily in favour of a valiant defence just weeks ago, and new ambassadors were sent to the Spanish by a jittery Signoria. The reply: Soderini must resign and the tribute would now have to be sixty thousand ducats.

Ominously, there was also one new demand: the Medici were to be allowed to return to Florence, though only as private citizens. It might be a Spanish army they were facing, but it was Pope Julius, no doubt now wholly under the influence of Cardinal de' Medici, who was setting the terms.

Soderini and the Signoria were shocked, divided, and unable to come to a decision. Some, particularly those like the Salviati brothers and their *ottimati* friends, were wholeheartedly in favour of accepting the Spanish terms, while others were just as energetically opposed. The threat of violence seemed ever present, and came closer on the last day of August when a group of young pro-Medici noblemen invaded the office of the gonfaloniere, manhandling him and demanding that he surrender and accept the Spanish terms. That seemed to make up a shaken Soderini's mind for him.

'You know as well as I that these ruffians represent those who have for years wanted to get me out of here,' he told Niccolò. 'I fear it will come to blood.'

'No! We won't let them near you again!'

But even as the hot words came, doubt assaulted his confidence. He remembered, all too clearly, the head of Paolo Vitelli on a spike down below in the piazza. Had that not been the act of a mob enraged? Did he really believe that such scenes could not happen again?

'Oh, it's not for my blood that I fear.' Soderini was now completely calm. 'But I will go from this place, and willingly, if it prevents riot and bloodshed in the streets, whether the offences are committed by my partisans or my enemies.'

Niccolò found nothing to say in response to that sentiment; it was typical of Piero Soderini to put the safety of the state above his own ambitions. And so the gonfaloniere went quietly into exile as Cardinal Giovanni's younger brother Giuliano entered the city to a rapturous welcome from the Medici family's partisans, chief among them Alamanno and Jacopo Salviati.

Giuliano de' Medici was ostensibly no more than a private citizen, but that fiction was soon abandoned. It took just a month for he and his brother to dismantle the republic, disbanding the Great Council and rewriting the constitution so that they could take full control of the machinery of government.

Niccolò and his colleagues in the chancellery were instructed to remain at their posts, and so he turned up every day as usual. At first he was confident that the new regime would, once it had settled down, recognise that it needed his skills and experience to keep the government going. He would demonstrate that he was a true servant of the Florentine state, and that he would willingly serve its governors, whoever they might be. The fact that he had been saddened and distressed by the suddenness and manner of Soderini's departure, he kept to himself.

But it wasn't long before he was forced to recognise that something fundamental had changed.

Every committee was soon stuffed with Medici clients and supporters, who ostentatiously snubbed him whenever he opened his mouth. The new focus of power had shifted to the Palazzo Medici, over on the Via Larga, and most of the important decisions that affected the state were now being made there, not in the Palazzo della Signoria, where there was a tense and gloomy atmosphere in the chancellery office, all the old joking camaraderie gone. Even his closest colleagues were increasingly circumspect, not avoiding him exactly, but being very careful in what they said to him and in his earshot. He began to feel like a prisoner waiting for his sentence to be handed down.

When the end came, it was at the hands of an embarrassed Marcello Adriani, who told him in the stiff and formal language of the proclamation that would be published throughout the city later that day, 'dismissed, deprived and totally removed' from all his remaining posts. Worst of all, he was prohibited from entering the Palazzo della Signoria for one year.

He was not alone: Biagio had also been dismissed, presumably an act of spite, since he was the only one of Niccolò's close friends who lacked the shield of aristocratic parentage that protected Agostino Vespucci and Filippo Casavecchia. It was comforting, though, that when they left the building, both Agostino and Casa insisted on escorting them out, arms linked and keeping up a defiant commentary on the injustice of it all to any and every official they passed by on their way out.

A miserable Christmas followed, at home in the house in Santo Spirito, where he spent hours brooding. Even his beloved books offered no solace; over and again he picked one out from the bookshelves in his study, flicked idly through the first few pages, and threw it down in disgust. What use was all this book-wisdom in the face of the brutal realities of politics? Everything seemed useless and pointless.

It was February, a cold but sunny day, when one of the servants interrupted an early family supper to announce breathlessly that there was an officer of the Signoria at the door, accompanied by half a dozen guards. Though filled with foreboding, he greeted the young constable with as much affability as he could summon. 'Well young Giulio, what brings you out on a dog-cold day like this? And with such a fine escort!'

'I am sorry Messer Machiavelli,' the young man said, a genuinely embarrassed look on his face. 'But I have a warrant that has been sworn out for your arrest. I am to take you to the Bargello.'

'Upon what charge, am I allowed to know?'

'I do not know myself, Messer. I am simply charged with conducting you to the prison.'

378

He had no option to go with them, leaving a pregnant and tearful Marietta standing at the door, and be conducted, humiliatingly, through the streets of Florence to the square stone mass of the Bargello, part-prison, part-courthouse. There his courteous treatment ended—the prison guards, a rougher lot than young Giulio and his escort, threw him into a dark and rancorous cell, lit only by a tiny window set high in the wall.

It was a nervous, near-sleepless night. It had all happened so suddenly that he could not quite take it in. What, he wondered, could he be charged with that would justify this kind of treatment? He could not believe that the new regime would be so depraved as to entirely abandon the rule of law and begin arbitrarily imprisoning those whose only crime was to loyally serve its predecessor. Unless there was something that had been going on behind the scenes of which he was completely unaware, some plot to trap him into an indictable offence. His mind went round and round, trying to put a shape to that idea, but every possibility turned to mist when subjected to any kind of logical examination. Eventually he gave up and fell into an exhausted sleep.

In the morning, his gaolers reappeared and conducted him, blinking in the light, across the courtyard and up the stairs into a plain room where he was only slightly surprised to be confronted by Alamanno Salviati, standing calmly and holding a sheaf of papers. Behind a small desk placed in one corner sat a magistrate, a big ledger book open before him. The only other occupant of the room stood beside the magistrate's desk, a short and muscular man who regarded Machiavelli impassively.

'Niccolò Machiavelli. You have come down in the world.' Alamanno's voice sneered as he consulted the paper he held in his hand. 'You did manage to acquire quite a list of titles—second secretary to the Signoria, secretary to the War Committee, secretary to the Nine of Militia, sometime ambassador to the court of the King of France, etcetera, etcetera. Now just plain citizen Machiavelli.'

'I am quite aware of my history, Ser Alamanno,' Niccolò said, his voice much calmer than he felt. 'I am, as you say, now no more than a plain citizen of the republic. But surely like any other citizen I am entitled to know with what I am charged?'

Salviati's laugh was without humour. 'We will get to that. Do you know a young man named Pietro Paolo Boscoli?'

The question was so unexpected that it took Niccolò a moment to understand what he was being asked. He searched his memory, frowning. 'I have the vaguest recollection of someone by that name. He came once to the Palazzo della Signoria with a petition of some kind, I can't remember about what.'

'The defendant knows Boscoli,' Salviati muttered to the magistrate, who duly made a note in his ledger. 'What about Luca Capponi?'

'That name I have never heard before today.' Capponi was an illustrious name in Florence, and in all probability he had met this Luca at some time or another, but he decided it was better to deny all knowledge until he knew what this was all about. 'Who are these men? And what have they to do with me?'

'They were arrested two days ago on suspicion of treason. When interrogated, they confessed that they planned to murder Giuliano de' Medici. Your name was on a list found in their possession, a list of citizens who they believed would support them in their plot.'

Niccolò was so astonished he could not restrain himself from laughing out loud.

'You think this is a joke, Messer Machiavelli?' Salviati's eyes had narrowed dangerously.

'No, no, of course not. But surely, Ser Alamanno, the idea that I would be a party to such a foolish conspiracy is absurd. They might have put my name on their list, but they never approached me and, if they had, I would have told them the whole idea was deeply stupid.'

'Yet your name was on the paper. They must have believed you would have sympathy with them.'

'I told you, the one I have met only once, and the other not at all. How could they know whether I would favour their cause unless they can read minds from halfway across the city?'

Salviati stared at him for a few moments and then shook his head. 'I am not persuaded of your honesty, Machiavelli.'

He gestured to the two gaolers who had been standing quietly behind him. They grasped his arms and hustled him through the door into a larger, higher chamber, which contained nothing except a rope that dangled from a heavy hook in the ceiling, with a leather strap fastened to its end. Suddenly, horrifyingly, he knew what was to come. Twisting in his gaolers' hands back towards the door he let out a shout of protest. 'No, Alamanno! You can't do this!'

But Salviati was nowhere to be seen. The door was shut, and only the magistrate and the short, muscular man stood in front of it. Neither said anything as the two gaolers took Niccolò into the middle of the room and tied his wrists behind his back. Meanwhile, the other man set about lowering the rope that dangled from the ceiling, until it was at the height of Niccolò's waist, and then passed the strap through the bonds that held his wrists.

Niccolò's s heart was pounding and he felt a rivulet of sweat run down his forehead into his eyes, forcing him to blink them clear. He knew what was about to happen, and he was frightened, but he was angrily determined to give his torturers no satisfaction whatever.

The chief torturer, for that was what he was, began to turn a drum around which the other end of the rope was wound. As it tightened, his arms were pulled away behind him, then wrenched upwards, and he felt the most searing, burning pain he had ever experienced across his shoulders and back.

His feet left the ground and he was hauled higher and higher, until he was a dozen or more feet in the air, suspended only by his wrists. Every fibre of his being wanted to scream, but he forced his teeth closed, biting his tongue in the process and adding another jolt of suffering. He didn't know how long he was suspended there, probably only a few seconds, but it felt as though it was going to go on forever. Then he heard the sound of the torturer releasing a lever, and he dropped a few feet, before jerking to a halt, causing another excruciating jolt of pain.

The magistrate looked up at him and shouted. 'Confess, Machiavelli, and this will all end!'

'There is... nothing... for me to confess to,' Niccolò panted. The magistrate gestured, the winch clanked, and he dropped another few feet.

'We know everything already Machiavelli,' the magistrate shouted, trying another tack. 'So there is no point in your resisting.'

'If you know everything…you must know that… I have nothing to do with this conspiracy,' Niccolò panted.

The magistrate's face tightened. 'Everyone confesses after a few drops of the *strappado*, Machiavelli. You will too.'

Niccolò said nothing, just shaking his head to clear the sweat out of his eyes, and spitting the blood out of his mouth, getting some minor gratification when drops landed on the magistrate's face.

Another sudden jerking fall, and then another. The same questions, the same denials, which he could now barely mutter through teeth clenched against the pain. The magistrate's angry expression was beginning to be tinged with wonder: Niccolò knew that few people resisted more than four drops, but he was damned if he was going to confess to these absurd charges, and once again just shook his head in denial.

Two more drops, and his feet were dangling within a foot of the flagstones. Niccolò was on the very edge of consciousness, but before he finally passed out he had the satisfaction of seeing a look of utter frustration on the magistrate's face as he finally ordered that the prisoner be released.

When he woke back in his cell, his whole body seemed to be on fire. His shoulders were bruised and swollen, though he could move his arms a little, albeit at the cost of great spasms of pain. At least his shoulders were not dislocated; either he had been lucky, or someone had attended to his injuries while he was unconscious. Six drops of the *strappado*! Through the pain, he felt a grim satisfaction that he had survived such extreme torture.

Mysteriously, he was never questioned again. Day after day, his only human contact was with his gaolers, who dutifully appeared twice a day to provide food and drink, but otherwise left him alone. Neither the magistrate nor Alamanno Salviati appeared to ask him again about this supposed conspiracy. It must, he decided, have been entirely made up in order to discredit him; no doubt the perpetrators had hoped he would confess quickly to save himself from the pain, and then he could be safely imprisoned, exiled, or worse. Who had dreamed this scheme up? He could only assume that it was Salviati himself, though his chances of proving that, or getting any kind of justice for that matter, seemed remote.

382

Ten, eleven, twelve days went by, and then he had, quite unexpectedly, a visitor.

'Biagio! Forgive me if I don't embrace you, old friend. My arms are somewhat out of joint!'

The feeble joke brought tears to his friend's eyes, and Niccolò suddenly realised what he must look like, filthy, unshaven, dishevelled.

'Come on, cheer up Biagio. I am in a better state than I look, which would admittedly not be too hard to achieve. I am hungry for news! Tell me what has been going on. How is Marietta bearing up? And the boys?'

After Biagio reassured him that his wife and family were well, though worried to distraction, and having promised to take a note of reassurance to them as soon as he left, Biagio turned to more political news. 'The Medici are well back in the saddle, Niccolò. They used the Boscoli conspiracy to tighten up their grip on all the principal offices of the state and round up anyone else they thought might have cause to oppose them.'

'An old trick,' Niccolò murmured, 'using a conspiracy as an excuse to impose tyranny. It doesn't even have to be a real conspiracy, if you are clever.'

'Yes, well.' Biagio frowned as he processed that thought. 'Anyway, Agostino tells me that everyone in the chancellery is keeping their heads down, all afraid that they might be following you into this stinking place.

'But the biggest news is that Pope Julius is dead. A fever, apparently. And Cardinal Giovanni has gone hurrying back to Rome for the conclave; the rumour is that he might even come out of it as the new pope! How would that be? A Medici pope!'

Should it come to pass, the election of a Medici pope would indeed bring extraordinary benefits to Florence, as papal wealth flowed through the hands of the Florentine bankers. Left alone in his cell, he felt disconnected from the world, which seemed determined to forget him. How long he was going to languish there, he could not tell. That his gaolers had turned from surly to genial was of little comfort, for though it suggested he was no longer under suspicion, they acted as if he was going to be their guest for a long time to come.

Then, astonishingly, the door to his cell clanked open, and with an ironic little bow, his chief gaoler conducted him out into the sunshine of the Bargello courtyard, there to be greeted with the smiling faces of his friends, Biagio, Casa, and even Agostino. Beyond the gates, he could hear the shouts of celebration that told him all he needed to know.

'Our Cardinal Giovanni de' Medici has been raised to the papal chair, and is now pope Leo X,' Agostino shouted over the noise as they emerged into the street. 'And in celebration of his election, he has commanded a general amnesty for all prisoners.'

Hobbling, held up by his friends, he could not help grinning as inanely as everyone else at the stupefying wonder of it. He was free!

Chapter 35—On Principalities

With a shout of triumph that could be heard out in the street, Niccolò swept the last of his checkers off the backgammon board. His opponent, Rafaello the innkeeper, gave him a mock bow of submission, acknowledging the victor in today's little tournament. The other onlookers, Giovanni the miller from nearby Falciani, Angelo the butcher from up the road in Spedaletto, and a couple of kiln workers from the same town whose names he could never remember, applauded and raised their beakers of wine in a shouted toast.

'So that's... let me see... fifteen *denari* you own me, Rafaello.'

'Fifteen! Who taught you to count, Nico?' The innkeeper was spluttering with indignation. 'Ten *denari*, that's all I make it.'

'Nico is right, Raf, it's fifteen,' the butcher said, running his stubby fingers down the column of figures he had jotted in chalk on a piece of board as the two protagonists had finished each game.

Niccolò let out a loud whoop. 'It's you who can't count, Rafaello! Come on, pay up.'

The innkeeper scowled and reluctantly dug into the small purse that hung from his belt. 'All right, all right. Here's ten, and you'll have to take the rest in wine.'

'You mean the wine that comes from my vines? That you water down and sell to unsuspecting passers-by? By God, you'd cheat your grandmother!'

'Who do you think taught me to water my wine? Anyway, that's the deal, take it or leave it.'

Niccolò scooped the coins into his purse and nodded his agreement. 'All right. But I'll take payment now and share my winnings with everyone else.'

That brought another cheer from the onlookers and, in a few minutes, everyone was happily gathered around the fire and toasting Niccolò's good health. *This is my little court,* he thought, *my little circle of admirers.* Rough men, and honest enough, but a far cry from the kings and princes and the famed *condottieri* whose company he used to keep. They knew who he was, what he had been, but they preferred to think of him just as their Nico, a local farmer who was made of much the same stuff as them, but who told better stories.

He settled into his chair facing the fire, with his back to the door as he always preferred (who knew what Florentine dignitary, on his way south to Rome and stopping in for an ale or a wine, might recognise Niccolò Machiavelli, former secretary of the defunct Florentine Republic, and wonder at his dirty clothes and ragged coat? No, better to stay incognito than to be recognised and pitied.) and waited for the inevitable request.

'Come on, Nico, it's story time!' This from one of the kiln workers, a brawny lad with a thatch of blonde hair and bright blue eyes.

'All right, but it will have to be a quick one today, else I will have Madonna Marietta in here demanding to know why I am wasting my time with you rascals instead of working on my account books!'

'Don't worry, Nico,' Rafaello said from behind his counter, 'the door to the tunnel is unlocked.'

Many years ago, his father had cut a tunnel between the basement of the Machiavelli farmhouse and the tavern so that they could easily move barrels of wine across without being interrupted by wagons and carts travelling along the busy road down to Rome. It was also a handy escape route for Niccolò from his increasingly tyrannical wife. 'I am safe then. Now, let me see. Did I tell you about the toothless whore I met once in Rome? No? Well...'

It was the kind of story they loved, bawdy and scandalous, with a hint of danger. Though it was true, he exaggerated the details, embroidering the facts with increasingly improbable incidents that, by the end, had them roaring with laughter. He was right at the climax of the story when Luca, the farmhand who had accompanied him to Imola all those years ago, sidled in through the front door and came up to whisper in his ear. 'Madonna Marietta sent me to find you, Messer Niccolò.'

'And did you find me here, Luca?' It was a routine they had perfected long ago; he and the young man were natural conspirators.

'No, Messer Niccolò, there was no one here except Luca.'

'Good lad. Make sure you take at least five minutes before you report back to the mistress.'

The lad slipped away and Niccolò stood up, gathering his coat around him. To the last cheers from his friends, he made his way down to the cellar of the inn and through the dank, chalk-walled tunnel to his own house. Climbing up from the basement, a small side door opened out onto a flat terrace furnished with a table and some benches, a pleasant place to enjoy some bread and cheese, and perhaps a little wine, while contemplating the vista that stretched away to the north of the Machiavelli farm.

Beyond the vine-laden slopes and open valley dotted with farmhouses he could see Brunelleschi's great dome, the gilded cross on top glinting in the afternoon's sun, and the tower of the Palazzo della Signoria, and beyond that the steep hills that climbed up to Fiesole, the Etruscan city that had given birth to modern Florence. It was a scene he had looked upon innumerable times since his childhood, but he had never been bored by it and had always found solace in its permanence.

He was still lost in contemplation, propped against the table and arms folded across his chest to ease the pain in his shoulders when the familiar voice of his wife broke the silence. 'There you are, Niccolò. I sent that useless Luca out to find you half an hour ago and it seems you have been skulking here all along.'

Struggling to eliminate the smile that his lips seem determined to form, a smile he knew Marietta would interpret as a smirk deserving of an angry tirade cataloguing his many faults, he turned and unfolded his arms into a gesture of peace. 'Hardly skulking, my dear,' he said mildly. 'Merely enjoying a few moments of solitude.'

She looked at him suspiciously. At thirty, Marietta was no longer the uncertain young girl he'd married eleven years before. Four children had thickened her figure and the years as undisputed mistress of his household had set her features in a hard, practical and above all, no-nonsense expression. Her complexion was still good, though, and there was mischief in her eyes whenever she was not using them to survey the misdemeanours of the household servants and rascally tradespeople. Or, as now, her too-clever husband.

'I am not sure I believe that. I swear that I heard your voice coming from across the road, though Luca swears there was not a soul there except that villain Rafaello.'

Well done, Luca, he thought. *I must make sure I put something extra in your pay this month.* 'He told the truth, though I *was* there earlier for a little, on my way back from the woods.' A small lie would serve to mollify her, he hoped. She always liked it when she caught him out.

'Ha! I thought so. How are the woods coming along?'

It had been his main task for the day—going down to the bottom of the valley and supervising the efforts of a team of woodsmen who were clearing away a patch of trees so that he could plant more vines. In truth, it had not taken all that long, and he had soon slipped away to spend a pleasant couple of hours sitting under a tree reading his copy of *The Divine Comedy*, the silence broken only by the occasional birdsong and the tinkle of a little spring that ran down towards the valley floor. Wandering home, he'd run into various people from the district, each of whom had wanted to chat about all those things that are vital to rural life—the price of wine, the size of the olive crop, the villainy of itinerant labour, the gossip from the local villages. And so eventually, he had made his way to the inn and an afternoon of backgammon.

He gave Marietta a highly edited version of all this, using his considerable persuasive skills to make it seem that he had been busy all day, diverting her with the village gossip he knew she loved to hear. By that stage, she had forgotten her suspicions and they were walking arm-in-arm towards the solid brown bulk of the house. Inside, dinner was ready—some roast chicken, spiced veal, goats-milk cheese and a platter of vegetables, washed down with wine from their vineyards. His sons, ten-year-old Bernardo, and Lodovico, a year younger, were already seated, waiting for their parents.

As they ate, Marietta talked about her day, summarising everything with her usual admirable efficiency, and Niccolò offered her more bits of gossip in exchange. The boys maintained a well-mannered silence while they wolfed down their food until Niccolò asked them about their day. They told their parents about their boyish escapades in a garrulous stream, breathlessly interrupting each other as they competed for their attention. As he entered into their childish world, Niccolò offered up a little silent prayer for the soul of his daughter Primerana, long dead of an unexplained fever.

388

The meal finished, the children were sent off to bed and he rose to go to his study, stopping by to bestow a kiss on little Guido, the latest addition to the family, fast asleep in his crib. There, he stripped off his filthy working coat and hung it on a peg set into the wall. From a coffer, he took out a loose-sleeved blue doublet, rather old-fashioned in cut, which he slipped over his shirt and buttoned up. Next came a scarlet pleated tabard that he slipped over his head, standing in front of a mirror to arrange the pleats to his satisfaction. With the addition of a black velvet hat, he completed his transition. In his mind, he was no longer a country farmer and had instead become a sophisticated courtier, ready to do verbal battle with friend and enemy alike.

Thus attired, he settled down behind the desk that was set in the middle of the room, facing a tall window in the middle of the only wall that was not covered with bookcases. Someone, Marietta probably, had already lit candles set in sconces all around the room, providing a pleasant soft light as the sun gradually receded.

*

It was almost twelve months since he had been dismissed from office and so savagely tortured that his arms and shoulders still ached from the damage that had been done. Though he was only forty-three years old, his career in public service was over, and he had decided that he would devote the rest of his life to quiet study and contemplation, and correspondence with his friends. And for the first few months after he moved up here to Sant'Andrea in Percussina, that was what he did.

His thoughts went often to the demise of the republic to which he had given his adult life. He had thought Florence would become as great a model of republican governance as the ancient Rome that he and his father had studied so carefully. Instead, it had proven to be a flimsy thing, blown over when the winds of fate gusted too strongly and from the wrong direction. But he was too sanguine to feel any passionate hatred against the new regime. Fate had dealt its blows, and he must accept them, and adapt his life as best he could against the prospect of better days that must come eventually.

Events beyond his quiet rural world continued without him, though his friends often wrote to keep him up to date. He sent them letters in return, filled with what he hoped were still acute observations and critiques. And he started writing a book, which was almost finished. It was not a long work, but he had poured into it all that he had learned from his public career. He called it *On Principalities*. When Niccolò told Agostino what he was doing, he was enthusiastic.

'Send it to Giuliano de' Medici,' had been his surprising suggestion. 'Who knows, Niccolò, perhaps when he reads it, he will see what a jewel you are and what use you can be to him. Stranger things have happened.'

As the last of the sun went on this December evening, he sat in contemplation. It was usual for him to spend a little while thinking about whatever subject came into his mind before ever putting pen to paper. He allowed his thoughts to wander among the classical authors for a while, imagining that Caesar, Tacitus and his beloved Livy were in the room with him, speaking their words for him to hear and dispute. This was a kind of intellectual cleansing exercise that prepared him for the real work of synthesising his accumulated experience into his little book.

Images of Cesare Borgia swam into his mind. Not the wasted, dispirited Cesare as he had last seen him, but the laughing, confident, powerful Duke Valentino he remembered from Imola and Cesena. He had been reading the night before the little pile of notes he made all those years ago, the day he'd received the news that Borgia was dead. No doubt that was why he was present in his mind. He had never found the time to do what he had planned to do with those notes and turn them into a biography. But perhaps he didn't need to; the dead duke seemed to inhabit every other page of *On Principalities*. He smiled as he thought about the irony of it—he, Niccolò Machiavelli, would make that extraordinary man's achievements (and failures) live through the ages, long after the man himself had faded from the public memory, even in Italy.

Then he laughed. *Stop dreaming, Niccolò. Your little book will probably never be printed, let alone be read by future generations.* Besides, Agostino was right. His real audience was just one man—Giuliano de' Medici. Sitting up straight in his chair, he drew a single piece of paper towards him and began to write.

> *Men who are anxious to win the favour of a prince nearly always follow the custom of presenting him with the possessions they value most, or with things they know especially please him; so we often see princes given horses, weapons, cloth of gold, precious stones and*

390

similar ornaments worthy of their possession. Now, I am anxious to offer myself to Your Magnificence with some token of my devotion to you, and I have not found among my belongings anything as dear to me or that I value as much as my understanding of the deeds of great men, won by me from long acquaintance with contemporary affairs and a continuous study of the ancient world. These matters have I now diligently analysed and pondered for a long time, and now, having summarised them in a little book, I am sending them to Your Magnificence…

The End

Historical Note

When Niccolò put pen to paper to write *The Prince* (as it eventually became known), he was in exile from the republic he had worked for all his adult life; it must have been particularly cruel to be able to see the dome of the cathedral and the tower of the government palazzo from the farm at Sant'Andrea in Percussina and know that he was barred from visiting his beloved city, let alone returning to the halls of power he had known so well. Giuliano de' Medici died before Niccolò could send the book to him, and so he had to rededicate it to Giuliano's younger brother and successor, another Lorenzo. It seems probable that Lorenzo never read it.

Though *The Prince* failed as a job application, Niccolò never gave up hope that he would one day be recalled, and he was indeed eventually rehabilitated as a citizen, ironically through the offices of Bernardo Rucellai, the *ottimato* leader who had stormed out of Florence when Piero Soderini was elected. Machiavelli became something of a raconteur, and busied himself writing plays, histories and a much more substantial work on political theory, *The Discourses on the First Ten Books of Livy*. Cautiously, the Medici regime began to use his services. In 1518 cardinal Giulio de' Medici commissioned him to write a history of Florence, and in 1525 he went off to resolve a trade dispute with Venice.

But the Medici regime came to a sudden end in 1527, partly as the result of yet another war between Spain and France, and a new republic was proclaimed; in a case of supreme irony, Niccolò was by now regarded as being too close to the expelled Medici, and was once again denied the opportunity to serve in the new government. In that same year, he died, aged 58, a disappointed but, I would like to think, still optimistic man.

Researching this book has been an extraordinary exploration for me. At the start, I knew little about Machiavelli, though I had read *The Prince* when I was in university. But the deeper I dug, the more I read, the more he intrigued me, and the more I realised that whatever Niccolò Machiavelli was, he was not Machiavellian. What came through from his despatches and his letters, and the letters to him from his friends, was a remarkably modern man, possessed of a cheeky and irrepressible sense of humour, who was both penetratingly intelligent and at the same time a little naïve. I hope I have captured some of that in the book.

One cannot understand Niccolò without understanding the city where he was born, that nurtured him, and that he loved passionately. I was fortunate, therefore, to have had the opportunity to have lived in Florence for best part of a year while I was writing the first draft of the novel. Being able to walk around a city that has not actually changed all that much since his day, and being able to get a train to so many of the cities and towns that he visited on his journeys, added a layer of understanding that I could not have got any other way.

Most of the events that are recounted in the book actually happened (in fact, there was quite a lot I had to leave out!), and where possible I have either used Niccolò's own words or paraphrased them for modern ears. There is no direct documentary evidence that Niccolò and Leonardo da Vinci were friends, or even knew each other, but in a city such as Florence it does seem more than likely that they did. Agostino Vespucci certainly knew Leonardo, for it is due to his writings that we know who the subject of the *Mona Lisa* was.

Similarly, it doesn't stretch credulity too far to suppose that Machiavelli might have met Thomas Cromwell in Florence, and I rather like the idea that a man who was to be seen in his later life as the arch-Machiavellian might have contributed something to Niccolò's own career.

The other figure at the centre of the drama, Cesare Borgia, is another whose character remains something of an enigma. He was without doubt bloody and ruthless, though in truth probably no more so than most rulers of his time, but he was also capable of great charm. Whether he really wanted to lead an Italian unification crusade and throw out the foreign powers that dominated the peninsula is open to question, but I the idea of him as a proto-Garibaldi is not completely far-fetched. And the fact that he looms so large in Niccolò's later writings certainly suggests that their relationship was more complex than that of simple adversaries; Machiavelli is in many places full of praise for the young adventurer.

Florence and Melbourne, 2019-2020

Made in the USA
Middletown, DE
19 March 2021